Lower Than the Angels

Lower Than the Angels

CHLOE GARTNER

Five Star
Unity, Maine

The Author asserts the moral right to be identified as the author of this work.

Five Star Romance
Published in conjunction with Kidde, Hoyt & Picard Literary Agency.

Cover photograph © Alan J. La Vallee

February 2000

Five Star Standard Print Romance Series.

The text of this edition is unabridged.

Set in 11 pt. Plantin.

Printed in the United States on permanent paper.

Library of Congress Cataloging-in-Publication Data

Gartner, Chloe, 1916–
    Lower than the angels / Chloe Gartner.
      p.   cm.
    ISBN 0-7862-2351-0 (hc : alk. paper)
    1. World War, 1939–1945 — Influence — Fiction.
  I. Title.
  PS3513.A7415 L69 2000
  813´.52—dc21
                                            99-055802

Lower Than the Angels

1

The bells of Glasgow tolled for the fallen. The slow, sonorous notes rolled across the roofs of the smoky city, echoed in the dusty squares. Pedestrians paused, motor cars braked to a halt, trams stopped as the switch in the power house was thrown. No hawkers cried the news; no mother in the Gorbals bawled out of the window to her child in the street below to stop that ball bouncing.

In Glasgow Green a dog barked at a squirrel and was silenced by its master. It wagged and danced an apology. The owner gave it a covert caress and whispered, 'Good lad.' The squirrel scurried from its retreat.

In George Square the dignitaries waited at the cenotaph. The bugler held himself at attention and moistened his lips, preparing to play the reveille. On the stroke of eleven the flag on City Chambers would be lowered to half-mast, hats would be doffed, heads bowed.

On the River Clyde the ships sounded their deep-voiced hooters. In the shipyards the riveters laid down their hammers, carpenters their tools. The gaunt davits paused in mid-air, the machinery clasped in their grips swung in slowing arcs.

As the echoes faded in the damp, windy air, the ship's clock in Charlie Maccallum's office chimed six bells. The fusillade of Miss Maclean's typewriter ceased. Silence held the city in thrall.

Charlie Maccallum, or 'young Mr Maccallum', heir to the

shipyard, laid his pen across the pages of the order book and stared at it unseeingly. He was the fifth Charles Maccallum to sit at the ornate, two-hundred-year-old library table, so broad that the first Charles and his brother, David, worked at it sitting opposite one another. The office was little changed from the time when those founders had occupied it. Pictures of later, newer ships had been added to those of the first Maccallum-built ships. The dark oak panelling was almost hidden by them.

The old leaded windows had been replaced by a long, wall-to-wall window which overlooked the yard and was double-glazed to deaden, as well as it could, the clamour of the yard. Gas lamps had given way to electricity. Steel filing cabinets flanked the old oak ones, and a comfortable swivel chair was now the only chair at the desk. The Trafalgar chairs with their dolphin legs and anchor backs in which the founders had sat stood primly against the wall under the portraits of the first Maccallums. Solemn portraits, and watchful. Charlie's father said that when he had taken over the desk after *his* father's death, he often fancied he had heard them speak to him.

They were frowning now because Charlie was not in the yard with the men, observing the two-minute silence. He had left that pleasure to old Mr Robertson who was retiring from the board at the end of the year.

'It would be a privilege and great honour, lad,' Mr Robertson had said, 'to lay the wreath on the new monument dedicated to the workers killed during the air raid. I put a bit of cash towards it myself, and it will be my last opportunity to mingle with the men. I was here that night, you know, and helped Reid get your father to the hospital. Then I came back to lend morale and see to it that the injured chaps were taken in care. Yes, it would be an honour, unless you feel you should do the job yourself.'

Charlie was glad to agree. He would have had to linger after the ceremony, speak to this man and that, inspect something or other, chat up the gaffers, hand out the cat biscuits he kept in his pocket to give to Tanker, the yard cat. It was time he could not spare. The war had been over for two years, but orders still poured in for vessels to replace those which had been lost, orders for merchantmen, cargo ships, flat-bottomed river boats meant for African rivers and lakes, liners, yachts, ferries, cruisers. There wasn't a shipyard from Glasgow to Greenock that wasn't booked with orders more than five years ahead. There were ships on the stocks, skeletal keels, rust-red hulls, and some glistening with fresh paint, waiting to be launched. The skyline along the River Clyde was jagged with poles and davits and iron-grey cranes, flying cradles and tall arc lights which turned the sky lurid at night and cast long, quivering reflections on to the river. Men worked on the Sabbath for exorbitant wages. Overtime was a way of life. Charlie often worked until ten at night. At weekends he always looked in and, once there, lingered for hours.

Meg, his wife, said he would have a nervous breakdown at the pace he was going. She resented the late hours, the warmed-up meals, the all too little time they shared. 'There *is* a life outside Maccallums' Yard, but I suppose it is bred in the bone.'

Bred in the bone, though Charlie had not known it when he was a child. He had known only that from the first time he had seen the yard he had loved it and felt that he belonged to it and it to him. He had been told that he was the son of one of Fa's wartime friends who had been killed in action. When his mother had been dying of leukaemia she had appealed to the Maccallums to take her five-year-old son, and thus he had come into the family in memory of that friendship.

Eventually his name had been changed from Charles Sutton to Charles Sutton Maccallum, but it had not been until he was a young man going off to Spain to join the International Brigades, that he had learnt the truth. The morning before he left, Fa had told him that he was, in fact, his real son, the result of a wartime love affair between Fa and Charlie's mother, who had been a nurse at Étaples.

Now he understood Fa's cautious but special love for him, and the reluctant affection from the Memsah'b—as Charles's wife was affectionately called in recognition of her Indian upbringing. He had gone to her, then, to thank her for having taken him in. She had given him a steady look and said, 'Why should I not have done? You are not only Charles's son, but you were a thoroughly nice child. You needed a home, a brother and sisters. We provided those things.' She had made it sound like a business deal.

'You provided more than that. You gave me my father and a future.'

'If you are talking about the shipyard as a future, you are welcome to it. It disappointed Charles that Carlos hates the yard. He wants no part of it. So you had better keep safe playing at soldier in Spain and come back to play at building Maccallum ships.'

That had been before Carlos was killed. Good old Carlos. It was Carlos of whom Charlie was thinking when he looked down on the silent yard. Rain blurred the window. The Maccallum pennant at half-mast flapped heavily and wrapped itself around the pole. The gaffers held their dusty bowlers across their hearts, the poppies in their buttonholes as bright as new blood. On the Clyde a tug had cut its engine and bobbed in the water as it drifted slowly downstream.

Charlie did not need poppies or a two-minute silence to

remember. In dreams he fought his way uphill through the icy blizzard, or the gale which lashed their faces at Teruel, swam the muddy yellow flood of the Ebro as it darkened with the blood of swimmers who were strafed as they tried to swim to safety, marched under scarlet banners in Barcelona, heard the voice of La Pasionaria, '. . . you are going home. Many are staying here with the Spanish earth as their shroud . . .'

Carlos was one of the many. That had been their war: the war which had solved nothing.

Far away and so faint that he thought he must be imagining it, he heard 'The Last Post'. The yard bashed into activity with a shriek of metal and the chatter of the electric riveters. A man in a flying cradle hit a white-hot rivet with a hammer, showering fiery sparks into the rain. The tug on the river spewed a white wake of grey-green water. Charlie returned to the table and picked up his pen. The ceremony was over for another year.

Miss Maclean knocked, came in, and wordlessly laid letters for signing on the polished surface. Her eye makeup was smeared. For whom had she been crying? A father, a brother, a lover?

He thanked her. She made an inaudible reply as she closed the door. Her perfume lingered in the room, spicy-sweet and flowery. The portraits of the long-dead Maccallum brothers frowned as if the scent had reached even their nostrils.

The rain which had gusted in from the Atlantic, drenching the countryside to the north and east of Glasgow, had moved on to the city. A mist so heavy that it was not unlike rain remained, lowering over the Campsie Fells and the village of Blanelammond. There, in the square around the war memorial, the umbrellas were still open, clustered together like a field of gigantic mushrooms. Fionna's feet were wet because her boots needed resoling. Her arm, which had taken the same shrapnel that had killed Carlos in Spain, ached from the damp. She wished she were home by the fireside having a hot cuppa with a little something in it. She wished she had refused when she had been asked to place the wreath. It was because she was Lady Lammondson née Maccallum. 'The *old* Lady Lammondson did the honour back in 19—.' Of course she had. It had been Lammondson money which had paid for that costly chunk of Italian marble. 'You may not remember. You were but a lass then.' A Girl Guide, standing in formation with the others. Lady Lammondson in her weighty weeds had been tottering so much that her only son to survive the trenches, Sir William, had had to hold her arm to steady her. She had died the year after—of sorrow, the village said. Memsah'b had said there was a bit more to it than sorrow if the village but knew. She hadn't visited London every few months just to buy lingerie, and the tottering had more to do with tippling than with sorrow.

Willie was not going to hold Fionna's arm no matter how much it ached, nor did she plan to die next year. A Girl Guide was going to assist her with that cartwheel of a wreath.

The Committee had outdone itself this year. So had the village. Urns, jars, and tins of autumn flowers surrounded the memorial. Hydrangeas dark as Spanish *rioja,* red berries, heather, roses of every hue. Gardens had been stripped and the containers had had to be rearranged at the last moment to make room for the wreath.

Fionna was laying the wreath for Carlos. His name was not on the memorial and never would be. Not that he would have cared. 'Bugger the Government and its sanctions against Spain. They'll pay in the end.'

One day she would return to Spain and put a stone at the spot where Carlos had been surprised by death. Her fiancé had been killed at the same time. Of the two, she regretted her brother more.

She closed her eyes, remembering the canvas walls of the hospital tent swelling and falling in the wind, the sun dazzling on the silver body of the Italian plane as it dived, the red flash of its guns, the tent toppling in slow motion, Carlos lying in the stubbled grass where he had been sleeping.

Fionna felt a pang of bitter nostalgia for that dirty, passionate war when she, Carlos and Charlie had been most alive.

As the notes of 'The Last Post' died someone in the crowd gave an audible sob. Fionna whispered, 'Oh, dear.' Willie gave her a quick, questioning look. She shook her head to indicate that nothing was wrong. One day she would go back to Spain.

Fionna's five-year-old son, standing stiff-backed beside his father, sighed loudly, heavily, and shifted his weight. His eyebrows were drawn straight across his forehead in a fierce line of rebellion. His russet hair escaped in wiry curls from beneath his tweed bonnet. His freckles sparkled in the rain.

A Girl Guide had been chosen to assist his mother to lay the wreath. By rights, as a Lammondson, it should have been he.

'We cannot take all the glory,' his mother had said. 'We must share.'

'Huh! Some glory! You said your very own self, and I heard with my very own ear, and I am no' deef, that you think it a dreary task.'

'One must do what one must do.'

One must stand in the rain waiting to hear the Girl Guides sing 'The Flowers of the Forest'. A cissy song. Not that girls could sing fine tunes like 'Scotland the Brave' or 'Blue Bonnets Over the Border'. One must listen to Father Timothy's blether, which was yet to come. One must tolerate the name

Jamie which was fine in its way. But when he grew up he would be a Sir like his father, then he would change his name to Seamus. Sir Seamus had the grand sound of a man who would do high deeds. Brave, bold things such as those described by Liam about *his* father. Liam. There was another grand name. Liam was the son of their Irish maid, a year older than Jamie and therefore an oracle.

Jamie's mother and Effie Murdochson stepped up to take the wreath. Effie curtsied to his mother. Her tie was askew, but what could one expect of a ninny whose real name was Euphemia? It sounded like a disease that would carry off a body in a day. She was only a Brownie at that.

The wreath was laid and Effie curtsied again. Folk would think she had weak knees. Jamie snorted. His father winked at him. His father was not a bad soul. When he had been young he had gone on safari in Africa. There was a grand photo album with pictures that made Jamie almost feel the heat and dust and smell the wild smell. Sometimes, hiking in the Campsie Fells, he pretended he was on safari. The sheep were *simbas*. That was an African word for lions. And danger lurked behind every rock.

He wished he were on safari in the Campsies with his Grandfather Maccallum and his Aunt Mairi right this very minute.

Aunt Mairi had come to visit from Germany and what a business it had been to get her here. It was all because long before Jamie had been born, long before the war, she had married a Jerry and gone to live in Germany and had given up her British passport. She was as beautiful as Snow White, and she lived in a castle called a *Schloss*, which was far larger than the castle where the Lammondsons had lived for ever so long and where Jamie and his father and mother lived now. She called Jamie *Schatzi* and *Rotharrig* and told him about the storks which came every year to build nests in the chimneys. She had promised he should come to visit one day when the Yanks who were occupying the castle were gone.

When asked if she would attend the wreath-laying, she had said, 'If I did someone would probably spit on me. I have already been snubbed when I tried to buy toothpaste in the village shop. I'll walk the Campsies with Fa, the way we used to do after the other war.'

If anyone tried to spit on her, Sir Seamus would spit on them. Spit gathered in his mouth just thinking about it. Who, with any wits about them, would come to a wreath-laying when they could go on safari in the Campsies?

A tide of mist lapped against the slopes and flooded the valleys between the smooth hills, blurring the distances. The only sounds were the cries of the curlews and the bleating of sheep. Dead bracken crushed soundlessly beneath their feet, and the wet grass whispered as it brushed their trousers.

'In the old days we heard the band when the wind was right. A few notes to remind us,' Mairi said.

'There is no band now. Those men are long gone and the younger lads . . . well, the war made a difference in the village.'

'It takes getting used to, doesn't it, Fa?' She took his arm. Dear, handsome Fa. 'Isn't there a quotation about being between two worlds?'

'One dead, the other powerless to be born. Matthew Arnold.'

'Of course. Matthew Arnold. That's me. Scotland is no longer the world I knew when I was young. And the Germany I went to with Erich changed so radically that we were no part of it. I am not sure I shall be a part of the Germany that is being reborn. I feel chopped in half as it is. Imagine Germany without Berlin!'

'Your mother and I have been wondering . . . must you go back? Could you . . . would you stay? We could bring your young son, Hannes, over here. I know the proper channels now. Possibly Frau Trötzen as well. Your mother and I are growing older,' he hurried on, seeing the growing protest in her expression. 'Milkstone will be yours when we die. The estate belongs to your mother, you know. You are the eldest. Carlos is lost and Fionna is now Lady Lammondson and Jamie is heir to that property.'

'What about Charlie?'

'He could not inherit Milkstone. It's entailed and he is not your mother's child.'

'He is so like you, Fa, that one forgets that. More like you than Carlos ever was. He is managing the yard well, isn't he?'

'Extremely well, and he loves it, which Carlos never did, bless him. Will you stay, Mairi?'

The plea in his voice hurt her. It was difficult to tell him that she did not want to stay. She found post-war Britain depressing. In Germany the release from twelve years of fear and evil rule was intoxicating despite the hardships, the Occupation, the hordes of homeless people. There was rebuilding to do and the satisfaction of doing it. Amends to make as purging as confession. And always the triumph of surviving to live another day. God willing, there would one day be a brave new world and a peaceful one.

'You don't have to give me an answer now, Mairi,' he probed gently. 'You must have suffered terribly.'

'Nothing like so much as many have. And the first years of the war weren't that bad. You see, the Nazis were afraid to make us unhappy. We had wine and cheese from France, milk, butter and meat from Holland and Denmark, luxuries from every conquered country. Mutti Trötzen had a summer in Spain. I visited friends who have a villa at Lake Como. Life went on. We weren't happy with the war, but we hadn't been happy since the Nazis came into power.

'It wasn't until the round-the-clock bombings started that life became difficult. And from mid-1943 on, all any of us could think about was getting rid of Hitler and his crew. That man led a charmed life right up to the end. And any hint of rebellion was put down immediately and cruelly. I know it sounds strange but we almost have suffered more under the Occupation. Some of them treated us like children who have been very, very naughty, and some made no distinction between those of us who were opposed to the Nazis and those who supported them. As for food, if it hadn't been for our garden and barter, we would have been hungry all the time.'

'We aren't so well off here ourselves, as you have seen, but I think we could manage to feed you.'

She took a deep breath. 'Fa, it is time for me to go home. I *must* be at the *Schloss* where Erich and Edu will expect to find me when they return.'

'If they return. The war has been over two years. If Erich were taken prisoner when Poland was overrun, should he not have been released by now?'

'I don't know. Exchanges are still taking place. If he has written, the letters are probably lost in the two-year backlog of mail. I doubt it will ever be sorted out even now that the ban on writing or receiving letters has been lifted.'

'And my grandson, Edu? Shouldn't you face the fact that he may not be alive?'

'I refuse to lose hope. Other young men who were reported missing, even dead, have returned. Towards the end records got hopelessly muddled.'

'At least your daughter is safe.'

'Yes. Life in post-war France is a bit easier than in Germany. Lilli's marriage is a good one. I had my doubts at first because they were both so young, and of course it had to be kept secret as it was forbidden to have anything to do with our prisoners of war. Not that we paid much attention to that edict. We became very fond of our French prisoners. They were so jolly and so glad to be out of the fighting that they kept up our spirits. I told you they did our gardening and took care of the vineyard and made the wine which we are still drinking.

'Fa, I may change my mind—if I lose all hope. But now, at the present, I *must* go back. Please understand.'

'All right, my dear. The offer remains open. Your mother will be disappointed.'

'Only briefly, if I know her. But she has changed. She is almost subdued, which is not like her.'

'I suspect she is seething underneath and one day will erupt like a volcano. She had a great deal to worry about during the war. You, her father in Assam where the Japanese were trying to break through into India, the violence caused by India's independence, and of course, Carlos. She has never quite got over his death.'

'Of course she hasn't. Carlos took after the Tolmies in features and colouring. Looking at the pictures of Memsah'b's brothers was like looking at Carlos. No wonder he was her favourite child.'

It was Carlos of whom his mother, Veda, was thinking during the two-minute silence. Carlos and India. Her mind shuttled back and forth between both of them: She could do nothing about Carlos. Death had its finality. But India—she must do something about her father. She must go back. She could feel India calling to her, compelling her to go. She be-

18

longed there as she had never belonged here, would never belong here. She must force Charles to let her go back.

She looked at the wet, black umbrellas, the drab raincoats, the pale-faced people, and wondered why she had not gone walking in the hills with Charles and Mairi instead of meekly doing her duty and attending the service.

This is the last year I shall attend, she told herself. It isn't as if it is post-1918. It meant something then, before we grew old without growing wise. This is the last time I shall listen to Father Timothy's blether . . .

Her attention was suddenly caught by his words, to which she had shut her ears. He was saying things he had never dared to say before. 'Many have fallen, not by the sword but by the will of evil men. Many have followed the Pied Piper into the mountain of destruction. Too many have joined those whose name is legion.'

Poor Timothy, Veda thought. Early on, years before the war had broken out, he had confessed to her that although he had still a shred of faith he had lost all hope. 'We are not only less than angels,' he had said, 'but close to being the spawn of Satan.'

He had been vicar of the small, stone church since she had first come from India. It was his first calling and he and she had become fast friends. The village had thought there might be a marriage, but both Timothy and Veda had soon realized he would never be more than her friend, confessor, and mentor.

'. . . Blessed are we who mourn, for though we mourn, we know no comfort. Blessed, we say, tongue in cheek, are the peacemakers who blunder and fail and bring forth further wickedness.'

Dear God, did he know what he was doing? She saw the uneasiness in those gathered around the memorial.

'But let us leave judgment to God and time and history. *Nox praecessit, dies autum.* The night is past and the day is at hand. Let us therefore cast off the works of darkness and put on the armour of light.' His voice thundered across the square like that of an avenging angel. 'Amen!'

In the startled silence the music master whispered a word to the Scouts and Guides, put the pitchpipe to his mouth and raised his hands.

Bless him from whom all blessings flow . . .

A thin smile twisted Timothy's lips as he caught Veda's gaze.

Bless him all creatures . . .

The villagers joined in uncertainly. Willie's voice boomed above the others.

A sudden wind ripped open the clouds, revealing a bar of blue sky. Watery sunlight gleamed on the marble thistle which topped the monument.

The weather continued to vary between rain, mist, and fragile sunlight. Then the temperature dropped. There were two clear, moonlit nights. Frost glistered on the Campsies. Mairi prepared to return to Germany.

As Fionna and Willie walked from Milkstone back to the castle on the night of Mairi's farewell dinner, low clouds darkened the moon, erased the stars, and blacked out the Campsies. The wind smelled of the far north.

'I should have brought a torch,' Willie said as Fionna stumbled over a rut and grasped his hand to keep from falling.

'Not to mind. We gave her a jolly send-off, didn't we? It was a fine party. We haven't danced so much for years. A pity Noel Coward broke it up. "I'll See You Again" always makes me weepy. If we weren't such stoic Scots there wouldn't have been a dry eye in the house.'

'Veda seemed to think it appropriate.'

'Memsah'b can be a sentimental fool. I doubt we'll be seeing Mairi when spring breaks through again. Fa pulled every string he knew to get her over here now and he desperately hoped she would agree to stay. He always was closer to her than he was to Carlos and me.'

'Did you mind that?'

'No. Carlos and I were loners. Oh, there were times when I wished Fa would give me the same look of approval that he gave Mairi, instead of an amused smile as if I were an aberration.'

'Is that why you agreed to marry an impoverished duffer old enough to be your father?'

'Freudian nonsense. I had a crush on you from the time I was a wee girl. You were so—so romantic.' Willie gave a bark of laughter. 'You were. The castle. Your wife deserting you for an Italian count. The kilt you wore instead of a sober business suit like Fa. Your safari to Africa. The time you took Margaret and me on a picnic to Inchmahone and you sang the Skye Boat Song as you rowed us to the island. Oh, it was ' ,vely!'

They had reached the castle and Willie fished the keys out of his sporran, the huge iron key for the ancient lock and the new steel one for the modern lock. The heavy door creaked open. 'I thought you told Maureen to oil the hinges.'

'I did and she didn't. I'll speak to her again.' Fionna put a hand on her husband's arm as he turned from locking up. 'Willie, don't ever leave me. Promise?'

'Why would I do a daft thing like that?'

'I don't know.' But as the hinges had cried out she had had a premonition. A feeling of finality.

'Snow, snow, snow!' Jamie shouted as he entered the dining room the next morning. He had been to the kitchen to fetch his bowl of steaming porridge, a ploy to persuade the cook to give him an extra nub of butter to melt in the centre and a second, forbidden spoonful of brown sugar. 'The Campsies are all over white. Did you see?'

'We saw. Say good morning to your father, Jamie.'

'Top of the morning to you, father, and may your day be blessed. That's what Liam said is proper to say. Do I have to go to school? It's going to be blizzards, the road'll be half-buried and you'll have to come a-searching and find me frozen to an icicle.'

'I doubt there will be a blizzard or that the roads will be impassable. And if you insist on extra sugar you will go without before the next ration is due.'

'The roads were buried last year. That was a grand winter, that was. Everybody snowed in and Liam and I making tunnels and igloos. It's going to be the same. Liam is having his porridge at the deal table and he said. "Blizzards, Seamus. Mark me words." '

'If Liam said so, the snow will no doubt reach the top of the tower before noon,' Fionna said. 'Blizzards or not, you are to go to school.'

Jamie wagged his head over his porridge. 'It is a hard thing to have parents who will sacrifice the heir to the title for a bit of schooling.'

'It would be a harder thing for an heir to disgrace a title which goes back to antiquity.' Willie frowned in mock ferocity and took a swallow of tea, wishing it held a wee dram for strengthening.

'Aye, but you went to a posh school. Why canna I?'

'I went first to the village school because it is the right and proper thing for the Lammondson heir to do. And we cannot afford a posh school right now.'

'Because England is bleeding Scotland white, Liam said, just as it bleeds Ireland.' Jamie picked up his bowl and drank the last of the porridge. 'Och, aweel, then. I am off. But mind, if the snow deepens you must fetch me with the Rover or find a dead heir by the roadside.'

'If the snow deepens the Rover couldn't get through. Let us leave the weather to God and be surprised.'

Jamie searched his mother's face for some betrayal of seriousness or humour. She was totally inscrutable. He capitulated. 'I'll no' be surprised.'

'Nor shall I. Do you have your piece?'

'Liam's bringing it along with his. Why d'you call my lunch a piece?'

'Because that is what the shipyard workers call theirs. And Lammondson aside, you are part Maccallum.'

'Shall I have to work in the shipyard like Uncle Charlie? Does he take a piece?'

'God forbid both! You'll have this estate to cope with, debts and all.'

'Debts, indeed, wife!' exclaimed Willie. 'The money will come. We'll soldier through somehow.'

'Liam doubts it,' said Jamie.

'Liam is fortunate to be safe in Scotland. He and his mum came near to being blown up along with his raving patriot of a father.'

'I'm away then. God keep you in my absence. That's what Liam says to his mum.' He slammed the door behind him to assert himself. Already he was bellowing towards the kitchen.

'Ho, Liam! We're away. Be so kind as to bring my piece along with you, eh?'

'Liam is a bad influence, talking insurrection at his age.'

'You cannot blame the lad,' Willie said mildly. 'I doubt he will inspire Jamie to blow up the ancestral home. But, speaking of debts, I have a plan. One that won't please you, I suspect, but it might bring in a bit of cash.' He rose and went to the broad, timeworn cheese and wine cupboard which dated from the sixteenth century, and took out the whisky bottle. Holding it to the light to see how much was left, he grimaced. Carefully, he measured a spoonful into his tea. 'It's to do with our pheasants. If we had a larger flock we could hold shooting parties in October. Place advertisements in *Scottish Field* and like magazines. A week's lodging in an ancestral castle, bed and board, tramping, shooting, fishing. It would appeal to Londoners and folk in the south. What do you think?'

'I think you have gone off your head. Guns popping all over the place. My God, Willie, wasn't there enough killing during the war without starting the slaughter of bird and beast?'

'If this is another bad winter the deer on the Busby will have to be culled.'

'The deer are why we have meat on our table and I don't fancy their gracing the tables of London. The house full of strangers expecting enormous meals. Your advert would have to say traditional, hearty Scottish fare so they wouldn't expect Fortnum's. Of course, they would have to bring their ration books, wouldn't they?' Fionna stopped, realizing she sounded as if the scheme were going to take place. Over her dead body. 'Be sensible. You would have to hire beaters, extra chambermaids, a pastry cook—those Londoners would expect something better than trifle and shortbread *every* night. Caledonian cream and a selection of cakes. Cheese and nuts and a savoury. You would have to install another bathroom. Provide sherry and whisky and brandy. Serve a midnight meal of sandwiches and coffee. Card tables, as they would probably want to gamble.'

'Give over, lass. You have set more obstacles in the path than Christian encountered on his progress. It was only an idea. No more than six guests, five-day limit. Arrive a Sunday evening, leave Saturday morning. Any longer and they would decimate the flock.'

'A mythical flock, so far. You would have to charge for the Sunday evening meal. Make Saturday breakfast free.'

'We need an extra bathroom in any case. I talked to the joiner in the village. He said there are a lot of fine fixtures in the junk yards in London from houses that were bombed out. He reckoned he can do it on the cheap.'

'I see your mind is made up.' Fionna emptied the teapot into her cup and motioned towards the whisky bottle. 'I have a wee headache after Fa's party last night. All right, Willie, I promise I shall think about it. I don't fancy playing grand lady to a lot of Sassenachs, but rates and taxes are as certain as death, and it is better than taking to the streets at my age.'

The clock in the hall coughed, cleared its throat, groaned, and struck eight o'clock. As the last rusty notes died Fionna said, 'Mairi will be away now. Just crossing Clyde Bridge. Poor Fa, he didn't succeed in saving his darling from the lions.'

Mairi was not away. The train's departure was delayed. The engineer, the conductor, blue-coated workmen, hurried up and down, shouting to one another. Other trains departed. The London train stood impotent and immobile.

The passengers, surrounded by luggage and wellwishers, shivered in the wind sweeping through Glasgow's Central

Station, driving dust and tattered papers before it.

Charles Maccallum Senior looked at his wife and daughter, huddled in their coats, their faces pinched against the cold. 'A pity we cannot wait in the hotel lounge,' he said. 'But if we did we might miss the train altogether. I doubt that any tip would be large enough to hold the train while a porter fetched us.'

'Don't even think of it.' Veda's voice was muffled by her fur collar pulled up about her face. 'As it is, Mairi may miss the night boat train.'

'You and Pa are freezing, Memsah'b. Why don't you leave? It can't be delayed much longer.'

'We shall wait, shan't we, Charles?'

'Certainly. Mairi's visit wasn't half long enough with nine years to make up.'

'But we all know I was fortunate to be able to come at all. If it hadn't been for your affidavits and those of Major Kimball I would not have been given permission either to leave or to enter Britain.' And the money she had received by selling the Meissen coffee set to the Major. It had been in the Trötzen family for three generations. There was no coffee to drink from it these days.

Veda sniffed. 'That was little enough your Yank Major could do for you after moving into the *Schloss* and forcing you to live in the servants' quarters in the cellars.'

'He could have given us an hour's notice to pack up what we could carry with us and get out. That is what usually happens, as I told you. Anyway, we are glad to have him and his staff there. Otherwise we would have had five or six or more families living with us. Families who had been bombed out and have no place to go. The American flag waving from the staff on the tower is better than a drawbridge and moat.'

She had helped Major Kimball pack the coffee set to send

to his sister as a wedding gift. He had said, 'I wish I were going with it. I'd like to be there to give Annie away, since Dad isn't alive to do it. Oh, well, war's hell, isn't it?'

He didn't know the half of it. The conquerors never did.

'We'll arrange for you to return again soon and bring Hannes with you. We have to meet our most recent grandson,' said Charles.

'Fa, surely you realize that I was not very popular in the village. I am a Jerry, an enemy, even though the war is over. Some were downright rude. One spat as I walked out of a shop, a woman who is probably otherwise rather nice.'

'You are also a Maccallum.'

'Who gave up her British passport when she married a German, long before Hitler was ever heard of.'

'Have you never been sorry?'

'No, but ashamed of the Nazis, yes.'

A small, embarrassed silence settled over them. They had said everything one says when it is goodbye, said everything during her visit. There were no more words.

Veda broke the silence. 'I hope you will be able to go back to Saarbrücken to recover the things you had to leave behind.'

'I'll try now that the travel ban has been lifted. But later. I told you before that travel is too difficult with half the railroad tracks unrepaired and too few carriages, and the Saar in the French zone. The crystal, the china, the silver trays, the ornaments are all *things*. Things I do not need the way I am living.' Didn't Memsah'b understand that the world would never be the same?

'*Things,*' Veda said, accenting the word as Mairi had done, 'matter. Beauty, graciousness is all we have left. It is not only lives that have been destroyed. It is values. War is a damned wicked business!' She glared at them as if they had caused it.

'I am bloody sick—yes, Charles, bloody. Bloody sick of it and its consequences.'

'Everyone is, my dear.'

Conversation while waiting for a train. Mairi had not told them how bad the first winter after the war had been when there was no coal, no food, no money because all bank accounts had been frozen, no transportation, a curfew, and gatherings of more than five people forbidden. The endless lines of refugees from every war-blighted country who had nothing but the rags on their backs and were willing to raid a garden for a raw turnip or green potato.

'It's over now, Memsah'b. The world will be rebuilt somehow. We will find our values again and new beauty.'

'So Timothy would have us believe.' Veda touched the arm of Mairi's coat. 'I am glad you have a warm coat. The crimson suits you.' Her voice indicated this was a kind of apology for her outburst.

'Thanks to the sister of my Yank Major. I don't like to wear it in the village. It is so much better than anything anyone else has. Some of the clothes she sent are beautiful, but completely useless. I doubt I'll ever go dancing at the Eden or Adlon again. The Eden is a pile of rubble and the Adlon has nothing left but its basement where they actually serve tea.'

'Perhaps your Yank will take you to his club.'

'There is no club in our village and he isn't *my* Yank, in that way. The only thing between Major Kimball and me is that I am a sort of substitute for his sister, just as he calls Mutti Trötzen "Mother". He is not quite young enough to be my son, but he certainly is very boyish. The Yanks seem to take a long time to mature.'

'An older woman would be good for him. He must be fond of you. He asked his mother and sister to send their castoffs. And some castoffs they are! I recognize the labels. Off the peg, but a very expensive peg.'

'His sister didn't want them now that the New Look is in.' What nonsense they were talking.

'Don't disillusion your mother, Mairi. It pleases her to think you have a little affair going with your Yank.'

At that point the conductor called for the passengers to board the train. Mairi and Veda kissed, clung tightly to one another. Then, without speaking, because she could choke out no words, Mairi followed her father along the platform and on to the train. He stowed her luggage on the rack, then they stood looking at one another until she flung herself into his arms. 'Oh, Fa, I shall miss you.'

'And I shall miss you, dear girl. Please keep in touch. Write often. Your mother gave you plenty of writing paper and ink, didn't she? Let us know if you hear anything at all about Erich and Edu.'

'Of course. *Auf wiedersehen,* Fa.'

'Take care, Mairi. God bless.'

He stumbled slightly as he stepped out of the compartment, blinded by tears. He and Veda waved until the train jerked and huffed and slowly moved away, leaving them lonely and chill in the dim light.

The first small, icy flakes of snow ticked against the window as the train left the station and moved on to the bridge across the Clyde. Flakes coated the steel-grey water and slowly dissolved. The sky was low over Glasgow. Smoke rose from the chimney stacks of the soot blackened buildings.

Mairi was glad she had the compartment to herself. She had had scarcely a minute alone during her visit. She needed time now to collect herself, to sort out who she had been once and who she was now. The visit had warped the past and the present, revived memories, some tender, some that opened like unhealed wounds to bleed old sorrows.

It was the first time she had seen her family since 1938. Veda and Charles had visited her after the Munich pact had been signed. They had toasted that uneasy peace every night, peace at whatever price. The next year war had come, bringing seven years of silence, of not knowing whether one another was alive. Then Fa had sent a letter via the Red Cross in Geneva. She had answered the same way, using Major Kimball's paper and borrowed pen.

In one way the letters had been better than the visit. Letters left unsaid things one did not wish to tell. One could remember people and places the way they had been, which was easier than facing the reality.

She had been shocked to see how her parents had aged, as she supposed she had aged. Fa had lost an eye when the shipyard had been bombed. Memsah'b—how silly to call her that all these years after she had left India—seemed weary, less alive. Fionna, too, had changed.

'It was the war in Spain that changed her. It was seeing Carlos die.' Memsah'b's gaze had rested briefly on her son's picture. His was the only family picture on the Sheraton table in the south drawing room, a wreath of ivy on the silver frame. 'It changed all of us.

'When I first took on your father's bastard son I thought the day would never come when I would be glad to have him. But I have been glad many a time. Most of all after Carlos—it was Charlie who kept your father sane.'

Mairi had felt a surge of pity for her mother, a woman she had always thought to be beyond the need of pity. Proud, beautiful, self-contained, a kind of goddess. It must have been a blow to her vanity when she learned about Charlie. Although she too had had her share of affairs.

Glasgow was disappearing into the curtain of thickening snow. It had been a mistake to have come, yet once she had realized that the trip was possible, she had been able to think of nothing else.

'I am going home to see my mother, the grandmother you don't know,' she had told her young son, Hannes.

'*This* is home,' Hannes had protested, with a six-year-old's logic.

'So it is.' And so it was, and she was going back to it gladly. To be at the *Schloss* where her elder son, Edu, and Erich would expect to find her if by some miracle they should come.

'Give them up, Mairi,' Erich's brother, Maxl, had said to her, not once but many times, too many times. 'Erich must be in Siberia by now, otherwise he would have been exchanged. Once they are sent to Siberia, they never return.'

But she would not give up. Not yet, no matter what Maxl said.

'If Erich doesn't come back, I may marry Maxl,' she had told Fa. Now, as the train crawled through the outskirts of the city, enveloping itself in a streamer of smoke, she doubted that she would marry Maxl, father of young Hannes. It had been inevitable that they had become lovers when he came back from the Eastern Front. There had been a bond between them since she had been a new bride and he a lad of ten, a bond which had strengthened over the years. He had the flippancy and lightheartedness that dependable, romantic Erich lacked.

But marriage? Something had happened to that idea during this separation. *Marry* Maxl? A small, still voice told her, 'You will not.'

The snow fell faster, whitening the earth. Patches of brown weed and dead summer gardens jutted above the thin layer. Another cold, bleak winter lay ahead.

She could no longer see the old smoky city. Snow coated

the grimy windows of the train, enclosing her in secrecy. She opened the book Fa had given her to read on her journey. 'It was a comfort to me throughout the war,' he had said. She had laughed at the idea of such comfort and smiled now as she read:

> It was about the beginning of September, 1664, that I, among the rest of my neighbours, heard, in the ordinary discourses, that the plague had returned again in Holland . . .

The train crossed the bridge over the Clyde, the red lights of the last car dimmed by snow. As they left the station Charles took Veda's arm, more as if to elicit her sympathy than to escort her. His hand found hers and he interlaced his fingers with her gloved ones. 'So she has left us.'

'You could not really hope that she would come home after all these years.'

'I hoped that she would want to. I wonder she doesn't feel alien there now, that she hasn't had enough of a sick Germany.'

'Dear man, after all this time she feels like an alien here. My impression was that she hopes Germany has learned its lesson and will rise from the ashes like a phoenix. As Timothy said, put on an armour of light.' She gave his hand a compassionate squeeze. 'Naturally she wants to be there if Erich comes home. I wonder if he is still alive.'

'She has a long, unpleasant journey ahead of her and we had no way of easing it.'

'We eased it with one of Willie's pheasants, half a dozen hardboiled eggs from the Gunns' chickens, a bottle of your precious *fino* and a flask of whisky. That should see her across the Channel and well into France. Of course, it is nothing like a hamper from Fortnum's. No paté and water biscuits, no lobster mousse, no *petite fours,* no Brie. I agree, I don't envy her the journey.' She gasped as they left the station and the snow, hard as sand, stung their faces.

'Cold.' Charles guided her to the first taxi in the rank of ancient vehicles awaiting fares on Gordon Street. The driver blew on his hands, touched his cap, and opened the door. 'Where to, sir?'

'Maccallums' Shipyard.' All streets in Charles's life led to the yard. Had their house at Milkstone not been twenty miles from Glasgow, had it not been for petrol rationing, Charles would be there every day.

The driver tucked a tatty tartan rug with some fringe missing around Veda's feet. She shrank from it for it, too, was as cold as if it had never known warmth.

'Pity I haven't a stone hottie bottle, ma'm,' he grinned, showing tobacco-stained teeth. 'One of them wouldny stay hot long in weather such as this.'

Veda smiled, acknowledging his kindness. As the driver eased out into the traffic of Hope Street, Charles again took Veda's hand. 'Mairi isn't having an easy time of it.'

'She has Maxl to comfort her. Marry Maxl, indeed! He was a filthy little Nazi until the Party became so atrociously bad that only a blind idiot wasn't disillusioned.'

'His seems to have been a thoroughly shattering disillusionment to have risked execution by deserting from the army. He put the entire family into danger.'

'There was a jolly fine chance he would have been killed if he had stayed on the Eastern Front. But putting his mother and Mairi at risk was damned cowardly. I refuse to believe that she is in love with him. In need of a man, as any woman is during a war. Men provide a kind of—what shall I say? Completeness.'

'It is nice to know that my place in life is to complete yours.'

'You do more than complete it or I should not have stayed with you all these years. Look at this traffic!' They had turned left on St Vincent Street. 'You would never know that petrol is still rationed. Will it never end? How long do we have to go on living in this way? It makes me feel so tired. So old.'

'Old! My dear, you are in the prime of life. Time cannot wither you.'

'Sixty-one is a bit past the prime.'

'Nonsense, especially in your case. You are none the less beautiful, none the less enchanting, none the less mysterious in the way that all charmers are mysterious.' He saw that she was wryly pleased and amused by his compliments. 'What you need is an affair.'

'What an outrageous suggestion.'

'Perhaps an admirer is what I am recommending.'

'Admirers no longer grow on trees and drop into one's lap, fully ripe and ready to be devoured.'

They were out of the city centre, speeding down Dumbarton Road, the snow whispering under the worn tyres.

'I am glad they are rare. I would be jealous and afraid that you would leave me.' He spoke teasingly.

She gave him a flirtatious smile. 'To leave you would be altogether too much trouble. We would never be able to separate our belongings. Besides, it would be you who had to leave. Milkstone belongs to me.'

'I tend to forget that, don't I?'

'So, no need to be jealous or to worry. I haven't the energy for affairs or admirers these days. I feel half-starved most of the time.'

'We do better than most.'

'So we do. The back doors of the shops are always open to

34

the Maccallums.' There was asperity in her voice. 'Are you going back to the yard after our luncheon with Meg?' Charles nodded. 'Then you must drop me off somewhere. I'll go to the art gallery. I don't like being alone with her, and I suspect she doesn't like being alone with me. We seem to have no common meeting ground. She keeps a distance between herself and the rest of us, as if we make her uncomfortable. Almost as if we overpower her. Perhaps we do. The truth is, Charles, your Charlie is the only normal one of us. Even he has picked up a few of our quirks. Our children, yours and mine, were hatched from cuckoo eggs. Carlos became more Spanish than the Spaniards themselves. Mairi became a German hausfrau—did you notice, she even has a slight accent? You would never know that English is her mother tongue. Fionna became a nurse, wiping someone else's bum, for heaven's sake! And married to a man old enough to be her father. Not that Willie isn't our dearest friend.'

'I have always heard that marriage to an older man is a compliment to one's father.'

Veda looked at him in disbelief and scorn. 'Wouldn't you like to think so?'

'It wasn't what we expected of Fionna, was it?'

'I never knew what to expect of Fionna. She eluded me.'

'If our children came from cuckoo eggs, you know where the eggs came from.' He was laughing at her. 'Your Aunt Katherine was an iconoclast, bless her. And your father did the unthinkable after your mother died. Married what is known in India as a wog.'

'A wog, but a lady.'

'Oh, yes, definitely a lady and a very beautiful one.'

'You can't say ours haven't been interesting offspring.'

'They have been a joy and very dear.'

'Not always.' She could think of times when they had

been anything but that.

They had reached the Clydeside shipyards now with the long row of davits and cranes lining the riverside, the wind-scudded smoke, and the endless clangour and bashing and chatter of riveters, noise like physical assault. As they pulled into Maccallums' the gateman saluted smartly. Charles paid the taxi and Veda followed him into the office.

Reid, the head secretary, had retired at the end of the war. He had been there since he was a boy, and for the past ten years Charles had longed to pension him. But Reid knew no other life and he had agreed, reluctantly, to leave only when he had reached his eighty-fifth birthday and could no longer cope with the inadequate post-war transport.

In his place was Miss Maclean, a trim, milky-skinned, efficient young lady with eyes as dark as lapis lazuli and hair as golden as honey. Veda considered her clothes a disaster—but what could one buy these days with coupons?—and her hair in need of an expert hairstylist who would turn that thick tumble into something that would cause people to turn and stare as Miss Maclean walked down Buchanan Street. Perhaps a rise in salary and a few suggestions.

But it was none of Veda's business. The girl had a tremulous smile and a hesitant, unsure manner. Unfulfilled, Veda decided. Too many young women would never be fulfilled, never have a lover. Too many young men lost in the war.

Miss Maclean all but genuflected when they entered the office. She blushed and for a moment seemed at a loss for words. Then, 'I'll tell Mr Maccallum you are here. You, madam, will want to sit in the board room. There is a nice coal fire. He told me to see to it, and a chair drawn up beside it.' She dimpled. 'Shall I send for tea and biscuits from the canteen? They are digestives today. And is the train away? It is sad, is it not? My mum said, how sad to see the eldest go off.' She clapped her hand to her mouth. 'Here I am blather-ing like an old wife. Mr Maccallum said I tell him far more than he wishes to know. I am to curb my tongue else he will dismiss me. I think he would not because I am ever so effi-cient. You should see the muddle Mr Reid left. I am still sort-ing it out.'

Veda decided nothing could salvage Miss Maclean if she didn't learn to hold her tongue. Mentally she withdrew the smart frocks, the hairstylist, and the lover. Miss Maclean would talk him into deafness. 'Thank you. The board room will do nicely. So would some tea. I brought a book to keep me occupied.'

It was *For Whom the Bell Tolls*. She had had it for a long time but had not been able to bring herself to read it. Fionna had said, 'Memsah'b, you *must* read it. It would help you to understand what Carlos wanted to do.'

Help to assuage the loss of Carlos. She removed her coat and gloves and, still shivering, settled down before the coal fire. With a sigh, she opened the book.

He lay flat on the brown, pine-needled floor of the for-est, his chin on his folded arms, and high overhead the wind blew in the tops of the pine trees . . .

She could see Carlos there. His bracken-coloured hair glowing in the sunlight. Fionna and Charlie had said he had grown a 'fierce' red moustache. It would have suited him. She wished there had been a picture.

Miss Maclean came in with the tea and two pathetic diges-tives. She made a great business of drawing a table close to Veda and pouring the tea. 'Is there anything else, Mrs Maccallum? It's not grand, but it's the best we can do these times.'

'Nothing else, thank you. This is very nice.' Which it wasn't. She put down the book.

Miss Maclean caught sight of the title. 'Oh! You are reading that? It—it's beautiful!'

Well, well, the girl could read.

'My brother—' Miss Maclean blushed. 'Perhaps I should not tell you, but I hope it will do no harm. He was in the International Brigade.' She looked as frightened as if she had confessed that he was a murderer.

'So was our son. And of course you know that the present *young* Mr Maccallum was also.'

Miss Maclean's eyes widened. 'No. He never said. But then, it isn't a subject that comes up in the ordinary day's work, is it?'

'I shouldn't think so. Did your brother come home safely?'

'Yes. In time for the next war. The army wouldn't have him at first. Called him a Red. They took him in the end, when they needed even the Reds. He was killed in Italy. It nearly killed my mum. Women set great store by their sons, don't they?'

'I suppose they do.' Too much so. 'Carlos did what he wanted to do. What he believed in.'

'So did Finlay, my brother.' She closed the door softly, leaving Veda to the coal fire, the tea, and Hemingway.

The tea was as weak as coloured water. Where, oh where, were the teas of yesteryear? Awaiting shipment in the confusion of independent India.

All year the independence of India had been in the news. There had been two long, rambling letters from her father, complaining about the United States Army during the war. They had hired the tea workers away to build their damned military road through to Burma and The Beyond. They said the road was necessary but the way they had built it was a crying shame and it was a mess when they had finished. Destroyed jungle, felled trees, slaughtered wildlife. Didn't know a poisonous snake from a harmless one. Slaughtered them all. Didn't understand that the Hindus and Moslems could not share the same food or eat together. Some Yank officer had commandeered the manager's house as his headquarters. May have been an officer, but no gentleman. As for the independence, that had opened Pandora's box. The British Commander of the Assam Rifles had stood down like the gentleman *he* was and turned over the Independence Day parade and ensuing celebrations to his Indian deputy. The tea plantations gave the workers a holiday, though half the workers didn't know what they were celebrating.

Then, the pleasantries over, the Muslim and Hindu workers, who had always got along and been friends, began murdering one another. It didn't make any sense. Nothing made sense these days. He assumed it was senility. He would like to see Veda again, but he was too old to travel and this was no time for holidaying in India. He had shipped *some* tea, but it was poor stuff.

Poor stuff, indeed, Veda thought, draining her cup. Miss Maclean was rattling away on her typewriter. Beyond the walls and the incessant noise of the yard, the hoot of tugs, the cries of the men, was a special kind of hell. She put aside the book and paced the room. She circled the long, heavy, fumed-oak table at which the directors sat and weighed decisions. Old men, conservative men, clinging to old ideas and ideals, suspicious of new methods, xenophobic. Charles did what he could to convert them to new ways. His suggestion of appointing Fionna to the board had come close to causing the old gentlemen to walk out. He thought he could pull it off yet, but he hadn't told Fionna. It was to be a surprise.

She stopped at the window and looked out at the swirling

snow. Mairi's train should be in the Midlands by now, blackening its trail with smoke.

My mum said how sad to see the eldest go off.

How sad to see any of them go off. *Women set great store by their sons, don't they?* Yes, of her three children she had loved Carlos the most.

She went back to her chair and picked up her book. Nine years was too long to mourn anyone.

Meg stood at the window watching the snow fall on Blythswood Square. As quickly as it fell it disappeared into the melting black ice which had covered the square for the past few days.

'Even the snow is grey in Glasgow,' she said aloud to no one but herself. Better to say it to herself than to Charlie. Better than to say it to her in-laws who were coming to luncheon after putting Mairi on the train.

Five years of marriage and she had not yet learnt to be at ease with them. Often, alone downstairs in the evenings, after young Charles had been put to bed, waiting for Charlie to come home, she thought that she had married too hastily.

Had she been in love with him, or was it because he had seemed so different from the other young men she had known, or because there were so few young men left in the village? All had 'gone for a soldier', and the list of casualties at the post office was a long one for a village of that size.

Some she had fancied. The son of the local distiller. 'You would live comfortably,' her mother had said. 'They are well off, and should be, considering the thirst of Scotland.'

'Too loud and jolly. He never opens a book.'

The owner of the local newspaper, ink-stained from helping to set type, a reader longing to be a writer, always sending job applications to the papers in Inverness and Aberdeen.

But, 'Weak lungs,' her father had said. 'He'd leave you penniless in a few years' time with bairns to rear on ha'pennies and thruppence.'

Then the conscientious objectors' reforesting camp had been established in the hills outside the village in some old World War I training barracks. The village hadn't accepted them at first, especially after reading the newly tacked-up list of casualties. Her father had said judgment was God's business, not that of men.

Charlie had been one of the conchies, as the conscientious objectors were known, and one of the few who had attended her father's church. There had been few churchgoers among them and most who did attend church went to the grey stone Church of Scotland, or the 'Wee Frees'. Even fewer came to the library, but Charlie had come every Saturday. They had talked. He had walked her home when the library closed. He had come to tea after church. He had shared the packages of treats which his family sent regularly.

'He was Sent,' her mother had said. 'There is no such thing as an accident. It was Meant.'

She had pushed Meg into it and Meg had allowed herself to be pushed. It had all happened too suddenly when Charlie had had to leave the camp and return to Glasgow to take over the shipyard after his father had been injured when it was bombed.

They had been married by special licence and had caught the one o'clock train to Glasgow immediately after the ceremony. Not even a wedding breakfast or a proper wedding night until they were installed in the house which had belonged to Charlie's grandparents.

The stone hotwater bottles had crashed out of the bed and rolled across the floor. The fire had gone out towards dawn, and by morning they were so cold that not even the blankets, let alone their passion, warmed them.

There had been no food in the house, but Charlie had said he didn't need breakfast. He had to go to the hospital to see his father and to the yard from there. He would grab some tea and bread at the canteen. He had given her some money, drawn a map to show her where the nearest shop was, given her a quick kiss, and gone out of the door. Then come back to say he would telephone the cook, Mrs Bacon, if she could believe the cook was named that, and the maid, Carrick, and tell them to report for work. In fact, she should give Mrs Bacon the ration books and let her do the shopping. Unless, of course, she was hungry.

Hungry! She was ravenous. Wandering through the house, more appalled by it every minute, she finally found the staircase that led to the downstairs kitchens, vast, gloomy caverns with a gigantic stove and a small electric plate for, Meg had assumed, making late cups of tea or filling hotwater bottles. There was a labyrinth of cupboards, larders and pantries, but no food and no tea in any of the caddies despite their romantic labels: Lapsang Souchong, Tolmie's Tiger Assam Tea, Earl Grey, Gunpowder. She had found some dusty bottles of ginger beer and decided that would do to wash down the remains of dried sandwiches and cake her mother had given them to eat on the train.

She had eaten in the drawing room where Charlie had started a pathetic fire before he had dashed off. She reminded herself of that now. She had known then and still knew that she disliked this house and would never be happy in it.

A pair of Wallie dogs by the fireplace, faded etchings of the first Maccallum ships, furniture that looked as if it pre-dated Victoria's marriage to Albert, plush patterned wallpaper, patterned Templeton carpets, cabinets in every corner filled with curios, dark gloomy pictures of impossible landscapes, and heavy velvet curtains.

She had replaced a picture of a dead fowl hanging by its feet amidst fruit and crockery with a print she bought at Kelvingrove Gallery: a Monet hillside with sun and red poppies and poplars. It looked as out of place in the room as Meg felt, and she liked it for that. It was one of the few changes she had dared to make. Fortunately, Charlie thought it 'nice'.

She had succeeded with the picture, but failed with the dishes. She had always thought that when—and if—she married she would have a certain pattern of white china with a border of ivy. The dinner service in the house was earthenware, with the first Maccallum paddlewheeler in the centre afloat three stylized, blue waves, a blue rope looped around the border with the date 1865.

'Could we have some different dishes?' Meg had asked.

Charlie had looked amazed. 'Don't you like these? They are symbolic of what we are.'

Symbolic of what the Maccallums were, but Meg did not yet think of herself as a Maccallum. The family had certainly tried to make her welcome, but they were far more complicated than any people she had ever known. They were more like characters in a bizarre novel than real people. At first she had thought of them in that way and even saw herself in a similar role. Now she knew they were real and would remain real, and the novel had no ending.

She told herself that every new bride went through some form of disillusionment. Even now she was not sure what she had expected of marriage. Not being left on her own for close on eighteen hours a day while Charlie was at the yard or conferring with his convalescing father. Not a grey wartime city where one felt the rationing far more severely than in a country vicarage. Not the confinement of the city. She missed the glens, the sea, the lonely hills, the simple village life.

But she knew she could not, would not dare to leave. She had not the courage to face her parents' disapproval and disappointment, the gossip of the village. So she had gritted her teeth and smiled at Charlie and stuck it out, trying to feel happy and in love, telling herself it would be better once the war was over.

That expectation was soon dispelled. The yard was busier than ever. Charlie was never on time for dinner and food was too precious to be spoiled by being 'kept over' for whenever he might arrive. Mrs Bacon left promptly at six, so it was Meg who made Charlie's supper. She didn't mind. She liked cooking, and often he sat in the kitchen with her, drinking an ale and telling her all that had happened during the day. He would eat at the big deal table, bleached white with the scouring of long years, and she sat opposite him, listening and nodding like a puppet wife.

On Saturdays Charlie slept away half the morning. Sometimes they went walking on the heath beyond Glasgow, but more often they took the train to Milkstone where Charlie and his father vanished into the study and talked shipyard, leaving Meg with Veda.

Last week Meg had decided she could take no more. She would pretend she wanted to make a short visit to her parents, but would let the visit draw out until eventually everyone would become accustomed to the fact that she was not returning. Then she had found out that she was pregnant again.

She did not want another child, with young Charles not yet three. But there it was and there she was. Charlie did not know yet and she was not about to tell him until it was so obvious he would discover it for himself.

He would be pleased, of course. His father would be pleased. One would think they wanted to populate all of that great, grey, gloomy city with Maccallums. 'We'll have at least six,' Charlie had said after young Charles had been born.

Indeed we will not, Meg had replied silently.

The tall, solemn clock in the hall struck eleven sonorous notes, sending them resonating up the stairs and throughout the house.

She had told the cook to put the onions in to bake at eleven. The eggs, courtesy of the Gunns who lived in the forester's cottage at Milkwood, would be made into an omelette after Charlie and the elder Maccallums had arrived and had their sherry. There was a scrap of Spam, minced to add to the eggs with some fresh herbs. Old bread to be toasted. No butter, but plenty of heather honey, sent from her mother.

It wasn't much of a meal, but it would have to do. Once when she had said that she found it difficult to manage on such short rations Memsah'b had said, 'But, Meg, don't you know where the side doors are? Of course one pays a bit extra, but one gets a bit extra.'

'That doesn't seem honest.'

'Honesty is the first casualty of peace just as it is the first casualty of war. I am not going to suffer because the Government cannot manage peacetime any better. If they had stopped that dreadful man when he marched into the Rhineland we would not be in this predicament. Mairi said there was a strong underground at the time and Hitler was quite prepared to back down. He was surprised to bits when neither Britain nor France raised a hand to stop him. The devil take them all. The next time Bacon goes shopping go with her. She will know where the back entrances are. And say the magic word, Maccallum.' She had accented the word sarcastically, as if it may be magic to some, but not to her.

The snow piled up on the cold, dark roofs, frosting the window ledges like icing on a cake and making an eiderdown on the front steps. Carrick was busy setting the table. Meg would have to sweep the snow off the steps herself. Undoubtedly her mother-in-law would be wearing her elegant, pre-war shoes instead of boots like a sensible woman. She would come in, back up to the fireplace and hitch up her skirts at the back, which always made Charlie laugh. 'Cold bum, warm heart, Memsah'b,' he would say. The same joke every time. That ridiculous nickname. Memsah'b. Meg choked on the word and tried to avoid using it. The diamond in her nose. She was a thoroughly ridiculous woman, but Charlie was fond of her.

'She took me in when she need not have done. Not one of them ever made me feel that I didn't belong.'

Meg checked to see that there was enough coal on the fire, then climbed the tall staircase. She might as well have been climbing Everest. She would get young Charles dressed for his grandparents, wrap him up well and let him play in the snow while she swept the steps.

She stopped in her own room to check her hair, touch up her lipstick, and put on her woollen hat and heavy sweater. Her solemn reflection in the mirror startled her. Did her unhappiness show so plainly? 'Oh, God, dear Father,' she whispered to the mirror. 'Help me to escape. Soon.'

Charlie would have been astonished had he known that Meg was unhappy. He did realize that she resented the long hours he was forced to spend at the yard, but it puzzled him that she did not like the house. He liked everything about it: being near to the centre of town, the sound of traffic, the proximity of other people and, most of all, the big, grey, granite house itself with the vast, high-ceilinged rooms, the ornate fireplaces, carved corniced ceilings, and all the old-fashioned clutter which had enchanted him as a small boy. It had been like a curiosity shop, a museum.

The elder Maccallums were the only grandparents he had ever known. His mother's parents had disinherited her when they had learnt she was about to present them with an illegitimate grandchild. All the affection he might have given to them, he gave to the elder Maccallums.

He had Grandfather Maccallum's pocket watch. It had been given to Carlos as a wedding present. It was one of the few things Fionna had been able to take when she had cleared out Carlos's apartment in Madrid after his death. There was a note in the box which Carlos had written soon after the Civil War had started:

> If I am killed, and since Tina's death I don't much care
> if I am, Charlie is to have the watch. It belongs to him
> more than it belongs to me. He, poor devil, is heir to the
> bloody shipyard.
> ¡Salud!
>
> Carlos

It was an enormous turnip of a watch that chimed the hours and quarter hours. The fob on the chain was a gold model of the first Maccallum paddlewheeler steamer, and the small paddlewheel actually turned.

Once, on a special occasion—it had been Fa's birthday—he had considered wearing it. Meg had said, 'Of course, it is sweet, but a bit too much costume ball, isn't it?'

He wished he had a waistcoat of grey satin like Grandfather Maccallum to stretch the gold chain across, and a capacious pocket for the watch. He would like, one day, to hold young Charles on his knee as Grandfather had done with him, and take out the watch when it was chiming the hour, costume ball or not.

Instead, the watch had joined other memorabilia in one of the many glass-doored cabinets. Charlie kept it wound and the faint tinkle of its chimes sometimes caused the corners of Meg's mouth to tighten.

Perhaps he should let her have the dishes she wanted. The Maccallum service could be used for breakfasts or late suppers, simple luncheons such as today when Fa was present.

The luncheon had gone well. Young Charles in his red leggings and tartan tam had met them on the steps, jumping up and down, clapping his mittens together and shouting, 'Gran'fer, Gran'fer, Gran'fer! Mem! Mem! Mem!' One did not call Memsah'b grandmother.

He had led the way into the house, redolent of honey-glazed baking onions. 'Smell!' he had commanded.

They had had two sherries each and lunched in the cosy back sitting room. Young Charles had been allowed to join them, seated on three encyclopedias.

They had talked of Mairi's visit and departure, the unexpected snowfall and, of course, the yard and orders, payroll, employees, while Memsah'b and Meg looked bored. Meg had escaped by carrying away young Charles, who by then was covered with honey. He had howled all the way up to his room because he had not been permitted, in his sticky state, to kiss Gran'fer goodbye.

Now Fa and Memsah'b had returned to Milkstone, the early dark was closing in, the arc lights in the yard glowed in a halo of snowflakes. Charlie had cleared his office desk by the time Miss Maclean came in with the day's letters to be signed. She stood at almost military attention by his desk while he read them over and added his signature.

'Thank you, Miss Maclean. All very neat and accurate, as usual.' He smiled. What a remarkable shade of blue her eyes were.

She made no move to go and he waited questioningly, sensing she wished to say something and was wondering how to phrase it.

'Excuse me, sir, I hope I am not being cheeky, but Mrs Maccallum—the one here today, not *your* Mrs Maccallum—told me that you were in Spain. Like my brother. With the Internationals. I wonder if you knew him?'

He searched his memory. 'There were so many of us. Maclean . . . Maclean . . .'

'Yes sir. Finlay Maclean.'

'Hold on.' He tousled his hair as if it would stir his memory. 'Of course! Fin Maclean. He was a hero! At Ebro after he had swum the river, he kept going back to help those who couldn't quite make it. Some were wounded. He didn't have a stitch—' Charlie stopped at the sight of her blush. 'We had left our clothes behind except for our—uh—drawers. Somehow, Fin had lost those as well. But it didn't stop him. How is he? I'd like to see him.'

'He was killed in Italy, sir.'

'I am so sorry. What a filthy shame. After all he went through.'

'My mum says you can't escape your fate.' She paused at the door. 'Sir . . . why does Mrs Maccallum wear a diamond in her nose?'

'I have always wondered that myself.'

As she closed the door she said, 'It seems a funny kind of place to wear an earring.'

He looked at the empty desk top, its polished surface gleaming under the light of the desk lamp. He should not be going home early. There was too much work to be done. There was always too much work. He wondered if they would ever catch up. Orders continued to pour in, the drawings piled up on the desks of the designers, the delivery dates were pushed further and further ahead. The money, despite running seven days a week and paying double on Sundays, was almost alarming. He had never dreamed there would be so much, and that he would be responsible for it all.

But this evening he was too tired to think. It had been late when they had returned to Glasgow from Mairi's farewell dinner. The house had been cold and while Meg had looked in on young Charles, he had stirred up the fire in the bedroom. They had sat beside it for a while before undressing, not talking much.

Meg had looked tired and he thought of the nights that she waited up for him to cook his supper when he returned at nine, ten, often past ten.

'I'm sorry I invited my parents to luncheon after they put Mairi on the train,' he had said. 'I can always change it when they come to the yard tomorrow to pick me up. I can take them out for a meal.'

'It's all right. We can manage something. It would be wrong to change it.'

'They always enjoy seeing the bairn.'

'Of course.' Then, 'It was a nice party. I enjoyed it. I didn't know they could let loose like that.'

'We don't go out often enough, do we? Tell you what, I'll come home early tomorrow night. We'll both be tired and we can have an evening catching up with one another.'

'It's Bacon's afternoon off.'

'Better yet. We'll do toast and cheese over the fire and have tinned fruit for dessert.'

Meg had made a mock face at him. 'I'll believe your "early" when I see you walk through the door.'

'Promise. Have the toasting forks ready. I'll slice the cheese myself. Bacon makes it too thin and it flops.'

They had undressed then and got into bed. He had

touched her tentatively, but she had given no sign that she was aware of it.

He telephoned for a taxi, turned off the desk light, and went to the window to take one last look at the yard before he left. Snowflakes whirled in the wind. The arc lights' reflection shone in the dark mirror of the Clyde. Every berth held a ship in various degrees of completion.

He locked his office. Miss Maclean had left the light in her office burning for him. He turned it off and locked the door behind him, went down the narrow staircase and walked across the snowy yard to the gateman's house where the taxi awaited him.

Miss Maclean stood in a queue waiting for the tram. Charlie caught sight of her as his taxi left the yard. She wore no boots or hat. A heavy scarf hooded her head and the wind tugged at it so she kept readjusting it. Charlie lowered the window and called to her. 'Let me give you a lift.'

She hesitated. The woman behind her gave her a nudge and she ran through the slushy street and climbed in beside him. 'It's ever so kind of you, sir. My shoes'll be ruined. If you'll drop me off at St Enoch's underground, please.' She sat stiffly in the seat, hands clasped, not daring to look at him or lean back.

'You should have worn your boots. But we didn't know it was going to snow, did we?'

'I haven't any boots. They wore out ever so long ago and coupons being what they are—' She shrugged.

'Have you far to go after you leave the underground?'

'Not all that far, sir. My shoes'll not suffer any more that wee way than they have done.' She turned and smiled at him. 'You are a funny kind of boss, worrying about boots and the like.'

'Who would do the letters and keep the office in order

if you caught a cold?'

'There are plenty of others.'

'But you and I have grown accustomed to one another's ways.'

She looked at him again, her eyes wide, dark pools. Lord help me, thought Charlie. She thinks I'm making a pass at her. He laughed uneasily. 'Perhaps I am getting old and set in my ways. I appreciate the order you have made since Mr Reid left us.'

'It is what I am employed to do, isn't it, sir? I am glad my work pleases.'

They sat in uneasy silence the rest of the way to St Enoch's, unspoken words hovering in the air between them. As she got out all she said was, 'Thank you, sir. Goodnight.'

The taxi eased its way back into the traffic. Her scent lingered in the chilly air. He wondered if he had been a fool, opened the invisible gate in the invisible fence that exists between employer and employee. He almost dreaded facing her the next day. Even worse, he felt as if he had been unfaithful to Meg. Puzzling, but there it was.

Veda had to admit to herself that Meg's luncheon had been a success. Charles had enjoyed being there and it had helped to dispel his gloom over Mairi's departure. He had praised Meg's menu and asked Veda why they never had baked onions at home, had played clap-hannies with that incredibly sticky youngest Charles Maccallum, and praised Charlie for his diplomacy in handling a labour problem which had arisen.

Meg had been more silent than usual, and Veda felt that she herself had not made as much effort to draw her out as she should have done. Should she have stayed on after the men had gone? Meg had looked almost wistful as she had seen them off, Charles and Charlie to return to the yard, Veda to spend an hour or two wandering through Kelvingrove Gallery. She never grew tired of escaping into the foreign landscapes and the company of the people in the ancient portraits. Perhaps she should have invited Meg to accompany her. Could it be that Meg was lonely and unhappy? In Veda's opinion anyone would be miserable living in that memorial to the almighty Maccallums, whose ghosts probably walked at night. But what could one do while rationing persisted in making life miserable? Fresh paints, new carpeting, modern furniture that would do wonders were unavailable.

Meg had brought few things of her own. No furniture at all. A few impractical things, the sort a romantic girl collected for her trousseau and scarcely ever used: a cut-crystal bowl full of rainbows, a lacquered Russian box, a crate of books, a carefully mended Paisley shawl, and some other bits and pieces.

The shawl now covered a monstrosity of a table which had been no beauty to begin with. It had been scarred by Charles and his brother. They had been given their first Christmas pocket knives and put them into immediate use by carving their names on the table top. The top had been waxed and polished and displayed to visitors to show what clever rascals those Maccallum lads were. It could not be taken to the Barras to be sold amidst the rabble of discarded furniture with ne Maccallum name scratched large and crude upon it. Charles said it should be burned.

'Not on your life, Fa. It is a part of family tradition.'

Charlie was too keen on family tradition, Veda thought. The shawl worked a transformation, even covering the ugly, deformed legs. Today the crystal bowl held chrysanthemums the same deep red as the shawl and the armour of the knight on the Russian box.

But a bowl and flowers do not work miracles. Perhaps Fionna could talk to Meg. Fionna could ask without causing offense, '*How* do you put up with this house?' Fionna could tell Charlie to spend more time being married to his wife than to the yard, which might need husbanding, but not a husband. The war in Spain had forged a deep, loving friendship between Fionna and Charlie.

Yes, Veda would turn the matter over to Fionna. That resolved, she focused her attention on the pictures in the gallery. She had been wandering about the corridors scarcely noticing the exhibits in the current show.

Cold draughts stirred in the long corridors. So few people were there that the echo of her footsteps followed her. Today the pictures offered small solace. The serene landscapes with cows and leafy trees bored her. The people in the elegant portraits were lifeless. The rose-cheeked Dutch wives were too content. The dazzling light of Monet and Cézanne belonged to another time, another France.

She wandered restlessly, conscious of the cold and of her weariness, before turning into a smaller room where she found that for which she had been unconsciously searching. A picture by Gerald Gunn which the gallery had bought.

Gerald had offered it to Veda first by showing it to her as he did everything he painted. He did not expect her to buy, but he always gave her first choice. Many she did buy, but not this one. Veda had insisted on installing Gerald and Margery in the forester's cottage at Milkstone after the death of their daughter, Tina, wife of Carlos. An artist's income was uncertain at the best of times, and the depression years of the Thirties had been the worst of times. The living arrangement and friendship had continued and Veda and Charles assumed it to be a permanent one.

Gerald called them his patrons. If giving them free rent in

a chilly stone cottage made them patrons, Veda supposed they were that. But patron or not, this was one picture she had not wanted to buy.

Nights in the Gardens of Spain. No resemblance to the music of de Falla. Not the power of *Guernica*. Veda had made a special trip to Paris in 1937 when it had been hung at the World's Fair.

Gerald's painting was more personal than Picasso's, more sorrowful, less enraged. In the foreground was the grey and barren earth of the graveyard where Tina had been buried. Bombings had opened the graves, uncovering half-decayed corpses and scattered bones. Tina lay there, her shroud ripped, her face green in death, her lips drawn back in a grimace of despair. The middle ground was Madrid under air attack. The only light was the burst of flame flickering on the ripped and dying gardens, the torn flowers, the shattered trees, the faceless houses. Overall was the night sky, filled with stars exploding like bombs.

Veda could not have lived with it, but she returned to it again and again. Charles said she was being morbid.

There was nothing wrong with that. Everyone was too busy being little ladies and gentlemen to beat their breasts and howl with sorrow, rub ashes in their hair and drape themselves in gloom's grey veils. There would be less need for psychiatry if everyone let loose now and again.

You are getting fanciful, Veda told herself. Thinking a lot of nonsense. You are also slumping like a crone.

She straightened up, stretched her back, then took out her mirror to make sure that her hair was not wafting about her face making her look like a distraught tragedienne. In the mirror she saw the reflection of a man standing hesitantly in the entrance of the gallery. Their gazes met. He gave a half-apologetic bow.

Hastily she replaced the mirror in her handbag and snapped it shut. As she rose, embarrassed at having been caught, he came into the gallery. She took him in at a glance. One of the Polish officers who had been stationed in Glasgow during the war and, either from choice, rejection or fear, had not yet been repatriated.

His high boots gleamed, his uniform, smarter than those of the British, was worn but immaculately pressed. He carried the inevitable briefcase, and under his arm was the wonderful hat, the tall, square, towering *chapska*.

She liked his face, the broad, high cheekbones, the Tartar eyes, the chiseled, hawk-like nose, and the thin sensitive mouth beneath the waxed moustache.

He bowed again. 'Forgive me, please. I disturb you.' His voice was gentle, deep, with only a slight accent.

'Not at all. I should be going.' She should not be going. She had another hour before she was to meet Charles.

'Please,' he held up his hand in protest. 'Do not go. I watched you, forgive me again, so deep in thought of the picture, I did not like to disturb. I, too, am in deep thought of the picture.' He nodded towards it, his brows drawn in a frown, his eyes sad.

'You like it?' She had not intended to become involved in conversation, but she felt drawn to him.

'That, I think, is not the word. Always I return to it. It has not the anger or the power of *Guernica*, which I have seen only in photographs in the journals. But it has great sadness. The poor young woman has the look of ultimate sorrow.'

'She was the artist's daughter.'

The eyebrows rose in quick surprise. 'But Gunn, that I think is not a Spanish name. Does she indeed lie in Spanish earth or did she but model?'

'She is dead. It is a long story.'

'You will tell me the long story, please?'

Veda hesitated, then sat down, thinking this was no chance meeting, but one beyond her control. With a 'May I, please?' and without waiting for an answer, he seated himself beside her.

She had never told the story before. The story of her son, Charles, always called Carlos, a geologist mapping the un-mapped regions of Spain. Of his marriage to Tina and of breaking his leg high in the empty reaches of the Sierra Ne-vada, and how Tina went for help, leaving her passport be-hind in her panic and hurry. Of her death from a freak accident on a narrow Spanish road and because of her dress (they were camping), her espadrilles, some foolish earrings, and no passport, the police had assumed she was one of Spain's innumerable poor. No one had come to identify her and she had been buried there in the paupers' graveyard, wrapped in that shroud. Veda gestured at the picture and fell silent. Her voice was beginning to tremble.

'Holy Mary!' Impulsively he took her hand. 'Once more, I ask forgiveness. I should not have asked for the long story.'

'I could have refused to tell it.'

'Your son, Carlos? You see, I demand more.'

'He was found after a few days by a shepherd, but by then Tina had been buried. He stayed in Spain to continue his work. Somehow—he belonged in Spain. When the war came he fought for the Loyalists. He was killed at Ebro.'

'I was with the Dombrowsky Brigade.' He said it simply as if she would understand. When she looked bewildered, he added, 'In Spain, I, too, fought there. Afterwards I could not go back to Poland. I remained in France in one of the prison camps for those of us who had fought. When the later war came, I rejoined the Polish government in France. When

France fell, we removed to Britain. So, I am here.'

'For how long?'

'For my life, I think. There is nothing left for me in Poland. My family were killed. My business which had been in the family before me, belongs now to the State. First one political party then another is in power and both no good. I stay here. It is not easy. I have been given some government work. There is a training programme for civilian jobs. But it is not easy.'

'New beginnings are never easy.' There, she had said the trite thing which never brought comfort. 'What was your work?'

'A small publisher of rare books in all languages. We also set type for other publishers, French, German, Dutch, because we could do it more cheaply than their own printers. It required knowledge of languages, of course.'

'But Spain?'

'Ah! Spain. That was a sudden idealism; the need to go tilting at the windmills of Fascism, to save the world so books would not be burned as were many of those we had printed. To save innocent people of another race, another religion, another political persuasion. The Gipsies, the Jews, those who spoke out against evil, those who spoke truth, those who tried to act. I did a rash, foolish, but worthy thing.' He swept a gesture at Gerald's picture. 'And in the end nothing was solved and the great, dreadful war followed. And many more died.'

'Mr Churchill called it the unnecessary war.'

'Did he? But he waged it ardently.' He smiled at her suddenly, his face transformed, his dark eyes sparkling with humour. 'We talk like two old friends and we have not yet presented ourselves. I am Major Tadeusz Kosciuszko.'

'And I am Veda Maccallum.' She opened her handbag and

took out her card. He accepted it gravely, read it, and put it in his briefcase. If Mrs Charles Maccallum meant shipyard to him he did not say so. It was nice to be accepted as herself.

'Are you descended from Tadeusz Kosciuszko the patriot, who freed his serfs and fought with the Colonies during the American revolution?'

'You know of him? A learned lady! I regret, I am not a descendant. Because of our name, my parents named me Tadeusz in his honour. Perhaps they hoped I would be so glorious.'

'You did fight for freedom.'

'Mine was a lost cause.' He looked back at the picture. 'You must know the artist if your son's wife was his daughter. Is it possible to meet him? Was he, too, in Spain?'

'Only to help trace her and identify the body. I think he would enjoy meeting you. Our telephone number is on my card. If you will give me yours where I can reach you, I shall arrange something.'

'When I meet him, what shall I say? Is it better not to pursue such a thing?'

'It is your choice.' They shook hands, smiling. Again Veda's footsteps echoed in the empty halls, but she did not notice this time. She was thinking of Major Kosciuszko, of arranging for him to meet Gerald. And Charlie, of course, and perhaps Fionna. They would all talk about Spain. A party. It would give her something to do now that Mairi had gone, leaving Milkstone empty.

2

It seemed as if the exhausting journey would never end. The constant changing of trains, the passport and papers examined again and yet again. Detours where tracks had been destroyed and still not replaced, where bridges were nothing but twisted iron tilting into the rivers. Uncomfortable, ancient coaches, filthy toilets; refugees squatting in the aisles when there was no more seating; people going home, if home was still there; sleek, well-dressed black marketeers with quick, calculating eyes, and their women trying to separate themselves from the other travellers.

She would be glad when she finally reached Koblenz where she would transfer to the narrow-gauge line which would take her home. Home to Mutti Trötzen and Hannes. To be greeted by Corporal Braun's 'Howdy, may-yam', and Major Kimball's 'Hi, Mairi'. She had come to depend on her conquerors in a way she did not depend on Maxl.

Maxl. There it was again. The worm of doubt. During the war when everything crumbled, love—physical love—had been a necessity. The need to cling to someone, to touch, to feel. She and Maxl loved one another, but they were not in love. Now their relationship had to be reevaluated. They must distance themselves from one another. There was always the chance that Erich would return. Wouldn't he? She was no longer sure.

Mile after mile her thoughts ran the squirrel cage of memory and hope. She dozed, and wakened cold and stiff. She stared dully out the window at the rubble and snowy desolation. She opened Defoe again . . .

They had dug several pits . . . into which they put perhaps fifty or sixty bodies each; then they made larger holes wherein they buried . . . from two to four hundred . . .

Buchenwald. Major Kimball had shown her the pictures. 'How could you not have known?' he had asked.

She tried to explain: the controlled press and radio, the lies, the climate of fear, trust no one, wear a blindfold. 'We knew and yet we did not know. Especially, we did not know how bad they were.'

'Yeah, they all say that. "We didn't know." Dammit, Mairi, you must have known.'

'And if I had known, what could I have done? You wanted heroes? We would have been dead heroes. We were prisoners, too. Prisoners of fear, of torture, of the knock on the door in the middle of the night, fear for our families, the future. Fear is a powerful weapon. As powerful as any bomb.'

'Ah, hell. Argue with a Kraut and you get philosophy.'

When she got home she would tell him what Fa had said. 'We are caught in the web of our own time.' And a web of deception.

While she waited for the train at Koblenz she had a wurst and beer. They tasted almost the way they had tasted before the war, and she was hungry. Memsah'b's hamper had long since been emptied and there had been no food on the other trains. She felt as joyful as a child when the small, grumpy engine and its two coaches puffed on to the narrow-gauge track. It was like a toy train at a carnival, made for fun rides, and it would carry her home.

The coaches were third class with wooden seats, but the

aisles had been swept and there was a fire in the stove. The conductor doffed his hat to her and swung her luggage aboard. He had been on the line as long as Mairi could remember, been called up to serve in the *Volkssturm*, and survived to return. He dusted a seat near the stove for her, and threw in another piece of coal. She was safe now, did not have to guard her luggage from theft, show her papers, or change trains again. She relaxed and fell asleep. The conductor awakened her just before they reached the village.

There was the *Schloss* topping the hillside. The wedding cake frosted with snow, mouse-nibbled by bombs and shrapnel. A slice cut out of it where the northwest tower had once been. Home.

Old Herr Breurer was still *Bahnhofvorsteher*, though everyone knew he had been an enthusiastic Nazi, and wondered how he must have lied so effectively on his *Fragebögen*, the questionnaire that all German citizens had been required by the Occupation to fill out. He bobbed and bowed as he took her luggage from the conductor, saying, 'Welcome back, welcome, *gnädige* Frau. How was your homeland? No need to try to carry your luggage. I shall keep it safe and you order that Yankee Corporal to come down in his jeep and fetch it for you. You insist on carrying that one case? Is it not too heavy? I would assist but I cannot leave my post, you understand. That Corporal must come for the other. You are still the mistress of the *Schloss* despite their intrusion.'

She escaped him and plodded through the cobbled street. Snow blanketed the mounds where there were flattened houses, yet to be rebuilt. The church tower was no longer a needle-thin spire, but a squat, square one. Wind blew snow into her face. She put down her bag to rest. Once there had been benches in the town square, but they had disappeared to stoke someone's fire.

Frau Binding opened her door and waved to Mairi. 'Welcome back, *gnädige* Frau Doktor Trötzen. Did you bring this weather from Scotland?'

After a few pleasantries Mairi picked up her bag again. The road up to the *Schloss* looked insurmountable. Tyre tracks muddied the way. Corporal Braun must be out in his jeep or perhaps it was the Major. The iron gates with the wrought iron unicorns stood open. 'How come these pretty old gates didn't get melted down to make cannons?' she asked.

'I suppose no one knew they were here.'

'It'd be a cryin' shame to lose them.'

The crying shame had been the loss of the windows and a corner of the roof on the southwest tower when the bomb had struck the northwest one. Rain dripped into the attic and into the room below. They had not enough tubs and buckets to catch it all. The rooms there were dark with boarded-up windows, but the cellars where they lived now were darker still. Memsah'b had been angry when Mairi had told her they lived in the servants' quarters. She called the Yanks bad names in Urdu and refused to translate.

A small figure ran out of the huge, arched, iron-studded door. The wooden bridge over the filled-in moat thudded under his footsteps. He sent snow flying as he pelted down the hill and nearly overbalanced Mairi as he threw his arms around her.

'*Mutti, Mutti, Müttilein!* I thought you would never return. Time can be so long, can't it? Did you bring a surprise? Is it in the case? I shall carry it.'

'The case is too heavy for you, but you can help. Take this handle and I shall hold the other. Were you a good boy while I was away?'

His blue eyes—Maxl's eyes—twinkled teasingly. 'Am I not always good?'

'You know very well that you are not. I met your cousin Jamie who is just your age. He has hair as red as a bonfire and *Sommersprosse* all over his face. They call them freckles in English.'

'Freckles?' He tried out the word. 'Why does he have hair like a bonfire?'

'Because his mother did when she was small.'

'Who is his mother?'

'My sister. Your *Tante*.'

'Do I have a sister?'

'You know you have. Lilli is your sister.'

'I forgot. She went away with Georges, didn't she? You went away but you came back. Uncle Maxl went away . . .'

Mairi looked down at his animated face. Snowflakes landed on his eyelashes. He winked them off. 'What did you say about Uncle Maxl?'

'He went away. After you went away. He said some bad words and when he left Grossmutti cried. Lean down and I shall whisper the bad words.'

'Never mind the bad words. Where did he go?'

Hannes shrugged. 'Grossmutti knows. He hugged me when he left.'

'Is he coming back?'

Hannes shook his head. 'If he were coming back, he would not have hugged me, would he?'

They trudged through the snow in silence. Mairi thinking furiously, wondering, damning Maxl for not waiting for her return. Of course, he may have heard of work, paying work. Not the kind he begrudged that would bring the vineyard back to life, make a garden to provide food, restore some comfort to the *Schloss*.

'When I go to bed tonight will you sit beside me and tell me about my cousin with the bonfire hair and about what you ate? Were there mountains of food?'

'Not much more than we have. But they grow vegetables in a greenhouse and raise chickens and your *Tante*'s husband raises pheasants, and your grandfather has a cellar of good wine and can afford to buy whisky.' She would like a hot whisky and lemon right now. She would sip it drop by drop to make it last as long as possible.

'Does my grandmother still have a diamond in her nose?'

'Always.' They had reached the door. Hannes opened it then helped her with the case into the huge central hall off which all the other halls opened. In the old days log fires would have been burning in the head-high stone fireplaces. The Oriental rugs would have glowed like coals on the polished stone floor. There was no wood to waste warming halls these days. The rugs had been looted by the first wave of Yanks who had come through and were probably rotting in the mud and snow somewhere.

Corporal Braun's typewriter rattled in his office. His radio crackled out an American song sung by a Blues-voiced female. 'That Dinah Shore, she can sing to me any ol' time,' Corporal Braun had said. She was singing to him now.

Honey, I been down, down to Memphis town . . .

'Memphis is in Egypt,' Hannes had told Corporal Braun.

'Not this Memphis, kiddo. This Memphis is where you hear the Blues.'

'Blue is a colour so how can you hear it?'

Oh. Lordy how that trombone can moan
It sounds just like a sinner on revival day . . .

'Do you understand that song, Mutti?'

'The words, yes. It's just a Yank song, Hansi.'

Firmly, Mairi closed the door on the hall leading to the cellar steps, shutting out Dinah Shore. The hall windows were covered with glazed paper, giving the effect of a winter morning in the Arctic. The porcelain stove stood cold and white as an iceberg. They bumped the suitcase down the curved stone staircase, the steps hollowed by centuries of wear.

Mutti Trötzen sat by the iron stove, but she got up as Mairi came in and welcomed her with a smile. She was beautiful when she smiled, and she still stood erect, her chin high, a proud lift to her head. She may have been conquered, but she was a lady unconquered in her soul.

'Dear Mairi, you have come back to us. Hannes said you would come today. He must be psychic. The visit must have been a good one. You look better.'

'I'm glad to be home.'

Hannes danced around them. 'She brought a surprise for me.'

'For both of you.' She took off her coat and gave an involuntary shiver. Even with the stove going the room was dank. 'What is this about Maxl?'

Mutti's eyes signalled 'later'. 'He went to look for work,' she said lightly.

'Not that there isn't enough work here.'

'He was restless.'

'I had noticed that.' Mairi knelt and unlocked the suitcase. 'Your grandmother first, Hannes. Look, wool to knit. They still make heather colours. And a sweater. It isn't quite new, but it is cashmere and Memsah'b said the skirt she wore it with is *kaput*.'

'I can imagine how *kaput* it was. Your mother is too generous.'

66

'Chocolate biscuits. Seconds from the factory, but they taste all right. Their shape isn't quite what it should be. You may have one now, Hansi. And look at this. Tea! My grandfather in Assam sent it.'

'Me, me, me,' Hannes chanted, leaning over the case.

'Yes, you. Here. They belonged to your Uncle Carlos when he was a little boy. I remember him playing with them in the garden at Milkstone.'

Carefully he opened the box. She admired his long, slender fingers, his narrow hands. She smiled at his awed face and the delighted sigh.

Black knights and white, archers and lancers, stonecasters, towers and banners, drawn up in the box facing one another, each army led by a king wearing a crown.

'It is the most splendid gift I have ever been given. Did my Uncle Carlos not want them any more? Is he too old to play with them?'

'He didn't need them any more.'

'It takes away the sad part of your being gone.'

She started to say, 'Take good care of them,' but she knew he would. If he did not, what did lead soldiers matter? They had outlasted Carlos.

'I am going to show them to Corporal Braun and Major Kim this very minute.'

'Ask first if they are busy. You must not disturb them, Hannes.'

'Corporal Braun is never too busy. He likes to be interrupted.'

'Very well. Go along.' As soon as he was up the stairs she turned to her mother-in-law. 'Maxl?'

'He left ten days ago. He said he was sick of doing the work of a peasant. Sick of the *Schloss,* sick of the Americans living in it—' She paused.

'And of my friendship with them.' Mairi finished the sentence. 'He told me that often enough. My so-called friendship has helped to put food in his mouth, hasn't it?'

'I think he resented that, too. He said you would never come back. That once you were in Britain you would listen to all the lies about Germany and not return.'

'Didn't we listen to lies for twelve years? Does he think I am so innocent that I don't know the difference between lies and truth? My God!'

Frau Trötzen twisted the skeins of new wool in her lap. 'He said he wants to go back to the university, back to study architecture. That was his subject, you remember.'

'At his age? Where is he planning to get the money to live on?'

'He took twelve of the silver plates.'

'The service plates? The silver ones? He had no right! They have been at the *Schloss* for how many years? A hundred and fifty? They have the family crest on them. We—you and I—buried them to keep them from being looted. Mutti, how could you have *allowed* him to take them?'

'He said he had a right to them because he is a Trötzen. He said his father told him they would be divided between the two of you, Erich and you and Maxl and his future wife, when I die. He took only twelve. I don't know why I am crying.'

'And I do not know why I am angry. We shall probably never again have a party for a hundred people, not even when Maxl marries. You used them at my wedding feast, I remember. But what do twelve plates matter these days?'

'Nevertheless, when he marries, Maxl shall be given thirty-eight plates. It is his own fault he won't have fifty.'

'I must go and ask Corporal Braun to bring my bags from the station when Kim returns with the jeep. It looks as if it's going to snow forever. Make us a cup of tea and we shall each have a chocolate biscuit, and I insist on you listening all about my trip. It was lovely, but oh, I am glad to be home.'

'How can you be glad to come back to this?'

'I belong here now.' She picked up her bag to carry it to her bedroom which had once been the butler's pantry.

'Mutti, mail call!' Hannes said it in English. 'That is what the Yanks call it. The post came while I was showing Corporal Braun my knights. Major Kim isn't back yet, but I am to go up when I hear the jeep. Here is a funny-looking letter. All over stamps and crazy writing.'

It was the most recent letter Mairi had written to Erich. Like all the others it was returned, stamped in Polish, German, and Russian: 'Undeliverable'. And in English, the Red Cross stamp: 'Unable to obtain information about this person'.

She put it in the drawer with the others that had been returned. With them was the last word she had had from Erich. A postcard on flimsy, wartime paper stamped: 'Passed by censor'. The postmark was faint and blurred but after examining it under a magnifying glass they had decided it said 'May 1946' and 'something Silesia'. The message was impersonal: 'Beloved, I am still here. I do not know when I shall be (the rest of that line was blacked out). Pray for me. Love to all.'

They had pondered over the censored words. 'Exchanged', 'moved', 'sent home', or something far worse?

'I don't know why I go on writing. It is a waste of paper and time.'

'Perhaps some get through.'

Maxl's voice echoed in Mairi's mind. 'Give up, Mairi. Erich is probably in Siberia by now. Still mining,' he had added.

She carried her bag into her room. Snow banked against

the narrow, high windows gave the room a grey half-light. Snow would be filling the shell of the northwest wing which had been blown away in the bombing, taking with it a Dürer, a Max Ernst, old etchings, family photos, books, Biedermeier furniture, Oriental carpets, beds, warm bedding, and small treasures.

It would be snowing in Siberia.

Wearily, she sank down on the bed and cupped her face in her hands. No tears came to assuage the anger, the disappointment, the loneliness, the hopelessness.

'What a damned, hellish, bloody homecoming!' She whispered it so Mutti Trötzen wouldn't hear. Hellish or not, she was half-glad that Maxl had gone.

The Arctic wind battering the cliffs of the North Cape drove snow across Lapland, howled through the forests of Finland, tossed the dark waters of the Baltic, and smothered northern Europe with snow. The shards of coal which blackened the grounds around the mine, blackened the snow as it fell. The window frames of the mine offices leaked sharp knives of frigid air, stirring the papers on Erich's desk.

Two years and eight months since the war had ended and he was still in Silesia. He had been there when the Russian armies had rolled past in their race to Berlin. Speer himself had ordered him to stay. The Reich needed coal now that the Allies had taken the Ruhr and put an end to production there.

What could he do but stay? There was no way he could cross Poland and Germany in the wake of the Russians. Now there was no way he could leave. He knew little of what was happening in Germany now. He hoped that all the Nazis were dead along with the Führer, their dreams bile in their dying, their pride soaked in blood.

Yet . . . had he lifted a hand against them? He had joined

the party before the war, mockingly, rather than lose his position as *Bergassessor*. He had allowed his children, Lilli and Edu, to join the Hitler-Jungvolk and the Jungmädels rather than risk harm at school. He had been passive, accepted everything with a helpless gesture. What would protest have gained? Imprisonment? Torture? Death?

Was he not a prisoner now? The Governor of the mine had just left the office. The floor was too cold to melt the dusting of snow that had blown in when he had opened the door. Erich picked up his pen again, but the figures on his desk blurred under his eyes. He was being transferred to the Kuzuetsk Basin. *Lieber Gott,* where was that? He remembered hearing about it, reading about it when he had been at university, but its location had never taken form in his mind. The second largest and richest coalfield in the USSR. Ten thousand acres of coal? Or was it ten thousand miles?

'Why?' he had asked. 'Why me?'

'Because, comrade, you were an assistant director in the Ruhr and the Saar. You are needed to help assemble the equipment we are transferring from Germany. You have been chosen from above.' He said it as if it were an honour. 'I shall miss you,' he had added with a smile. He had two stainless-steel teeth at the front which made his smile slightly sinister.

Erich said dutifully, 'And I shall miss you. For a moment I had hoped you would be going with me.'

The Governor had laughed and given Erich a friendly slap on the shoulders. 'No, no. I am secure here. For a while. One never knows, of course.' His voice was cautious, as if he had glanced over his shoulder to see if there were someone listening.

'I suppose there is no hope of my being repatriated?'

'You are not happy with us?'

'I miss my family. There is a child I have never seen. And a grandchild, half French. My daughter married one of the French prisoners who worked our grounds. France and Germany wed at last.'

'Believe me, comrade, you are better here. The Germans are starving. Berlin is rubble. The country is in chaos because the British, Americans and French have no experience in handling the situation that exists.'

'I also have a wife waiting for me.' If she was still alive. He had understood why there had been no word from her during the first two years, but now the ban to write or to receive letters had been lifted, and there was only silence.

As if he had not heard, the Governor continued, 'Furthermore, you are a special case. You were not of the *Wehrmacht*. Your papers show you joined the party under obligation to hold your position. You have worked well with us. A special order from above would be required for your release. That will not come as long as you are needed. You are to travel with some German workers we have retained to assist you. The machinery will follow separately, under guard.' He laid a finger to his lips and smiled around it. 'A special case, you understand. Freed under the noses of the British.'

Stolen. The polite word was 'freed'.

'And after the machinery is in place and working?'

'That will no longer be my concern. The Governor you will work under—no, let us say, work *with*—is Comrade Janek Okhlopkov and he will be the one to decide that.'

'And the Germans assisting me? War prisoners? Former soldiers?'

The Governor spread his hands and shrugged. 'I was not informed. Only that they would join your train somewhere along the way.'

The wind moaned under the eaves, driving a funnel

of snow past the window.

'I believe it is a kinder climate.' The Governor looked out the window. 'Your papers will be ready this evening. And of course, I shall see you off tomorrow.'

'Tomorrow?'

'That will give you time to finish your paperwork and say farewell to your *katya*.'

'She won't be going with me?'

'My dear fellow, there will be other *katyas* in the Kuznetsk. We send them in once a week to service the prison workers. You will have no trouble finding someone permanent and willing.' He smiled, a man of the world. 'She was fortunate to have you as long as she did. We will recommend her to your replacement. No need for concern.' Erich wanted the man to get out before he lost his temper. Recommend her! What would happen to Marya?

'I am glad you understand. Yes, get on with it. As I said, I shall miss you.' He had left in a flurry of snow. It was an hour yet until noon, but Erich could do no work. The figures ceased to make any sense to him. There was no future, no hope, nothing.

The house he shared with Marya was only a few steps from the offices, but the wind was so strong he had to fight for every step he took. Even though he walked with his head down, the gusts of snow blinded him. And when he reached the house he would have to break the news to Marya.

She was at the stove stirring soup. As he forced shut the door she smiled radiantly at him. 'The storm wants to come in and warm itself.' She was too thin, yet her figure was comely and the bones of her face were good, so even the thinness was beautiful.

She kissed him and touched his arm lovingly. 'The soup is ready and there is bread today and cheese and a little ginger cake. Frau Ebert gave me a bit of sugar. It is a feast.'

He forced himself to smile at her. 'And I am hungry.' The truth was he had no appetite at all, knowing he would have to tell her.

She ladled the soup into the brown earthenware bowls. It was thick and fragrant and the colour of burgundy from the beets she had hoarded all winter. He ate in silence, finding the soup good and that he *was* hungry, and eating kept him from talking, from telling.

'*Liebchen,* there is something wrong. Tell me.'

He dipped his bread into the soup, bit into it and swallowed before answering. 'I am to be transferred. To the mines in Russia.' He saw the fear in her eyes. 'Tomorrow.'

'To the mines? Oh, God. Tomorrow! Just like that? And—me?'

'No.' He would have explained, but she pushed her bowl away and pounded the table with her fist.

'Is that all I have been to you? A *katya?* A bedside rug?'

'I asked if you could go. He said it is forbidden. Marya, it is not my doing. You know that. What can I do?'

Her anger cooled as suddenly as it had come. 'I know. We can do nothing against them just as we could do nothing against the SS. We are less than animals. Insects to be stepped on. Exterminated.' She began to weep. 'God help me, God help me, God help me.'

Erich rose and put his arms around her, drew her to her feet and pressed her body against his own, her helplessness stirring his desire.

'No, Erich. Later. Bed will not make it right. Our soup will go cold and our little cake. Later. Let us finish our meal. We will not have many more together.'

Long before the late northern dawn came, they were at the

station. The platform was lit by a single bulb, and the concrete slab was slippery under its coating of snow. The Governor was there before them, pacing up and down, leaving a network of black footprints in the snow. He smiled a greeting, his steel teeth gleaming in the pallid light. He shook hands with Marya. 'Yes, yes. No worrying now. I shall see to it you are taken care of. One of the *good* Poles, eh?'

She did not return his smile.

They heard the train coming long before its headlight punctured the darkness. Marya clutched Erich's hand. Her eyes shone with tears. Anything Erich could have said would not have comforted her, and it remained unsaid because of the Governor's presence.

The stationmaster came out, swinging his lantern, casting quick shafts of light into the darkness. The train crept to a stop, driving snow before it. The conductor swung down the steps, exchanged a word with the stationmaster, glanced at Erich and gestured at him impatiently as if to hurry him aboard. Erich and the Governor shook hands, the Governor stepped back and nodded at Marya, giving her permission to make her farewell. They exchanged a quick, passionless kiss and she thrust a package into his hands. 'Food for the journey. A little message is enclosed. Goodbye, darling one. Do not forget me. Please. Remember me, Erich.'

He stood in the vestibule, waving as the engine dragged the train into the darkness. The Governor saluted. Marya stood motionless, a slight, shadowy figure, hugging herself against the cold. Soon snow and darkness blotted them from view.

Except for three other passengers, the carriage was empty. They looked at him with incurious, lifeless eyes, their breath steaming from their mouths as they grunted a greeting. Erich chose a seat near the stove though no fire glowed in it. Frost crusted the ash and dead coals. The fuel box was empty of anything but dust. A kerosene lamp swung with the motion of the train, casting pale light against the ceiling.

Without removing his gloves, Erich opened the package to extract the 'little message'. He was dismayed to find that Marya had given him her ration of sausage and cheese, half a loaf of black bread, two boiled eggs, sugar lumps, and the ginger cake. Better that he should go hungry than she, but there was no way to return it now. He unfolded the enclosed paper. There were three sentences.

'In the spring there will be a child. I had planned to tell you as we ate our cake. It was to be a celebration.'

She had not signed it.

The unborn child accompanied him on the journey. Waking, he thought of it. Sleeping, it haunted his dreams. It took various forms. Often it was the bald, aged face of a newborn with enormous blue orbs for eyes, swaddled in clouds as if emerging from outer space. Sometimes it was a toddler, fair-haired, rosy-cheeked, who held his hand as they walked in a meadow blood-spattered with poppies.

At other times it was the mirror image of himself as a child, standing solemnly on the shore of the North Sea while Maxl ran up and down in the shallow waves shouting at him to play. Or the lad who had clung to Grossvati's arm as they watched the remnants of the defeated army march home from the Western Front after the first war. No bands played. No flags waved. The sullen crowds which had thrown flowers four years earlier surged forward and spat on the men, tore the epaulettes and medals from the officers' uniforms. Grossvati's tears had fallen on Erich's hands. He awakened now to find the tears were his own.

A child he would never see, who would never know him, his father. He choked on the ginger cake when he tried to eat it. He broke it into thirds and gave it to the other passengers who mumbled surprised thanks. Otherwise they remained strangers, isolated in silence, perhaps in fear.

Snow coated the windows and high noon was like early twilight. Every seven or eight miles the train stopped for the crew to get out and shovel snow off the tracks. Intermittently the wind whined, followed by the silence of a dead world.

He lost track of the days, but always the unborn child was with him. Occasionally there was a station where he could buy a greasy sausage or a bowl of hot, watery soup and some flat, grainy bread. The stations were ghostly. Everywhere were burnt-out freight cars, tanks and troop carriers, rusting artillery, frozen water tanks. It was as if the war had been yesterday.

The pine forests bent under the snow. The trees were ripped and scarred by machine-gun fire. Trenches zigzagged through them and the frozen roads were cut by tank tracks, lined with wrecked trucks, burnt tanks, scraps of cloth and, sometimes, bones. The villages were black hulls, and everywhere were shell holes filling with snow.

In some villages there were lines of prisoners, shackled together, guarded by guns, working to clear the ruins. They wore ragged *Wehrmacht* uniforms. Some were barefoot except for rags wrapped about their feet. They were like spectres from a painting by Bosch.

One passenger left the train in the middle of the wilderness. He took his pack from the rack, gave them all a nod and a grunt, and left. They watched him flounder into the white wilderness, sinking to his knees at every step, until the thickening snow turned him to a grey shadow.

Near Stalingrad the train was stalled for five days while the tracks were being repaired. The crew built a sauna out of scrap lumber from half-burnt buildings, heated stones and threw snow on them. Passengers and crew sat in the steamy fog, letting the heat burn into their chilled bones. Erich remembered hot summers on the Costa del Sol, with Mairi turning to bronze beside him on the beach; fish dinners on the esplanade with paper lanterns flickering in the hot wind, and pitchers of dark sangria.

That was reality, lost forever. The tracks were repaired and he climbed back on to the train to be carried further, ever further towards the east.

The cold weather continued without a break. Snow feathered down from heavy skies. Glasgow's streets were grey liquid which froze at night and thawed at midday. Old dears out to do their frugal shopping spilled like comic tumblers, breaking their fragile bones.

Two Sundays after Mairi had returned to Germany, Meg and Charlie drove to Blanelammond to call at Milkstone and the castle. The Campsie Fells looked as soft as down, and Milkstone, when they started up the drive, looked as if it were sculpted from ice.

It was good to be out of the city. With petrol rationing there were too few such treats, though Meg could not help wishing they were going to some place other than to visit Charlie's relatives. It was useless to suggest such a thing, just as it was useless to suggest that they should move out to Kelvinside or Dowanside where they could have a garden for Charles to play in. Such a suggestion would be met with a shocked disbelief and flat, but kindly refusal.

Not to mind. The narrow driveway was banked with snow and the barren branches black against it. In summer the air was sweet with greenery, wallflowers bloomed in the stone dykes and rhododendrons were towering scarlet trees. Behind the house was a dell that in May was a lake of bluebells, and beyond it a small lochan with a minuscule island on which grew wild roses and a single tree.

Meg liked the house. It had a helter-skelter disorder which was comforting. Pictures covered the walls, books and magazines overflowed from tables and were stacked on the floor beside chairs, carpets covered worn places in other carpets, petals fell from bouquets, and there were cats everywhere because Veda adopted every stray. Just inside the entrance hall was a very old, very dusty, stuffed cobra, hood spread ready to strike. Young Charles adored it and always gave it a kiss. Veda would have given it to him, but Meg had refused the offer, and Veda had said that in any case, it was half-promised to Jamie, but she was afraid if it were moved it would fall to bits. Charles loved to hear the story of how it had been found in the bath and the servants had refused to kill it because it was sacred, and one of Veda's brothers had dispatched it by breaking its back as it was about to strike.

Already Charles was jumping up and down in anticipation of seeing it again. Charlie let him out of the car as soon as they drew to a stop, and he paused only long enough to point at the Dutch-tile guard dogs set in the wall beside the thick, iron-bound Gothic door, and announce, 'Dogs!' before beating on the door with two small, clenched fists. When the door opened he hugged his grandfather's knees with screams of joy, then released them to greet the cobra.

Veda, wearing a floor-length wool skirt and a heavy turtleneck, came to greet them. The cobra was forgotten.

'*Talli, talli badja baba,*' Charles clapped his mittened hands together.

'He remembers!' Veda had taught him the Urdu 'clap hands' on his last visit. '*Ucha roti . . .*' she prompted.

'Yes. *Ucha roti schat banaya!*'

'That's enough,' Charlie said. 'Memsah'b, you're looking smashing as usual.'

He never says that to me, Meg thought. Perhaps I don't look smashing.

'Sweet lies, laddie. You should recognize the skirt. It's an old blanket which used to be on your bed.'

'I thought I recognized the latticework border.'

'Well, come along to the fire. We have a lovely bottle of Highland malt, brown as peat and sweet as sin, awaiting you. Mr MacCrae who minds our croft on the Kyle sent two bottles. Pure luck his still has never been discovered.'

They followed her into the south sitting room which ran the length of the house, with a fireplace at each end, both ablaze today. Over one fireplace was a Monet haystack glowing in the French midday sun, and above the other a Joan Miro whimsy. Dark oils mingled with silver-framed family snapshots and Gerald Gunn's watercolours took up the rest of the wall space. Dapplegrey, the old hobby horse, had been brought down from the nursery, which was too cold and too remote for carrying coal to warm it for young Charles's brief visit. He mounted at once and galloped away to foreign parts, wearing the tea cosy as a helmet. 'Whilst the tea goes tepid,' Veda sighed. 'Better tepid tea than a howling child.'

If the sitting room at Blythswood looked like this, Meg thought, she could be happy. She could be happy at Milkstone, too, but there was no chance it would ever belong to her and Charlie. It would be Mairi's and what would she do with it, living in Germany? Perhaps she would lease it to them.

After the second whisky the talk turned inevitably to the shipyard, and whether to accept orders from the Admiralty for anti-submarine frigates.

'We have enough orders to keep us busy without taking on the frigates, haven't we? The next war is going to be all Hiroshima and Nagasaki, if the Yanks have their way, and God help us all.'

Veda stood up. 'Come, Meg, if they are going to talk shipyard we'll go to the other end of the room.'

And what shall I find to talk about? Meg wondered. She was saved by her son who tumbled off Dapplegrey and demanded a walk to the lochan.

'Good idea. Sweep the cobwebs out of our heads. Want to come, Meg?'

'I would like it. I miss walking in the country.'

'Come out whenever you feel the need. It's good for the wean, too.'

When they reached the entrance hall Veda unhooked her skirt and stepped out of it, revealing a pair of baggy trousers underneath. She laughed at Meg's surprised expression. 'Too many cold passages in this house. I prepare for indoor blizzards. Will the coal shortage EVER be over?'

Out of doors there was a watery gleam of sun, too weak to melt the snow. Charles galloped ahead of them. They walked in silence for a little way, then abruptly Veda asked, 'Meg, are you happy in town? In that house?' Damn! She had intended to leave that question to Fionna.

'It—it hasn't the charm of Milkstone.'

'Huh! Charm! It's a dreadful house.' Veda kicked a pebble out of the path. 'Always has been. Every stick of furniture in it should be done over. One would think it a National Trust monument.'

'As far as Charlie is concerned, it is.'

'He can be a very stiff-necked young man. He must have more than an ounce or two of those hidebound English grandparents of his. That in combination with the

Maccallum grandparents can be a disaster when it surfaces. Fortunately it doesn't surface often. Overall, he is a dear.'

Is he? 'I have been thinking of going to visit my parents.'

'One needs that, doesn't one? I have been thinking the same. In fact, I considered asking if you and Charlie would stay at Milkstone with Charles while I was away. I don't like the idea of his being alone and there isn't much companionship in household help.'

'When are you going?'

'Not at once. Charles won't hear of it until things settle down. But I think about it, dream about it, and plan. I could never live contentedly if I didn't see Papa once more before he dies.'

'I am sure Charlie would be agreeable to staying here.'

'The real decision is yours.'

'Is it?'

'It should be. Speak up to him, Meg.'

Young Charles trotted back from where he had been breaking a path through the drifts. He pointed through the dark, leafless grove of trees which divided Milkstone property from the Lammondson. Distant, above the tree tops, they saw the blunt square tower of the castle.

'Aunt Fee. Jamie,' said the little boy.

'Yes, that's where they live. We shall see them after we leave here.'

He nodded and trudged on towards the lochan.

'He's quite intelligent, isn't he? Be careful he doesn't turn into pure Maccallum.' She gave Meg a quirky smile. 'Carlos didn't, thank God.'

Jamie met them at the door of the castle and took immediate possession of Charles. 'Come, child. Liam and I are going to explore the Bushby. I'll watch him, Aunt Meg. Tether him to me the way mountaineers do. If he gets tired Liam'll carry him pick-a-back. He's fierce strong, Liam is.'

Fionna came into the great hall. 'Away with you, Jamie. Meg, Charlie, come in where it's warm. Don't worry about Charles. Jamie feels like the Great Protector and has given his oath there will be no derring-do.' She slammed the door upon the lads and herded Meg and Charlie into the enormous formal room. 'Sherry, whisky, Maureen's oatmeal cakes made with real butter churned from our own cow. The blessings of country living in times like these. You must take a pat home with you. Don't let me forget. Willie, love, do pass the booze.'

Meg forced herself to relax. All these people were so confident, so at ease with one another. They seemed to melt together so each personality played counterpoint against the other into a complex composition. Veda's words had been the first intimation that *she* was no Maccallum, but a secret rebel.

But Meg wondered about Fionna. She had always been jealous of the close relationship between Fionna and Charlie. 'But we were in Spain together. With Carlos,' Charlie had protested. 'It's nothing to be jealous about. It's simply something we shared that the others didn't. Just as you and I shared special times. The conchie camp, for instance. And those days in the library . . .'

'I suppose you have heard,' Fionna was saying. 'Memsah'b is at it again. She met a Polish officer in Kelvingrove Gallery and is determined that all of us shall be as enamoured of him as she is.'

'Hm, that is a bit ominous. I hope she isn't planning to have an affair with him. She really should begin to act her age.'

'I had the impression that she felt a bit of a fool for having acted so impetuously,' Willie said. 'Actually, it's Gerald he wants to meet. He was admiring the picture. You know the one I mean.'

'Oh, she mentioned how much in common Charlie and I would have with him as he, too, had fought in Spain. I thought it was one of her famous cover-ups.'

'I want to meet him,' Charlie said. 'I thought the Dabrowski Battalion was all but wiped out in the siege of Madrid.'

'A few of them ended up in my ward at the hospital,' Fionna said. 'Very few.'

'He must be one of those. So bring him on!'

'Oh, she intends to bring him on. She is planning a party—if you can tear yourself away from the yard one evening, old dear.'

'Actually, Fionna, that is what we called to discuss. Old Mr Robertson has finally decided to retire. A great relief to all of us as he falls asleep during board meetings and his snores are so loud and distracting that we end up shouting at each other. The point is, there will be a vacancy on the board. Fa and I want you to fill it.'

'You are off your head, both of you.'

'Wait a bit, lass. I think it's a capital idea.'

'Throwing me to the wolves, Willie? What would those old gentlemen say when you announce I am taking Mr Robertson's chair?'

'Never mind them. Will you do it, Fionna? After all, you *are* a Maccallum and you have a head for business. There's a stipend with it. You could use the cash, couldn't you?'

Fionna held out her glass for a refill. 'You know, Charlie, that Carlos and I were never all dewy-eyed about the yard. Mairi was. She should have been the son. But the mention of a stipend has seduced me. All right, you have bought yourself a board member. Now perhaps Willie will give up his daft scheme for shooting parties.'

'Too late, lass. The adverts are away at *Country Life* and *Scottish Field*, all paid for and scheduled to appear in the January issues.'

'January! The shoot isn't until October.'

'I need the deposits to pay the joiner for the bath appliances.'

'Damn, damn, and double damn. Sorry, Meg. I am often given to blasphemy, a bad habit I learned in Spain.'

Willie smiled and refilled glasses all around. 'You'll enjoy the gentlemen, lass.'

'The devil I will. As your shooters come in the front door I shall dart out the back.'

They drove back to the city in darkening twilight through which hesitant snowflakes fell. Young Charles slept in the back seat, covered with a tartan rug, and neither Meg nor Charlie spoke much for fear of awakening him. Charlie seemed absorbed in his own thoughts, and Meg's spirits sank the nearer they drew to the city.

The city was dark, as electricity was still curtailed, and Blythswood Square was darker still, the houses shuttered against the cold, and no lights seeping through.

Charlie carried the sleepy child up the steps, leaving Meg to unlock the door. The chill greeted them. The fires had burned down to coals dark as garnets. The door knobs were icy to touch.

'No use building up any fires except in the back room,' Charlie decided. 'We can eat off the tea cart.'

Of course, Meg thought. He expects to eat and Mrs Bacon gone for the evening. It would have to be another omelette made from the eggs Memsah'b had sent back with them, with cold, sliced venison on the side. 'I shall grow antlers soon,'

Meg thought. 'To think that venison is considered a treat!'

Charlie stood indecisively in the hall, still holding the drowsy child. 'How about if you put him right to bed and let him have supper there?'

'Yes. All right. Put a shilling in the heater, please,' she added. No need for all of them to have chilblains.

'He won't need it in his bed.'

'He will need it while he eats and while I sit with him to see he doesn't spill. Please, Charlie. Don't be so—stoic.'

'What else is there to be these days?' His voice came back down the stairwell.

She hung up her coat and pulled on her old workaday cardigan. 'I too shall take up blasphemy,' she told herself, as she carried the basket from Milkstone down to the kitchen.

Astonishingly there was still a faint warmth in the coal range in the kitchen. Meg put her hands on the black lids, feeling warmth seep through her.

The basket which Memsah'b had given them contained more than eggs and cold venison. There was a jar of pickled beetroot, a rhubarb tart, turnips, and a flask of the precious malt whisky. Feeling reckless, Meg poured some into a cordial glass and sipped it as she fixed young Charles's boiled egg and toast.

Charlie was already rattling at the fireplace in the small sitting room. Obviously he hadn't hung about to undress his son. *That* was woman's work.

When she carried the tray up to the nursery she found young Charles kneeling in front of the shilling heater, struggling with his socks. He smiled angelically as he pulled one off and waved it in triumph. 'May I have a hottie in my bed?'

'Of course. And you may eat on your little table before the fire. Fetch your small chair and I'll go back down for the hottie. The water is almost on the boil.'

'Shall I eat in my clothes then? Father said to eat in my jams.'

'Whichever.' Meg set the tray on the small table and her son sat down and solemnly surveyed the egg in the blue-ringed bowl and the toast fingers.

'I'm glad it is not porridge.'

She read *The Tale of Mr Toad* to him while he ate. The heater went off and in the brief silence before she recklessly added another shilling they heard the whisper of snowflakes against the window.

She helped him undress and brush his teeth, then tucked him in and turned off the light. The red glow of the heater warmed the room with its light. 'I'll send your father to kiss you good night,' she promised as she closed the door.

Surprisingly, Charlie had put a cloth on the tea cart and laid the flatware and dishes on it. By the time he returned from telling his son goodnight their meal was ready and he wheeled it in.

It was probably the whisky working, but as she ate she realized how tired she was. This new, secret pregnancy was sapping her strength. She must apply for extra rations due pregnant women, but if she did, Charlie would know at once. And she did not want him to know. Not yet.

'You seemed to get on better with Memsah'b today,' Charlie said, pushing the cart out of the way so he could stretch his legs towards the fire.

'Yes. We talked about our staying with your father when—if—she goes back to India.'

'No problem. Fa is determined she shan't go. Almost fifty years in Scotland and she told him she still feels closer to her home there. Is that something that comes with old age?'

'It isn't confined to old age. I miss Caithness and the empty country and the North Sea.'

'I think of it sometimes myself. I used to feel at peace with myself when I got away from the barracks or was off from the others, squatting in the dirt, planting trees. I sorted out a lot of problems that I hadn't known I had.'

'I was thinking . . . I . . . I'd rather like to go back for a visit.'

'In midwinter? And travel the way it is today? You're daft, Meg.' He smiled affectionately. 'It's too late for the heather. Wait until spring when the broom is in bloom.'

By spring she would be distorted and awkward. Later she would be trapped with a new baby.

'No.'

'No? . . . Meg, I realize I don't spend as much time with you as I would like these days. I can't even guess how soon the worst of the rush at the shipyard will ease off. At the rate orders are coming in we'll soon be booked six or seven years ahead. I'm sorry. It isn't what either of us expected. I'll try to make better arrangements, I promise. But as for going north now, in this weather, and trains running with old equipment over tracks that haven't been repaired since '39 . . . It's plain foolish.'

'One man's foolishness is another's logic.'

'Are we having an argument? I suppose we are. Tell you what, I'll think about your side of it and you think about my side of it, and we'll talk about it tomorrow.'

'Will it be any different tomorrow?' she mocked. 'Will the trains be running on time and the snow melted?'

'I promise I'll think of it objectively,' he grinned at her.

'You'll be in such a hurry to get to your precious yard and order books that you'll gulp your breakfast and rush off without having time to talk.'

Charlie got up and stretched. 'Meet me for luncheon at Sloan's. They serve a decent meal in spite of rationing. We'll talk then.' Before she could answer, he wheeled the tea cart out of the room and down the passage to the dumbwaiter singing,

> A Spaniard who hails from Alcala,
> When angered would shout *mucha mala*,
> He tossed a grenade . . .

Meg closed the door which he had left open behind him. She would enjoy tossing the grenade herself.

He kissed her goodbye while she was still asleep. 'Going in early so I can take a long lunch hour. Meet you there at one. It's snowing billy-o, so take a taxi. I've left a pound note by your comb.'

While she was still struggling to wake up, he was gone.

At ten she placed a call to her parents' house. The lines crackled and whistled as if the storm affected them. Meg imagined them silvered and heavy with ice. The dark trees bending in the wind from the sea. The sea itself, ice-grey and boiling. Snow drifting against the tombstones in the church-yard beside the vicarage, filling the crevices of the stone dykes which enclosed the house. Then the telephone was ringing and in the midst of a ring the receiver lifted and her mother's voice, brisk, despite the faintness, announced, 'The Vicar-age, Mrs Sinclair speaking.'

'Mother, it's Meg.'

There was a cry, faint as a bird call, then, 'Meggie. What a coincidence. Not that your father would call it that. He would say it is God working. We tried to ring you yesterday on the cheap rates, but you were out. Should you be calling on day rates? They are so dear.'

'It doesn't matter. I wanted to talk—'

'You are all right, aren't you? Not ill? Is the sweet wean all right? And dear Charlie?'

'Yes, yes. Everyone is well, but I—'

'Good. It gave me quite a turn there for an instant. In this weather one never knows. So many colds and catarrh and spills on icy walks. Poor Mrs Scovil fell and broke her wrist. She is that old, you know. We hope it will heal properly.'

A sudden thought seized Margaret. 'You and Father are all right, aren't you? Is that why you were calling?'

'Fit as ever, Meggie. But we have such a lovely plan. Mr MacPherson—you remember Mr MacPherson, don't you? He butchered and gave us an entire lamb. And your father said, "Una, we'll never between us eat all this meat. Meg and Charlie must have some. But transport being what it is these days and packages shunted about and all, and of course meat as scarce as figs on a thistle or pound notes in the collection plate, you—" meaning me, Meggie "—must deliver it to them in person." So, if it is well with you and you are to say if it is not, I am taking the Thursday train to Glasgow. And I am bringing some lovely wool from the mill. Heather tones to knit sweaters for your Christmas which will keep my hands busy while we chat, and potatoes Mr Finlayson gave us instead of his usual tithe of honey, and ever so many other things. And if Peggy calls with her fish from Wick before the train and I wrap it in snow to keep, I'll bring a nice haddock. I'm all atwitter. Just fancy, I've never seen your house or met the elder Maccallums or seen a shipyard. It's a pity your father can't come as well, but he is so busy during Advent and of course I must be back for the Christmas services, much as I should like to spend it with you. It *is* all right, isn't it, Meggie?'

Meg drew a deep breath. 'Of course. Of course, it is, Mother. I'll be glad to see you. It will be lovely.' The connection was so bad she felt certain her disappointment didn't sound in her voice. Charlie would have his way after all. God must be on the side of all males.

Charlie had a double sherry awaiting her when she arrived at Sloan's and had ordered eggs mayonnaise and roast chicken.

'I might have wanted haddock.' She was still seething, unfairly, at the fact that she had lost, was trapped again.

'Not on a Monday,' he grinned at her over the rim of his glass. *'Slàinte!'*

'Slàinte!' she echoed.

The grin turned into an affectionate smile. 'Well, love, you will be interested to hear that Fionna said I am being beastly and if you want to go to Caithness you should be allowed to go with no interference from me.'

'You told her?' What right had he?

'Of course I told her. I telephoned her about coming in to meet the other board members—informally, of course—and during the conversation I mentioned you wanted to brave post-war transport and go to the north. She called me a dominating male, inconsiderate, obstinate and selfish.'

'You are,' Meg said, softening it with a wry smile.

'Sharper than a serpent's tooth, you two ladies. I told her that I told you you could go in the spring—which you may, Meg, I promise. But in this weather—' he broke off. 'She said you should go now. She—she asked if you are pregnant. Are you?'

'How dare she?'

'She's a nurse, for heaven's sake! She said she recognized the look. Something about your eyes. *I* don't know about these things. Are you?'

She gulped down the last of the sherry. 'May I have another?'

He looked as if he were about to refuse, then he signalled

the waitress. They sat in nervous silence until the drinks came. Meg sipped at hers before answering. 'Yes. Yes, I am. That's why it can't wait for spring.'

'Why didn't you tell me?'

'Because I don't *want* another child. Not yet, anyway. There *are* more things in life than being a cow. A mother. Don't you see? I had to get accustomed to it myself.'

'I suppose it will make you angry if I say I am pleased.'

'I knew you would be.'

The eggs mayonnaise were set before them. 'You can go north, Meg. But hurry back. I need you. You're my touch-stone, my balance wheel. It's heaven to come home to you at night, finding you waiting for me.'

'Resentfully.'

'Rightly so. As soon as we finish lunch I'll telephone Miss Maclean and tell her I'll be late. We'll go to Central Station and arrange for your ticket. When do you want to go?'

'I *can't* go! I telephoned my mother to tell her I was com-ing—yes, even though you were against it—and found *she* is coming *here*. Laden with mutton and ham and potatoes and yarn. And pots of honey like Pooh Bear. She's so excited I couldn't say no.' Tears gathered in her eyes and spilled over into the mayonnaise. 'Damn. I'm crying.'

Charlie reached over to take her hand. 'Meg, Fionna's right, I have been a beast. Forgive me.'

'What else can I do? I'm pregnant.'

'I am pleased even if you are not.'

'Men always are. It's some sort of perverted pride.'

'If it helps any, Fionna said, "Poor girl." '

'Tell her I'm grateful for the sympathy.'

They finished the eggs mayonnaise in near-hostile silence. When the chicken was served Charlie began to speak care-fully about her mother's visit: what they could do to entertain her, what gifts they could give her in return for all that she was bringing. When had she last been out of the Highlands, had a journey?

Not since the summer of '39. Meg and her parents had spent a shimmeringly hot fortnight in France seeing Paris and Chartres, concluding with a breathless jaunt to Avignon, wondering all the while if war would start before they had to go safely back to Scotland. The anxiety of teetering on the last days of peace had added spice to the journey. A hot summer like that of '14, her father had remarked.

Glasgow would be neither hot nor shimmering like France. But perhaps it wouldn't matter. It was escape which was of value.

By the time they finished their sliver of cheese, Charlie was glancing at his watch. 'Do you mind if I get back? I really should flee. You stay and have a coffee.'

Of course he had to flee. Didn't he always? 'I don't want a coffee. I should get back as well.'

Snow still swirled down, turning Argyll Street into a dark, slushy river. The tyres of the few motor cars churned it into spray which slapped the sidewalks.

Charlie hailed a taxi. 'Come on, Meg, you can ride to the yard with me, then the cabbie can drive you home.'

'No. No, I—I promised Charles a surprise. A red ball,' she added with sudden inspiration. 'Jamie had one Charles took a fancy to.'

'All right. But take a taxi, won't you?' He drew her close enough to kiss her, but she turned her face so he only brushed her cheek. Then he slammed the door and she barely had time to retreat from the filth flung out as the taxi spun off.

Caught in her lie, she knew she would have to shop. She had wanted only to be alone, to walk in the snow and think.

Reconcile herself to the fact that there was no escape. Not yet.

People dressed like bundles, heads sunk deep into their mufflers and collars, hurried along the street, bumping one another with their 'messages' bags and muttering an apology, if they bothered to apologize at all. Meg turned her face up to the falling snow. When she was a child her father had told her that snowflakes were kisses of angels. She needed those kisses now.

She walked all the way home, having a good long think. Sometimes she paused to gaze into a shop window, and sighed at the number of ration coupons required for the simplest frock. It was wishful thinking, as in another few months she wouldn't be able to fit into them.

She turned off Buchanan Street at St Vincent Street and followed it to Blythswood Square. She was tired and cold and resentful. No taxis were in sight and in any case it was only a few more blocks to the square. The walk had done little to calm her, yet she was glad when she finally reached the house. The grim mausoleum. But as she closed the door behind her, the wide, shabby hallway was almost welcoming. She hurried into the sitting room before she even took off her coat, and stretched out her chilled hands to the fire, smelling the steam from her coat, hat and gloves. The flames set off sparks in the crystal bowl, heightened the smell of lavender-scented beeswax with which the furniture had been polished and repolished over the long years. Her mother would like this room.

Slowly Meg pulled off her sodden, knit-lined leather gloves, and as she did so she seemed to hear her father's voice comforting her after they had forced her to break off her engagement to tubercular Angus Colquhoun, and breaking Angus's heart as well.

'Remember, daughter, God never closes one door without opening another.'

'It wasn't God who closed it. It was you and Mother.'

Charlie had walked in the door God had opened. And the next door seemed firmly shut.

The arrival of Meg's mother coincided with the evening of the dinner which Veda was giving for Major Kosciuszko, and a friend, Captain Chmura. 'He would so enjoy, if I may impose,' Major Kosciuszko had said when he telephoned to accept Veda's invitation. 'He is young and lonely and lost both brothers in Spain.'

'Do bring him along, by all means,' Veda had agreed, hoping the food would be adequate. 'It will make it a real party.'

She had telephoned Fionna directly afterwards. 'I have taken on another refugee Pole. Do you have any candles?'

'Tapers or votive?'

'Don't be cheeky. I have nothing left but white and with all this snow and austerity, they give the table a chill.'

'I have some red ones. I was saving them for Christmas.'

'Christmas will take care of itself.'

Will it? Fionna wondered. It never had done.

'Red will do nicely. Did you know Meg's mother is arriving the same day? I hope she brings her ration book. Perhaps her visit will calm Meg. She seems to be in a state.'

'She's pregnant. Couldn't you tell?'

'Dear God, no. Poor lass. I must be extra kind to her.' (Fionna groaned inwardly.) 'Can you send Liam and Jamie over with the candles?'

'It's nearly dark when they get home from school. I'll bring them myself.' Not that she wanted to be caught up in Memsah'b's bustle. One would think she had never given a dinner party before. She must be far gone on her Polish officer. Poor Fa.

Afterwards Fionna thought that a wicked fairy must have read her thoughts. For she recognized Major Kosciuszko as he walked in the door, his tall square *chapska* under his arm, his diffident smile, his bowing over Memsah'b's hand, leaving the kiss an inch in the air. When he was presented to Fionna he gave no sign of recognizing her. Such were the effects of his sedation in the dusty hospital at Escorial. That was eight years ago and since then the world had changed.

Fionna sensed that Meg had been apprehensive about introducing her mother to Memsah'b but they took to one another immediately. Memsah'b was in high spirits. Obviously the party was a stimulant. Heaven knew, austerity had become a leaden weight to everyone.

Mrs Sinclair reminded Fionna of a merry pixie with her triangular face, sharp little chin and mop of black curls which bobbed as she chattered, wagging her head expressively. There had been an awkward moment when she had been introduced to Fa. She exclaimed, 'But you and Meg's Charlie are the very image of one another. One would think Mrs Maccallum had no part in his creation at all. I know it sometimes happens.'

Veda had laughed. 'It does indeed. I always tell myself that Charlie sprang like Minerva, fully formed, from Charles's head.' She exchanged a mocking look with Charles, and betrayed her nervousness by backing up to the fireplace and hitching up her skirt.

Mrs Sinclair giggled like a girl. 'I always want to do that and sometimes I do when I am alone, but it isn't the proper thing for a vicar's wife, you know.'

Veda dropped her skirt. 'Nor for a proper hostess. Charlie always tells me cold bum, warm heart.'

'I don't know how many warm hearts there are these days, but there are certainly plenty of cold bums. I told Meggie she must keep the wean's room warm. Forget the shillings. The pounds will take care of themselves.'

It was then that the Gunns arrived with the Polish officers, Gerald having volunteered to meet their train with Fa's car.

Everyone was very formal at first. The Poles were obviously overwhelmed by the elegance of Milkstone, but Fa's whisky soon changed that. Soon Major Kosciuszko was looking at Gerald's pictures and they were having an animated discussion about art. Captain Chmura was being boyishly charming with the ladies, and Charlie and Fa were, as usual, discussing the yard. Fionna felt as if a curtain had closed on the present, a play was done, and she was back in a past, warped and remoulded into a different shape. She could almost smell the heat and blood and dust and antiseptic, hear the dull, distant thud of artillery and feel the room shudder. She looked at her husband and saw a stranger. She was glad when dinner was announced.

The only light in the dining room was that of candles. 'Candlelight is more flattering to ladies my age,' Veda maintained. She had filled every sconce—so much for Christmas—and the four nine-branched candelabras on the table, with red and white candles. The lace tablecloth was over a red undercloth which Fionna recognized as an ancient, much-mended tester from one of the fourposters. Red berries and carnations filled the white ironstone epergne. Memsah'b knew her drama.

But she was not prepared for the reaction. Major Kosciuszko stopped with a gasp, then he kissed Veda on both cheeks. Captain Chmura clasped Memsah'b's hands and kissed them. The Major kissed Fa. Chmura saluted him.

'Madam, sir, you honour us. Poland's colours for poor exiles. Never will we see our homes again, but you bring the colours to us, the memories, the welcome.' Tears shone in his eyes.

Fionna had to hand it to Memsah'b. She made a quick recovery. 'But it is you who honour us.'

Fa opened the champagne he had been hoarding—and how had Memsah'b persuaded him to part with it? He proposed a toast to Poland and for a moment Fionna thought the glasses would sail through the air and crash on the hearth. Major Kosciuszko spared the crystal by toasting Scotland. Captain Chmura toasted the Maccallums. Charlie toasted the International Brigades. Formality disintegrated.

Fionna, seated down table from the Major, could not keep her eyes off him. More than once his eyes met hers and a puzzled frown passed over his face.

After dinner they broke into groups in the long south drawing room. Charlie inevitably sat with the Poles. Veda and Charles settled down to get acquainted with Mrs Sinclair. Meg and Marjorie Gunn found that both were reading *The Scarlet Tree* and were busy with the Sitwells. Willie was telling Gerald all about his projected shooting parties. And I am the spectator, on the fringe, Fionna told herself.

'You are very quiet lass,' Willie turned suddenly to Fionna.

'I was thinking how much Carlos would have enjoyed being here to meet the survivors of the Dabrowski Battalion.'

Charlie looked up at the sound of her voice. 'Fe, come and join us. You were there. You were a part of it.'

Almost reluctantly, she walked the length of the room, conscious of the three men watching her. She was glad she had spent her coupons on a new gown, bronze lace over brown silk jersey which clung to her figure while the lace rippled. With it she wore the long strand of brown amber which

Memsah'b had given to Tina when she and Carlos were married. When Fionna had gone to Spain after Tina's death, Carlos had thrust the beads, almost savagely, into her hands. 'Take them. Take them away, Fe. *She* wore the amber in Malaga, one of the last nights we had dinner together before she died.'

Fionna touched the strand of beads now as she walked across the room self-consciously, aware that the three men were watching her. Touching the amber was something to do with the hand which wasn't holding her drink. As if in response to her nervousness, the old wound in her arm twinged suddenly in pain.

'Fionna was in the medical corps. Her ambulance picked me up when I was wounded. It was the first time we had seen each other since we had been in Spain.'

She sat facing them, a little apart, waiting her acceptance. Then, abruptly, she asked Major Kosciuszko, 'Do you still have your violin? Do you still play Chopin waltzes and *"Zigeunerweise"?* You asked for it in the hospital at El Escorial and Captain Chmura found it and brought it to you. The Yank in the bed next to you taught you an American song, "The Red River Valley", but in Spain we sang "There's a valley in Spain called Jarama . . . where so many of our brave comrades fell . . ." '

'Where I, too, fell, but I survived.'

'Did your wound heal?' she hurried on, knowing she was talking too much, too fast. 'You left half your stomach in Spain.' She thought, I know your body as well as I know my own. Better than I know Willie's. I have never seen his flesh laid open and watched the doctor pick out shrapnel, counted the sponges, changed the dressings. I heard you cry out for the wife and children who died when Warsaw was bombed. I wiped away the tears you didn't know you were shedding.

He closed his eyes and crossed himself. 'Jesus, Mary, and Joseph. I dreamt of you but your face was that of my wife. I asked for you. They told me you had gone.'

'I went with the field ambulance. The doctor was my fiancé. Teruel, Ebro.'

'Ebro is where I lost my violin. I could not swim with both that and my gun. After, I took up the guitar. There are many guitars in Spain.'

'I was wounded at Ebro and of no more use. I went to Barcelona and from there to Italy. And finally, home to Scotland.'

'I apologize, I did not recognize the nurse who tended me with compassion. Yet, there was the haunting throughout dinner which I could not capture.'

'Because I am not dressed in fatigues and in need of a bath and a shampoo.'

'So, you too were wounded. And your fiancé? You married in Spain?' He gave a questioning nod towards Willie.

'My fiancé was killed in the same strafing. Our brother, too. Sir William and I were married after I came back to Scotland.'

At that point Fa broke up the groups. When he had had enough malt Fa lost his reserve. He loved a singsong, a dance, what Memsah'b called a chaos. He insisted they all follow him to the second-floor ballroom where the fires were already cutting the chill. He put a polka on the phonograph, caught Meg's astonished mother into his arms and carried her across the room, whirling and laughing. Veda grabbed Gerald, Willie clasped Meg, and Charlie, Marjorie Gunn. Jan Chmura bowed over Fionna's hands.

After that there were Scottish reels to be taught to the Poles, jigs, sambas, tangos, and finally waltzes. 'I am very drunk,' Fionna kept telling herself as she and the Major were turning, arm's length apart, to the strains of the old sentimental waltzes of times past, times lost with the Austrian Empire.

'You knew him in Spain?' Willie said as they walked home, Fionna in her brogues, her party shoes in Willie's pocket.

'Yes. As a body in a bed whose dressings I changed when I was on duty. The Dabrowski Battalion was almost completely wiped out. It's strange seeing them again. We hadn't expected him to live and I never thought of him again. There were too many others.'

'I wonder if it was like that in the Great War? Did they never think of us again?'

'Did you have a mad crush on some Rose of No Man's Land? But you weren't wounded, were you?'

'No. Lucky for me. But you remember, I lost my brothers.'

'Well, we cannot live in the past, can we? There is always tomorrow.'

She dreamt that night of dancing over the surface of a broad blue river. Completely alone.

The Monday following the party was the date of Fionna's first meeting with the members of the board, and she was nervous by the time she reached the yard. Fa was already there, having taken an earlier train, and was in the board room having tea with the other members.

'He might have waited and taken me in,' Fionna told Charlie.

'I'm going to do that. He is reassuring them that having a woman—especially as she is a Maccallum—on the board does not mean that the yard will declare bankruptcy. They had a difficult enough time accepting Miss Maclean sitting in to record the minutes.'

'Do I look sedate enough?'

'Perfect. By the way, I am lunching with Tad Kosciuszko and Jan Chmura. Want to join us?'

'Ye—e—s. Thank you. I'd—like it.'

'You sound hesitant.'

'I am not sure it is wise to re-open the past.'

'What nonsense, Fionna! It isn't as if you are being unfaithful to Willie. You know it bores him silly—same as it does Meg—to hear us rattle on about Spain.'

'Is Fa coming?'

'He and Memsah'b are taking Meg and her mother to luncheon. It will be we four.' He took her arm. 'Come along. Are you ready to beard the old lions in their den?'

The meeting went off better than Fionna had expected. She made a little speech that Willie had helped her write about the honour of having been asked to serve as a board member. About the even greater honour of having been voted in (not unanimously, she knew, but did not mention), after her name had been put forward. She realized she had much to learn and would try to hold her tongue until she *had* learned, and would always be glad to hear their advice whenever they felt like giving it.

One gave her a nod, a smile, and a thumbs up as she sat down.

'I think I am going to like being a board member,' she told her father after the meeting. 'They aren't such old bears after all.'

'They growled like bears when Charlie and I put your name forward. I think you reassured them. Will you join us at luncheon? Veda and I are taking Mrs Sinclair out.'

'I am going with Charlie and the Poles.'

'I thought he would ask you. Be careful.'

'What do you mean by that, Fa?'

'I think you know.'

'I am too old for that sort of thing, Fa. I promise—No, I don't. I promise nothing.'

He kissed her forehead and left her standing by the window, staring out into the yard. The arc lights glimmered like will-o'-the-wisps in the dense fog. Fog obscured the river and lapped at the window. Only the mournful bawling of fog horns indicated there was a river with vessels cautiously feeling their way along it.

She should not be going with Charlie. She knew it and knew that she would go. Not all the warnings in the world could keep her away. Already she felt dizzy at the prospect of seeing Tad again.

In Germany there was rain, continuous, unrelenting rain. The Rhine rose seven feet in twenty-four hours. Saarbrücken was cut in half by rising water. The Moselle, and all the tributary streams were in flood. *Schloss* Trötzen was surrounded by a torrent of mud and broken trees. The river was loud at night with its roaring, carrying away chunks of earth and rocks, and levelling the terraces of the winter garden. The saturated earth swelled so the doors of the *Schloss* did not close properly, a thing unknown in Mutti Trötzen's memory.

Corporal Braun spent a day re-banking the winter garden, but by morning it was washed out again. 'Well, diddlydamn, look at that. I'll have to do the whole thing over again.' He sang 'Tomatoes, tomahtoes, let's call the whole thing off . . .' as he worked.

'I don't understand that song,' Hannes said to Mairi.

'Don't try. Just be glad he is trying to help.'

Corporal Braun loved helping. 'I'm a farm boy, ma'am, and how I got attached to that stupid typewriter would be hard to say. But that's the army. A guy's natural talents don't mean a thing.'

'Your natural talents have kept us fed.'

He leant thoughtfully on his shovel, rain dripping off the lock of hair which hung over his forehead, and off his wide, puckish nose. 'You know, Frau Mairi, this weather, gardening's gone to pot. You can't do much with frozen ground under four feet of snow. 'Bout the only thing I can think of now is mushrooms.'

'Mushrooms?'

'In your cellars. We used to raise them at home. They're good for you, and versatile. Soups, sauteed, raw, pickled in wine—and you got plenty of wine.'

'How do you grow them?'

'You just say the okay and leave it to me.'

'Okay. They sound wonderful.'

'Now about Christmas which is coming on like gang busters—'

'Yes. I told Hansi not to expect miracles. There's to be a special sweets ration for the children but as yet there are no toys in the village shop and not a candle to be had for the tree.'

'Major Kim and I had been talking about that. The PX in Frankfurt has a few things that might help. You just give us a list and sizes and the like and we'll see what we can do.'

'You are very kind.'

'Yeah, I suppose so. Way I figure it, we didn't ask to be here and you sure as God didn't invite us, so it all comes out in the wash.'

What did not come out in the wash was a letter from Maxl, the first since Mairi had returned from Scotland. He was coming home for Christmas. Mairi handed the letter to Mutti Trötzen, who when she had finished reading it said, *'Ach so!'* and put the letter on the table.

'I almost wish he wouldn't come,' Mairi said. 'He resents

everything so much. He will make it uncomfortable. I know it has been hard for him, but bitterness doesn't help, and these men are kind to us, not like some of the others one hears about.'

'You should have stayed in Scotland for the holidays.'

'I couldn't do that to you and Hansi.'

'Perhaps Maxl will behave himself.'

Mairi had little hope that he would. She was glad when his arrival was delayed because of storms, and a few days later something occurred which took her mind off Maxl.

During the night snow replaced the rain, and by morning it had covered the rain-rutted, sodden land. Drifts moved like small glaciers, carried by the streams underneath. Low, grey clouds darkened the already dark morning. No one moved in the streets of the village and only a few thread-thin skeins of smoke rose from the chimneys.

Mairi helped Hannes get ready for school and decided to walk as far as the bottom of the hill with him. Dinah Shore was singing to Corporal Braun that her mama done told her.

'Uncle Maxl doesn't like those songs,' Hannes said.

'Uncle Maxl doesn't like anything about the Yanks.'

Defeat had changed him. She, too, had changed. She was stronger now, more objective, clear-sighted. She had learnt to be in order to survive.

It was difficult walking downhill. She and Hannes clung to one another, slithering, slipping, laughing.

'We need our skis,' Hannes said. 'Or a sled.'

'We need springtime.'

'Will my papa come home in the springtime?'

'I don't know.'

'If he does come home will the Yanks go away?'

'No.'

'Shall he come home *some* day?'

105

'I hope so, Hansi.' And would he accept the lie that Hansi was his son? Would Maxl keep silent about whose child he was? What a fool she had been.

'All right, off you go. Can you manage the rest of the way?'

'I could have managed the hill but I knew you liked a walk. There's Dieter. Hey, Dieter! Wait!' He ran, waving his arms to keep his balance, his school bag thumping on his back.

Mairi watched until he caught up with his friend, and they trudged off together towards the school. No one but children were about. The snow was heavy as fog, blotting out the railway station and the houses at the furthermost end of the village.

There was a light in the shop window and she decided to visit it in the hope that Christmas candles had come in, and perhaps some papier mâché toys.

As she emerged from the shop with twelve red candles which had cost as much as rubies, and a set of wooden construction blocks in various shapes for building castles and walls, she almost collided with a young man, gaunt with hunger and with circles as black as death under feverish eyes. His *Wehrmacht* uniform was ragged; sockless toes protruded from the broken leather of his boots.

There were fewer refugees these days, straggling back from captivity. This one looked young and ill, and she thought of Edu, still listed as missing. He was about Edu's age, and for a fleeting second she wondered if he were her son. But I would know Edu, she told herself.

'Do you need some help?'

'I am looking for Frau Trötzen. Is that the *Schloss* there on the hill? Why's an American flag flying from it?'

'I am Frau Trötzen, and that is the *Schloss*. A part of it is US Army-occupied—for our small village, you know.' She smiled at the ridiculousness of the village needing parole. 'Why do you want me?'

'Edu sent me.'

She clutched his arm, feeling the bone beneath the flesh-less skin. 'Edu? He's alive? Where? Oh where?'

'Slovenia. He's a war prisoner. Has been since '43. Me as well. We weren't in action a day before we were wiped out. Thirty-two of us were all that was left. Not even an officer, but they were scum anyhow. Ready to lick the Führer's ass if he ordered 'em to. Excuse me. I know it isn't proper to say such things in front of a lady, but we hated them. They ordered us to attack when *they* knew and *we* knew it was hopeless. Same as suicide.' A fit of coughing shook his body. He wiped the bloody phlegm from his lips with his cuff.

'You are ill. Come, take my arm. We'll go to the *Schloss*. You can rest and have some food. We haven't much. Soup, some bread, some vegetables.'

'Edu said you were kind. He made me promise to come after I had been to my home first.'

His home couldn't have done much for him, Mairi thought.

'Our house isn't there. The whole street was blown up. A woman told me there used to be notes on the wall telling where the people had gone, but the storm blew them away. I tried to find the priest but the church isn't there any more either and no one knew where he was. Someone thought he hadn't answered the *Fragebögen* properly and he was in jail. I can't believe that of a priest, can you? So I came here. My name is Josef Beier, but you can call me Jo.'

They made slow progress up the hill. Jo shivered and coughed and several times they had to stop for him to rest. When they reached the hall Dinah Shore had given way to Count Basie. Jo grinned. 'Decadent music, *ja?* Black stuff. A chap I knew before the war went to the States to visit his uncle who'd emigrated because he had a Jewish wife, see? He brought back a lot of records. We used to play them secretly. Armstrong, Basie, Goodman. *Wunderbar!*'

He made her wait in the hall until 'The One O'clock Jump' ended. 'It's like medicine. It made me feel better. I almost forgot about my feet.'

'Which are probably frost-bitten.'

'Do you think I will lose my toes?'

'They haven't turned black. Here are the stairs. We live in the cellars. You can see a part of the *Schloss* was bombed.'

'And the Yanks took the good parts.'

'There are only two and they are very kind.'

'They play the right kind of music anyway.'

Mutti Trötzen took command after her initial shock. 'First some soup and hot wine, then a bath. Fortunately Corporal Braun repaired the plumbing in the upstairs bathroom so there will be hot water and I shall ask him for some army soap. I can find some of my husband's nightshirts and warm sweaters in our old rooms. You are to go straight to bed.'

'She's bossy like my grandmother was.' Jo grinned at Mairi.

Mairi wanted to hear about Edu, but Mutti said that must wait until Jo was in bed. 'Let him rest a little, then it will all come spilling out.'

Mairi thought the bath had made him weaker for he had continuous fits of coughing which left him gasping for breath. Mutti tore up an old sheet for him to use as handkerchiefs. As soon as they were soiled she carried them to the fire. But weak as he was, he was not yet ready to sleep. 'I promised Edu, you see. I want to tell you now. Sometimes when I go to sleep I wonder if I shall wake up. That is why they turned me out. They said I would give it to the other prisoners. They knew I was going to die so they let me go.

'They marched us from camp to camp and there wasn't enough food. One meal a day. Bread and some grey water they called soup. Some of the men who were wounded couldn't keep up. We had to leave them by the road. I suppose they must have died there where we left them. Good men they were, too. We ended up in Jugoslavia. Summer came and it wasn't so bad except we had to work hard. Twelve, fourteen hours a day. The prison was bad in winter. No blankets. They didn't beat us, but we couldn't write to our families to tell them we were alive.

'Edu's clever. You know that, *ja?* He learned the language and they used him as a translator. It's a big camp but our group stayed together. When they turned me out, all our comrades wanted me to find their families and tell them to send Red Cross boxes. I came to you first because—because Edu said you lived in a *Schloss* and I thought you must be rich. Rich people have a way of getting food that poor people don't. But I have to keep my promise and find the other families and tell them. So I won't hang about and bother you for too long.'

'You will hang about until you are well enough to go on. We can write to those families. The ban on sending letters has been lifted, so we can write.'

He closed his eyes. 'Then, it is well, what I did. I kept my promise.'

Jo's admittance into the household gave Mutti Trötzen something to do. Her face became animated again. The socks she was knitting for Maxl became socks for Jo. She took his temperature, she concocted pastes of pepper, wine and precious flour for his frozen feet, water was constantly on the boil to provide him with hot water bottles.

She badgered Major Kimball into giving him a room

above the offices. 'It's empty. You don't use it. He must not be near Hansi because he is infectious. Tuberculosis is on the rise now that we can't eat properly. He must be in isolation. There, I can make a *klein* fire for him and he can hear Corporal Braun's naughty records. I like them myself. So merry, so—you say—swinging.'

Kim threw up his hands. 'What the hell. Just so long as HQ don't find out. He'll have to fill out a *Fragebögen*, you know.'

'That he will not. He was born after 1919. He is a mere boy and far too ill to cope with all those *dummkopf* questions. No one bothers to read them anyway.'

'I am afraid somebody does bother. Well, Mutti, it can wait until he is better. Why the hell am I letting myself be talked into this?'

'Because you are a very fine gentleman with compassion and love for your fellow man.'

'I am a sucker is what I am. Bewitched by beautiful German ladies. Every one of you is a Lorelei.'

'You are so funn-ee! As if an old lady could bewitch you.'

'Lady, you just have done. Move him up and tell him to send his musical requests to Braun. Braun'll be only too happy to oblige.'

For the next few days Mairi wrote letters to twenty-four parents—all that were left of the thirty-two soldiers taken captive. Some of the addresses she could scarcely read because rain and snow had soaked the pocket of Jo's uniform. But she did her best, taking dictation from him—small personal items about each one—and sent them off to destinations she suspected had been bombed out of existence. Meanwhile she wrote on her own to the Red Cross prisoners-of-war division, informing them of the situation and asking their help in repatriating her son and the sons of others.

The flood waters receded and froze. Snow continued to

fall. Mutti placed an Advent wreath on the table in the entrance hall and suspended another from the cellar ceiling. There were no candles and every Sunday during Advent she bewailed the fact.

'Even during the war we had candles for the wreath. Why is peace so difficult?'

'Because, like Faust, we sold our souls to the devil.'

'Perhaps in the old storage cellars where we kept the beer casks. The servants used candle lanterns when they went to draw beer.'

'We used those candles when we had no electricity.'

'So we did. How prodigal we were.'

Mairi thought it scarcely prodigal. She had found shreds of old Christmas paper and ribbons, and an Advent calendar which she had given to Hannes on the first of December. Every day he carried it up to show Jo the new picture behind the door that was opened.

A week before Christmas Kim made a trip to Frankfurt. He returned with candles for the wreath. 'They cost the earth even at the PX,' he confided to Mairi. 'But they seem to mean so much to the old girl I got them anyway.'

There was only one Sunday left in Advent. Still Maxl had not come. Every day Jo grew weaker. Not all the potions which Mutti concocted helped him. He slept fitfully and cried out in dreams. Already his face was skull-like, his eyes sunken in their sockets, his cheeks hollowed, and his skin bone-white except for the red fever spots.

'He is dying,' Mutti said, 'and soon he will lose his foot. After Christmas I shall go to his village myself and try to find his parents. Someone must know where they are.'

'You can't do that. Travel is too difficult.'

'I can and I shall, Mairi. At the same time I shall go to Cologne and find out where they buried my man, if they found enough of him to bury. I shall look out our house and see if anything was salvaged from the wreckage. I should have done so as soon as the travel ban was lifted.'

'Then I shall go with you.'

'You are needed here with Hansi.'

Mairi sighed. 'We'll discuss it later.' Perhaps by Christmas Jo would be dead. Perhaps Maxl—if he ever arrived—would convince his mother not to go.

He arrived the Monday before Christmas.

As soon as Maxl had written to his mother telling her that he would be home for Christmas, he regretted it. It was almost unbelievable that he had so little desire to see Mairi whom he had worshipped since he was a child. He told himself it was because she had changed since the war had ended. She had betrayed them by going home for a visit, she was too tolerant of the Occupation, too friendly with the Yanks. But in all honesty, he knew that he, too, had changed.

He was ashamed of having cuckolded his brother, resentful that he had promised never to acknowledge Hannes as his son and half angry that Mairi and his mother had expected him to rot at the *Schloss,* playing at being a peasant. He hated the sweating work, the smell of soil, the poverty which should not be their lot. His grandfather had dropped the 'von' from their name after the first war, but Maxl knew it was still there, a small word which elevated them above other people.

Every day men long considered dead or dying in some Soviet labour camp drifted back across the border. One day Erich might come. Then there would be no place for Maxl in Mairi's bed or Mairi's life. And he no longer wanted a place in either of them. It was like the popular song, 'Everything passes, everything fades away . . .'

He was not ashamed of having deserted from the Eastern

Front when the Führer had ordered them to fight to the last man. He had had enough of the Führer. But the humiliation of defeat and the Occupation had soured him. The Yanks to whom he had surrendered had done their best to humiliate him. To make him feel it was the act of a coward and a traitor. The famous battalion which had surrendered *en masse* were not treated as he had been treated. They had been disarmed, questioned and sent home. He had been kept for eight months, questioned, and re-questioned, filled out the *Fragebögen*, been bullied and mentally spat upon.

A general had wandered into the room one day where Maxl was undergoing yet another interrogation. He had picked up Maxl's file and shuffled through it, then slammed it back on the table.

'This is pure crap!' he had said, unaware that Maxl knew English. 'You're wasting your time and his. Sure his old man had to join the Party. He had a high position, a family to think of. Sure this guy was a Hitlerjugend. For Christ's sake, they were all Hitlerjugends. He found out it was all a pack of lies. He had to desert, didn't he? What the hell's the difference between desertion to a lost cause and surrender to a lost cause? Why the hell don't you send him home? You're as bad as the fucking Nazis, trying to force him to condemn himself. Don't you have worthier victims sitting in Nuremberg? Send him home. That's an order and if you want it in triplicate, I'll give it to you in triplicate.'

Maxl was released that afternoon. He had walked for three days to get back to the *Schloss*, to Mairi, to the son he had promised he would never acknowledge . . . and found the damned Yanks installed in the *Schloss*, and Mairi and his mother living in the servants' quarters in the basement and considering themselves fortunate.

By unspoken agreement, he and Mairi had not resumed

their war-time liaison. He had been shocked at how old and drab she had looked. She had been shocked by his bitterness. He had isolated himself from them as best he could for the remainder of the winter. In the library, where the books were suffering from the cold, he found things he had always intended to read. He would sit there in his great coat, mittens and knitted hood reading Schiller's *Maria Stuart*, Egmont, *Faust*, Sudermann, while the damned Yank corporal played his lousy music and the hoarse voice of Louis Armstrong accompanied *Death in Venice*.

The American army had given him a sack of seed to take home with him. Mairi had been delighted, and as the warm spring days thawed the earth she insisted that they make a garden. Spinach where there had once been roses; onions edging the formal walks; turnips and beetroot amongst the surviving daphne and camellias. Mairi's pale skin had tanned and she had laughed as she knelt in the earth, kneading it through her fingers. Her beauty had returned and he had hungered for her again, but dared make no move.

When the first pale-green shoots appeared they had had to ask the Yank corporal which were weeds and which vegetables.

'Holy Cow, where you folks been all your life you can't tell the difference between an onion and a weed?'

Maxl had not deigned to answer, but Mairi had laughed. 'We left it up to our gardeners.'

'Yeah, I reckon you did, living in a castle and all. Some folks are born lucky and ignorant.'

They would not have known how to do anything if it hadn't been for Corporal Braun. He showed them how to plant the potatoes, how to set up poles for the peas and beans, told them when it was time to pull the onions, when the lettuce was ready for salad and the beets for boiling.

He taught Mutti to can, examined the kitchen larder and showed her which old, faded, half-useless spices to use for pickling. When the fruit trees bore fruit, molested by birds as it was, he 'requisitioned' a ladder and was up on it handing the fruit down to them. During the summer Maxl sorted through the rubble of the bombed tower and salvaged what he could, but rebuild it he could not. It remained a shell where wildflowers blossomed in its depths and ivy inched its way up the wall, a cherry tree sprouting from a seed dropped by a bird.

By autumn he could no longer endure the rot that was creeping into his bones and the stagnation of his mind. He was thirty-two, too old to go back to the university, but that was what he wanted to do. To take up his interrupted education. He wanted to help rebuild Germany, re-educate it, resurrect it. He wanted to be shot of all old things and begin anew like Mies van der Rohe and the American, Frank Lloyd Wright. He wanted new thoughts, new attitudes, new architecture, a new world.

He told no one. But when Mairi went to Scotland, he asked Mutti for some silver plates to sell, and set off for Heidelberg. Now, like the sentimental fool of a German that he was, he had come home for Christmas.

The sight of the *Schloss* wrenched him with nostalgia. He remembered the happy summers they had spent there and the Christmas times as snowy as this one, when they had skated on the frozen lake, ridden to church in the sleigh, had every tower room filled with cousins and aged aunts and uncles and guests. It was no longer the same. The Persian carpets were gone, bartered. One small prayer rug had got them fifty pounds of potatoes when those they had planted ran out. A Vermeer had got a case of grapefruit juice from the PX, and the silver plates had got him enough money to return to the university, buy a second-hand suit and a sweater on the black market, and have his *Wehrmacht* uniform turned, retailored, and dyed. He had black market cigarettes, a cashmere sweater and shawl for Mutti; a gold necklace and gloves for Mairi; books, a soccer ball, and a second-hand Tyrolean jacket for Hansi.

As he climbed the hill he wished he had not come. It had been a long, cold journey, for the trains had had to be re-routed around flooded tracks, washed-out bridges, and rails still unrepaired after bombings.

The drumming of Gene Krupa blasted his ears as he opened the door.

The visit went off better than any of them expected. Maxl managed to be half-way decent to the Yanks. He spent hours with Jo, listening, sympathizing, and exchanging experiences on the Eastern Front. He promised that he would stop off in Jo's village on his return and try to learn the whereabouts of his parents. He taught Hannes to iceskate. He cut the Christmas tree and helped to decorate it after Hannes had gone to bed. He even found the box of decorations in the attic and some tarnished tinsel.

They toasted Christmas and the speedy release of Edu and return of Erich. They went to the old music room and Mutti and Mairi played duets of old carols. The Yanks joined them and they carried Jo down to be with them.

It was not until Maxl prepared to leave, not even remaining to see the New Year in, that Mutti tried to persuade him to stay. 'We've been promised an election in January. We are to elect our own town mayor. As a Trötzen you would surely be elected.'

'Why would I want to be mayor of this village?'

'It is *our* village, Maxl. If you don't run, old Herr Breurer will surely be elected and it is a wonder he passed the *Fragebögen*. We all knew he was a Nazi.'

'He passed because he is the *Bahnhofvorsteher* and the only one who knows how to run the train signals. He'll be a great mayor. He'll kowtow to the Yanks and get privileges no one else could manage.'

'He is still a Nazi at heart.'

'You will have to put up with him. I have better things to do. Let Mairi run against him if you are so keen on having a Trötzen in office. She kowtows to the Yanks, too.' Then, before Mairi could lash out at him, 'Anyway, I'm thinking of getting married. I have met a student—she is studying economics. We get along well. We have plans for the new Germany once the Occupation leaves us. She has agreed to move in with me which will save us both a bit of cash, and she has a job promised to her as soon as she passes her doctorate. Her parents have a little country house on a tram line where we can live. I will be doing the planning and building of our cities—new, modern, efficient housing and office buildings. We have to wipe out the past twelve years. We must be reborn.'

'She cannot be much of a lady if she will move in with you before marriage. What can her parents be thinking?'

'She is enough of a lady that she hasn't sold herself to the soldiers for a pair of nylons or cigarettes. Her parents are greatly relieved that she is settling for a well-bred German of ɔod family.'

Mutti wiped her eyes on a frayed handkerchief. 'It is all very sudden and very unusual and I am not sure that I am pleased.'

'The important thing is Maxl's happiness,' Mairi put in quickly. 'When summer comes you will bring her to meet us. You could be married where all the Trötzens have married.'

'That will be up to her. I am glad you know now.'

'I, too.' No more guilt. No more fear that Maxl would let slip anything of their relationship if Erich ever came home. 'We must send her a gift. What is her name, Maxl?'

'Viktoria. I'd like one of Grossmutti's rings.'

After a moment, Mutti said, 'Yes. I suppose it is only right that you should have one. Though I should like to have met her parents. Very well. I'll fetch the jewel box.'

When she had left the room Maxl leaned across the table. 'Vikki knows about Hansi. I want him, Mairi, once we are settled. I want him, if only for a part of the time. Holidays.'

'That is impossible. You promised you'd never claim him. What will Erich think?'

'He'll think I am a very devoted uncle. We can discuss it later, but I—this is a warning. I want my son a part of the time.'

'You'll have children of your own by Viktoria, surely.'

'She doesn't want children. She is what your Yanks would call a "career girl". But she is willing that we should have Hansi for holidays.' He gestured with his cigarette. 'A readymade child without the disfigurement of pregnancy and the smelly baby days.'

'She sounds a very cold potato.'

'I assure you, she is not cold. But she knows what she wants.'

'Maxl, I pity you. I really do. But you should be a good pair. You always knew what you wanted, too.' She broke off as Mutti returned with a ring box, and they all bent over it to inspect the rings which were left.

'They are all very old-fashioned settings,' Maxl said. 'Never mind. She can have it reset for the price of the gold.' He chose a ruby and diamond dinner ring in a setting which Mairi thought elegant and charming.

He left the next morning. 'I should feel sad,' Mutti said.

'But Maxl was always the troublesome child. We spoiled him after the first war because of his sickness. I am glad he is doing well, though I don't know about that *Mädchen*. He was good with Jo, wasn't he?'

Jo died on Epiphany. He was buried in the family churchyard and three choir boys sang *'Ich hatt' einem Kamerad . . .'* in high, young voices. Corporal Braun and Kim attended the funeral and Hannes laid the Advent wreath on the grave.

To Mairi's surprise, Maxl remembered his promise to Jo. He stopped in his village near Kassel and located the priest, cleared of his questionable *Fragebögen*. Both parents and a younger brother had been killed during a raid when their house collapsed on the cellar in which they had taken refuge.

'So they did not know their son was alive and he did not know his parents were dead. It seems very sad, but somehow, perhaps better, for they would have had him only a few weeks before they lost him again. War does very strange things.' Mutti blew her nose and wiped her tears on one of the handkerchiefs Kim had given her for Christmas.

As they left the churchyard snow was covering the newly turned earth.

Erich had been at the mines six weeks, yet still the equipment which he was meant to assemble had not come from Germany. The Governor, Janek Okhlopkov, told him it was expected daily, but due to the torn-up railway lines, the difference in rail gauges, and, perhaps, the Occupation's reluctance to be relieved of the equipment, there were bound to be delays. 'Be patient, my dear fellow. Soon you will be busy enough for two men.'

Meanwhile, the Governor did his best to be affable and entertaining. 'You are not a prisoner, you understand, but our guest and colleague and director of equipment. You have your own house and you eat as well as I do. It is not Maxim's—you have been to Paris?—but neither is it as the prisoners eat.'

Erich's house was a one-room, earthen-floor cabin of squared logs with a thick coat of plaster inside. There was a small entrance hall with a thick door so the wind did not enter the house after the outer door was closed. A huge brick fireplace served both for heating and cooking. A crippled old woman came twice a day, first to make Erich's breakfast of flat brown cakes of bread baked on the hearth, and later to cook his dinner of cabbage or turnip soup, pickled cucumbers and green tomatoes, and sometimes a haunch of squirrel or rabbit.

Once a week he and the managers were invited to the Governor's house for a meal. The menu was the same, but there was more meat, for the Governor was a hunter, and the soup was thicker, based on a meat broth. After dinner they played cards or sang while the Governor pumped a player piano of which he was immensely proud. His repertoire was astonishing: Strauss waltzes, Russian folk songs, Tchaikovsky, Shostakovich, English music hall songs, American songs from the Twenties, and army marching songs.

Often the Bokhara and Samarkand rugs were thrown back and the three managers would dance together, stamping their polished boots on the blue-painted floor and swinging their hands.

At the end of the evening there was always a toast to peace. They would throw the burning vodka down their throats and embrace one another with tears in their eyes.

By day, Erich was free to inspect the mines, which were the most extensive and richest he had ever seen. What Germany could have done with these! There would have been no defeat. Ten thousand square miles of coal, Janek told him proudly, both underground and open pit. Before the war they were taking twenty-three million tons a year from the mines. With the new equipment and improved methods they would double or triple that figure.

In any other situation Erich would have found it exciting to be a part of such a project, but in the circumstances it was depressing. The mining was done by prisoners of war of every age and from every conquered country. Their uniforms were rags and few had boots. Their log barracks was unplastered, so wind knifed in. They slept on tiers of wooden shelves, and had one meal a day.

At first Erich had tried to speak to them, but he had given up because it made him feel ashamed. He had searched their faces, thinking he might find someone he had known, but hunger and slave's work had made their faces curiously alike.

He visited the prison hospital where, the doctor told him, he had every imaginable kind of case: typhus, typhoid, acute bronchitis, tuberculosis, rheumatism, and every possible kind of venereal disease.

Once a week whores were brought in by lorry. The guards lined up the prisoners outside the barracks. Twenty were allowed in at a time for ten minutes. A whistle would blow, the door would open and the next group entered.

Four women came for the Governor, managers and overseers. 'Clean women, no sickness,' the Governor explained to Erich. 'As our guest, you may have your choice.'

At first Erich refused. The memory of Marya and the child were too much with him. As for Mairi, she had become a shadowy vision, a half-remembered dream.

At last he asked for a pale, blonde girl who looked no more than sixteen. Her unconcerned efforts, expert as they were, her lack of modesty, her practiced, unemotional performance, sickened him. He decided he preferred celibacy.

Days and nights and weeks crept by. One night sitting before his fire Erich heard the strains of *'Tannenbaum'*. He thought he was dreaming. He opened his door to a shock of cold air. Stars rimed the sky and snow lay on the scarred terraces of the open pit mines.

The song had ended. The frozen branches of the trees cracked in the wind. He was about to close the door when the voices rose again, blown on the wind like the voices of souls long dead. *'Heilige nacht, stille nacht . . .'*

He closed the door, returned to the fireside and wept. How could the prisoners have known it was Christmas?

At the end of January a few pieces of equipment arrived, but so many parts were missing that Erich could do little about fitting the hydraulic machinery together. Since Christmas he had been keeping a makeshift calendar on his wall. Each day that he marked off seemed like another day in a coffin of eternity.

In March there was a typhus epidemic. One hundred and eight men died in one day. Erich asked the doctor for their identification tags, thinking that if he ever got home he would notify their parents. After he had collected more than three hundred tags, he simply copied names and numbers in a small notebook. Soon it, too, was full. In April more equipment arrived, and he was too busy to visit the hospital.

3

1948 began almost unchanged. The coal ration was increased, the bread ration cut down, and the snow level rose to five feet in the countryside. Jamie and Liam were ecstatic. Their half-days were spent tunnelling through the castle grounds, and they battled their way to school with snowball fights against arch enemies and fast friends.

Willie trudged the countryside with hay for the deer and grain for the pheasants. 'Poor things. Think of the ones who have no one to bring fodder.'

'Think of that when you hold your slaughtering parties this fall.'

'One asks forgiveness of the beasts when one kills.'

The January board meeting at Maccallums' had been concerned with the building of shallow draft vessels needed to open the undeveloped companies in Africa, South America, and the Far East, and the replacement of river boats sunk during the Burma campaign. Most of the old men were against taking such orders. Weren't the needs of Britain far greater than those of a lot of natives? The yard was still behind in replacing the merchant ships sunk during the war. Passenger ships were still on back order. It would be ten years before they could double the normal requirements.

'By then,' Fionna said, 'aircraft will be carrying freight, same as they did during the war. In the States the Flying Tigers have already become freight carriers, and their future plans are to expand to the Far East and Europe.'

'But that is in the States, my dear Lady Lammondson. Aircraft will never replace ships.'

'They carried combat troops during the war. Have you seen the advertisements in the papers for holiday flights to New York and California? Planes are getting larger all the time. In my opinion they will be giving us a good bit of competition. I vote for the shallow draft vessels. Those countries have no airfields yet and they are accustomed to shipping by water.' She was talking too much, making herself unpopular, just as Charlie and Fa had feared she would do.

The matter was put aside to be taken under consideration next month. Fionna decided to do some research in order to present facts at the next meeting. She refused the usual invitation to lunch with Charlie and the Polish officers.

'I thought you enjoyed your luncheons.' Fionna didn't answer and Charlie grinned. 'I think you're gone on Tad.'

'I am not *gone* on him, but I think he might be going or gone on me. I am not available.'

'You could let him know that.'

'I'd make a muddle of it. I don't know how to be graceful about such things. I was always odd girl out.'

'Don't tell me that. In Spain you could have had your pick.'

'That was different. Females and life were in short supply. Nothing lasted there.'

'Would your Yank doctor have lasted?'

'I doubt it. He wanted me to go back to the States with him.'

'Tad can't take you back to Poland.'

'Charlie, I am not like Memsah'b. She could manage several harmless affairs all at once. It flattered Fa in some strange way that he had something other men wanted. The only one he got really angry about was Wallace Crawford because it got gossiped about.

'All right, Charlie. I do like Tad. When our luncheons are over and he puts on that beautiful *chapska* and goes marching down the street all stiff and proud, I want to run after him and beg him not to leave me. And I can *not* do that. Not to him, not to Willie, not to myself.'

'I shouldn't have teased. I didn't know it was that serious.'

'It isn't, but it could be. Can you imagine the effect on Willie? He had one woman walk out on him. Not that she wasn't a total besom. He is a dear man and I will not betray him for a romantic officer in a fancy dress hat straight out of an operetta. We would probably find it was all a dreadful mistake anyway. You don't build a relationship reminiscing about a lost war.'

'It will be difficult to avoid him since Memsah'b and the Gunns have taken him up. They have invited him and Jan for the weekend, by the way.'

'Then I shan't go near Milkstone and if she invites us, I'll invent a migraine.'

Riding out to Blanelammond on the unheated train which seemed uncertain whether it would last long enough to reach its destination, Fionna regretted her decision. She and Tad found so much to talk about besides Spain. Books and art, politics and political theory, Communism and Toryism, the days he had spent in a prison camp in France after Spain, life in Poland and the family he had lost. He carried pictures of his parents, his wife, and small sons. 'But one cannot continue to mourn about that which is lost. Life is today and tomorrow, not yesterday which does not return.'

He had hoped to start a small publishing business in Scotland like that he had had in Poland. Art books, illustrated classics, new works which had been printed by underground presses during the war and had very small, safe audiences, books long suppressed, and literature gone out of print because it did not meet with popular taste. But at present he was impoverished and must wait. Fionna wished she had the money to lend him, but knew it would interfere with their friendship even if she had had it.

The Rover was waiting where she had parked it that morning. She had to brush an inch of snow off the windscreen and the bonnet. As she sat warming the engine, she wished again that she had stayed in Glasgow. Lunch at the castle would be warmed-over soup, too thick with barley, and bread which was unpalatable even when toasted. All because she had been a fool and fallen for a man who played, unconsciously, on her sympathies.

The Rover roared and she backed out too fast, skidding as she did so. Easy, lass, she thought. You are in a bad way if he has that effect on you.

Smoke poured in white cotton skeins out of the chimneys and the castle itself looked as if it were posing for the December cover of *The Scots Magazine*. The old red sandstone blocks were bright against the white land, the hill they called the Bushby dark and its foliage snowtufted. What a muddle the building was. The old, square, 11th-century keep surrounded by Georgian additions on the one side, the Victorian addition on the other, its acre of roofs and chimneys, laced with ivy which prodded green fingers between the bricks and stones. The Lammondsons had had no eye for architecture, once they had started adding on. As a child she had thought it beautiful and romantic. When she had returned from Italy and Spain in '38, the castle and Willie had been a haven and refuge. Willie had been comforting, gentle, passionate, and grateful for her love.

But that was nine years ago. Now she felt nothing but stagnation. Was it the fault of post-war Britain where life was more austere than in the war years and without the excitement and incentive? Or was it herself?

She had thought that serving on the board would stimulate her. Today's meeting of short-sighted old gentlemen had depressed her.

She turned off the engine and sat for a few minutes gearing herself to face the remainder of the day. Liam and Jamie crawled from one of their burrows looking like snowmen. Jamie pummelled the windows of the car. 'Did you bring us a sweetie?'

'Nary a one. The sweetie shop has shut down due to the sugar shortage. I've two biscuits each from the canteen, but they are scarcely worth eating.' She handed them the biscuits as she climbed out. 'It's a wonder your noses aren't frozen.'

'It's almost warm under the snow, 'cept the snow benches are cold on our bums. You're home early.'

'So are you. Dodging classes again?'

'It was half-day at school. Remember? Father has a surprise for you.'

'Then I'd best go in and be surprised.'

The hall was as cold as it was outside. The plumbing fixtures had been removed and Fionna could hear, in the distant wing, the joiner's hammer. She wondered if that was the surprise.

A feeble fire smouldered in the drawing room. She added a log and used the bellows on the small, uncertain flames.

Wrapped in her coat, she went through the rooms looking for Willie. She found him at last in the tiny vestry room off the old castle chapel which he used as an office. It was so small that the minuscule fireplace heated it comfortably. He had added shelves to the vestment cupboards to hold his papers, and used an ancient washstand as a typing table. He sat at it now, poking with two fingers at the keys, his spectacles sliding down his nose and a stack of letters on the chair drawn up beside him.

'Lass, you are back early. Didn't Charlie take you to luncheon? Seems the least he could have done.'

'I wanted to get home early in case the snow starts again.'

'Wise. Look what the post brought!' He pulled *Country Life* from under the stack of papers. It was open to the page where his advertisement appeared. 'Rather good, isn't it? Well placed, dignified, but attractive.'

'Yes. It's very nice, Willie. But I half-hope there won't be any responses, much as your heart is set on this daft idea.'

'Och, lass, but there are.' He gathered up the papers and waved them at her. 'Came on the same delivery. Eleven of them. Now it is a matter of choosing which to accept and putting the others on a waiting list. Between now and October any number of things can happen.'

'Eleven! So it *is* going to happen.'

'It is. You must help me select the guests. One chap wants to bring his own retriever dog.'

'That is going too far.'

'I don't know. A chap gets used . . .'

'Willie, next they'll be wanting to bring their valets, then their wives, if not their mistresses. We are not a resort hotel.'

'Quite right. And we cannot take any more than six.'

'Any more than six and I should have to leave home.' She gave his shoulder an apologetic pat. 'Do as you like about the dog. I promise I shall read the letters later. Now I am going to ask Maureen to heat some soup and make a cup of tea for me.'

Thank heavens October was a long way off.

The assassination of Gandhi coincided with the weekend that Veda had invited the Polish officers to visit them.

Charles heard the news on the wireless and immediately went in search of Veda. He found her in the greenhouse, sitting on a packing box, discussing salad greens with Gerald.

'I have told you before,' Gerald was saying, 'that there is not enough sun these days for tomatoes to ripen properly. I cannot produce lettuces when there is five feet of snow on the ground. Hullo, here's Charles. Perhaps he can convince you that coleslaw is just right for venison because it's made of cabbages and I have plenty of those. Eh, Charles?'

'Yes, fine. I like cabbage in any form except boiled beyond recognition.'

Veda heard the deadness in his voice and noticed the solemnity of his face. Something was wrong. 'Charles! Tell me! Is it Fionna? Jamie?'

'Gandhi was assassinated this afternoon. Five-twenty, India time.'

'No! No, Charles. There has been a mistake. One of those wild rumours. No one would assassinate our Bapu.'

'I am afraid it is true, my dear. Nehru is scheduled to speak soon. The funeral is tomorrow.'

'I don't believe it.' She pulled herself to her feet, and stood trembling as tears streaked down her face. 'Never mind lettuces. Coleslaw will do very well.' Without waiting for Charles, who was about to take her arm, she dashed out. They watched her run blindly towards the house.

'I didn't know she cared so much for that little man. I should have thought she would be a Memsah'b to the end.'

'Veda? No, Gerald. You forget she had a Hindu stepmother and half-brothers. She believed passionately in freedom for India. She is a very complicated lady. Best I go to her.'

She sat on the floor beside the fireplace, her knees drawn up, her arms clasping them, her head resting on them. At his step she looked up. She had smeared ashes on her forehead. Ever the dramatist, Charles thought. What an actress she would have been.

'Poor India! What will happen now, Charles? Will there be more slaughter? Was it a Moslem who killed him?'

'A Hindu. Had it been a Moslem the violence would have erupted more violently than before. There have been some riots in Bombay. Come, my dear, I'll pour you a stiff drink.'

'I think a drink is not appropriate.'

'Gandhi was a saint. You are not. I shall pour a drink and you shall drink it. Remember, you have two weekend guests coming tomorrow. They will not enjoy a house of mourning and their hostess in tears.'

'We must make excuses. Perhaps Fionna could take them at the castle.'

'Veda, pull yourself together and be sensible. Fionna's guest rooms are torn to bits preparing for Willie's mad scheme for autumn. She is having a hard time of it with all the shortages and the neglect of the rooms being shut off all these years. She told Charlie that one is almost hopelessly mildewed. All the Chinese wallpaper must be torn off. We shall have Tad and Jan here as planned. Now, I am going to fetch your drink.'

'I'm going to telephone my father. He will be in a state.'

'I suspect all lines to India will be engaged, but try anyhow.' It would give her something to do.

He was right. It was impossible to get through. By the time the whisky had taken effect she had decided to try again in a few days. Meantime, she telephoned Fionna. 'Have you heard?'

'Yes, Willie told me. Are you very upset, Memsah'b?'

'What a foolish question. Of course I am upset. I know you and Willie are bored to death by my Polish officers but you must change your mind and come tomorrow to help me. I don't feel that I can be light-hearted and amusing.'

'Nonsense. You blossom at parties.'

'Don't be heartless, Fionna. It would be different if Charlie and Meg were coming. But she is so Victorian about her condition that she scarcely sets foot out of the house.'

'It isn't a time that one looks one's best, is it? Perhaps you could persuade Charlie to come without her. He and the Poles can fight the great battles all over again.'

'I need another woman.'

'You have Margery Gunn. She's good company.'

'But Tad and Jan like you.'

'Memsah'b, I *cannot* come. I have far too much to do here. I have to sand the mildew off the walls of the north bedroom so the painters can begin on it on Monday.'

'Why don't they do the sanding?'

'Because I can't afford them. Besides it is Maureen's weekend off and we should have to bring Jamie. Without Liam he would be restless and whining.'

'You must come. I appeal to you.' Veda heard Fionna's heavy sigh and knew she was capitulating.

'All right. Willie will probably thank you for saving him from shifting furniture. He still lives in the days when menials did all the work. What time do you want us?'

'Early, but not for luncheon. I haven't enough food and I couldn't ask them to bring their mess chits.'

As Fionna put down the telephone she shrugged. She had accepted, not to help her mother but because it meant she would see Tad again. Why was she trying to fight it?

It did not surprise Meg that on Saturday morning Charlie changed his mind about going to Milkstone for the weekend. For January, it was a rare day. Even the grey snow of Glasgow sparkled under the sun in a pale-blue sky. Puddles of slush appeared on the sidewalks. Icicles wept slow tears. Snow packs on roofs broke into individual glaciers and started slow paths down the sloping tiles. A gentle wind blew from the west, driving small balloons of white clouds before it.

'It will be glorious in the country. We could go for a long walk.'

'A long *muddy* walk?'

'But it's sunny! It would be good for you. And Memsah'b needs cheering.'

And so do I, Meg said silently. She hadn't felt this sluggish and uncomfortable when she was carrying young Charles, but she had been healthier then. She had still had a reserve of strength from the good country food that had helped them through the early years of the war. She had been strong from the clean air of the Highlands, so unlike the fog of Glasgow. Unlike this massive tomb. The vicarage had been warm and snug and she had had the daily stimulation of her work in the library.

'You go and take Charles. I'll have a long nap and a simple supper. I may not even dress, but stay in my robe all day.'

'I think a day in the country would be good for you, but if you want to be shot of us for the day, that might be good for you in a different way.'

'It's just that I am tired all the time.'

'You should get a nanny for Charles.'

'Nannies went out with the war, Charlie.'

'Perhaps we could get an au pair from France.'

'Any girl who would come to post-war Britain as an au pair wouldn't last two months.'

'Fionna's Maureen might know of an Irish girl.'

'That is a possibility. Or a Spanish girl who was on the wrong side in *your* war.'

Charlie frowned at the slightly accented *your*. 'Yes. A Spanish girl might be glad of the chance. I doubt she would know any English.'

'All right. I'll think about it. If you have really decided to go I'll get Charles ready. Don't let him get too tired or he will be a beast by evening.'

'I'll give Memsah'b a call to tell her we're coming.'

Meg was exhausted by the time she had wriggled Charles into his clothes, packed a small bag with a change of clothing and his brogues for when he changed from his boots. His favourite bear had to be dressed in *his* sweater, cap, boots and mittens which Meg's mother had knitted during her stay.

They went downstairs, Charles via the bannister. Charlie was waiting in the hall. 'It's all set. Fionna changed her mind and will be there, too, and she is having to bring Jamie, so the lads will have each other. I got in touch with Tad and told him I would pick up him and Jan. We'll go by the yard first, old chap, and then off we go.'

The long-case clock coughed and struck the half hour as Meg waved them off, glad to see them go. Closing the door, she debated whether to go back to bed with the latest Ngaio Marsh or—or what? The telephone interrupted her indecision. She had half a mind not to answer, but she did, to stop its insistent ringing.

'Fionna here, Meg. Memsah'b just now told me you are coming. I'm so glad. It's a glorious day. Real sunshine, though a bit watery. What I wanted to suggest is, why don't you stay overnight? We have one decent spare room and the lads can share. Don't expect too much. It's Maureen's weekend off. She goes to her Irish friends where they all talk revolution and IRA and Sinn Fein and throw out the English and have a good weep and a rousing good time. Will you stay over?'

Fionna was overwhelming. Meg thought that the patients Fionna looked after in hospital must have recovered to escape her energetic prodding.

'It is only Charlie and Charles who are coming. I was too weary to consider it. Charlie has already left. For the yard, of course. I doubt he will answer if I ring there. Tell him I said to stay over. I'd be glad of the change.'

'I should think you would be. The lad must be exhausting these days. Pregnancy is hell. Pity they can't be bred in a cosy bottle in a lab and picked up already cooked like fish and chips, wrapped in a blanket printed with yesterday's news. Do you think I can persuade Charlie?'

'You can if anyone can. Tell him I could have a long lie-in tomorrow and could just potter about all day.'

'Right. I'll use force if necessary. You have a good lie-in and don't so much as take off your nightgown and robe. I'll send them home after Sunday night supper. How's that? And do eat properly, Meg. Promise that.'

'I shall, of whatever there is. I'd like some unattainable things.'

'Do you remember clotted cream and strawberries with sponge cake? Prawn paste on real toast? Veal with walnut pickle? Mutton hams?'

'There's nothing remotely like that in our cupboard.'

'Nor here. Go back to your bed and dream of them, or read and sleep and read some more. Cheerio, then.'

The silence of the house closed around her. There was the loud tick of the old clock, the mutter of the fire and clink of coal, the creak of snow on the roof, the incessant drip of melting icicles, the tinkle of the crystal fobs on the chandeliers and, beyond the windows, the sounds of the city.

It was the silence of solitude, of being alone. No child played in the nursery, no cook clattered in the kitchen, no maid dusted, waxed and polished, trying to move as if she weren't there.

Meg sat on a footstool and held her hands out to the fire just as she used to do at home while her father read Dickens aloud. Coal fires did not have the smoky flame and scent of peat fires. The scent of the Highlands, of long-dead moss and bracken and ancient seas.

When she had said during her mother's visit that she wished she were going home with her, Mrs Sinclair had been shocked. 'You are a married woman now, Meg, living in a grand house, with money and a lovely gentleman for a husband, a dear wee bairn and another on the way. Oh, a visit would be all right. That is what you meant, isn't it, dear?' Her voice was doubtful.

'Yes. A visit.' It was not what she had meant. As the ten-fifty train to Inverness moved out of Queen Street station, Meg had cried. Not because her mother was leaving, but because she herself was not. Why wasn't she? Why hadn't she?

Now, sitting alone in front of the coal fire, she suddenly felt daring, and went to her room, packed her bags, and called a taxi. While she waited she wrote on a large square of paper, 'I have gone home.' She tried to think of something else to say but nothing seemed suitable and the taxi driver was already coming up the steps. She indicated her luggage and followed him out of the door. She folded the note and dropped it through the letter slot where he would see it when he came home on Sunday night. To a dark, fireless, empty house.

Meg's 'defection', as Fionna called it, shocked the family. Fionna reluctantly took young Charles to the castle for a few days, with the firm understanding that Charlie would get some kind of nannie, ersatz or otherwise, to take him over.

There were endless discussions as to what could have 'got into that girl'. Had she planned to leave when she insisted on staying at home that weekend, or had it been a sudden aberration? 'Pregnant women often go off their heads,' Veda said. 'I have seen it time after time.' She had been laughed into silence.

Charlie had rung the vicarage every day and spoken to a distressed Mr Sinclair and a tearful Mrs Sinclair. Neither understood what had upset Meg. Meg refused to come to the telephone.

Fionna, who had helped interview the prospective nannie, refused to console Charlie. 'You spent almost no time with her, you wouldn't allow her to make this her house as well as yours. She had almost no friends. The only women she met were young wives with nothing in their heads but knitting and nappies and rationing. No one shared her interests. You refused to let her do volunteer work at the library, and you haven't taken a holiday since you were married. If the shipyard is that important to you, Charlie, you best marry it and forget Meg.'

'I expected you to be more understanding, Fe.'

'Pooh. *I* knew she was unhappy and I saw very little of her. Memsah'b knew it and she is about as perceptive as a lamp post. You are her husband. Why didn't you know?'

'We had some good times. And we did take a holiday. We went to the Lake District for a week last year. Things were in a mess when I got back. Fa had only half tended to things. He hadn't entered the new orders or acknowledged them but left them all on my desk with notes attached.'

'So's not to intrude on you. Well . . . perhaps she'll get over it. If I were you I'd go up there and woo her. If you can leave the yard long enough.' She got up and drew on her gloves. 'On second thoughts, wait until the baby is born. You will be expected to be at the christening. She will be herself again by then, if she ever *is* herself again, whatever herself is.

'Hire that woman, Partland, Charlie. She will lavish young Charles with the love she lavished on the child she lost in the air raid. She has a decent accent, good manners, and obviously needs work. And stop going about looking like a wet weekend. Even Miss Maclean waylaid me after the last meeting to ask, "though she knew it wasn't her place", whatever was the matter. Tears fell when I told her. So do pull yourself together.'

'I wish you would stay for lunch.'

'I am lunching with Tad, but don't tell Willie. Ever since that fateful weekend when Jamie fell madly in love with Tad and Jan, he keeps asking when Koko, as he calls him, can come to visit us. Willie has been clinging to me like ivy.'

'What was so fateful about that weekend?'

'You idiot. That's the weekend Meg left you. And Koko and I exchanged a passionate kiss in the hall while everyone else was involved with the BBC news. Very romantic. I had just emerged from the hall loo and he was waiting to enter.'

'Oh, Fionna, you will break his heart.'

'More likely, he will break Willie's. Perhaps this is heart-break season.'

The weeks went by. The thaw came, flooding low-lying areas. Snow and ice packs slid off the roofs with whooshing sounds followed by earth-shaking thuds as they hit the ground, often taking the drains with them.

Young Charles no longer cried for Meg or asked when Mummy was coming home. Charlie took Miss Maclean to Sloan's for luncheon on her birthday and learnt that her first name was Amelia.

The castle smelled of paint and varnish as the rooms for

the shooting party gradually took shape. Paint was still on the list of shortages. The only available colours were grey or green. Fionna was inventive. For rooms with mildew, she added shoe blackening to the green paint so it became the colour of fir trees and covered the darkened spots on the walls. She shifted white damask curtains from other rooms and put down white sheepskin rugs. For the grey rooms she dyed much-faded and mended curtains cherry-red. The ancient furniture was sanded anew and waxed; the chimneys were swept, the brass fenders polished, and bunches of herbs hung in the corners to sweeten the air.

Jock MacPherson and Rob MacDonald were called back from retirement to act as beaters, maids were hired, plates polished, and some decent wine acquired from a man who knew a man who had a boat and made small excursions to France. Willie said he must also know the excise men.

Every week Mrs Sinclair asked Meg if she didn't think it time she went home.

'I am at home.'

'You know what I mean, dear. Your place is with your husband. And what of your wee bairn? Don't you miss him?'

'A little, but only a little. He was all Charlie's. When Papa was reading *Dombey and Son* the other night I was reminded of young Charles. "Papa, what is money? Father, what are ships? Take me to see the ships, Father. Shall I build ships some day, Father?" In his piping wee voice. He is already tainted.'

'You're very bitter for a mother. I find that difficult to understand, Meg. It isn't natural.'

'If I am a burden, Mother, I'll leave.'

'Oh, no. We are delighted to have you here. It's just that you are a married woman and you have responsibilities now.'

'You don't understand how comforting it is to be here.'

'I do understand. In a way. But Meggie, one must break the ties. And I don't know what to tell my friends. They are so curious and they do wonder why Charlie hasn't been up to see you.'

'Do you have to tell them anything? I suppose you do. Why don't you tell them what I told you to tell them when I came? That the doctor thought I should get out of Glasgow's foul air until after the birthing because I had a lung congestion. And that I wanted the child to be born here so Father could officiate at the christening.' But of course, her mother was a hopeless liar. 'And Charlie is too busy at the yard to come up, but that he telephones weekly. Is that so very difficult?'

'It is certainly difficult when he telephones. I wish you would speak to him.'

'I don't want to so much as hear his voice.'

'You can't hate him, Meg. You were in love when you were married.'

'I'm not sure that I was. I was bored and infatuated. Emotions during war are different from emotions during peace.'

Mrs Sinclair put down her knitting, took off her glasses and stared at her daughter. 'Are they indeed? I was married to your dear father during the war and I find no difference in my so-called emotions. I loved him then and I have never ceased to love him, and my hope is that we shall die together for neither of us could bear to be without the other.' She wiped her eyes, got up and stalked, plump little figure that she was, out of the room.

'Some people are just lucky,' Meg called after her. 'Mother, I'm going for my walk.'

New green pierced the graves in the churchyard. Small flowers bloomed in the stone dykes. The broom was in bud, but not yet in bloom. Young lambs tottered in the meadows, and only the deep sunless folds of the mountains still held a silver gleam of snow.

The long, narrow stretch of beach was empty. Meg walked in the sand rather than on the rim of the turf, still soggy from winter. She was sorry she had been so severe with her mother, but she was weary of being asked when she was going home. Weary of old acquaintances in the shops who exclaimed over her and asked about her husband.

She was glad she had come, though her arrival had been more of a consternation than a welcome. She did not regret anything she had left behind because she knew Charlie would keep her possessions safe, confident that she would return.

She walked, digging her heels into the sand, until she was tired. The sea was calm today, indigo blue and without a wave. It licked harmlessly against the shore and retreated leisurely, soundlessly. She sat down to rest, leaning against a rock, and sifted empty winkle shells through her fingers. The sea pinks were not yet in bloom, but there was a breath of warmth in the air. A softness, half-promising that winter was gone.

She slept and was awakened by someone kissing her fingers. Opening her eyes she saw it was a black cat. She reached out to stroke it and it surveyed her carefully, then arched its back and rubbed against her hand.

'Oh, but you are beautiful. What are you doing by the sea?'

A whistle answered her and the cat looked up and started to dash away, then paused as a young man walking on the turf leapt down a few yards away. 'Oh, sorry! I could have landed squarely on you. Is Cyprian bothering you?'

'Is he yours? No. He wakened me and high time, too.'

The cat gave her a golden look, then strolled to his master and curled against his legs. The young man bent down and gave the cat's ear a tender tug.

'He likes to go walking with me, but sometimes he gets ahead, and just as often lingers behind to investigate something which interests him.'

'He is beautiful.'

'And highly intelligent. You like cats, do you? Some don't, more fools they.'

'I haven't had a cat for a long time. We had two before I left home. What did you call him?'

'Cyprian. For the black saint.'

'That would please my father.'

The young man studied her with eyes as dark as the sea. Cyprian unearthed a winkle shell, sniffed at it, flicked it away, chased it and pounced.

'You must be the vicar's daughter. I heard you were back from Glasgow and about to lamb.'

Meg blushed. 'It's rather obvious, isn't it?'

'You're no sylph.' He sank down, cross-legged in the sand. 'What's happening in Glasgow these days?'

'I haven't been there since the end of January.'

'Is it so long? I knew you were here. Gossip gets about. It meant nothing to me because I had no idea I'd be meeting you. I live in the next village and I decided to take advantage of the good weather and have a walk by the seaside. You must enjoy this after Glasgow. Reekie old city, it is.'

'I wish I had never left here.'

He raised his dark scimitar eyebrows and appeared to be thinking. 'I thought you'd a husband. Shipping tycoon. No, wait a bit. Shipbuilding. Um. Right? I must listen to the gossip after all without knowing I hear it.'

'What else does the gossip say?'

He dribbled sand through his fingers. Then he grinned.

' " 'Twas a wartime marriage, you know. Special licence. No banns posted. He was a conchie. Och, a fine lad. I remember him well. Not like some of them. Real Reds, some were. But him, a gentleman. They say it was her mother set the cap for him. Whatever. There's one bairn. Off she went and left the wean behind. Heartless, I call it. But she had a congestion, they say, and the doctor said the foul air of Glasgow—and it's ever so smoky, you know. A body can scarcely breathe and the clothes on the line black again as soon as they're put out—the doctor said she must away or lose the new 'un and herself as well. So back she is, but we understand the husband will be up for the christening and no doubt he'll carry her away back. But *I* shouldn't wonder it's a real separation. And you know yourself the vicar's opinion of divorce." '

Indignant as she was, Meg could not help laughing in his imitation of the voices and facial expressions of the gossips in the shops. 'You're perfect! I can almost hear them. My poor mother. So that's what she has been going through.'

'It's cheeky of me, but now that I have met you . . . I too am curious. Will he be here for the christening, and will he carry you back? Or is it a real separation?'

'Do you want to be the bearer of news from the horse's mouth?'

'I do not gossip. They shall never know I met you. I—merely wondered.'

'I wonder as well. I don't know yet. Now you know more than my mother does. More than the gossips do. And I must be getting back.'

He helped her to her feet, and his hands were warm and firm on hers, holding them a second longer when she was standing up. 'All steady?'

'Yes. Thank you.'

'Do you walk here often?'

'When I can escape.'

'Perhaps Cyprian and I shall see you again. Tell the lady goodbye, Cyp.'

The cat rubbed against her ankles, looking up at her with golden eyes, and purred. She leant over and stroked him. 'Goodbye, Cyprian. That is, *au revoir*.'

Before she had gone more than a few steps, she turned. He stood where she had left him, looking after her.

'I do not know your name.'

'Ian Henderson.'

'*Au revoir*, Ian Henderson.'

'*Au revoir*, vicar's daughter.'

She smiled and waved, then turned resolutely homeward, conscious of her heavy body and plodding steps.

As her mother cleared the tea things away that evening, Meg asked her father, 'Do you know a young man called Ian Henderson?'

He was filling his pipe and without looking up from a business he took seriously he said, 'Aye. I know who he is. He comes to early morning prayer now and again. Not regularly, but that is not surprising considering petrol rationing.' Satisfied with his pipe, he searched his pocket for a match, and smiled at her. 'Why do you ask?'

Her mother re-entered the room and Meg hesitated before answering. 'I met him when I was walking on the beach today.'

'Met whom?' Mrs Sinclair demanded.

Mr Sinclair answered. 'Ian Henderson.'

'Meg, you should not take up with strange men.'

'Meeting someone in passing on a walk is scarcely taking up with him, Mother.'

'There's no harm in young Henderson,' her father said between puffs at his pipe.

'His cat was walking with him. It is black and named for Saint Cyprian.'

'You see, my dear? Quite harmless.'

'He must be new here since I left. I don't remember him.'

'His parents lived in London. Ian was in the service, of course. His aunt, Miss Henderson—she never married. I believe her intended was lost in the first war. She left Ian her house when she died and he moved up here a year or two ago. Apparently has independent means.'

Mrs Sinclair knew. 'Oh, yes. Miss Henderson left him a packet and his parents did as well. They were killed in a car crash. But no matter how wealthy, it seems not quite right for a young man to be idle.'

'Perhaps he isn't idle, mother. Perhaps he is ill.'

'He is not that, or we would know.'

'I am sure we would, my dear. The doctor's wife does not reveal the patients' illnesses, Meg, but she books their appointments so we are all alerted for life or death. She should be required to take an oath of silence.'

'He certainly knew all about me.'

'He didn't!' Mrs Sinclair was scandalized. 'Oh, Meg, I do hope no one saw you. There might be talk.'

'Land and sea were empty as a desert place, Mother dear. And from what he said, there is quite enough talk.'

'People *do* wonder, Meg. Dear, dear, there's the telephone. Is this Charlie's night to call?'

'Does he have a special night? If it is he, I am not in.'

Mrs Sinclair frowned at her before leaving the room. Her father puffed at his pipe until it went out. 'Tobacco is no good these days.' Patiently, he retamped it and applied another match. 'I hear MacKay's gatehouse is empty. Lodger chap they had there took a position in Aberdeen. It is snug and fully furnished—well, I suppose a few necessities such as bath towels, teacups and the like are missing. I doubt the furniture is anything much. Castoffs from the big house. Nothing like what you had in Glasgow.'

'What I had in Glasgow should have been in the Victoria and Albert.'

He raised his eyebrows in surprise. 'Your mother told me it was grand. But she is impressionable. About the gatehouse, if you and the bairn should decide to stay on, it might be just the place for you. Privacy. Your mother is a fine woman, but she does go on. And she couldn't fuss constantly over the rearing of the bairn.'

'That's the place across the bridge and up that narrow road along the river, isn't it?'

'Aye. Just the proper distance away. Tsk. It is out again. I should give up smoking, but even a vicar is allowed one harmless vice.'

'Would you object terribly if I stayed on, Father? I am not sure that I shall. I am not sure how I feel. I am not sure where I belong or what my loyalties are or anything. But I should like to be alone so I could think properly and sort myself out. What would Mother say?'

'Everything that came into her mind. Later, I hope she would become accustomed to the situation. Of course she would enjoy the new child. As for my objections, I hope that I am a tolerant man and one who forgives human frailties. It was a hasty marriage. Neither of you knew one another well.' The pipe was going again. 'I have missed you, but parents must learn to release their young, and I did so, hoping it was wise. Now you need wisdom and understanding of yourself, your life, your husband. I will give advice if you ask for it, but I shan't expect you to take it nor shall I be offended if you don't.'

'Could we look at the gatehouse tomorrow?'

'It's the Ladies' Guild Day and your mother will be busy

in the afternoon. If the weather holds, I think it would be understandable if we felt the need of a wee walk.'

Mrs Sinclair returned, bristling with indignation. 'That was Mrs Forbes, if you please. President of the Guild, Meg. She wants everyone to contribute an egg and a spoonful of sugar so she can make a sponge for tomorrow's meeting, and a twist of tea for the communal pot. Really, I do think in such times as these the Guild could hold a meeting without refreshments. And a sweet, of all things! I know we are all hungry for sweets, but is it right that we, the Guild, should indulge ourselves?'

'Perhaps the Guild ladies who hunger and thirst after righteousness hope that they shall be filled.'

'If it were righteousness it would be quite a different matter. And what I shall say when they ask how you are keeping, Meg, I do not know.'

'Tell the truth and shame Satan, my dear.'

'Never!'

'Tell them that my husband is coming for the christening.'

'Is he then? Will you permit it?'

'For your sake.' She would be living in the gatehouse by then. She and Charlie could battle out their lives in privacy.

Mairi spent the spring working for Edu's release. With the use of Corporal Braun's typewriter, she wrote countless letters, only to receive standard letters in reply. The matter had been referred to the proper department; prisoners were being repatriated daily; there was no record of any prisoners in the area she mentioned; the name, rank, serial number, date of birth, name of parents will be required before action can be taken in this matter.

It was difficult to be patient, knowing that Edu was alive,

and having seen Jo's condition. Kim said, 'Look here, if they are using him as a translator he is probably getting a bit more food and some special treatment. And while you are writing all those letters, you should write to HQ and put in a claim for damages to the *Schloss* from those bombs. From the looks of what was lost you ought to get a nice bundle of good old US of A dollars.'

'Are you serious?'

'Of course I'm serious. I thought you knew about it or I would have mentioned it before. I'll see to the forms if the village doesn't have them. Everybody is making claims.'

'I would have no idea how much to ask.'

'List everything that was destroyed and get a carpenter or stonemason to tell you how much it would cost to rebuild. They'll cut down any figure you ask so make it big.'

Mairi set Mutti Trötzen to making a list of the furniture and things lost, but remembering them depressed her so much that Mairi took on the task herself.

Meanwhile the garden had to be planted, and this year Maxl was not there to help. In the village was a young man who had lost a leg in the Battle of the Bulge. He was newly home from the hospital, having been fitted with an artificial limb.

He came to the *Schloss* looking for work and Mairi hired him. She had been doubtful about giving him the job, wondering how he could kneel to plant. He was not yet accustomed enough to his new limb to be sure of his balance. He managed the pruning easily enough, but planting the seeds and the tiny seedlings he had to do lying prone on the earth and dragging himself along.

Nor did he like taking suggestions, or orders when suggestions failed. Once he asked Mairi who was doing the gardening, her or him. But he was a hard worker and the beds he prepared were far better than last year's which Maxl had done.

Mairi was showing him where she wanted the spinach when Corporal Braun ambled out and asked, 'How y'all doin'?'

Jurgen did not look up but went on turning earth with renewed savagery.

'It looks great, doesn't it, Walt?'

'Super. You're a real professional, Jurgen. And with a game leg, too. How's the new one? Getting used to it?'

Jurgen did not answer.

'Jurgen, Corporal Braun is speaking to you.'

Jurgen answered in German. 'I don't talk to Yanks.'

'It is the Yanks who gave you your new leg.'

'It was the Yanks who took the old one.'

'I kinda think I'm not wanted here. You got a good worker there, but he could use a lesson in manners. See you, Frau Mairi.'

'I'm sorry, Walt.' She turned back to Jurgen. 'All right, Jurgen. He won't bother you again, but he has been very kind to us and helped with the garden last year which he did not have to. I am disappointed that you feel as you do.'

She said to Mutti Trötzen, 'He will have to go. I had hoped to keep him on to do the weeding and odd jobs around here, but I cannot have him acting that way. And I am not sure I have the courage to tell him.'

Jurgen solved the problem himself. One day he did not limp up the road nor did he come the next day, nor the next. The new seeds needed watering and Mairi put Hannes to work under Corporal Braun's direction while she walked down to the village.

She found him sitting on the steps outside his house. He did not stand up or answer her 'good morning'.

'Why haven't you come to work, Jurgen?'

'Because I don't work for *verdammt* Yanks.'

'You are working for us, Jurgen, and it was agreed your mother would have some of the vegetables and potatoes.'

'Better she starve. You can kiss their arses if you want to. A fine example of German womanhood you are. But you aren't a German. Are you? You're a *verdammt* Churchill-lover. Serves you right your man never came back from Russia. But you probably have that *scheiss* corporal or the *scheiss* major laying you, same as the Yanks are laying all the German girls who ought to have their legs sewn together and their tits cut off. If the Führer were still alive, he'd have the lot of you in the bake ovens, same as the Jews.'

Mairi was trembling so much she did not trust herself to answer him. Anything she said might have brought on another tirade. She turned quickly so he would not see the tears that came without her wanting them. Before she had gone more than a few yards from the house his mother caught up with her.

'*Gnädige* Frau Doktor Trötzen, please forgive my Jurgen. The gardening was too difficult for him. He suffers pain always in the leg which is no longer there, and the new leg chafes so much it is torture to wear it. And of course he is bitter. If the Führer but knew the sacrifices that were made for him he would have found a way to carry on to the end. But he was lied to and betrayed by the men around him and had to fight alone, as we all know. Göring, Himmler, men he trusted, they were all jealous of our love for him. It is tragic, is it not, but it will not bring back our Führer, Jurgen's leg or his friends or his father who died in the *Volkssturm*.'

'Nothing will.'

'About the vegetables he planted . . .' She twisted her hands together and bit her lower lip.

'I shall see to it that you get your share.'

'Thank you, *gnädige* Frau Doktor. Thank you. I knew you would treat us fairly. And please, forgive my Jurgen.'

'We all need forgiveness, Frau Becker, but for some it is easier than it is for others.'

April and May passed without news of Erich or of Edu's release. The authorities no longer acknowledged Mairi's letters with more than a printed card reading: 'We are in receipt of your recent communications. Investigations are under way. You will be notified of results in due course.'

Neither was there any word from Maxl. His mother's birthday in April passed unnoticed. She pretended not to mind. 'He is busy with his studies. It is not easy to return to school at his age.'

In June the new currency transformed life. Mairi herself carried the permitted number of Reichmarks to the small bank to be exchanged for the new Deutschmarks. A few days later foodstuffs and consumer goods no one had seen since early in the war appeared in the two shops.

'It was there all the time,' Mutti said bitterly. 'We starved and shivered, and there it was, packed away. I will have none of it.'

The greatest surprise was the reappearance of Herr Berger. Mairi was in the village buying flour when she saw him coming along the main road, wheeling a cart top-heavy with belongings, pots jingling at the sides. Frau Berger followed, a heavy basket on each arm.

'Herr Berger, you've come back. We had given you up for—well, we thought perhaps the camps . . .' Was it quite nice to mention such a thing?

'No, Frau Doktor Trötzen, we have been quite safe, tucked away in a little mountain village in Switzerland. We got there before the boat was full, you know. Afterwards they turned so many back, poor things, to be caught and sent to the ovens. We were blessed by God to have seen the way while there was time enough to escape.'

'And you have come back!'

'Of course, Frau Doktor Trötzen. It is our home. Is our small shop still there?'

'Yes. Standing empty all these years. The yellow star on the door has almost faded. The priest boarded up the windows so they would not be broken, and a good thing as they would have been shattered when we were bombed.'

'Tsk. I see the *Schloss* has lost a tower. But you are all quite safe?'

'Not quite.' Quickly she told him of Erich, Edu, and Vati Trötzen. Frau Berger wept and had to put down her baskets to search for a handkerchief to blow her nose.

'Yes, yes,' Herr Berger nodded. 'They were evil times, but perhaps like the phoenix we shall all rise from the ashes. Blessings, Frau Doktor.'

'And to you. As soon as the shop is open we shall need new curtains, thread, ever so many things.'

He patted the mound on the cart. 'I had the *Schloss* in mind.' He winked. 'The Trötzens never quibbled over the price.'

'Should we have done?' Mairi smiled.

'The prices were fair, but some thought—only a few—that because we are Jewish, we enjoyed a bargain. It was they who enjoyed it Frau Doktor. We were often the losers.'

Mairi went on through the village, telling everyone she met of the Bergers' return. The last she met was the postman on his way up to the *Schloss*.

'Well, that is a relief to me. I have been keeping a box of mail for them ever since their disappearance. One does not destroy government post, you know, Frau Doktor. It is against the rules. But I have been wondering what to do with it as not all bore a return-to-sender address. Very good. I shall call on them as soon as I have delivered your post.'

'Shall I take it so you need not cycle up the hill?'

'That would not do at all, Frau Doktor. It is my duty to deliver to the address. Besides, there is mail for the Major to be signed for and that I cannot trust to you, with all due respect.'

'I understand.'

'There is also an official letter for you. Perhaps it would do no harm if you were to have it now.' He reached into his bag, looked over his glasses at a handful of letters and extracted an envelope.

'Red Cross!' Trembling, Mairi tore it open and scanned it. 'Oh, Herr Reiter, they have found him. My son, Edu. He's alive. "Negotiations are under way for his release and that of twenty other prisoners." Edu is alive!'

She ran the rest of the way up the hill and when she reached the door she had to lean against it until she could breathe normally. She pounded on Corporal Braun's door, then stuck her head in. 'They've found him! They've found Edu. They're working on his release.'

'Hey, there!' His chair tipped over as he stood up and marched over to her. He caught her in his arms, kissed her and whirled her around in time to the music. 'Happy days are here again!'

'Yes, yes, and I must tell Mutti. Do put me down, Walt. I'm breathless enough. I ran all the way. It is a day of surprises. Herr Berger is back, too. Oh, you don't know the Bergers. It's that small, boarded-up Jewish shop. They have come back. All this time we thought they were dead in some awful camp. Oh, and the postman is on his way with letters to be signed for. He wouldn't trust them to me, of course. It would not be official.'

'Um. I think I know what they are. Didn't expect them so soon. You go on and tell your good news, honey, and I'll tell the Major. He'll be real glad that is cleared up. He was about to request the CO to get on the tails of those guys.'

'He can request him to get on to them about Erich,' she called over her shoulder. Somehow, somehow, she thought, everything would be all right. It was a day of miracles.

She and Mutti opened a bottle of champagne and were sipping it happily, reading the official letter over and over, when Corporal Braun and Major Kimball tapped at the door. They, too, had a bottle of champagne, a Dutch cheese and a box of crackers.

'Not exactly caviar and *foie gras,*' Kim apologized, 'but the best we could do on the spur. We have a little celebration of our own to share with you. First, let's toast the return of Edu and the future of the Herr himself.'

Mairi was already feeling a bit drunk, but it was a special day. Mutti's nose was quite pink and her eyes shining.

'Now, then. I don't know how our news will go down. In one way, you ought to be happy. Old Walt, here, he's being discharged and sent back to Texas. It's the "first in, first out" policy and he's been in a long time. So our loss is Texas's blessing. Friedrichsburg, isn't it, Walt?'

'Right on. Old German settlement. Those early Germans just plain loved Texas. Planted vines and made their beer.'

'Myself, I've six months yet to go. But the powers figure your village doesn't need me any more. I'm being transferred to SHAEF in Frankfurt for six months, then home. You ladies can move back upstairs where you belong. We'll help you move before we clear out. And we'll have one last grand party. Invite the whole town. It's on good old Uncle Sugar.' He stopped. 'Mutti, why are you crying? It's a celebration.'

'It is the champagne, I think. No, it is you. You have been

like sons and now you go away and leave us. Sons always do.'

'I'll be in Frankfurt. I can come often before I go home. I'll come again to say goodbye, I promise you. I'll bring diamonds.'

'I have diamonds, you foolish boy. It's that—I've grown used to you. I have learnt to love my enemy.'

'Haven't we all?'

The *Schloss* seemed empty without Corporal Braun's music; the rooms cavernous after the snug servants' quarters in the basement.

'How did we ever fill all these rooms?' Mutti asked over and over. 'It is not right for us to have so much when there are still homeless people whose houses were destroyed.'

'Do you want to start a hostel, Mutti?'

'Dear God forbid! A lot of strangers and most of them not quite fine. It is the emptiness . . .'

Mairi knew. It was the men who were missing or dead.

There were fewer DPs now. The village had never suffered the masses of homeless wanderers that larger towns and those on main thoroughfares had. There was little for them here. No housing, no odd jobs. The city dwellers had drifted back to their cities, hoping their homes were still standing or that there would be room at the relocation camp. The worst influxes had been in 1945 and '46. Then those who had drifted through had seen the American flag on the *Schloss* and swarmed up the hill. Corporal Braun had become expert at 'sending them packing'. He had a supply of Red Cross and UNRRA packages that he handed out, directed them to the nearest relocation camp, and told them to 'get on their diddlydamn way', using force to make them leave when it was necessary.

Any who came by train, riding the baggage cars, clinging

to the roofs of the carriages, were not allowed to get off. *Bahnhofvorsteher* Breuer and *Schutzmann* Bohr marched up and down on patrol while the arriving goods were unloaded. That done, the train was whistled off with a flurry of signal flag-waving, and jeers and curses from the disappointed wanderers. The village acquired a reputation of a good place to stay clear of.

In July the days were warm, the garden flourishing. Mairi had received a cheque of indemnification for 54,000 marks. It had been suggested that she apply for a widow's fund but she had refused. She was sure Erich was alive somewhere, and to accept a pension would be like sealing his fate.

Mutti Trötzen was receiving a widow's pension. Major Kimball had helped her fill out the papers which both Mairi and Mutti had found baffling. With all the money coming in Mutti urged Mairi to buy new sheets, new blankets, new clothing, new everything. 'We have lived like beggars long enough.'

Mairi ordered the bedding and material for the curtains from Herr Berger, but decided that her clothes, courtesy of Kim's sister, would do a bit longer. Memsah'b had sent her a few issues of *Vogue* and she realized her clothes were hopelessly out of style. But she was so accustomed to her poverty that she felt guilty every time she bought anything. She had even put off rebuilding the tower because the cherry tree growing out of the ruins had birds' nests in it. 'I do not want to destroy their homes. I have seen enough destruction.'

One late July day had been particularly warm. They ate supper on the upper gallery overlooking the village and distant hills, and lingered on until moonrise. Owls hooted mournfully and bats circled on sudden, silent wings. In the cherry tree a nightingale sang. A plane flew over, low on the horizon, coming in for a landing in Frankfurt. It was still surprising to see a plane with its lights ablaze and no sirens howling, no far-off rumble of falling bombs.

' *"Über allen Gipfeln ist Ruhe."* I, too, am at peace tonight,' Mutti said. 'I have not felt so in a long, long while.'

Was there peace where Erich was? Did birds sing there?

They said good night and went to their rooms, leaving the windows open to the warm air, 'too warm to be harmful', Mutti said. Mairi looked in on Hannes who was in bed reading. 'You will be a slug-a-bed in the morning if you do not leave Crusoe and go to sleep.'

'But he has just found Friday.'

'Friday will not go away again before tomorrow.'

Mairi had just floated off into her own sleep when she realized Mutti was standing by her bed. 'Mairi, Mairi, there are people in the garden. They must have been waiting until we slept.'

Mairi reached for her lamp, but Mutti stayed her hand. 'No lights.'

'What shall we do? Let them take our food?'

'No! It is ours. The Red Cross and the armies feed them. We are two defenceless women. Oh, I wish our Corporal were here. He would dispatch them.'

'Go and wake Hansi. I'll go to the balcony and call out.'

'What can a child do?'

'I don't know, but he has more of a man's voice than I do.'

Four formless, ragged scarecrows in the moonlight were busily digging up the precious potatoes, trampling the beet greens and the turnips, working furiously, stopping long enough to gnaw at a raw, dirt-encrusted vegetable.

'Who's there?' Mairi called. 'Is it my neighbours?'

They froze, then there was a mocking laugh. *'Ja,* neighbours, hungry neighbours.'

'Neighbours come by daylight. Go away.'

'Not yet, you old swine.'

She shrank back into the shadow. 'You are trampling the garden. If you come tomorrow I will give you food.'

'*Ja,* you'll give us food and have the police here.'

Mutti and Hannes joined her. 'Keep back!' she whispered. 'There is nothing we can do. Let them take what they want.'

'I have a gun,' Hannes shouted. 'I will shoot if you don't clear off.'

'We've been shot at before.'

Hannes stepped forward and took aim. Mutti tried to pull him back, but as she grasped his arm he shot once, then again.

There was a howl of pain, followed by curses. A second later a hail of rocks was hurled on to the balcony. Mutti cried out and stumbled, slumping suddenly against Mairi and nearly throwing her off balance.

'Mutti, are you all right?'

Mutti moaned, and in spite of Mairi's trying to support her, sank to the floor.

'Hansi, *Grossmütterchen* has been hurt. Put down that gun and help me.'

'Can't. I'm reloading.'

'I command you . . .'

Another wild series of shots interrupted her.

'They're leaving,' Hannes announced. 'Running as if tanks were after them. I think I should alert the police. Do *Schutzmann* Bohr good to get out of his nightcap and nightshirt and see some action other than marching around town bowing to the ladies.'

'You will go nowhere. You will help me carry *Grossmütterchen* to her bed. She has fainted. Turn on some lights so we can see what we are doing.'

They made a makeshift stretcher of a blanket and rolled the frail form on to it, then half-dragged, half-carried it to the bed. 'She weighs no more than a kitten,' Hannes commented. 'Even now that there is more to eat, she is still a tiny *Grossmütterchen*.'

Her temple was bleeding from a large cut and already the skin around her eye and cheek bone was discolouring. Mairi massaged her face, then slapped it gently, but she did not waken. Smelling salts had not yet come back on the market, and the small silver vial of salts which had been as much a part of Mutti as her handkerchief since Mairi had known her had long since dried up.

'Fetch cold water, Hansi, and some brandy. Do hurry.'

Hansi looked frightened. 'Did they throw stones because I shot?'

'No, they were saying bad things to me. They were bad men. Go quickly.'

The pulse was slow and uneven, and despite the pressure of cloths applied to the temple Mairi could not stop the bleeding. The brandy trickled against the pale lips, but there was no sign of swallowing. Mairi chafed Mutti's hands and wrists, which seemed as cold as stone. The pulse under the thin flesh fluttered like a moth's wings. Often Mairi lost it altogether, only to feel it surge again to resume its uneven flutter.

'Hansi, you must fetch Frau Binding. What a stupid village this is with no doctor.'

'Frau Binding does nothing but deliver babies. Why do you want her?'

'She knows a bit about nursing. Fetch her, Hansi. Oh, before you go—put the gun away and not a word about it. Where did you get that gun anyway?'

'From Grossvati's gun room. It is the one Uncle Maxl used to hunt squirrels and rabbits when he was here. To make our stews. They were better than the meat we have now.'

'You should not have used it.'

'Corporal Braun said I should. He said, "Do you have a gun, kiddo?" He always said "kiddo", didn't he? And I showed him the gun room and he chose that one for me and showed me how to load it and gave me ammo—that's what he called it. Ammo. He said I am the only man here now and there could be trouble. He knew, didn't he?'

'Yes, he knew. Put it away, go and get Frau Binding and don't tell her about the gun. Just tell her what happened. Not about the gun, understand. I think we are still forbidden to have guns.'

'I'm glad there is moonlight.'

'So am I. Go safely.' He was seven years old, but he looked very white and small as he gave her a Corporal Braun salute before he left her. She heard him skipping through the halls, humming a song Walt had sung the last few days before he had left—'Gonna take a sentimental journey . . .'

No sooner had he gone than she remembered the door would be unbolted. It would be all right. The marauders had fled. But the *Schloss* was full of whispers, and finally she went through the wide, silent, stone halls and down the staircase hollowed by the footsteps of generations of Trötzens. Hannes had left the heavy front door ajar. The scent of trampled earth and night-blooming stock filled the hall. She stood, indecisively, wondering if anyone had entered, if one of the men had stayed behind and was even now going through the rooms, seeking her or, more likely, food and loot.

She waited, listening. The garden was silent. No wind stirred the leaves, the staircases connecting the three towers were silent. Then the nightingale sang a long, joy-filled *Nachtmusik* and was answered from a distant hill. Mairi closed the door and bolted it. She returned to Mutti's bedside.

It was too late. She was dead.

She had said, 'I am at peace tonight.' And so she looked now.

Mairi covered her face with a new pink sheet, a parting gift from the PX and Corporal Braun, then she went down the hall and sat on a stiffbacked chair beneath the ancient armour to await the return of Hannes and Frau Binding. No tears came. She felt nothing but an emptiness.

She had no idea how much time had passed before she heard their voices and footsteps on the paved entrance. She rose stiffly and found her hands almost too numb to unbolt the door.

Frau Binding took immediate charge. 'I will wash and pre- pare her. Hannes must fetch the priest. You will have to ham- mer on the door, *mein junger Herr,* as he sleeps all too soundly. You, *meine Frau Doktor,* must have a stimulant, then some rest. There will be much to do. Show me the kitchens and then leave me to do what must be done. I never thought this day would come. Peace, they call it. Yes, times are better, but where is peace?'

When they were alone Mairi said, 'I am afraid, Hansi, that you must fetch the priest. Or shall I go? You must be very tired.'

'No, Mütterlein, I shall go. First, though, I must tell you something. A secret. Can Frau Binding hear us?'

'No. She is in the kitchens boiling water and doing who knows what.'

He put his mouth up to her ear. 'There is a dead man in the garden. I am afraid I killed him. Is that a great sin?'

'My God! It is terrible! *You* killed him with all those wild shots? Oh, Hansi, Hansi!'

'I didn't aim at anyone. I just shot to frighten them. What will *Schutzmann* Bohr say?'

'I don't know.'

'Will he send me to prison?'

'Certainly not!' But she was not sure what action could be taken against a child, even though the killing had been to protect them.

'Perhaps he will forgive me because we are Trötzens. Perhaps no one need know.' He glanced over his shoulder. 'Diddlydamn, here comes the Frau with her buckets of water. I'd best run for the priest or she'll wonder what ails us.' And in English, 'See ye!' He ran out of the door before Frau Binding came into sight, toiling up from the kitchens with her steaming buckets.

The night was like a bad dream. Weariness and shock made Mairi move by rote rather than logic. Frau Binding was in charge. After the priest had done the necessary things, she took care of the body. Then she called the priest and Mairi into the room where she had arranged a small circle of chairs for the three of them. There was a table with cups and cakes and precious coffee.

Mairi thought it was macabre to sit there in silence, munching cakes and averting their eyes from the death bed. She could not keep her mind off the other body lying in the garden. Presently, when Frau Binding and the priest were nodding in their chairs, she startled them by saying, 'I need some air. I'm going for a walk in the garden.'

'It has been difficult for you. It would be forgiven if you slept a little,' Frau Binding said.

'The air will rouse me.' Mairi knew full well that to sleep a little would not be forgiven. There were rules to be observed for death and the dead. 'I shan't be long.' As she closed the door she heard the priest and Frau Binding clucking in sympathy.

The door to Hannes's room stood open and his lamp was burning. He was lying on his bed, fully dressed, staring at the ceiling. He turned his head and looked at his mother with round, bleak eyes.

'Hansi, come with me. We must hide the body before morning.'

'I was thinking the same, Mutti, but I did not know what to do.'

'We shall put him in the barn. Tomorrow, when I can think more clearly, I'll decide what to do.'

They crept down the stairs, conscious of the sound of their footsteps in the silent hours. Moonlight cast black shadows over the grey landscape, silvered the leaves of the trees, turned the white stones of the *Schloss* to snow.

'There,' Hannes whispered. 'In the carrots.'

It surprised her that she could look at the body without horror. It was skeletal, dressed in rags and broken shoes from which blackened toes protruded. Nothing was left of the face, dark with blood, but the mouth twisted in a toothless grin, jaw hanging askew. Was this the one who had called her an old swine? It did not matter. A hungry, homeless wanderer had died, and there was little compassion left in the world.

'Fetch the wheelbarrow, Hansi. In the charity box in the barn are some old blankets. Bring one and a shovel.'

Waiting, she gazed at the ruined garden. Vegetables were ripped from the earth, the spinach flattened; gnawed carrots, half-eaten, had been tossed aside; the poles for the peas and beans were broken and the vines limp on the ground. Anger and resentment choked her. She was half-glad that the man lay dead, and was ashamed of her gladness.

The wheelbarrow creaked. Mairi hoped the thick stone walls would prevent the sound from penetrating the death room. Gulping with revulsion, they shovelled the body into the blanket and, using it as a sling, lifted the body into the barrow. The man was so thin he weighed almost nothing.

Hannes wheeled the barrow into the barn, Mairi walking beside him. It was too dark to see well, but they concealed the barrow in the back as best they could and locked the door after them.

'Go to bed and get some sleep, Hansi. We'll think what to do tomorrow.'

Hannes pointed to the east where a pale, grey line edged the horizon. 'It's already tomorrow.'

'So it is.'

Hannes tumbled into bed, fully dressed and was asleep before Mairi closed the door. She returned to join Frau Binding and the priest, slumped in their chairs, snoring in unison. Uncomfortable as it was to sleep sitting up, Mairi slept herself and did not awaken until the room filled with golden dawn.

The day was one of bustle and sorrow. Hannes slept until noon, then went to work repairing the damage done to the garden. Mairi faced an endless parade of callers from the village. They ran out of coffee and had to switch to wine and schnapps. Although she only sipped at the schnapps she felt it making her drunk because she was so tired.

She thought afterwards that it was because of the schnapps that the shocking solution to the problem of the dead man had come to her. The grave-diggers had arrived mid-afternoon to prepare the grave in the family plot. When Mairi went to pay them, Hannes accompanied her, carrying a tray of cold beer and cheese. The day was hot and the men were sweating. They thanked Mairi graciously and sat on the pile of earth to drink.

'Hard work for such a day, *ja?*' one said, his lip moustached with foam. 'But we do not mind. She was a fine old lady. Always a kind word to us. We made it deep and strong so she will rest well.'

Hannes and Mairi gazed into the dark shaft, then their eyes met in startled agreement.

Mairi set her alarm for midnight, and roused Hannes. Mutti Trötzen's body had been removed to the church, where stone angels guarded it by candlelight.

They carried no lantern or torch, for fear some restless villager would see them. Their shadows walked before them and clouds drifted across the moon, turning its light cold. The wheel of the barrow creaked but there was no one now to hear.

Superstition aside, Mairi felt a qualm when they reached the burial ground. The place was eerie. The markers where long-dead Trötzens slept were white reminders of all mortality where stone endured. Angels knelt, wings unfurled, carved helmets from ancient battles, a climber's axe and rope, a toy drum, and the black, dank shaft where Mutti Trötzen would lie tomorrow.

'It's scary, *nichts?*' Hannes's voice quavered.

'Yes, it is. I hope we are doing the right thing. Perhaps we *should* have told *Schutzmann* Bohr. Too late now.'

Together they lifted the blanketed body and dropped it into the grave. Then each took a shovel which the gravediggers had left behind, and shovelled earth until both were panting from the labour.

'I think that must be enough, Hansi, but I'll come out tomorrow as soon as it is light and make sure that—that nothing shows.' She was feeling decidedly queasy. 'Off to bed.'

Hannes took the handles of the barrow, then dropped them. 'I'm going to be sick.' He ran across the graves to the far end of the ground and leant over the low stone wall. Mairi heard him sobbing as he retched and vomited. When he returned he leant against her. 'I'm sorry.'

Mairi hugged him and stroked his hair. 'I feel sick myself, Hansi. Go to bed. I'll take the barrow back to the barn.'

'I'll go to church with you tomorrow, but must I come *here*, too?'

'No, *Schatzi,* everyone will understand.'

'Thank you. For I think I should be sick again if I did.'

Mairi started to wheel the barrow away, then she stopped, turned back and looked into the grave, feeling that she should say something. 'God, please forgive us if we have done wrong, and gather this poor man unto your gracious mercy and protection.'

The next morning, shortly after dawn, Luise Margrete Maria Trötzen's coffin was lowered on to the earth which covered the other body; bedded in death with an unknown man.

Maxl arrived in reply to Mairi's letter telling him of his mother's death. He no longer wore his dyed *Wehrmacht* uniform, but was so well dressed that Mairi felt shabby. At the same time she wondered how he got the money to buy clothes.

'I have a job. I am working for Viktoria's father at his factory. He manufactures wireless sets. We will go into television when supplies are available. It is still experimental with us.'

'I thought you wanted to be an architect and rebuild Germany. What happened to university?'

'It is more important to eat than to study. There were no textbooks and most of the professors were Nazis. Still are. It's a good job. I enjoy it. They are good people. By the way, Mairi, I want to take the Mercedes back with me.'

'You can't!'

'I damned well can. The Yanks would have requisitioned

it if I hadn't walled up that end of the barn. That is what happened to the Bekkers' car. Goddamned Colonel requisitioned it and when he left he took it with him. Shipped it back to the States.'

'That motorcar belongs to Erich.'

'He doesn't need it wherever he is.'

'He will need it when he comes back.'

'*If* he comes back. Now that Mutti is gone there are a few things I want. She has—had—some pearls—'

Mairi interrupted. '*Had!* We sold them right after the war ended to buy food.'

'I'd like to go through her things.'

'Maxl, you are a ghoul. Come back in a few months, but not now. It was dreadful enough without this. You have changed. Or were you always like this and I didn't see it?'

'I haven't changed. I have learnt. Sentimentality and idealism don't get you anywhere. I have learnt that the people we welcomed as liberators were no better than the Nazis. I have learnt the only thing they respect is wealth and the show of it. If you aren't royalty you get kicked in the teeth, when you aren't being kicked in the backside. I am using the "von" again which Grossvati gave up after the other war. It gives me status and it gives Viktoria's father status to have a "von" working for him.'

'If you have so much status you might try helping me to find out where Erich is.'

'I'll do what I can but I thought you had already gone through all the channels.'

'A *von* Trötzen with status might have more influence.'

'When are you going to start rebuilding the other tower? Do you like living in a ruin?'

They glared at one another, then Maxl broke the silence. 'Come, Mairi, we love one another. We must not fight. We have a child in common. I want to take him back with me for a holiday.'

'I need him here to help with the garden.'

'For God's sake, Mairi, hire a gardener. And some maids and a cook. What has happened to *your* standards that you are so critical of mine?'

'Go away, Maxl. Just go away and leave me in what little peace I have.'

'I'll go. Tell Hansi to pack his things.'

But when Mairi called Hannes in from the garden and said, 'Uncle Maxl wants to take you with him to Cologne. Do you want to go?' he stiffened and glowered at Maxl.

'Go away and leave my Mutti alone? That is *dummkopf*. What if the bad men come back? Who will protect her? I don't want to go to Cologne. I want to stay here. I want to be here when my brother Edu comes home.'

'Don't be *dummkopf* yourself. It will be a nice holiday.'

'No thank you, Uncle Maxl. I stay here.'

Maxl threw up his hands and stamped out of the room.

Before he left the next day, without the Mercedes or Hannes, Mairi relented enough to give him Mutti's wedding ring of heavy embossed gold, and a cameo pin.

He held the ring in his hand as if weighing it. 'I had forgotten it. I thought it had got lost.'

'It was lost for a while. Before the end of the war she was so thin it wouldn't stay on her finger. Corporal Braun found it behind the bookcase when he moved it to make room for his files.'

'And gave it back to you?' Maxl was astonished.

'He and Major Kimball were unusual men for conquerors.'

That summer the last of the mining equipment which had

been sent piecemeal arrived at the mine. Erich was glad to have work to keep him busy at last. He had used the interim to repair the old equipment as best he could but, as he told the Governor, equipment was not his speciality. Yes, he had studied it in his courses, but never maintained it. The Russian technicians knew almost more about it than he did. But the new German equipment he did understand and the very sight of it swept waves of nostalgia over him.

At night he dreamt of the Saar, of the house where wisteria grew outside the bedroom windows, and the long stretch of green garden which went down to the river. He dreamt of Mairi, who sometimes had the face of Marya. An infant's face appeared, vanished, and reappeared like a waxing and waning moon. Strains of music—but perhaps it was the Governor who often could not sleep but sat up until dawn playing his piano. When he was very, very tired and despairing, nightmares tormented him. Dreams of the last weeks of the war. The troops retreating without order or direction. The distant sound of bombardment, the burning of buildings, the bodies thrown into mine shafts, the hysterical, terrified civilians. He would awaken trembling—and pace the floor until the cold sent him back to his bed again. He wondered why he had been loyal to the orders of a government in which he had never believed, had paid only lip service for the safety of himself and his family, for the luxury of his life. There had been cowardice, too, after hearing the whispers of the camps. Men went through life making mistakes which they realized as mistakes in hindsight, but which seemed logical at the time.

He had written to both Mairi and Marya, letters which the Governor assured him would be sent. No answers came. No Red Cross representatives called at the mines in search of prisoners of war, and the summer brought malaria.

With the machinery in place the mines were in full operation. The rows of waste grew around the open pits and there was always the noise of electric power shovels and explosives.

Once a week Erich was driven to the site of the underground mines and spent a few days of inspection there, descending into the mines with the men, trying to say words of encouragement to them. But what encouragement was there for men who would never return to their homes, who would die young?

Now that everything was going well Erich asked the Governor if he would not be sent home. 'I can show the overseers how to repair the machinery if there should be problems.'

'No, no, my dear Trötzen. You are essential here. Already you have shown us ways to improve our production. Your record is known in higher circles.' He nodded in a conspiratorial way. 'You understand, of course. No, you must stay with us. What can we do for you to make you happier? A woman, perhaps? One to live in with you? Some men find their company a comfort. Myself, I prefer the occasional titillation, but on the whole my music and my own ways.'

'No. I do not want a companion. No woman. Perhaps when winter comes another blanket.'

'A blanket!' The Governor almost giggled. 'A woman would be warmer, my friend. But a blanket. Yes. You shall have a blanket.'

'I should like to do something for the prisoners—the workers. The Germans. They do not deserve this, you know. Their misfortune was being trapped behind the lines. Some Red Cross boxes, warmer clothing, blankets for them too, better food.'

'There I can do nothing. They are treated as well as can be expected. War crimes must be punished. No, do not mention this matter again. I warn you—for both of us.'

A bottle of vodka was delivered to Erich's cabin, and with it, a tin of caviar.

Summer waned. The aspen forests beyond the mines turned colour, then lost their leaves which flew in the air like gold coins. The mornings and nights were cold and the prisoners on their way to the mines shivered, their faces pinched, their bodies racked with coughing.

A factory was being built in Kuznetsk to manufacture mining machinery, and Erich was sent there as an advisor, along with an interpreter, actually a spy and bodyguard to keep Erich from escaping. It was good to be away, to talk about a business which he understood, to eat in a restaurant however poor the food, to walk along streets where there were shops and stalls and ordinary people.

He wrote again to Mairi and Marya, more confident that these letters might reach them. As he began to address the envelopes he had a sudden inspiration and sent them care of the Red Cross headquarters in Geneva, enclosing a slip of paper asking that they be forwarded to the enclosed addresses.

The postmaster looked at them doubtfully. Erich explained in his stumbling Russian that it was to thank them for the equipment they had sent to the mines.

'They will have to be examined, opened, you understand, for they have no official stamp. I will see what I can do.' He glanced around. 'The Red Cross found our son for us. He was captured and doing forced labour in Italy. He is back with us now.' He nodded. 'I think this is not to thank them, ah?'

'I don't know why you think that.' Erich was afraid of betrayal.

He grinned. 'Nor do I.'

When Erich returned to the mines he found his cabin had been whitewashed so his calendar of days was completely covered.

That Christmas the prisoners did not sing.

Charlie went north for the christening of Una Maccallum just as Meg had promised her mother that he would do.

She had written to him once, asking him not to telephone any more as it distressed her mother, and begging for some time to sort out her life. 'I am no longer sure of anything—what I want, how I feel, what the future is. I admit I sometimes miss you and small Charles, but I am not yet ready to return.'

She did not miss them in the way that she supposed she should, in the way any other wife and mother would. At times she felt almost guilty, but she was happy in the MacKays' gatehouse. She enjoyed her evenings before the peat fire, the shutters closed, the lamps lighted, her simple dinner on the tea cart, and a book propped open to be read as she ate. She liked the simplicity and lack of obligation, and because she was happy she was able to tolerate her mother's visits, all bustle and chatter.

She had not seen Ian Henderson again because she felt too awkward and misshapen to walk on the beach. But just before the child was born her father had mentioned casually that 'Young Henderson' had gone to London for a spell. He was still tidying up his parents' affairs.

'Did he take Cyprian?'

'Oh, aye. Mrs Gilbride who does for him said the cat has a special carrier, fancy as a sleeping car. There was no question of leaving the cat behind.'

By the time of the christening the walls of the gatehouse were hidden by yellow broom and the garden was a mass of bluebells. A scarlet rose bush climbed the grey wall to the window of the gabled bedroom where Meg slept. Rose-sprigged wallpaper and lambskin rugs decorated the small boxroom where the baby slept in the cradle that had been Meg's.

'You seem rather settled in,' Charlie commented. He could not keep the envy out of his voice.

'It was necessary to be so.'

'Was it? You could have come home.'

'Not yet.'

'I love you, Meg, but I admit I don't understand what has happened to us. I thought we were happy. And the way you left, without a word to me, without warning, and left our child! Have you no feelings?'

'I didn't know I was going to leave until I was actually on the train. As for Charles, he is well taken care of, isn't he? Children that young adjust quickly.'

'That is a heartless attitude. Does he mean nothing to you?'

'No. But in a way I can't explain. I feel I am objective about him. I don't want to smother him the way I was smothered. I want him to be a separate person. Una, too. I am determined neither of them shall cling to me nor I to them.'

'Nor you to me. That's it, isn't it?'

'I don't know. I did love you and liked you as well. But somehow—I wasn't myself any longer. It was as if in being married I had lost myself. I was expected to merge into the great Maccallum family and I couldn't. Wouldn't.'

'That is ridiculous. Just because of marriage you were still Meg Sinclair inside.'

'Meg Sinclair was stifled, overwhelmed, and not allowed to move so much as a teacup from the place in the cupboard where it had hung in your grandmother's day.'

'You could have done whatever you liked.'

'It's easy for you to say that now. I remember asking for some different dishes—'

'Oh for God's sake! Dishes! All right you can have your dishes. Fionna told me I was being beastly about that. Young Charles likes those dishes.'

'Of course he likes them. He's a Maccallum. He can eat off them.'

'Then what the devil is it? Do you love me or don't you? Do you want to be married to me or not? And if you don't, what do you want? A separation? A divorce? I suppose I could go off with some female and pretend to be unfaithful to you.'

'I want time to think. I should have taken time to think before we were married by special licence and whirled off to Glasgow together. Where the day after our arrival you left me in that cold tomb of a house and went off to the shipyard and stayed until nearly midnight and were off again at dawn.'

'We were at war. The yard was working a twenty-four-hour schedule. Did you expect the yard to run itself? That's all over now.'

'Is it? It was usually ten o'clock before you got home every evening. You were there Saturdays, Sundays . . .'

'Only long enough to check in.'

'I am selfish. I expect more of a marriage than that. It was nice when you were at the CO camp. When you came to the library on Saturdays and we talked. We didn't talk any more when we were married.'

'We made love. We ate by the fire in the small room. I still eat there, it isn't the same without you. Oh, Meg, what can I say, what can I do?'

'I've already told you. Give me time. Time doesn't cost anything—'

'Anything but misery. Loneliness. Sorrow.'

'Is it too great a price if it comes right in the end?'

'Does that mean it will? That you might come back?'

'I don't know what it means yet. I'll make a bargain with

you, Charlie. You don't have to accept it. I'll come back with you. There are some clothes I need, some things I want. My crystal bowl, my books, the Monet print—you can hang your Maccallum ship back up in its place. I shall see for myself if young Charles is all right. But I shall keep the key to this house and come back here for at least six months. Is six months too much time?'

'Yes. It is. But if that is what you want, if that is the bargain . . . I suppose I shall have to accept it. Reluctantly.'

'Six months is a month for each year we were married.'

He looked so downcast that she reached out and touched his hand. He grabbed hers and clung to it as if he were drowning in sorrow.

'I'm sorry, Charlie. I don't want to make you miserable or unhappy. I truly am sorry. You see . . . I am not even sure I understand myself.'

Going back to Glasgow was like going back in time. The minute she walked into the house all the unhappiness which she had managed to dispel in the north came flooding back. It was worse than she had remembered. The house was oppressive and ugly; the heavy Victorian furniture without charm; the chill like winter, although Glasgow was enjoying one of its sunny, balmy summer days. Charlie dropped the luggage in the hall, hugged Charles and left for the yard with a 'Back as soon as I can, I promise. Charles, take care of Mummy while I'm gone.'

Young Charles greeted her almost casually. 'Hello, Mummy. I'm glad you're back. See how tall I've grown. Is this my new sister? I have a toy ship for her.'

The new nanny, Mrs Partland said, 'There now, Master Charles' (Master Charles, for heaven's sake, Meg thought), 'the wee bairn is too young for toy ships, but you'll have grand times together when she is older. I'll take you to the boating pond and you can sail your wee boaties together.' She smiled at Meg. 'He's a grand lad, Mrs Maccallum, and ever so bright about ships. We go through the old album together and he can name every one.'

I'm sure he can, Meg thought.

'I told the maid, Annie, to put the cradle in your bedroom so you can hear wee Una if she cries in the night and needs to be fed. So much easier you know, just to take her into your bed.'

'Thank you. That was thoughtful, but I do not want the baby in my room. She had her own room in the north. And she sleeps through the night without a bottle, so I doubt she will awaken.'

'You don't feed her yourself then?' Mrs Partland looked askance.

'No, indeed. A scientific formula is much better for babies in these days of rationing.'

Mrs Partland stiffened visibly. 'I shall go and tell Annie to see to it the cradle is moved. Master Charles, do you want to stay and talk to your mummy while Partland sees Annie?'

'No. She'll be all right alone. Won't you, Mummy? She likes to be alone, same as me.' Without waiting for an answer, he followed Mrs Partland out of the room.

Meg drew off her gloves and dropped them along with her coat on a chair. It was a mistake to have come but she had to prove to herself that it was as bad as she remembered. She could not wait to be away again.

The train ride down had been uncomfortable both physically and psychologically, Charles tried to be warm and friendly and considerate. Once she had said, 'You are trying too hard, Charlie. Stop trying to ingratiate yourself.'

He had looked as if she had struck him.

He returned from the yard far sooner than she had expected him. Already she had a stack of books on the floor which she intended to pack to take back with her; but she had hoped to have them boxed and out of sight before his return.

He looked at them woefully. 'You're being rather hasty, aren't you? Shouldn't you give yourself time to be here? You might decide to stay.'

'I was under the impression we had a bargain.'

'Damn it Meg. You aren't even going to give it a chance, are you?' He shrugged when she didn't answer. 'All right. Do it your way. I did come home early to be with you, but I may as well have stayed at the yard and let you pack. Fa has things under control, thanks to Miss Maclean's tutelage. We are invited to Milkstone on Sunday, if you think you can tolerate it.'

'Will they want to see me?'

'Of course they want to see you. I am the one taking the blame for this whole stupid business. I'm the black sheep. You'd think I was a wife beater, the way Fionna acts. They don't know yet that you aren't staying. I didn't have the courage to tell them.'

'Would you like me to tell them?'

'I don't know. I still can't believe it's happening. I can't believe you are going back.'

'Do we still have the box I brought the books down in?'

'I think it is somewhere in the basement. I'll look for it.' He left the room, shoulders sagging.

She was being unnecessarily cruel, but if she gave an inch he would overpower her with promises and persuasion.

She spent the next three days packing. The cook, Annie, and Mrs Partland were curious, but none dared to question her.

Fionna telephoned. 'I'll see you on Sunday. Memsah'b

has gathered the clan. We'll all behave like little ladies and gentlemen and pretend you simply went for a visit. From the way Charlie is acting, I think *this* is the visit. I warned him a long time ago and much as I like him—and I *do* like him, Meg—he has a streak of English bulldog in him he must have got from his mother. We other Maccallums are more flexible, thanks to Memsah'b. The Tolmie family were iconoclasts.'

'Nothing is decided yet, Fionna. We made a bargain that I have time to sort things out. Charlie is so different here from the way he was when I met him. And Glasgow is rather overwhelming for a Highland villager.'

'Glasgow in combination with the Maccallums, even to a very sophisticated villager. I remember Mairi saying she went through something of the same sort when she first went to Germany and was engulfed by the Trötzens, but she soon proved herself stronger than any of them. I suspect they *heil*ed Mairi instead of Hitler.'

'You are being very kind.'

'And blathering on like a fish wife. Oops, there's Willie calling. Cheerio, then.' She rang off before Meg could say goodbye.

Meg felt a twinge of remorse as the train pulled out of Queen Street station. Everyone had been kind, happy to see her, and unaware that she had packed up to leave again. Charlie had been cautiously affectionate and companionable, even managing to get home at a decent hour in the evenings.

She had begun to wonder if the marriage could improve and she would eventually learn to be happy. Perhaps she had cast her die and there was no turning back.

Charlie's face as he kissed her was almost more than she could bear. She looked back as she walked down the long concourse and waved, and was surprised at the unwelcome tears which blinded her, so that she stumbled on the step into the train. The porter dropped her bags and seized her arm to help her. 'Partings are always sad, madam. You'll cheer up before you've reached Pitlochry. And *och* to be seeing the Grampians in the summertime. A sight I've never forgot.' He stacked the luggage, arranged a seat for the baby's bed, and took off his cap as he thanked her for the tip. 'God bless, madam, and a safe journey to ye.'

Glasgow's brief summer was over and a soft drizzle fell on the black roofs. She hoped it would not rain all the way to Inverness, the clouds low on the mountain tops and the green land wet.

Fionna's parting gift, a book, lay unopened on the seat beside her. 'Geoffrey Household's newest. All heat and olive groves and intrigue. Koko said you would like it.'

Koko was Jamie's name for Major Kosciuszko, who now worked in a bookshop on St Vincent Street. It was not publishing, he had told Meg regretfully, but it was 'with books'. Fionna was one of his best customers. He had smiled at Fionna in a way that made Meg envious of such admiration and affection.

Meg had asked Charlie if something was going on with Tad and Fionna. 'I have wondered that myself,' Charlie said. 'She said she wouldn't do anything to hurt Willie, but she always goes off with Tad after our board meeting luncheons. She gave him Carlos's guitar which she sent home from Spain after he was killed. I think, like me, she just has a special bond with him, a *¡Salud!* that no one else has. Same with Jan, of course.'

Meg thought it was more than a *¡Salud!* but she didn't say so. She envied Fionna and decided she would miss her. Perhaps in six months she would return. Perhaps not.

The train gathered speed, leaving Glasgow behind. Words from childhood sang in her mind with the rhythm of the wheels on the track:

> Faster than fairies, faster than witches,
> Bridges and houses, hedges and ditches;

What came next? She repeated the lines over and over, but all she could remember was the ending:

> Each a glimpse and gone forever!

Was Glasgow gone forever? She did not know. She picked up the book and began to read: 'The four graceful ships steamed out of Beirut harbour in line ahead, their holds and cabins packed with the French Army of the Orient . . .'

4

January came and went. February and a chilly March passed without word from Meg. There was no telephone in the gatehouse and Charlie no longer called the Sinclairs. Once or twice a month he took Miss Maclean out to dinner. He now called her Amelia, but he was still Mr Maccallum. Not even Fionna knew of this. There was no need, as it was quite harmless.

Ever since the end of the war Veda had been insisting that she must return to India to see her father before he died. The two tumultuous years after the Freedom made such a journey impossible. For her sixty-fifth birthday Charles gave her a return-trip air ticket to Calcutta and Assam. He was to accompany her as far as Rome where she would break the two-day journey. They were taking the night sleeper down to London and would fly from there. Because of these arrangements there was to be no birthday celebration.

'Anyway, I am too old for such foolishness.'

'You will never be old, Memsah'b. You will go on forever,' Fionna told her.

'And wither all at once like "She", or that poor soul in *Lost Horizon*.' Veda had already lost her beauty, she told herself. Which was not true. Her body was still slim and her face as unwrinkled as a girl's. Rationing had been beneficial. She lived almost entirely on the vegetables which Gerald grew. From her favourite Indian restaurant where she had eaten since she first came to Glasgow, she had got a yogurt starter.

Charles could not tolerate yogurt, but Veda mixed yogurt with cucumbers, nuts, onions, and tomatoes, and seasoned it with turmeric, or berries, when they were in season, and a sprinkling of cinnamon. She used it for a facial and a hand cream, and Charles asked why she didn't emulate the actress who bathed in milk, substituting yogurt. 'You have more than enough to fill a bathtub,' he said with a solemn face. For there were carefully blanketed bowls of it curing in warm corners of the kitchen, by the fireplaces, by the geyser in the bathroom.

Despite her protests that she was busy packing and wanted no celebration, Fionna, William and Jamie came to afternoon tea. To their surprise they found Veda in tears. 'It is Papa,' she explained. 'His birthday wishes came this morning. His letter had been posted before he received our cable.' She took the flimsy, yellowed paper from the table and handed it to Fionna. The ink was pale and the script as thin as a thread, wavering across the pages as if a spool had rolled across it, unwinding as it went.

Jamie, who at eight was tall and stalky, asked, 'May I have the stamps, please?'

'Yes, darling. The envelope is there on the table. I should have thought to give it to you.' She rose and began to pace the floor. 'Read it later, Fionna. I am going just in time. I should have gone before, but Charles would not allow it. One would t˙ ink I was a child. I could have forestalled this thing he is proposing to do.'

'What *is* he proposing to do, Memsah'b?'

She ignored the question. 'He is ninety now. He has never been the same since the war. You remember, my stepmother was killed in the bombings. Japanese or Americans, they didn't care where they dropped their bombs. My half-brother and some of his children were murdered during the riots between Muslim and Hindu before the partition. The tea garden has been taken over by the government. He is a stranger in his own land. He has outlived his time. All is vanity. Nothing of value remains. On and on he goes until he comes to the crux of the matter. He has been in Calcutta taking instruction to become a *Sannyasin*. I cannot allow it! I must arrive in time to stop him.'

It was Willie who said, 'I don't quite understand. I've heard of *Sannyasin*. A religion of some kind, isn't it?'

'The *Sannyasin* are wandering ascetics. Usually only Brahmins can become *Sannyasin*. Somehow, he has managed to become accepted. That is bending the rules. He has been taking instruction ever since the death of my stepmother, and is now in the last stage, that of renunciation. He must give away everything and he asks me to come, not knowing of course when he wrote that letter that I *would* be coming. He means to give everything to me, after that nothing is left but the ceremony, which I may attend, watching from a wall.' She backed up to the fireplace and lifted her skirt to warm herself, for although it was April, there was a chill breeze. 'He is too old. He would not survive six months.'

'If he is ninety, does it matter? Perhaps he wants to die, Memsah'b.'

'It matters to me. He is my last tie. The cords have never been broken in all these years. In all my dreams, I am back there, living a different life. I am glad Charlie is not here for I can say that I understand Meg. There are some places where we are born that we never leave. They are always pulling us back. We may transplant, but we do not thrive.'

'Memsah'b, you can't tell us that you haven't thrived.'

'I have lived a double life and I am adaptable.'

Father and daughter exchanged amused looks.

'It is some kind of monk, then?' Willie persisted. He did

not understand why Veda was upset. Surely a ninety-year-old man was permitted to know his own mind.

'Monk, yes, wanderers, beggars. They are allowed three possessions, a water gourd, the skin of a tiger or an antelope, and a staff. They live on alms and one meal a day for which they must beg. As I remember, they do not have a begging bowl, but I may be wrong.' She wrinkled her forehead trying to remember. 'I used to see them when I was a girl. Dreadful old men. Covered with ashes, to remind them that the body is transitory. Their hair all matted, uncombed and uncut, and full of lice. And their stink! Well, of course, all of India stinks. Do you know what they drink? Of course you don't. A sacred beverage made from the five gifts of the sacred cow. Milk, curds, ghee—which is a kind of butter, Jamie—urine and dung.'

'Pee, Memsah'b? Cow pee? They drink that? And dung like what Jock calls the dung heap? Crackers! 'Course the chickens and pheasants scratch around in it and peck at the stuff and we eat them after, but talk about stink!' He grabbed his nose and made a face.

'Be quiet, Jamie.'

'I am scientifically interested.'

'You'll learn more by holding your tongue instead of your nose.'

'Cow dung is rich in nitrogen,' Willie observed.

'If he had told me before I might have prevented it. I could have brought him here.'

'He would not have come, Veda. He wouldn't transplant, as you call it.'

'No. He would not have come. But why does he want holiness at his age?'

'Perhaps that is when one needs it the most.'

'How are you going to manage this trip when you can take

only fifty pounds out of the country?' Fionna asked. 'I know you've bought the ticket and all, but will fifty pounds see you through?'

'Papa will meet me in Calcutta at the Victoria Hotel. And of course, if he carries out this mad plan, he will have to give me all of his money.' She began to pace the floor again. 'The government compensated him for the tea gardens, and he has provided for his grandchildren. But I am to take whatever I want from the house and what he calls a "comfortable sum".'

'Isn't it a mistake to go? Shouldn't you let him do what he wants?'

'He asked me to come and I want to go, Fionna. Sometimes I think I never should have stayed here but gone back before I married you, Charles. Much as I have loved you.'

'The last time you went back, you came very close to staying, I remember.'

'But I heard you calling me.'

'I'll call you, Memsah'b, 'cause you are the only gran I have and the only one that's got a diamond in her nose. They always ask at school, is it real and how'd you get it there? I tell them it's magic and you were born with it. Some of them will believe anything.'

'Perhaps I should exchange it for an emerald. Emeralds are said to prevent dysentery, and there is enough of that in India.'

'Oh Memsah'b, do be careful. And don't drink any of Grandpapa's sacred beverage!'

'It wouldn't be allowed. I am not holy enough.'

The plane landed at Ciampino airport at five-thirty in the afternoon, when the slanting sunlight gilded the domes and steeples of Rome's churches, and turned the dusty air to mica. Veda had grasped Charles's hand as the plane descended, but now she released it and smiled at him. 'How many years since we have been here? Long before the war. Do you suppose that little trattoria where we ate pasta and drank bitter red wine is still there? Can we find it again? It was near the river, remember? We had walked in the Forum by moonlight.'

'We shall do the same again, if you aren't too tired.'

'Tired? Never! We must, Charles, because tomorrow evening I go on and early the next morning you go back to dreary old Glasgow. Will you be quite safe alone in Rome without me?'

'As the plane leaves at seven in the morning and I shall be short of cash by then, I think I shall be very safe.'

As they rode in the limousine towards the Hotel Quirinale, she chattered on and on about the things they must do. By the time they were in their room and she was running a bath, Charles thought her nervous agitation quite unlike her. He wished she would rest. She had a long flight ahead of her the next evening, and although he had booked a sleeping berth for her, he doubted she would sleep well. He wished he were going with her, but sensed that this was something which she must do alone. If he had not come this far with her, she would have flown straight through and overtaxed her strength.

She seemed calmer by the time he emerged from his own bath. She had dressed carefully in a flowing black chiffon dress with a scarlet sash and a thin scarlet shawl to wear against the night air. Sixty-five and she was still the most beautiful woman he had ever known. He loved her as much as he had done when he had married her against the wishes of his family and her aunt.

She had exchanged the diamond in her nose for an emerald and he laughed and touched it with his finger. 'Superstitious?'

'No. Respectful of ancient beliefs, for who knows but that they might be true?'

'Veda, promise that you will come back to me.'

'Where else would I go? There is no longer a tea garden that belongs to us. No longer the India that I knew.'

He was apprehensive as he saw her on to the plane. The twenty-four hours they had spent together had been idyllic. They had found the same trattoria, they had visited the places they remembered, walked the Spanish Steps, drank wine on the Via Veneto, visited Hadrian's Tomb, fed the cats in the Colosseum, visited the tombs of Shelley and Keats, and been driven on the Appian Way. They had returned to the hotel with a minimum of time for her to reach the airport to catch her plane. Charles realized afterwards as the plane rose into the still, sunlit sky, that she had planned it that way. No time for goodbyes. A quick kiss. A 'take care, darling', and 'last call for passengers . . . on flight 106'.

Twilight settled over a Rome that was desolate without her. The hotel room empty, a place to lie sleepless until the morning five o'clock call. A dry roll and coffee before he took the limousine back to the babel of the airport. Geneva with its fountain over the lake, and London at dead noon.

He took the afternoon train to Glasgow to resurface, like a diver who comes up slowly from the sea bottom to avoid 'the bends'. Then he telephoned Charlie, and the two womanless men drove the darkening road to Milkstone together.

Rome was silhouetted against a long stretch of violet sky, the domes dark, long, twisting lines of lights along the streets. Then they were over the darkening sea, the lights of Naples, the glow like that of a cigarette of Vesuvius.

Veda went thankfully in to her cramped berth, its lights

too dim to read the book she had bought, its blankets too thin to warm her. She was chilled with fatigue. Her gaiety had been an act for the benefit of Charles, so that he would send her off with a smile. Instead his face had been a tragic mask. In her life there had been moments when she realized how much she loved him. This was one of those moments, waiting for sleep, enveloped by the sound of the engines.

She awakened as the plane dropped altitude for its landing at Cairo's Farouk airport. She raised the curtain and saw the lights of Alexandria and the toy ships in a toy harbour. The Nile was a band of shimmering steel in the moonlight. Out of the dark sea of the desert the pyramids emerged like islands in a cubist painting. Then the land rose to meet them. There was the thud and bump as the wheels hit the earth, the scream of the engines as they reversed. And the swarm of humanity and all the sounds of the East.

She was glad when they were airborne again, rising over the squat villages and the moon-silvered network of small canals and fringed palms. She slept again, and in the midst of a dream was awakened for breakfast, though it couldn't have been more than three o'clock in the morning in Scotland. Wearily she dressed, nibbled at the breakfast she did not want, and stared listlessly down at the vast expanse of Arabian desert undulating with waves of heat. Wasn't there said to be a 'lost quarter' there? It was easy to imagine any number of lost quarters, ancient sand-buried cities, travellers turned to whitened bone.

The sky, which had been honey-coloured when she had awakened, had been bleached white by the sun. The Arabian Sea was oily and smooth, dazzling with the sun and the heat.

She was giddy with the time change, the meals at hours when she was not ready for them, and the sound of the plane, the almost imperceptible, unceasing vibration. From Bombay to Calcutta, she dozed, awakened confused and uncomfortable, then dozed again. When she left the plane she felt as if she were sleepwalking, yet back home it was just past noon.

She had expected her father to meet her, but as she searched the faces of the crowd she did not see him. It was not until someone called her name that she saw and did not recognize him. She hoped her face did not show her shock.

He was still tall, with the bearing of a prince, his once-piercing eyes clouded by the beginnings of cataracts, his white hair still a lion's ruff, but his body so thin that his flesh hung on him like rags. She felt, not his arms, but his bones as he embraced her, both of them crying.

They went to the hotel in a dilapidated taxi which crawled through the streets, the crowds parting before it like the waters of the Red Sea. When the cab was forced to halt, arms were thrust in the windows, voices demanding alms. Veda bent her head not to see them. 'It is horrible,' she said. 'Was it always like this? I never saw it before.'

'It was always here. We were privileged when you were young. When you are young, when you are the dominant race, you see with different eyes. The only misery is your own.'

'It is shocking, Papa.'

'It is India. But there is no more slaughter. No more violence. Nehru is a good man. The *Sannyasin* accepted him, bestowed their ancient symbols of authority on him. They went to him on the evening of the transference of power and bathed his head with holy water and put the sacred ash on his forehead. It makes him one of us.'

'Papa . . . why?'

He touched her hand with his, dry as a serpent's skin. 'Later. Later.'

Later. Time to think how to save him. She had come with

hope, but she felt it ebbing from her.

The air conditioning in the hotel was temperamental, first too cold, then powerless against the damp heat. Despite her weariness they talked late. She told him of the family he no longer knew. He listened, nodded, smiled, but she could see they meant nothing to him. They were strangers. It was his own fault, she thought angrily. Why had he not visited them more often? Why had they not visited him? But there had been the Twenties slump when half the men in the shipyard were on the dole, the tea slump of the Thirties, then the war. He rambled on about the war, '. . . we could hear the artillery . . . the planes always seemed to be off course . . . hordes of refugees from Burma . . . cholera . . . work stoppages called by the Congress for non-cooperation with the British war effort . . . the Tea Association opposed the Ledo road and the Americans . . . put as many legal stumbling blocks in the way as we could . . . no use in the end . . . yes, yes, my world has come to an end . . . a man outlives his time.'

'Papa, come back to Scotland with me.'

'When I was young, your grandfather sent Katherine and me to Scotland to school. Katherine never came back to stay. But I came back. The tea garden was mine and I wanted it. There were times when I longed for Scotland. It haunted me. Stevenson wrote something about the old huddle of grey hill, never again to see Auld Reekie. Never to set his foot again upon the heather. But he was dying in the South Seas and his letters were full of homesickness. Except for you, there is nothing for me in Scotland. There is nothing for me here. I have outlived two wives, their sons, India and my own time. I am full of years. I want no more of this life. It doesn't bear thinking about the kind of world your grandchildren will inherit.'

'Possibly it will be a better one. A peaceful one.'

189

'Vain hope. We have lost our humanity. We have chosen the wrong dream. We were always less than angels, less than devils, but there are devils among us, and there is no health in us.'

'Are you determined to do this thing?'

'The ceremony is tomorrow.'

'Tomorrow! Papa, not tomorrow!'

He stood up and kissed her with lips dry as a snake's skin. 'I am going back tonight. I have left the address there on the table. You may come tomorrow and say goodbye to me and, if you wish, watch the ceremony from the wall. After that, go to Assam, and take from the house whatever you want. It is all yours. The manager is expecting you. The money is in your name at the bank. Sleep well.' He hesitated at the door. 'Shall I see you tomorrow?' Wistfully.

'Of course, Papa. I shall come. I will not stand in your way any longer.'

He had discarded his Western clothes for a *dhoti*. His flesh was loose over his ribs and sunken belly. His long Scottish legs meant for kilts and hill climbing were sticklike. His feet were bare and calloused. His staff and antelope skin lay on the floor beside him. Choked with emotion, Veda could not speak.

He smiled ruefully and showed her a small ash-and-clay figure in the shape of a man. 'Do you think there is a resemblance?' He gave a small laugh. 'Do you recognize your old father? I am no sculptor. It was the best I could do. When you see it burn tomorrow, you will know it is the death of your old Papa, who then ceases to exist.'

'Papa, I am sorry I came. I don't think I can stand it.'

'Would it be different if you stood by my bedside and watched me suffer a death of disease?'

'I suppose not. But—' She stopped.

'Give me the gift of your acceptance.' A bell rang. 'It is time for visitors to go.'

She stood up, so full of sorrow she was not sure she could walk unaided. She clung to him as they embraced. She thought she saw tears in his own eyes.

'Papa.' It was one last desperate attempt. 'If you can cry when you tell me goodbye, you are not yet ready.'

'It wasn't a tear, but a mote in my eye.' He pushed her from him. 'Go in peace, my darling. Go in peace.'

She went, so blinded by tears that she bumped into another weeping woman. They clung to one another and went out together sobbing. That evening, as she sat at the window of her hotel room, they came past in a long parade, their bodies smeared with ash, their water gourds at their sides. If her father was among them, she no longer recognized him.

She left for Assam the next day, travelling through East Pakistan in a sealed compartment. There was no food on the train, and she could not open the window to buy tea from the vendors at the stations. In Assam she changed trains three times because of the different rail gauges. She managed to have some tea and rice on one, but the tea was murky and the rice grey. She wondered what water it had been cooked in.

The river steamer was better, and the air was cooler. She watched the shore pass and all the river traffic, the country boats, the mail boat, the tea rafts, the dug-outs and boats whose prows had painted eyes to see where they were going. She remembered them all from childhood, and they comforted her grief.

The wide teak doors of the house stood open and the manager was there to welcome her. She remembered enough of the language to greet him in Assamese.

The house was full of ghosts. She was always catching glimpses of them out of the corner of her eye. Her father's pipes were still on his desk. His clothes still hung in the armoire, a few hairs clung to his hair-brush. In her stepmother's room, clothes hung limply on their hangers. Sandals were by a chair as if she had just slipped out of them. Her jewels were there, her wedding ring, a bottle of scent, a jumble of bracelets.

Veda's room was just as she had left it after her last, long-ago visit. An unfinished weaving was on her loom. Perhaps she would finish it while she was here. Even some of her clothes were there, long out of fashion, insect-ridden, mildewed.

The old Daimler was in the car port; the tennis court where she and her brothers had played was overgrown, the net hanging there, torn, rotting.

She stayed a week, sorting, choosing, rejecting. When she grew weary she sat on a veranda, sipping her father's whisky and watching the river traffic, dreaming of the past.

The manager sympathized and told her not to fret. He would have whatever she chose packed, labelled, and shipped, then he would clear out what was left.

She chose some books which had not yet been eaten by insects or gone black with mildew, some faded photographs of her mother and father and the brothers killed in the Great War, a few sentimental objects, her stepmother's jewels, the heavy Victorian silverware, the silver platters and bowls, some small rugs, some prayer flags.

She cried when she left, knowing she would never see it again. In a few years no one would remember the people who had lived there. The ghosts would tire and vanish like mists. Again, the three changes of train, the sealed compartment. This time she had brought food with her, but the heat soon spoiled it. It was night when they finally crossed the border. She stared dully into the darkness, seeing only her reflection in the window. Her head ached and her stomach was uneasy. Somehow, she reached Calcutta, fought her way past the beggars, found a cab to take her to her hotel. By the time she reached her room she had diarrhoea and severe cramps. Four times in the night she vomited. Her lungs felt clogged and she was almost too weak to drag herself from her bed to the bathroom.

The maid came to make up the room. She looked at Veda, then turned and ran out of the room leaving the door open behind her. Presently there was a doctor standing by her bed, taking her pulse, her temperature, her blood pressure, and forcing her to drink some medicine.

People came and went. The room was in endless twilight. The doctor came again, his hands were cool on her pulse. She heard him saying to the manager, 'You must cable her husband. He must come.'

Charles. Yes. If Charles came she would be all right.

October was drawing near again. Willie's pheasant shoot was fully booked. They took eight guests now, having opened two more bedrooms. Fionna had spent the summer refurbishing the first six. She had replaced the make-do curtains with custom-made ones from MacDonald's, put in fitted carpeting, had the rooms painted colours other than green and grey. During October they subscribed to *The Times* so the gentlemen could keep in touch with London.

She had commissioned Gerald to do a small, coloured sketch of the castle and another of the pheasant shoot. These had been printed as complimentary postcards.

She still disliked the entire idea and dreaded the week of the shoot, but it brought in money. Added to that the money from her position on the board and her inheritance from Memsah'b, she and Willie were not only solvent, but 'rolling in it', for the first time.

Two years had passed and she still could not accustom herself to the idea that Memsah'b would never be coming home. Overcrowded as it was with furniture, Milkstone seemed empty, hollow, deadened. It had been a year before Fionna had had the courage to open the crates which had been shipped home, and even then she had wailed, 'What did she expect us to do with all this?'

Fa had offered her the diamond, but she had shrunk from it, refused to touch it. 'Why didn't you bury it with her? It was as much a part of her as her fingers and toes. How could you have done?'

'I thought you knew. She was cremated. I sent the ashes back to the manager of the tea garden and asked him to scatter them there.'

'And Grandpapa never knew?'

'I couldn't locate him. Perhaps it is just as well.'

Fa, too, seemed empty and more tired. His interest had shifted from the shipyard to politics. He had joined the Scottish National Party and was full of bitterness about the English exploitation of Scotland. They could no longer invite him to the shoot dinners because after a few drinks he got into shouting arguments with the guests.

Mairi had written, asking him to visit her, but he had replied that he couldn't make the effort. He said he would give her the money to visit him, but Mairi had a job now at the American Embassy in Bad Godesburg and was still involved in trying to locate Erich, whom she refused to believe to be dead.

Shortly after Veda's death, Fionna had given up resisting Tad. She, Charlie, Tad and Jan now lunched together once a week on Tad's afternoon off. They had long since ceased to fight the battles of 'their war', but the bond held them and their friendships had deepened. Jan was a designer at the yard, Tad still at the book shop. Fionna thought his salary a disgrace.

Occasionally after luncheon, Fionna and Tad went back to his place to round off some particularly interesting discussion. The flat was two rooms in a high-ceilinged, ornate, early-Victorian mansion which had been converted. The rooms overflowed with books and pictures, several by Gerald Gunn. A map of Poland was pinned to the wall above the mahogany Partner's desk which they had found, waterstained and disintegrating, in front of a rundown secondhand shop. The photographs he had once carried in his wallet were now in small silver frames which Fionna had found at the Barras. 'Nicked, no doubt,' she had said, 'but what are the odds now they've found a good home?' She had donated some furniture from the attics of Milkstone, and they had spent many afternoons haunting crowded, dusty antique shops for incomplete sets of dishes, odd bits of silver and crystal, 'for I shall not be giving large dinner parties,' Tad said; for rugs not too badly worn and chairs in need of reupholstering.

Fionna felt motherly about the flat. Hadn't she spent hours refinishing the desk, retying springs and tacking new cloth on the chairs? She made the tea, poured the brandy, fed shillings to the heater, took off her shoes and curled up on the sofa. One day, as a dark summer rain beat at the windows and it seemed as if the flat would never be warm, Tad suddenly asked, 'How long has it been? Our friendship?'

'Four years.'

'We did once kiss at Milkstone.'

'I remember.'

'You feel as I do. I see it in your eyes. But you are careful.

You put on armour. You blind Willie so he will not see.'

'Yes.' She rose from the sofa and in her stockinged feet paced the room restlessly. 'I am afraid he would know —somehow.' The marriage had seemed so right at the time and it had been right for fourteen years. Somewhere she had read, beware of the fifteenth year of marriage. It was even more dangerous than the seventh. Perhaps it was because she was forty-two that she felt discontented and unfulfilled. There was no longer any flavour to life. She suspected she was more deeply in love with Tad than she had ever been with Willie. Their shared afternoons made her feel alive for a little while. When she was not with him, there was a hollowness inside her. She stopped beside the heater and stretched out her hands to its warmth.

'I, also, do not wish to hurt Willie. He is solid, good, a gentleman. A little humourless, perhaps, but that is no great sin.' He, too, was restless, stopping to move a book, straighten a picture, pick up an object and put it down again. He came and stood beside her at the fire and stretched out his hands beside hers. 'I do not ask you to leave Willie. That would be wicked. We—you and I—could not survive as friends if we did such a thing. I ask only to share you. Love is expandable. The more one loves, the more one is able to love.'

'You've got it wrong, Tad. The more one loves one person, the less one loves the other. Our kind of love causes displacements.' She turned and put her arms around him, leaning her head against his shoulder. 'All right. I shall try it and see if I can live with it. Because I do love you very, very much. I think it started in the hospital in Escorial. Do you know what I remember? The way you raved on and on in Polish when you were sedated out of your mind. And when we were operating, all laid open and full of sponges and blood, you opened your eyes and looked at me. You were anaesthetized, but there was pain and wonder in them, and for a second, before you went under again, recognition. As if you knew me.'

'Perhaps I did, from another time, and we have met again.'

She had gone home almost drunkenly happy, so full of gaiety and affection that Willie remarked that she should go to town more often. It was obviously a stimulant. 'You are more like the lass you used to be. I have forced you to moulder here. What a selfish old duffer I am.'

After that there was no turning back. It was shameful to be so happy, but her happiness seemed to spread to Willie and Jamie. She was glad, because she wanted everyone to be glad as she was glad. She knew it to be borrowed happiness, but happiness nonetheless.

Ever since she had come into a part of Memsah'b's money, she had had an idea which she had been uneasy about putting forth. But towards the end of the summer she decided to try it out on Willie. It was an evening after she had been with Tad and he had been reminiscing about his publishing business in Poland.

'Willie, I've been thinking that with some of Memsah'b's money I'd like to back Tad and Gerald in a small publishing business. The kind Tad had in Poland.'

'Seems a risky project, lass.'

'It might be worth a go. I think it would have pleased Memsah'b. She was fond of both Gerald and Tad.'

'As you are. You and Tad seem to have a great deal in common.' He took off his spectacles and laid down the *Glasgow Herald*. 'You spend a good deal of time with him.'

'He is rather at a loose end on his afternoon off. And as long as I am in town anyway—' she shrugged.

'He seems to be good for you.' After a slight pause, 'In a way that I am not.'

'Nonsense, Willie.'

'I hope so. Well, talk to Charles about your scheme. He is the business head of the family. Have you mentioned it to Tad?'

'No. I wanted to talk to you first. He will probably go all haughty and proud and refuse anyway.'

'I imagine you could persaude him.' Willie returned to his paper.

She delayed mentioning the project to Fa. For one thing —it was probably her guilty conscience—she had the feeling that Willie was watching her. Twice he went into town with her and asked if he could join The Big Four at luncheon. While he was checking his coat and umbrella Tad raised a quizzical eyebrow at Fionna.

A few days before the shooting party was due to take place, Fionna went for a long walk in the Campsies and sat at the top of Dumgoyne overlooking the castle and Milkstone. She needed a good long think about Tad and Willie and her own life. There was no way she would divorce Willie and even if it came to that, in some unforeseen way, she had no illusions about whether a marriage to Tad would work. In fact, she couldn't think why any marriage worked. What was the adhesive that held a man and a woman together?

She had a good life, but it was all so predictable, even her afternoons with Tad were predictable. Sitting up there on Dumgoyne was not enough to sort it out, to make a decision—as if a decision were called for. She needed to get away and the best escape was to the old croft they owned up in the north near the Kyle. Since she had been a child the family had used it for semi-camping holidays, for retreats, as Memsah'b used to say, a place to restore their souls when the world was too much with them. It was to the croft that Memsah'b had taken the children and her polo ponies to sit out the last years of the Great War. There in a long-ago summer the

Maccallum youths and the young Trötzens had spent a summer, and Mairi and Erich had fallen in love. Fionna had gone there when she had returned from the war in Spain. Willie had followed her and they had been married at the village church.

Apart from anything else, she dreaded every October when the shoot took place. She had never got used to the 'rich English gentlemen' (damned Sassenachs, they were), and the sound of their guns, the talk of their 'bag', the drawn-out dinners, card-playing evenings, the bustle and invasion of it all. It was she who had to keep the maids in order and inspect everything they did to see that nothing was left undone; keep Maureen from warring with the extra cook and the pastry cook; stand by when the dishes were washed to see that the precious china and crystal were handled with care; check the shopping list before it went out every day, and check it again when the supplies were delivered.

There was one particularly obnoxious man—he was no gentleman in her opinion, and no sportsman in Willie's—who was coming this year. She had urged Willie to tell him they were fully booked, but he had booked before he had left the year before, and Willie could find no way to put him off. He patronized Willie, talked down to Jamie, ignored Liam, did not leave the maids a proper tip, and made sly passes at Fionna.

Yes, she must go to the croft.

The overcast sky had thinned, shredding the pale clouds until they disappeared. All of Scotland basked in sunlight and temperatures that broke October records. If the weather was fine here it would be glorious in the Highlands.

She walked down the hill feeling as if she had reached a turning point. Jamie was in the kitchen doing his lessons with Liam at the deal table. Willie was having a wee whisky, his wellies off and his slippers stretched to the fire, and Fionna's glass and a tray of cheese straws awaited her. Willie smiled at her over his newspaper.

'You are all aglow, lass. The walk did you a kindness.'

'I need more of them. I think I'm thickening around my middle. Don't shake your head. My skirts know. Willie, I want to go to the croft while the shooting party is here. I'm sick of the sound of guns, of dead birds and fish all over the place, of smiling politely to a lot of gentlemen I can't abide. You don't need me. Maureen has handled it long enough that it will run smoothly. It is all laid out, supplies, menus, drink, everything. Please, relay I go?'

He surprised her. 'Of course, lass. You haven't been right since Veda's death. Once or twice I thought to suggest a change. The Riviera or a visit to Mairi. The croft is the very thing. Silence. Long walks. Milk and eggs from the farm, simple suppers, no one to bother you. I know you don't like the shoots. You can take the Morris now that there's plenty of petrol. When can you pack up and go?'

'Tomorrow.' Meekly. 'Before they start arriving.'

'Efficient lass. I half wish I were going with you. We had a fine time there. You were mending from your experiences in Spain. Yes, it's a curative place.' He sipped thoughtfully at his drink. 'Once the shoot is over and if the weather is still holding I may join you. That is, if you could tolerate me.'

'I think I could do that,' she smiled. Though I'd rather not, she added silently.

She went off early enough to see the eastern sky turn light and silhouette Stirling Castle. Ground mists rose from the fields of Bannockburn, the ghosts of the warriors who had died in 1314. Stirling town was not yet astir except for a sleepy cat yawning in a doorway and a woman scrubbing the doorstep of her shop. She paused, mop in hand, and stared at the car speeding past. Fionna gave her a wave which was not returned.

It had been a long time since she had felt so free. 'And day's at the morn; all's right with the world,' she said aloud. Why had she felt unhappy and indecisive? The tingling of her glands when she was with Tad did not mean that she loved him beyond all else. Sex was really rather silly when one thought about it. Often she felt an awful fool shedding her clothes as soon as she walked in the door of his flat, and later getting up and dressing, all casual and glutted, and going home to Willie to pretend she had spent the afternoon going over the books with Charlie or going to a gallery or shopping for things which she never brought home because she hadn't bought them.

Tad would be hurt, but she really should give up on the whole thing. There! The problem was solved before she even reached the croft. Perspective. That was what was needed.

She had a pub lunch in Inverness and bought a few supplies. It was late afternoon when she turned down the narrow road along the Kyle, its water glowing with sunlight. There was the small hillside croft, a sea of purple heather almost engulfing it, the road overgrown with bronzed bracken.

She wanted to go to it at once, but she knew she must go to the farmhouse, tell Mr and Mrs MacCrae she had arrived, and buy any eggs they had to spare and a pitcher of milk for her tea.

Two sheep dogs came out to bark and wag. Mrs MacCrae came to the door. 'On my soul! Can it be Miss Maccallum? But of course it is and not changed a bit since she was a lass. But it's Lady Lammondson now, isn't it? Of course, I mind well you and Sir William marrying in our small church. A surprise that was for sure. Whatever are you doing here, Miss?

Mr MacCrae stir yourself. It's Miss—that is, Lady Lammondson—come.'

She ushered Fionna into the kitchen where Mr MacCrae sat in a rocking chair, stockinged feet on the fender, an orange cat on his lap, glasses perched precariously on his nose and a newspaper on the floor beside him.

'So it is! A grand thing to see yourself again. I'd stand but it would disturb Samuel here. He has been feeling a wee bit peely-wally of late, having fallen in the rain barrel, not knowing the top was off at the time he leapt.'

'Don't disturb him, please. I have come to stay a week or two at the croft since the weather is so fine.'

'Twon't last. It never do. But catch the butterfly on the wing, I always say. You'll find the croft in fair condition. There's a stack of peat round the side as always, the chimney's been swept, and all to do is to take the bed linen from the chest. Wife and I always say, you never know when the Maccallums'll turn up, for they are not folk who hum and hew once a notion strikes. So we keep it in order and the cheque from your father comes regularly as Hogmanay. We heard the sad news about Mrs Maccallum. Such a fine lady. Not like some. And to think of having to die in a foreign land! Now, wife, be getting the bedding for her and a few eggs for her breakfast and a gillikin of milk. There's fresh curd cheese, too, that would go nicely with some oat cakes the wife just baked. We can spare a few of those as she always overdoes it.'

When all was ready they refused money 'this time' for the supplies. Mr MacCrae apologized to Samuel for having to disturb him in order to go with Miss Maccallum to open up the croft and lay a match to the fire. Samuel accepted the apology with a sleepy yawn, curled up in the cushioned seat which had been vacated, and resumed his nap.

* * * * *

At last she was alone, the sheepskin mattress cover and downie on the bunk bed in the loft, a peat fire glowing on the low hearth, the earthenware dishes washed and put away except for her mug, from which she sipped sweet, milky tea as she sat on the steps in the twilight. The hills were dark against the western sky where a mauve glow lingered after the sunset. The eastern sky was deep blue with a few pinpricks which would become stars as darkness fell.

She promised herself she would be up at dawn, pack a lunch and be off for a long walk in the hills. Poor Willie, while she was walking in the heather he would be meeting the train, greeting the men as they arrived, directing those who had motored to the parking area, serving welcoming drinks, discussing birds, weather, and other banalities. She would telephone him Sunday week to tell him to hie himself to the Highlands for the cure.

Her ebullient mood lasted throughout the week. Every morning she awakened happy and she went to sleep in an almost divine contentment. On Friday afternoon she returned from another day-long walk. The weather was changing. Mist-grey clouds seeped down the craggy hills, the scent of damp heather was in the air, and the Kyle water dark as lead.

A piece of paper fluttered against the drawing pin holding it in place on her door. She took it into the house with her and lighted a candle. Mr MacCrae had been there and built up the fire. The room was cosy after the chill of evening.

Miss Maccallum, you are kindly asked to call your father at the castle at whatever hour you return. We shall not go to our beds until you come, so do not be fearful of disturbing us.

She read the note twice, feeling troubled. Mr MacCrae must have got it wrong and meant her husband, not her father. It was probably only Willie announcing his arrival and telling her which train to meet. She would have to tell him the weather had gone off.

She had not removed her coat, so she set out at once. She took her electric torch, intending to walk. Then set it down and fetched the car keys. Something about the note made her uneasy.

The dogs came out to bark a greeting. A lighted storm lantern was on the doorstep. The door was opened by Mr MacCrae before she cut the engine.

'I am glad you're back as soon as you are. I hoped the weather would drive you in. It was noon time Mr Maccallum telephoned. I would have come to fetch you, but I'd no way of knowing which way you went and there seemed no point in wandering the hills like a lost lamb searching out its mother.'

'I am sure it doesn't matter that much that you should have come looking for me. Did my father say what he wants?'

'Only that you were to call the castle as soon as you set foot under the lintel. He sounded unlike himself and sair distressed to hear you were away over the heather.'

Mrs MacCrae was busy at the stove. 'You'll stay for tea with us, Miss, after your call? That is to say, Lady Lammondson. A fresh-caught grilled fish and some tatties, a fruit tart and Orkney cheese.'

'Yes. All right. Thank you. The castle? I am to call the castle. Not Milkstone?'

'Aye, the castle. Tell her not to call Milkstone, he said twice over.'

It seemed forever before she got through. But finally Fa's voice answered. 'Fionna, are you there?'

'Of course I am here, Fa. What is it? Is it Jamie?'

'There has been a shooting accident. It's Willie. He is in Victoria hospital. You'll be needed, of course.'

'How serious is it, Fa?'

It took him a long time to answer. 'Serious enough. I am trying to manage things. The—uh—gentleman concerned has been questioned by our locals and has sent to London for his solicitor.'

'I'll wager my soul I know which gentleman it was. A rotten shot. He should not have been allowed to own a gun, let alone be a guest of the shoot.'

'So Jock MacPherson has told me privately. Anyway, I am here. The gentlemen have been asked to remain though no one thinks it was foul play. Maureen is wailing like the proverbial banshee, and I have had to bring Cook over from Milkstone. Margery Gunn is here with me, keeping the girls on their toes. I want you to get a good night's rest and don't break all speed records as your mother would have done. Go directly to the hospital and call me from there.'

'He isn't going to die, is he?'

'Let us hope not.'

'You sound doubtful.' She heard the tremble in her voice. 'I'd rather start tonight but I have the packing up to do and I might fall asleep on the road.'

'And I would have you, too, on my hands. I think you should plan to stay in town with Charlie as long as Willie is in hospital. You will want town clothes and Jamie will want to see you and you'll have to speak to the gentlemen, if they are still here. You might even manage to silence Maureen.'

'All right, Fa. Tell Jamie I love him. And Willie, too, of course. Thank you for calling and managing.'

'Good night, Fionna. Drive carefully.'

'I shall. Good night, Fa.'

The MacCraes tried to pretend they hadn't been listening.

'Bad news, was it, Miss Maccallum?'

'Sir William has been injured in a shooting accident. I have to leave tomorrow.' She sat down in Mr MacCrae's rocking chair. Samuel leapt into her lap and began to knead and purr. She stroked him absentmindedly. 'It's terrible because I have been so happy all week. I could have stayed forever.' It was her punishment for Tad.

Day after rainy day she sat beside his bed while Willie wandered in other places, other times. 'Tell Aloni to dig the chiggers out of my feet . . . there's a cobra in the latrine, fetch my gun . . . where are the bearers? It's time to pack up . . .'

He even spoke of his first wife. 'Gone? Gone, you say? She can't be gone. She left the bairn. No woman would do that. And took the family baubles.'

One day he sat bolt upright in bed. 'Lass, is that you? Why are you back? I was coming to join you at the croft. The weather held, just as we'd hoped. Not a cloud. Regular heat wave. I haven't seen the sun so bright and the sky so clear since I was in Africa. It's almost blinding.' He put his hand across his eyes and slumped back in sudden death.

There was much to do in the months that followed. The gentleman responsible for the accident was cleared of any blame or malice aforethought. He made a handsome monetary gift to be used for Jamie's schooling. Fionna considered returning it, but decided not to be churlish.

Willie's clothes were bundled up and sent to Oxfam, his papers sorted and those worth saving, filed. But his affairs were in violent disorder. The bank account was so out of balance that it took a month's struggle with the bank and the books to find whether there was any money and what taxes and duties had been paid or left unpaid.

Fa finally moved to the castle temporarily, to help. Together they ferreted through dusty ledgers, sheaves of ancient bills stuffed into desk corners, jacket pockets, bureau drawers, and even between the pages of a book Willie happened to have been reading when the post arrived.

A decision had to be made about the shooting parties. Fionna wanted to cancel them, but Pa said she would need the money. 'Jock MacPherson and I can handle them.'

'I'd rather register with the tour bus companies and serve teas and sell gimcrack souvenirs and postcards. No one would be killed that way.'

'Would you really prefer that?' Fa's expression was horrified.

'I would hate it. I don't even want to go on living in the castle. It isn't the same without Willie. And Jamie.'

For Jamie was eleven now and had been going to his 'posh' school in Glasgow for some time. He stayed with Charlie and was reluctantly very much supervised by young Charles's nanny, Mrs Partland. Because of Liam's exceptionally high marks, and on recommendation of the schoolmaster, Fionna had paid his tuition as well. He, too, lived at Charlie's, much to the suppressed objections of Mrs Partland. Liam, she told Cook, was a born rebel, and for all his brilliance—and he was that—would come to no good.

The shoots continued with Fa as host. During that week Fionna moved into town. The anniversary of Willie's death passed. Fionna sent off a letter and waited impatiently for a reply. It arrived a few days after Christmas. She hugged its contents to her and said nothing to anyone until the New Year when she told Tad.

Fa held a huge party at Milkstone to celebrate Hogmanay. The ballroom was decorated as it had been in the old days. The fireplace blazed, and the punch bowl was never empty.

The long table set up at one end of the room held game pies, baked ham, cold roast chicken, Scotch eggs, salads, black bun, shortbread, trifle, Venus cake, atholl brose, port and whisky.

Fa would have hired musicians but Fionna insisted that the phonograph was preferable. Dancing could be more varied that way for young and old.

Besides the family, the Gunns—who were almost family after all these years—were there along with their son and daughter-in-law and granddaughters. Jan Chmura brought a young artist who was apprenticing at Tad's publishing company. Neighbours, friends, members of the shipyard board, came, some lingering until midnight, others staying a short time, then going on to their round of calls.

Charlie was one who left before the New Year was rung in. He had promised, he said, to look in on someone in town.

Jamie tugged at Fionna's sleeve. 'You know who someone is, don't you? Miss Maclean. He's sweet on her.'

'Is he? I thought I had caught him looking at her as if she were the sixpence in the Christmas pudding.'

'He takes her out. Nights he says he has to work late.'

'However do you know that?'

'Maureen's seen them. They didn't see her, so don't tell. Do I get to stay up 'til midnight?'

'Of course.' So Charlie's broken heart was mending.

At midnight the music in the ballroom stopped. The windows were thrown open so they could hear the church bells in the village ring out through the chill, misty air. Solemnly a toast was drunk to the New Year and new hopes. And a new life, Fionna thought. Then the night was shut out and the party continued.

By three o'clock the fire was guttering, the candles pools of wax that sent up long flames. The chairs that had been drawn up to the hearth were empty save those two occupied by Fionna and Tad, sitting in silence, watching the glowing coals.

Twice Tad started to speak, then caught back the words. Fionna looked at him questioningly, her eyes filled with love and tenderness.

'I find I have not the courage to speak because I fear your answer. Fionna, marry me.'

'Why? What is wrong with our relationship as it is?'

'It is incomplete. It is not enough to have you for an afternoon or two, when it is convenient. I want—all of you.'

'You would never have that nor would I ever have all of you. There is always the past and the secret part of ourselves. Tad, I'm not ready. It isn't Willie. It is simply that as much as I love you and cherish you, I am not yet ready to make a commitment of marriage. It, too, would be incomplete.'

'But why? What are you going to do? You can't stay on at the castle alone, living half a life.'

'I am going to Africa. To Doctor Schweitzer. To make something of my life.'

5

Meg could not help wondering whether she was being a fool to break up her marriage. To stay in Glasgow in an attempt to reconciliate would not work. All that did was make her more resentful. The only solution was time. Time to know herself and to learn whether she loved Charlie enough to accept his pattern of life.

She was glad to be back in the MacKays' gatehouse, to have her few possessions around her. Yet she knew her being in the village distressed her father, happy as he was to have her company, and embarrassed her mother, who was buffeted by village gossip.

Meg attempted an awkward apology to her father. He silenced her with 'Nonsense! You must follow your heart. A loveless marriage is like whoredom. I don't approve of divorce because marriage is a sacrament and divorce is not, but neither do I wish you to be unhappy and make Charlie unhappy. Unhappiness is a contagious disease which would infect your small lad and Una.'

'My being here distresses mother. Perhaps I should move to another village.'

He blew a smoke ring. 'A little martyrdom will not injure your mother. I shall remind her that the blood of martyrs is the seed of the Church. I think she regrets the loss of the Maccallum status. After her visit to Glasgow she would have found the Celestial City shabby by comparison.'

'Do *you* mind if I stay on a bit longer?'

'It delights me to have you back. And your mother delights in your wee girl which you so brilliantly named after her.'

'I told Charlie I would take no longer than six months to make a decision.'

'Six months, six times six months. Nothing should be done hastily except the catching of fleas. Soon there will be some new village scandal to sharpen the tongues of the Mrs Grundys.'

Meg disliked living off the money which Charlie sent her, which was far more than enough for the simple life she led. When the librarian asked her to help out two afternoons a week, she accepted. Her mother enjoyed having Una to herself to spoil. Later, the school asked Meg to reorganize and update its small library and take over the hour after school. With those small stipends, Meg was now able to bank more than half of Charlie's cheque, telling herself that eventually she would return it all to him.

Six months passed and, to her surprise, Charlie did not remind her of the passing. Maccallums' was busy now producing ships for the Korean war. She suspected that if she did go back he would have little time to reforge their relationship.

One blustery spring day when her head felt full of the fug of winter, Meg left Una with her mother and went walking on the shore. She had done so several times since her return, but had yet to meet Ian Henderson again. She hesitated to ask her father if Ian had returned for fear he would wonder at her interest.

The wind blew sand and spume, and tried to push Meg backwards for every step she took forward. She wrapped her scarf around the lower half of her face and walked head down, enjoying the struggle with nature.

She did not see the figure approaching and was startled

when someone called out, 'Hullo! It's Mrs Maccallum, isn't it? So you came back!'

'So did you. Did you finish your business in London?'

'Business? Is that what you heard?' His mouth curled cat-like in a smile.

'Something to do with your family's estate.'

'The settlement of the estate will drag on for another half year, at the least. Father left his affairs in a tangled knot through which no sword of Damocles could cut. Actually I was breaking off an engagement. I discovered that we wanted two different things out of life. Have you broken off your marriage?'

'I am not sure.'

'Your man must have the patience of Job.'

'I think he's too busy building ships to notice that I have been away longer than I said I would be. The longer I am here the less I want to go back. I am disgracefully contented.'

'If contentment is disgraceful, I am disgraceful, too. I am relieved and happy now that I am shot of Celia. People do tend to get themselves into tight corners, don't they? It isn't always easy to get out. Look here, you are being blown to bits. There's a sheltered spot back a way where I left a thermos of hot tea. Enough for two. Will you share it?'

'It sounds wonderful. I didn't realize how cold and blustery it was when I started out.'

He took her arm and they trudged back the way he had come.

'Do you still have Cyprian?'

'Of course. He put his nose out and decided to forgo his walk. The wind disturbed his whiskers. I have his sister as well. Jasmine. Celia discovered she is allergic to cats as well as to me. Another good reason to break an engagement.'

'I have been thinking of getting a cat.'

'No home should be without one. Which reminds me, you are all sylphlike. You had the child?'

'In June. A girl. Una.'

'Are you still at the gatehouse? Before I left for London I overheard that you were living there. I thought of calling, but I wasn't sure it was quite the thing.'

'I am *sure* it wouldn't be quite the thing.'

'Is the little gabled turret your bedroom?' She nodded, surprised. 'You read late. I drove home that way the other night. The long way around, but—' He shrugged. 'Actually, I was wondering about you and took the road on a whim. I haven't been back long enough to catch much local news as discussed over the cabbages.'

'I think I am yesterday's news now.'

'Here we are. If we hunker down we'll be safely out of the wind.'

The sheltered spot was a break in a higher portion of the beach, where a chunk of land had collapsed in a storm. It formed a narrow, hollowed cove, wide enough to shelter two people, and seemed to have done many times as there were blackened remnants of old campfires in front of it.

Meg and Ian sat cross-legged in the sand, elbows touching, backs leaning against the earthen bank. He filled the cap and the fitted cup and handed one to her. 'I hope you don't take milk. The truth is, there is a lacing of Glenfiddich in it. Do you mind?'

'It's just what we need.'

'Good. *Slàinte,* then.'

They touched cups and drank. For a while they sat in comfortable silence watching the North Sea assault the shore. Meg thought, this is why I returned. To sit by the sea with Ian. She was well aware that she scarcely knew him, but she felt comfortable with him in a way she had not felt comfortable with Charlie for a long time. He interrupted her thoughts.

'Don't think me daft if I tell you something. Actually, I don't know that I should tell you, but I want to. You are a part of the reason I broke my engagement with Celia. One brief encounter and I couldn't forget you. I couldn't let go of the thought of you. And I didn't know what the devil to do about it. I couldn't swoop into Glasgow and abduct you from that damned husband of yours. So I thought the first step was breaking off with Celia.'

'I didn't forget you either. I have walked on the beach several times hoping I'd see you again. The trouble is—' she broke off to hold out her cup as he refilled it. 'The trouble is, we don't know each other. Who are you? Are you, as my mother would say, an idle young man who does nothing? What do you think about? What are your politics? What do you read? What are your future plans? I want to move cautiously this time. Of course we can be friends,' she added hurriedly. 'I don't mean I expect a—a relationship, which is a silly expression. It's that I seem to be full of questions. I want to know everything about you. I don't know why,' she added shyly.

'Don't you? I do. I was hoping we could work up to what you call a relationship. See if anything comes of it.'

'I *am* still married, but more and more I doubt that I shall go back. I'm happy here.'

'Then you were meant to be here, just as I am. For your mother's information, I am not an entirely idle young man. I mess about in my garden, grow my own vegetables, cut my own peat on my bog land because I like the scent of a peat fire. I do have proper heating as well. And I grind out books. Heroic adventure. Escape. A poor man's imitation of John Buchan and Geoffrey Household. Most of mine are straight out of Andrew Lang's *History of Scotland*.'

'Do we have the books in the library?'

'You do, but not under the name of Ian Henderson.'

'What name?'

'When you come to live with me and be my love, I shall tell you.'

She smiled. 'Then I may never know because that may never come to pass.' She glanced at her watch and gasped. 'My mother will think I have been swept out to sea. I must get back. I hope we shall meet again.' She held out her hand and he helped her scramble to her feet.

He had a way of tossing back his head when he laughed, the skin crinkling around his eyes, the laugh coming from deep within. 'Oh Meg, how formal you are. The very thought of your mother turns you into a proper lady. Of course we shall meet again. And again and again. I am going to help you cast off the past, toss out all doubts as to where you belong.'

'I have doubts because I feel guilty at having them.'

'Your case isn't a hopeless one.' He kissed her lightly and, as he had on the long-ago day, waited, watching her go. As she had done before, she turned once. This time she waved.

She walked home deep in thought, aware that her feelings for Ian Henderson were getting out of hand. She scarcely knew him, but it was as if she had known him always. Already she felt about him as she should feel about Charlie, and did not. He had a warmth and humour and understanding which Charlie lacked. She wanted to be with him and she wanted him to want to be with her.

On Sunday after Evensong, Meg had tea with her parents. While her mother washed up, her father walked her home, pushing the carriage in which Una slept, having exhausted herself with entertaining her grandmother. Her father said casually, 'Mr Henderson was at eight o'clock service this morning.' They paused at the crossing to wait for a lorry to rumble past. 'Disgraceful the way they thunder through the village. He spoke to me after. Asked if it would be improper to call on you.'

'Oh.'

'I told him to consult his own conscience, but to be aware of yours.'

'I met him when I was walking on the beach.'

'The day you were so late that your mother thought you had been set upon by ruffians? After he spoke to me, I suspected as much.'

'I like him. Perhaps it is because I long for male company.'

The evening air was chilly, but carried the scent of springtime and budding greenery. Blue smoke rose from the chimneys, the western sky was aglow, and silence surrounded the earth. Meg took the key out of her pocket and unlocked the heavy oak door. Mr Sinclair wheeled the carriage into the hall.

'Perhaps such a friendship would help to settle your mind about your husband. That must be done, Meg. For Charlie's sake as well as your own. Good night, my dear. Say your prayers before you sleep. Perhaps in dreams God will speak to you.'

'Does He speak to you in dreams, Father?'

'He speaks to everyone, but not all have ears.'

Meg helped at the library on Monday afternoons. She hurried about, tidying the house, so her mother who would sit with Una could not find fault with her housekeeping. Una was bathed and dressed, sitting in her pen, solemnly examining her toys. Both she and Meg were startled when the weighty lion's head knocker announced a visitor. It was too early—Meg hoped—for her mother. She opened the door to see Ian Henderson standing there, a cat carrier in his hand.

'You said you were thinking of getting a cat,' he said without so much as a how-do-you-do. 'I hope you will accept this one. It is Jasmine. She is not as happy as she should be in a bachelor household.'

'Oh, Ian, hello! Do come in. Yes, I'd love to have her if she will accept us.'

'Good. Jasmine and I were uncertain about venturing into forbidden territory. Hang on, I'll fetch her things. She mustn't be allowed out for a few days.' He set the basket down in the hall and went back to his car, returning with a pan, a bag of litter, and four cans of cat food. Jasmine mewed plaintively.

'It's all right, Jasmine.' Meg carried the basket into the sitting room and put it down close to the fire. Ian looked at the room approvingly. 'Nice. It suits you.' He opened the basket and the cat, black and golden brindled fur, emerged carefully, sniffed Meg's ankles then rubbed against them, keeping a watchful eye on Una who was gurgling and pointing, stretching pink hands through the bars: a prisoner begging favours. Jasmine sniffed the fingers from a cautious distance, then walked into the cage. Cat and child examined one another, equals, but careful equals.

'Well. It seems to be all right, doesn't it? Look at that! I hope she won't put out claws.'

'I hope Una won't put out hers. Oh, she is lovely. Thank you, Ian.'

'My pleasure. And Cyprian's. Will your charming young lady allow me to kiss you?'

'I think she is preoccupied at the moment.' Feeling a shameless woman, she went into his arms, accepting him.

They jumped apart as the knocker sounded again. 'It's my

mother. She keeps Una while I work at the library. What will she say?'

'Or not say? Let her in. I'll be the perfect gentleman. I have been known to tame dragons in my time.'

Mrs Sinclair looked from Meg to Ian, uncertain whether to disapprove.

'Mother, this is Mr Henderson. He brought us a cat.'

Jasmine left Una and came to greet Mrs Sinclair. She lifted a paw, miaowed, and rubbed round her ankles.

'Well! How—how—oh, she *is* a beauty. She reminds me of a cat we had when your father and I first married. Sheba, because she was so beautiful and beguiling. I still think of her. You must rub butter on her paws, Meg, so she will know this is home. How very kind of you, Mr Henderson. I heard you had returned.'

'Here to stay, Mrs Sinclair, except for brief, necessary trips to London.'

'It is peaceful here, isn't it, and the air is so pure. Meg, have you offered tea?'

'There hasn't been time and anyway I must fly or be late. Mr Henderson, you will have to excuse me. I work at the library on Monday afternoons.'

'May I drive you? It is a longish walk.'

'Well—I don't know.'

'Of course you must be driven, Meg. The weather has turned blustery again. Spring never seems to be able to make up its mind, does it? Off you go, then. I'll take care of buttering paws. And a bite of food, I think, to reassure her.' She saw them into the motor car and gave them a nod.

'I told you I could tame dragons.' Ian grinned and took Meg's hand.

'You aren't out of the woods yet. Nor am I. She took it very well, but we have a long way to go.'

★ ★ ★ ★ ★

Charlie had let the six months pass, waiting for word from Meg. It was her move and he wasn't going to prod her. He still worked long hours which, because he enjoyed what he was doing, did not tire him. Often Miss Maclean was kept overtime and it had become a habit to drive her home if the hour was late. He found her pleasant and undemanding, and she appreciated the overtime pay.

All in all, he was not unhappy, which puzzled him when he had time to think about it. He enjoyed going home to Blythswood where a simple late supper awaited him, and afterwards he could sit by the fire with a brandy, and finally go to bed to sleep. No recriminations, no resentments.

Fa demanded more of his time after Memsah'b's death and Charlie was glad to give it. They were closer than they had ever been. Fa talked to him of Charlie's own mother, Alison; told him how they had met and of their brief, wartime love affair.

There were bachelor parties with Fa, Tad and Jan, and sometimes the lads, Jamie and Liam were allowed to join them at dinner before being banished to do their homework.

Charlie liked having the boys there. They were lively company. He laughed at their boyish jokes, helped them with their studies, entered into their games. Young Charles, too, blossomed under their attentions. His vocabulary grew and he tried in his childish way to compete with them. When a ship was launched and there was a trial run, Charlie took the three of them with him. Once, when they had an extended holiday, he took a holiday himself. They sailed the yacht down the Firth and all the way into the Mull of Kintyre. He pointed out the land in the distance, lying low like mist, and told Liam it was Ireland.

'I could almost swim it,' Liam exclaimed.

'Not quite. But you are little more than a hundred and twenty miles from Belfast.'

'That's not as far as we've come today, is it, sir?' Liam's eyes took on a faraway look. 'Just to think, there's the land where I was born! Where m'dad's buried. Ireland.' It was like someone's saying, 'Amen.'

As time went on, Charlie missed Meg less and less and understood her less and less. Fionna shook her head over him. 'Charlie, few people ever understand what someone else wants out of life. Some marriages are made in heaven, some in hell, and most of both end up in limbo. Limbo is where I am right now, but Willie, dear man. is unaware of it.'

That, of course, was before Willie's death. Charlie had understood the limbo part because he knew Fionna was all 'mixed up' with Tad. But the marriage part he did not understand. Marriage was marriage, love was love, and a wife was a wife and mother.

'And never the twain shall meet,' Fionna mocked him.

It had shocked him when, after a long day, he had driven Miss Maclean home. Before she got out of the car she said, 'Mr Maccallum, I have to speak to you.'

He had drawn the motor up in front of the house. It was close to eleven o'clock and the damp streets were deserted, the houses dark. In the dimly reflected street lamps her face was pale as moonlight, her eyes black.

'I don't know how to say this, Mr Maccallum, because I like you and you have been ever so kind. But the thing is, I am thinking of leaving. I don't know if you understand how it is to be shut in a job and know there will never be anything else. I don't want always to be a secretary and grow old and pinched-looking and faded. Never to have anything else other than my work and, when Mum dies, a lonely house.' Before he could protest, she hurried on. 'For a woman there should be something else. For all too many, there *is* nothing else. But if there is something, I have to find it. I don't want to be like them.'

'Amelia, you would never be pinched and faded.'

'Wouldn't I just! It happens before you know it. You look in the mirror one day and suddenly you're old, drab, lonely, and nowhere to turn. Even now I am not sure where to turn. Maybe as secretary in some far-away embassy. It would be different, romantic. Maybe I'll emigrate. I don't know. I am looking into possibilities. But I thought it fair to warn you, so you, too, can be looking for a replacement.'

He sat in stunned silence looking into the wide, anxious dark jewels of her eyes, her brow wrinkled with seriousness, her lips half-parted, the scent of Fabergé faint, haunting and disturbing. Involuntarily he half-sobbed, put his head on the steering wheel. His shoulders shook as if he had a chill. 'Oh, Amelia, don't you leave me, too.'

There was a painful silence, then, 'I don't *want* to leave you, Mr Maccallum. It isn't you. It's—everything. I'm twenty-nine, next year I'll be thirty. There isn't one man I care about. At my age, there isn't much choice, thanks to the war. And I know I shouldn't expect anything else. There *are* class divisions, but I want to cross over into something better if I can. Not some Johnny or Ned who'll spend his Friday night pay in a pub playing darts or watching football games, who has never read anything or done anything or cared about anything except surviving.'

He turned to her fiercely. 'Stop that. You are far too good for what you are describing.'

'Am I? My mum says it comes from my allowing you to take me to dinner in all those posh places. She said I've got above myself and I should be grateful for my good job and my pay rises. And I am. But . . .' She left it there.

He sat up and faced her, moved by her beauty, wanting her as once he had wanted Meg, and knowing this was a gentler less hostile woman. 'Amelia, I understand. I have been demanding and unaware. I will not allow you to leave. Wait! Let me tell you.' He took her hand which clutched her handbag, loosening it so it lay quiet in his own. 'Wait for me.'

'Wait? For what? Until I'm thirty, thirty-five, forty? *Wait*, Mr Maccallum? Haven't you heard me?'

'I heard.' He put his arms around her, pulling her to him so the steering wheel hurt her ribs and she gave a little cry. He kissed her as once he had kissed Meg, but with a hunger long unsatisfied. With a desire he had not known existed. With a love only now manifesting itself.

At first she resisted, then subsided, returning his kisses with her own. He felt tears on her face. Meg had not cried with submission, but accepted him as if he were a sacrifice.

At last she broke away sobbing. 'It won't do. It won't do at all. I won't be—a whore for you. I won't be the gossip of the yard, having secret rendezvous, everyone whispering about me. Let me go, please, Mr Maccallum. I'll come in tomorrow, but I must submit my resignation.'

'Stop talking like a secretary, Amelia. Amelia, once I am free will you marry me? Is that something better? Better than a romantic foreign embassy? Will you?'

'You're off your head, Mr Maccallum. I'm working class. You're not. It wouldn't do. Best you sleep on it. I'll understand if you regret saying what you did. Anyway you must start looking for a new secretary.'

She opened the car door and edged out. She stood, her face shadowed now, and said, 'Don't see me in. Thank you for the proposal. I suppose it doesn't matter if I tell you that I've been in love with you for ever so long. That is why I'm leaving.'

6

The year following Willie's death had been hellish. At long last when everything was in order, Fionna felt as hollow as a jack-o'-lantern, with vacant eyes and lifeless smile, and no candle alight within. It was sad to learn too late how much another being was a part of one's own self, how necessary to one's life.

The castle too was hollow. No dripping Burberry hung from the antlered coat rack in the hall, no muddy wellies stood firm beneath it. The smoke from his pipe no longer wafted through the rooms, and the last of his hopeless avalanche of papers had been sorted and filed. The armoire in his dressing room now served as a storage place for the overflow from Fionna's own armoires, and the most recently adopted stray cat had taken over Willie's favourite chair.

Although a year had passed she still caught herself thinking, 'I must ask Willie . . .' 'I must tell Willie . . .' Restless and disoriented, she could not settle down. She longed to vacate the castle yet was loath to leave it because Willie would have wanted her there. She considered taking a flat in Glasgow as an escape hatch when she needed it. But she knew the city would depress her, especially with Tad there, waiting for her to agree to marry him.

Fa asked her to stay with him at Milkstone for a while. 'We are both alone now. We would be company for one another.'

It was difficult to refuse. She understood his own emptiness since Memsah'b's death. Gerald Gunn said Fa was drinking far too much. Fionna decided that comforting Fa and nursemaiding him would do nothing for her own morale. But she wondered if she was neglecting a filial obligation. So it was with guilt and hesitancy that she told him, 'I want to go away, far away, Fa. I have a plan . . . I—I don't know how to tell you because you'll think me daft.'

'Try me.' He was in the mellowing, three-drink stage, pleased to have her there to distract him, to help him keep the fourth drink at bay.

'Do you remember when I was a wee girl and wanted to go to Africa and have a medical station? I tried to learn Swahili and I was always operating on my dolls.'

'Could I forget it? What a delightfully different child you were. I remember, too, that Veda had to dismiss the nanny you had because the two of you couldn't get on.'

'It wasn't just myself. She threw out Carlos's collection of rocks. She was a terror. "Why ever do you want to go off to Africa, Miss Fionna?" ' she mimicked. ' "There's nowt there but black heathens and terrible beasts. Why don't you play nicely with your dollies as your sister does? Why must you always have them sick in their cradles or be a-cutting them open to remove their so-called organs. I am bone-weary of threading needles for you to sew them up again." ' She was pleased to see Fa laughing. 'I wish that old jampot had known that I ended by being a nurse and doing very well at it.'

'We all wish our enemies knew of our successes, but none of our failures. Is it Africa you are thinking about as a faraway place?'

They were sitting before the fire in the long south drawing room at Milkstone. The room seemed too large without Memsah'b. One of her cashmere shawls, as scarlet as field poppies, was draped carelessly across the back of a sofa. Once Fionna had tried to remove it.

'Don't,' Fa had said. 'I like to think she will come back

and wrap herself in it the way she always did.'

She isn't coming back, Fa, Fionna thought, but she had not said it aloud.

Fionna looked at the shawl now, wishing her mother were there. 'Yes. Africa, Fa.' Her voice sounded as if the young, callow Fionna had resurfaced. 'While I was at the hospital waiting for Willie to—well—to die, I met a nurse I had known in Spain. We were in the same ambulance crew. She and one of the Internationals were married there. The marriage broke up after the war. Marriages like that often do, don't they? She joined a field ambulance group in '39, did the Dunkirk thing, and later went in with the invasion and stayed on with the Red Cross afterwards. Then she went to the hospital in Lambaréné. You know, Doctor Schweitzer's place.' Fa nodded. 'She said they can often use extra help when someone wants to go on home leave or falls sick themselves. I got thinking about it, sentimentally, I suppose. Fulfilling a childhood dream and all that slush. I sent an application. I have been accepted for six months. The answer came just before the New Year. I told Tad after your party, when everyone had gone to bed. He isn't too happy about it. He doesn't approve at all.' She gave him a half-ashamed look. 'Am I being an awful idiot?'

'My dear girl, I think you are being enormously courageous. How many of us have the wisdom and enthusiasm to make a new beginning when they come to the ending of one life? To fulfil a childhood dream of swimming the Hellespont, climbing Everest, emigrating to Samoa, or re-establishing a career? I shall be disappointed if you don't go.'

'Are you certain? Jamie is resentful. Mostly, I think, because he cannot go with me.'

'Jamie's world is all before him. He is safe and busy, and Charlie enjoys having the lads with him.'

'A good job he does or I should never dare to do this.'

'And Tad's not enthusiastic?'

Fionna made a *moue*. 'He doesn't understand. I'm not sure I understand myself. In one way I feel as if I am flinging everything aside and leaving wreckage behind. Actually, I suppose I'm trying to run away.'

'Not in the way that Meg did. She was the one who left wreckage. She still had a life and responsibilities.'

'Fa, you must forgive her. Charlie shares a good bit of blame in the failure of that marriage. Has he told you they are divorcing or has he left it for me to break the news? He is going to do the proper thing and go off with some hired hint who will pose in her skivvies when a detective discovers them. Sordid, isn't it? I gather Meg's mother is very upset. Meg will never be able to take communion again or be remarried in the church. And apparently there is a man in the offing. Meg seems to be sailing tranquilly through it all.'

'She seemed a phlegmatic young lady to me.'

'I suspect there is a lot of flame and passion under that phlegm to which Charlie never succeeded in setting a match. I doubt he even tried.' She got up and paced the room, paused before the fire and stood with her back to it, pulling up her skirts just as her mother used to do. 'Well, it's done now. Willie's gone and I've turned down Tad, and who knows what lies before us? Where is that new day that dear old Father Timothy promised us years ago?'

'Still at hand.'

'As the Yanks would say, balls. Will I never get Spain out of my soul, Fa? Was that *my* day, just as it was Carlos's? Will I never have another?'

'Perhaps in Africa where you wanted to be as a child.'

'Memsah'b would have had an explanation for it.'

'Veda had her Christian, Hindu, Muslim philosophies so

intertwined she could explain everything.'

'Including infidelity. Did she never feel guilty? I felt so guilty about Tad that I thought Willie's death was my punishment.'

'Your mother and I always wondered why you chose to be married to Willie. He was a dear man but a dull one.'

'Steadfast. After Spain I needed that. Just as I needed Tad.'

'I hope you won't lose Tad.'

'Do you *want* me to marry him, Fa?'

'I think you should be married again. Yes.'

'I am not sure that I should be. That is another reason for going to Africa. To distance myself, so I can think. I am always running away, am I not? One would assume that at my age I would have learnt there is no escape.'

'Give it a try. Perhaps, as the young people say these days, you will find out who you are. Or is it, find yourself? I never had that trouble.'

'If that is my trouble, I hope I can solve the problem. "And Southward aye, she fled." '

By the time of her departure, Fionna knew she was making a mistake. Childhood dreams should be put aside with toys and other childish things.

Her men, as she thought of them, accompanied her to the airport. Pa kept giving her encouraging nods and Jamie stood close to Tad, trying to pretend that he wasn't gulping back infantile tears. Until now she had not noticed how tall he had grown during the past year. He was as tall as Tad.

Tad's face was so sad that she wanted to put her arms around him and comfort him, make rash promises that she was not sure she could keep. He had wanted to accompany her as far as Paris. She had refused to allow it. Now she wished he were coming so she wouldn't sit in Orly alone, beset by doubts as she waited for the Air France plane to Brazzaville.

Charlie kept asking if she was sure she had all her papers in order and warning her not to drink anything that hadn't been boiled.

It was a relief when the flight was called. She hugged Jamie and told him to be good, to which he replied that mothers did not say that to one his age.

'All right. Be braw, then, and be canny.'

'Aye, that I will.'

She told Fa to keep his pecker up and whispered to Charlie, 'Are you going to marry your girl?'

He whispered back, 'She won't have me.'

She clung to Tad the longest, but to him she had nothing to say.

She looked out the window as the last of Scotland vanished beneath the plane. What the devil did she think she was doing? Was this an early onset of middle-age crisis?

At Orly she wandered about, telling herself that she was as lonely as a cloud, but where were the daffodils? She wished Tad were with her being his extravagant Polish self.

Airborne again, a tingling of excitement hesitantly took over. Europe skimmed away. The Mediterranean was a shimmer of turquoise. By the time luncheon was cleared away, toy boats were bobbing at anchor in the harbour of Tripoli. Olive groves like old silver, black-green citrus orchards, tobacco plantations, and waves of grain edged into the lion-coloured land. The plane dropped altitude over mosques and arches and ancient, sun-stained buildings, and seemed in danger of clipping the flagstaffs on the roofs of the tall, modern buildings before it thumped on to the dusty, wind-blown concourse.

The captain asked the passengers to disembark during the refuelling, but warned that the on-going passengers would not be allowed to leave the building. The airport was a cry of confusion, a conglomerate of races and nationalities. There were fezzes and turbans, pugharees and kepis, shawls and purdah, caftans and cassocks, Yanks in wrinkled fatigues or government-issue suntans, French officers in their chic uniforms, and two British privates in Black Watch kilts and glengarries.

Her new seatmate was a black man wearing a cleric's collar and a carved onyx cross on the gold chain spanning his vest. He was gigantic in both height and girth, and his black suit was shiny with age. His grizzled white hair was cut close to his scalp and he smelled faintly of garlic. He bowed to her before seating himself. When the plane took off he drew a prayer book from his pocket, closed his eyes, and moved his lips in silent prayer.

Tawny earth danced and wavered in the heat. Once a long curtain of sand billowed in the wind and the seat belt sign came on as the plane rode the wind. Sometimes there would be a green oasis with stone-white houses set amongst it. A lone truck crawled in the vast emptiness. The endless drone of the engine lulled Fionna to sleep. Glasgow was a long time ago.

She awakened dry-mouthed and stiff. The sun had shifted; foreshortened shadows lay across the wooded savannah to which they were descending. She rubbed her gritty eyes at the sight of a long line of pyramids beyond the long, high wall encircling the town.

'Pyramids?' she said aloud.

'Ah, yes. But not of ancient time and not of stone. They are of sacked peanuts, the groundnut, you know? They are stacked so to wait for transport. We are coming into

229

Kano. Is it your destination?'

'No.'

'I did not think so. You are British?'

'Scottish.'

He smiled and there was laughter in his eyes. 'Ah, yes. There is a difference. I know of the SNP, the Scottish National Party. We have such politics in Africa. Everywhere in Africa there is nationalism. It was a happiness to escape for a while. I have been a pilgrim visiting shrines. My first being Canterbury. You have been to Canterbury?'

'No, but I know of it. There is a play, *Murder in the Cathedral*.'

'I know of the play also. I am named for Thomas à Becket. Father Thomas, you may call me. I would tell you my other name, but even if I wrote it for you, you would trip over the pronunciation. The British do not speak Zulu correctly. My father was a Church of England priest before me, and as a student in Oxford he once did visit Canterbury. The miracle touched him to become a priest. So I was named for Thomas whose tomb he touched.' He glanced out the window. 'Ah, we are landing and must again disembark. It is good for the legs to stretch.'

It was good to escape the plane. She no longer felt either excitement or doubt. Only the weariness of being shut in a plane with the unceasing vibration and sound, and the closeness of other bodies. She struggled to keep awake during the long afternoon while Father Thomas, in his high, curiously accented voice, went on and on about the shrines he had visited, the holy wells, Iona and Saint Columba. He fell silent at last and she looked out the window and gasped. All beneath was green, greener than a painted sea, wave-like under the wind. And cutting through the green, a ribbon of silver with amethyst and sapphire jewels moving, shimmering, on their setting.

'Ah, yes.' All his sentences seemed to be prefaced with 'Ah'. 'The Congo.'

'I have never seen a river so wide. It is like a Monet water-colour. Green, purple, rose-lavender, pink. What is it?'

'I, too, know Monet. It is the water hyacinths. Beautiful and terrible. A problem to shippers which will not go away.'

'I should hope not.'

'Ah, some beauty is deadly and must be destroyed. If God made beauty why must it be destroyed? Because it is Man who has corrupted beauty.'

'Shall we be at Brazzaville soon?'

'Ah, yes. Very soon.'

'Then I must comb my hair—tidy myself, if I may pass you please.'

'Your destination is Brazzaville?'

'Lambaréné, actually. I am going to work at Doctor Schweitzer's hospital.'

'You are a nurse?'

'Yes.'

'You did not tell me.' His voice was accusing.

'You did not give me a chance.' She stood and he stood to let her pass.

'Ah, an old Zuluman who talked too much to make himself important. Forgive me.'

'Father Thomas, there is nothing to forgive.'

He carried her hand baggage off the plane. He was to continue to Johannesburg. He detained her for only a moment. 'I bless you, if a black priest's blessing is acceptable. Remember, God has given His angels charge over thee to guard thee in all thy ways. Go in peace.'

'Thank you, Father Thomas. I am glad you sat beside me.'

'From here on, it is forbidden to sit beside a white. I was

fortunate for a little while.'

She stayed that night at the Air France Hotel in Brazzaville, for it was too late to go on to Lambaréné. The plane did not leave until morning.

Dinner was served on the terrace overlooking the vast expanse of the river, no longer silver but dark as oil except where the lights from the hotel rippled on the surface. Mesmerized by weariness, she felt as if she had wandered into a dream. She lay awake a long time trying to catch up with herself and understand the decision which had brought her to Africa. It had made sense in Scotland, but it made no sense now, and the fact that it did not troubled her.

Twice she got up and stood at the window, looking down on the black river and the swiftly moving islands of hyacinths which the terrace lights illuminated for a moment before they passed from view. This was not the Africa she had wanted or expected. That Africa had vanished fifty years or more ago. Gone with Doctor Livingstone and Burton and Speke. Gone with childhood.

She overslept and missed the plane, much to her relief. It was a bad start, but she knew she needed another day to adjust to her new beginning. She was even too listless to explore the town, but sat contentedly on the terrace, watching the river, writing brief letters home. It was only to Charlie that she dared to write, 'Don't tell the others, but I am suddenly not quite sure what I am doing here. I am beginning to wonder if it was an utterly daft idea.'

It was fatigue which had caused her doubts. By the next morning she was ready for whatever came. Even the antique plane which looked as if it could not lift off the ground did not daunt her. It was heavily loaded with a conglomerate of humanity, food, machinery, tools, baggage, crates, and mail bags. The passengers stared at Fionna, and she tried not to stare back. When she did meet their eyes they grinned at her. She was not sure whether it was in friendship or because she was a curiosity.

There were four stops before Lambaréné. Each time the plane dived through a hole in the clouds and descended into thick greenery, to land with a thud and bump across a narrow clearing. Each time it finally halted, just short of a wall of jungle.

At Lambaréné she and her belongings and two sacks of mail were moved to a jeep which jostled her to a wharf where she transferred to a dugout with four oarsmen. It rode low in the water of the Ogooué River and she wondered uneasily if there were crocodiles. Trees hung low over the river, trailing clumps of tangled vines in the water. Some were mottled and thick and resembled pythons. Had she been young she would have wished they were. Now she hoped they were not. That was what age did to one.

The oarsmen sang in polyphonic rhythm accented by the dip of their paddles. They interrupted their song long enough to shout to friends in passing pirogues or walking along the road which followed the river. Bells rang in the distance, reverberating, mingling with the sound of the water. One of the oarsmen grinned at her, showing a mouthful of white teeth. He said in French, 'They know you come now.'

As they rounded a wide bend in the river, she saw, set amongst the palms and foreign trees, the low sprawl of the hospital buildings. A crowd had gathered on the beach, and on the wharf was an old gentleman in rumpled clothes and a cork helmet.

The dugout slid against the wharf, bumping as the current tugged it. None too gracefully Fionna scrambled out of the unsteady craft and one of the oarsmen gave her a boost up. While she was still attempting to collect herself, she found her hand grasped and being shaken by the gentleman. His eyes shone with merriment. 'Welcome. We have been expecting you. We are glad you have come.'

She gulped, afraid that she would cry. 'Thank you. I, too, am glad.' And she was glad. It was going to be all right.

When Fionna was a student nurse, she had cried one day with frustration and anger over a stupid mistake she had made. Matron, who was rumoured to make mincemeat of nurses, had come across Fionna snivelling in the linen room, her arms full of sheets, tears streaking her cheeks.

Matron had looked at her grimly, then given her arm something that was between a shake and a pat. 'It wasn't a disaster, Maccallum. It was an incident. The patient will live—though her family might prefer otherwise—and you will learn. Whenever you get discouraged remind yourself that all beginnings are difficult.' As she walked out of the door she had called over her shoulder, 'Get along to B14 with those sheets. The dirty old bugger has soiled his bed again.'

More than once in the days that followed her arrival at Lambaréné Fionna thought of Matron. It seemed to her that everything about this beginning was difficult.

She had been given a bewildering tour of the grounds by Lisa, the young Swiss nurse whose place she was taking while she was home on leave. At dinner she had been seated across from Doctor Schweitzer—Lisa whispered it was always done on one's first night—and been interrogated about her experiences in Spain and during the recent war. She tried to answer intelligently between her struggles with cutting and chewing the tough cutlet, which Lisa told her was crocodile tail and in her honour. 'Usually it is carp which is nothing but skin and bones.'

Then he had invited her to assist at an amputation the next morning. The patient had removed a sand flea from under his toenail and the wound had got infected. Now the foot must come off. The doctor then delivered a lecture on the sand fleas which had come to Africa from South America during the last century, and the ills it caused.

After dinner there had been a hymn, a reading from the Bible, and a long discussion of the historical and allegorical significance of the passage. Towards the end Fionna had stifled yawns.

Lisa had walked her back to her cubicle in the dormitory in case she got lost on her first evening. As they left the dining room they heard a Bach fugue intermingling with the sound of cicadas and bullfrogs. 'He always plays awhile before he retires,' Lisa said. Bobbing kerosene lanterns lit the way of others going to their rooms. Fionna had forgotten to bring hers as it had still been twilight when the dinner bell had rung. Small cookfires glowed where the families of the hospitalized patients camped. The stars were thick, and close enough to touch, and the jungle beyond was full of the cries of night birds.

Lisa had waited until Fionna had lit the lamp on her table and hooked the sheet which served as a curtain across the window. 'Don't forget to use the water in the wine bottle to brush your teeth. It is boiled and that in the bucket is not. If you forget you will get a very bad bug.' She had giggled like a schoolgirl. 'I know. I once forgot. And don't forget to bring the other lantern when you go to dinner tomorrow night. Sometimes there are cobras. Usually they run when they feel the vibration of your footsteps, but if they are asleep, pow! they bite if you step on them. That would make you sicker than unboiled water. And do not forget to wear your helmet always! I sound like your mother, overflowing with advice. Sleep well and do not worry about the amputation. There will be others to help.'

Fionna had bolted her door and leant against it surveying her room, which Lisa had described as being quite nice. Not the adjective Fionna would have applied. A cell at Dartmoor would be larger. Her clothes, still wrinkled from being packed, hung in limp resentment on two nails hammered into the whitewashed wall. Her luggage was stored beside the chipped chamberpot under the iron army cot which was her bed. The deal table held the wash basin, a soap dish, bottled water, the two lamps, the cosmetics she had unpacked, and her writing case. Slowly, she had begun to unbutton her blouse. There seemed to be nothing to do but get ready for bed. What had she got herself into? A monastic order?

By the time she had washed she realized how tired she was. It had been a long day. She had turned out her lamp and sat down on her bed and had leapt up again immediately. The springs had squealed under her weight. She had tried again, more carefully, but at every move the bed protested. She had got into as comfortable a position as she could and remained rigid. In the next room someone dropped shoes. The floor reverberated like a drum. Further away there was a whispered conversation. Sick babies cried, sounding as if they were under her bed. The bed in the next cubicle rattled and protested more loudly than Fionna's had done. Somewhere someone used a chamberpot very noisily. Beyond the walls the cicadas and bullfrogs carried on their competition.

For a long time she had stared into the darkness afraid to move, wondering if she had done the right thing coming here, missing Jamie and Tad far more than she had thought she would. Feeling empty and lonely she fell asleep, turned, and was awakened by her bed, lay awake listening to the fretting babies, and finally was surprised to hear the sound of the rising bells and found milky morning light filtering into the room.

She unhooked the sheet and looked down the grassy hill to the Ogooué River. It glowed like an illuminated mirror, reflecting celestial light into the sky. Tall palms moved stiffly in the wind, and beyond the river the dark-green horizon seemed to stretch forever.

It was not the Africa in Willie's fading photo album, the Africa of the Serengeti Plain and the herds of animals, Kilimanjaro, and the frontier town of Nairobi. This was her Africa, and she was glad she had come.

By the end of the week she no longer heard the cicadas, the bullfrogs, the crying babies, the sounds from the other cubicles, nor her own bed. If Fa had expected her to find herself, as he had teasingly remarked, he had not known how busy she would be. Some nights it was as much as she could do to find her toothbrush.

There were always patients coming by dugout or pirogue from miles away, accompanied by every member of their family and their animals. There were always patients in front of the pharmacy waiting for their initial examination, slumped in chairs, lying on stretchers, waiting for medicine, for the operating room, a spare bed, waiting to give birth or to die.

There was leprosy, yaws, tuberculosis, every known variety of venereal disease, cancer, fractures, ulcers, tantrums brought on by low blood sugar, tetanus, and malnutrition. And sometimes death.

Once she had to accompany a corpse to the burial ground. The small child's body had been wrapped in palm leaves, and laid on a stretcher. The procession consisted of blank-faced family members, a goat, a boy with a pick and shovel, and Fionna with a Bible.

No one told her that there were no individual graves. She had been so shocked by the sight of the mass grave that, after the body was lowered and the red earth covered it, she could not find her place in the Bible to read the Burial of the Dead. The family watched her fumbling, their dark eyes inscrutable pools. Finally, in desperation, she pretended to be reading, but instead quoted Wordsworth: 'A slumber did my spirit seal . . .'

The family seemed satisfied. The Bible contained many things, and if the nurse with hair like copper chose to read it in her own language instead of French, it did not matter to them or to the dead child.

The weeks turned into months, and with the passage of time came contentment. Fionna felt more useful and dedicated than she had done in the hospital in Glasgow.

She was no longer shocked by the cats, dogs, goats, chickens and monkeys wandering freely in the wards, the blending and interdependence of all forms of life. Mothers slept under the beds of their sick children, wives at the foot of their husbands' beds. Relatives swarmed to visit, made little twig fires on the stone floor and fried fish, sharing it with the patient. Grandmothers, mothers, sisters, and aunts were present in the delivery room when a child was born, and afterwards stamped and clapped, danced and sang.

Activity was unceasing. The washerwomen were never at rest, but always surrounded by mounds of laundry. They sat in a circle around the tubs, their skirts tucked up between their thighs, chattering and beating their hospital linens. On the river bank women bargained, shouting, laughing, shaking their fists, for fish or crocodile. There were tailors, cobblers, carpenters and mechanics. A boy filling the lamps with oil, the natives haggling at the market place, the gardeners tending the vegetables, men cleaning the outhouse, politely known as the Hinter Indien.

Once a week she had an afternoon off. Often she went by motor launch to Lambaréné-Downtown. There she wandered about the shops buying souvenirs for Jamie, Liam and young Charles. Crocodile teeth, a gorilla skull, a cobra skin, some brass ornaments, a spear, and a bottle of cognac for herself. After that, she climbed the hill to the Air France Hotel where she sat on the terrace sipping Heidseick and writing letters. She took her own mail along to reread at leisure, because often at night she was too tired to remember what she had read.

'Isn't it strange,' Mairi had written, 'how we three have wandered? Carlos to become more Spanish than the Spaniards, and to die fighting for Spain's freedom; and now you to Africa where you have always dreamed of going. Will you ever return to the heather, Fionna, or are you a dedicated nurse now? I envy you. I am dedicated to nothing. Everything I do is done to fill time, waiting to hear whether Erich is alive. Edu would have me get involved in politics, but I am willing to leave the rebirth of Germany in the hands of the young idealists. Perhaps I have lost faith in everything and still suffer from the guilt. Fear sealed our eyes to the crimes being committed, made cowards of us all. Edu calls it our "moral ruin".

'Do write again, Fionna. I loved your description of the shower. The bucket with holes pierced in it and filled from the rain barrel. I could almost see you covered with soap and trying to rinse it all off before the water gave out. Like Carlos, you are our adventurer. First Spain and now Africa, and a life with William in between. Yes, I do believe I envy you.'

It was easy to envy at a distance, Fionna thought. Not that she was sure she was as dedicated as Mairi assumed. She enjoyed being away from the hospital, luxuriating in her leisure, and looking forward to a well-cooked dinner at the hotel of coc au vin, *pommes frites,* Brie and fruit. Sometimes it was steak—not crocodile—and rice cooked in a broth with herbs and cheese, and petits fours.

On one of these afternoons off, she met an American reporter there, writing, or trying to write, a story on the hospital, Gabon and the Congo.

'That covers a large part of Africa,' she had commented.

'In depth.' And when she looked puzzled, he had added, 'Every aspect. Culture, politics, future, and of course, the famous hospital of the famous doctor. I wrote requesting an interview with the old boy and was politely refused. Anything you can do to help?'

'Only tell you that he doesn't give interviews. You are welcome to visit the hospital. You will find he is a very busy man. It *is* a working hospital. And if you try to question him he will tell you that he is only a doctor working there.'

The reporter bought her dinner and they were lingering over cognac. 'Can't you put in a good word for me?'

'It wouldn't make any difference, Jake. Someone will show you around the grounds, you can have dinner there if you wish, and have a desire for crocodile cutlets. But he won't tell you anything that you want to know.'

'Then let me interview you. Get your impressions of him and the set-up there.'

She twirled the glass on the table, admiring the colour of the liquor in the candlelight. 'Let me think about it. I don't want to be misquoted or sound critical.'

'So! There are things to criticize!'

'No, no, no. I meant, if I told you about, say, the female relatives being allowed into the delivery room, it would sound unsanitary. But it isn't. You would have to see it to understand it, Jake, and—' She glanced at her watch. 'It's time to go back.'

'Why don't you spend the night here? With me?'

'No, thanks, but no. I'm not into that. Anyway, there's an operation in the morning.'

'Time you got into it. How long did you say your husband has been dead? Over a year. What are you saving yourself for?' He raised a questioning eyebrow. 'You could go back early enough for the operation. No one would know.'

'I would know and I am sure the doctor would not approve.'

'Is he your keeper?'

'While I am here, yes. I would do nothing that might offend him.'

'Except come to the hotel and get smashed on your afternoon off and eat something considerably better than crocodile cutlets and a hell of a lot more expensive.' He crushed out his cigarette as if he were crushing Fionna herself. 'Okay, babe, find yourself a motor launch and go back to the monastery and tell Big Daddy you have sinned.' He got up so abruptly he knocked over his chair, then strode off the terrace, his back stiff with anger.

She sipped at the last of her cognac, watching him go, and realized that the answer to his question was that she was saving herself for Tad. Never once in the early years of her refusing his advances, had he been churlish or anything other than gentlemanly and understanding.

She walked down the hill to the wharf and chose a pirogue rather than a motor launch. She wanted to go slowly, quietly, back to the hospital, with only the sound of the water purring against the craft.

A gibbous moon turned the river to quicksilver. The paddles made dark furrows in the shining water. As they left the lights of the town the vegetation became a dark, undulating wall. Water hyacinths drifted by, their scent lingering on the air. As men pulled the craft against the water they sang softly, as if not to disturb the darkness. Once she heard drums. Suddenly she wished that Tad and Jamie were with her sharing the experience. She felt close to them as she had not felt all her time here. She had been too busy to want them, but now she did. Tad she missed for his gently demanding, possessive need of her body as proof of her love. For her own need and willingness to give, as she could not, *ever,* have given to Jake Keely to whom she would have been just another lay. More than that it was Tad's gentleness, the good talks they had, the mutual understanding.

As for Jamie, she wished she could have shared the entire experience with him. He would have made himself a part of the colony, seen a sleeping cobra on every path, in every vine a hopeful boa, played with the children and learnt to speak to them, all the time thinking he was doing something grand.

As the pirogue drew up to the wharf she smelled the smoke of the small, individual campfires over which the families of the patients were cooking their meals. The flames were like fireflies in the dark.

A small group was drawn around one fire and was singing a psalm. They sang in French, but as she walked up the path she recognized the words, 'By the waters of Babylon we sat down and wept, when we remembered thee, O Zion . . . How shall we sing the Lord's song in a strange land?'

She thought, I should go home. It was almost as if Tad and Jamie were calling out, asking her to come. In another month Lisa would be back from Switzerland and Fionna would be free.

She went to bed in peace. She had known the gratification of helping a patient to recover, had gloried in the moments of small beauty, grown fond of the doctor and felt enriched by having known him, but to stay would never be enough. She was no martyr, no saint, no dedicated nurse. She had gone the full circle from her childhood dream and was going home to her beginnings.

The first early light awakened her. Lying in bed, smiling to herself, she mentally composed a long letter to Jamie, telling him she would soon be home. And another, a love letter, to Tad giving him hope that she was ready for marriage.

When she walked into the dining room for early breakfast the head nurse met her halfway across the room. She had an envelope in her hand.

'Nurse Lammondson, a cable came for you only a few moments ago. A launch brought it up from Lambaréné-Downtown. I was about to bring it to your dormitory.'

'A cable?' She felt her stomach contract in fear. Without sitting at the table, she stood beside the door and ripped it open.

Imperative you telephone immediately. Charlie.

Nurse Kottman watched her with anxious eyes. 'I think cables always bring bad news,' she said.

'Yes. I don't know. I must telephone at once. Will I be needed if I go to Lambaréné long enough to do that?'

'We shall manage. You must have some coffee and a bit of bread first. I told the launch to wait in case an answer was needed.'

'Thank you. I'll get my handbag.' She accepted the coffee cup that was thrust into her hand and the bread and cheese wrapped in her napkin.

She did not even stop to change, but grabbed her handbag and hurried to the waiting launch. Had something happened to Fa or to Tad or—dear God forbid—to Jamie? Her heart churned like the water churning in the wake of the launch.

She tried the yard first, but there was no answer, then she remembered that Scotland was two hours earlier than Gabon. Charlie was probably still at home, and after all the trouble of trying to put through the call.

While she waited she had another coffee and a brioche.

The dining room was empty. The waiters watched her eat and whispered together and laughed, slapping one another on the back and feinting with their fists.

She heard the telephone ring and was across the lobby before the clerk could page her.

The connection surged with a sound like water and wind as if both elements were involved in the transmission.

'Charlie? Charlie, it's Fe. What has happened? What is it?'

The line crackled and she could not hear his reply.

'What? What? Damn, what a rotten connection.'

'I said, I think you had best come home at once. Jamie and Liam are missing. We think—'

'*Missing?* What do you mean, missing? Kidnapped? How long? Tell me, for God's sake!'

'We think we know where they are, but it's a question of how to go about getting them back. No, not kidnapped. Not, I think, in any danger. That is—of their lives. But—Oh, hell, Fe, come home. It's a question of finding them and getting them back. Tad wants to try it. But I think you had better come. You could probably get to the bottom of it.'

'Bottom of what?'

'Look. I'll arrange for a ticket to be waiting for you on Air France from Brazzaville day after tomorrow. Can you make it?'

'I can probably make the milk-run this afternoon and be there to leave tomorrow. Try for a ticket for tomorrow.'

'Right. And if it isn't there—if they can't get a ticket that fast, there will be one the next day. I'll book you straight from Orly to London and Glasgow. If you have time, call me from Paris, failing that, from London.'

'Yes. All right.'

'And, Fe, don't worry.'

'Don't worry! I'm so worried I'm about to lose my breakfast. You call Air France the moment I hang up. And when I get home you'd better have your armour on, for I'm planning to clout you for not taking better care of my son.'

'Get off the blower, Fe, and go and pack. This call is costing money.'

'Aye, laddie, and it's cost me peace of mind.' She slammed down the receiver.

Jake Keely strolled across the lobby towards her. 'What are you doing here so early? I thought there was a big operation this morning.'

'There's an operation all right. Operation long distance to Glasgow and it's an emergency. Haven't time to talk now. If I don't see you, good luck with your interview.'

'Oh, did you speak to him?'

'Not yet, but I will. I'll warn him.'

Her departure was much like her arrival, with the bells ringing and everyone gathered on the beach to see her off, ambulatory patients, nurses and doctors, workmen, washerwomen and children. As she climbed into the launch they shouted *auf Wiedersehen* or *au revoir* and those who knew she would never return, *adieu*.

She waved until the launch rounded the bend of the river, shutting the hospital from sight. Before they reached Lambaréné-Downtown, they saw the milk-run plane skimming low over the green jungle, then dropping into it for a landing on the cleared strip. It would wait for her, and by evening she would be in Brazzaville.

Jamie had been four when Maureen and Liam came to live at the castle. To have Liam there was almost like having a brother, a hero, mentor and fellow adventurer. It was Uncle

245

Charlie who had discovered Liam and his mother and had been responsible for their move into Jamie's life.

Early in the last year of the war, Charlie had been in London on business. He had very nearly missed the train back to Glasgow. He had run the length of the concourse at Euston as the whistle was blowing, and swung aboard the last car as it was moving. The station master had slammed the door on his heels. He had a first-class ticket but the train was crowded. Even some navy brass stood in the aisle, smoking and grumbling resignedly.

Charlie had gone the length of the train crawling over passengers sitting on cases, perched on the arms of the seats, or hanging from straps, swaying with the movement of the train. He cursed himself for not having had the forethought to reserve a seat, but it had not occurred to him that the costly first class would be filled. He finally settled for leaning against the wall in a vestibule between coaches, having to move every time someone came to use the toilet.

Sharing the vestibule were a student dozing on his knapsack, an exhausted-looking young woman sitting on a battered suitcase, and a starved-looking lad with eyes as large and blue as those of a china doll.

Charlie smiled at him. The boy ducked his head, and under lowered lids, stared back. The woman gazed out of the window at the dreary backyards of London. Charlie unfurled *The Times* and tried to read, aware of the boy's eyes boring into him.

Presently the boy tugged at his mother who was now leaning back, her eyes closed, half-asleep. 'Mum. I'm hungry.'

'You'll have something when you get to Uncle Sean's.'

'But we're nowhere near and we haven't eaten since we got off the mail boat.'

Fresh over from Ireland, Charlie thought.

'Stop whining, Liam. It took all I had to buy our train tickets.'

'Some tickets! We should be riding free, no seats and all.'

'A good thing I had the cash to buy them or you'd be hungry on a park bench in London.'

'I'd beg.'

'The day I see you begging will be the day you see the back of my hand. You do not beg, even if the flesh hangs on your bones and your belly bloats. Think of the men in the prisons on hunger strike for the freedom and let me hear no more complaint.'

Well, well, another flaming Irish patriot, fleeing to the country holding hers in thrall.

'Like Uncle Frank.'

'Like him.'

'He died.' The lad thought for a moment. 'Like me Da.' A tear ran down his cheek. He brushed it away angrily.

Charlie tried to appear to be immersed in the war news. The student stirred suddenly and rummaged in his knapsack.

'I've an apple the wean can have. My granny gave it me when I left.' He held it out and the boy's hand crept out to reach for it.

'He cannot accept it.'

'Och, come away! It'll go rotten. You know why? She fed me so many apples while I was staying with her that the smell of 'em gie me to boke. Apple sauce, apple bake, apple pasties, apple with salad cream. My uncle in Kent sent her a barrel of them. What's left she's drying in the oven before they go off. I swear I was planning to toss it in the trash bin soon as we hit Central Station.'

'All right. Liam, thank the young man properly.'

The apple vanished, core, seeds and all. Charlie waited a decent length of time then said to the student, 'Guard my spot here and my briefcase, will you? I'm going to the buffet car to see if there's any food. I missed breakfast myself. Could I bring anything? A cup of tea, madam?'

'Nothing.'

He returned with four limp sandwiches, a pot of tea, and a cornet of greasy chips. He forced himself to eat one of the sandwiches, which he did not want on top of the hearty hotel breakfast he had had. Wiping his hands on his handkerchief, he said, 'I'm not as hungry as I thought. A pity to let these go to waste. How about it, old chap, could you manage one of these on top of that apple?'

The woman gave him a mocking smile. 'Liar.' It was little more than a movement of her lips, but he heard it and gave her a deprecating shrug.

By the time the train drew into Glasgow she had told him that her husband had been killed in an accident. Much, much later, when they had been installed in Castle Lammondson, he heard the story. They had gone to blow up the telephone exchange. The man who was supposed to have been helping had been arrested and Maureen, for that was her name, had taken his place. She had got out of the car to stand as sentinel, and her husband had remained to make a small adjustment to the mine. Suddenly there was an explosion. She had looked back and fainted.

When she came to she was in the hospital being treated for shock and minor cuts from bits of flying glass. She had told the authorities she had been passing by on her way home from work. She did not know who was in the car or why it had exploded.

The IRA had not allowed her to attend her husband's funeral for fear of reprisals on herself and Liam. They had bought her a ticket out of the country, and she and her son were on their way to her brother, Sean, in Glasgow where she hoped to find work.

At that time Fionna was still nursing at Victoria Hospital and household help was difficult to find. Women could make more money in the war effort than as cooks or chars. Fionna's interview with Maureen had been cursory because her mind was already half made up to hire the woman. She was more interested in watching the two lads together, at first eyeing one another warily as two strange dogs, then Jamie's feeler. 'Do you want to see my train?'

'I like trucks better. They're mobile and can cut across country where trains can't go. You can camouflage them with branches and turf and the soldiers'll be going so fast they pass right by.'

'Oh, well, war.' Jamie dismissed camouflaged trucks. 'Come on. It has a real whistle and a coal car with real coal.'

Maureen had interrupted Fionna to say sharply, 'Don't go far, Liam. It isn't your place.'

'Let them go,' Fionna had said. 'I'll show you the rooms you would have and you can see if they suit. A small sitting room, and a bedroom each. The furniture is a bit shabby, but if rationing ever goes off, we can improve that.'

'Oh, madam.' Maureen had choked back a sob.

'That's settled then, and I'm off to work. Tomorrow is my day off. If you can be here around ten we'll have the day to sort things out. Oh—here's the money for the train fare and I'll pick you up with your luggage at the station.'

Fionna had not regretted her hasty decision. Maureen proved to be the kind of cook who worked miracles with rationing, was intelligent and efficient, and located a housemaid where Fionna had failed to find one. Furthermore she was aware of her good fortune and quietly grateful for it.

If she wanted to take the *United Irishmen* newspaper it did not matter to Fionna, though Willie had frowned and hummed over it a bit. Fionna thought the Irish had had a rotten deal from the time of the Edwards onward, having their land handed out to Court favourites, and the religions set against one another so that Ireland united wouldn't turn against England. If Liam's heroes were Wolfe Tone and Kevin Barry—whoever they were—that was all right, too. He was well-mannered and clever, 'too clever by half,' Maureen said, and a good foil for Jamie. It was gratifying to see the pallor disappear from his face and flesh fatten his bones. Fionna should have been more aware.

Liam's indoctrination of Jamie had not been deliberate. Liam himself had been indoctrinated by the kind of life he had led. His childhood and that of his cousins had been anything but normal. They had heard little else but of one great-uncle's death in the Easter Rebellion of '16, his grandfather's death in the '22, his uncle's hunger strike and death, the plots which succeeded and those that failed, safe houses, friends and traitors. To Jamie it was fiction. Like Sir William Wallace and The Bruce, Robin Hood and Rob Roy, Kinmont Willie and Johnnie Armstrong, the Reiver. They, too, had harried the English. They exchanged tale for tale. It had taken Jamie a few years to realize that what Liam described was not the heroes of old, but of the near-present, and that Liam had known some of these folk and even touched them; that Liam's father had been blown to bits doing a grand thing. That Liam himself planned to do grand things as soon as he was old enough.

It sometimes seemed to Jamie that Liam had already done grand things. During the great snowstorm the year Aunt Mairi had visited, Jamie and Liam had tunnelled through the drifts. Liam had told Jamie how they tunnelled through the garden walls at home to move from backyard to backyard and avoid going into York Street. York Street was Protestant and it wasn't safe there. One had to get to Queen Street which was Catholic. But it was not always safe either because the Protestants were as apt to bomb it as the Catholics were to bomb York Street.

Liam taught Jamie a rousing song, 'She got up and rattled her bin, For the Specials were a-coming in, Tiddy-fa-la, tiddy-fa-la.' That was when the UVF came to raid the Catholic areas after dark and heave hand grenades through the windows. Anyone seeing them coming yelled bloody-murder, and everyone got up and banged their dustbin lids and pots and pans, until the invaders were driven off.

When Jamie and Liam were old enough they moved into Glasgow with Uncle Charlie to attend what Jamie insisted on calling 'the posh school'. Jamie's mother said the only thing posh about it was what it cost to attend.

Sometimes on Sundays Uncle Charlie planned something to do with the boys, but on Sundays when he was busy with other things they either went out to the castle or took the underground to Pollokshields to visit Liam's Uncle Sean. That was jolly.

The house was always crowded. People all talked at once and there was always singing and someone playing the Irish harp and the tin whistle. There was plotting and discussing and laughing and arguing. Maps were drawn and recipes exchanged for mixing something called Paxo. They even gave Liam one of the recipes, saying, 'One day you'll be given the fixings as well, lad.'

Despite rationing there was plenty of food, roast potatoes, oatmeal muffins, turnips mashed with carrots, and ginger beer for the young'uns and ale for the elders.

Smoke thick as fog on the Clyde from the pipes and cigarettes hung low in the room. Late in the afternoon, when folk were getting ready to go to their homes, Uncle Sean would give the toast, 'In the name of God, in the name of Tone's bleeding throat, in the name of Emmet's severed head . . . and for the countless dead . . .' and Liam's eyes would shine with tears as he added under his breath, 'And for my Da who died for Ireland.'

On the wall of Liam's room at Uncle Charlie's was a sign, all in big Gothic letters with a green border curlicued around it. 'England quake. Ireland awake!'

Uncle Charlie had laughed when he saw it. 'Liam, the SNP could use you. We'll put a sign in Jamie's room saying "Scotland Shall Rise Again".'

He was teasing, but Jamie could see it made Liam angry that Uncle Charlie did not take him seriously.

Visits to the castle were not nearly so interesting as those to Uncle Sean's. Jamie's mother seemed determined that Jamie should learn all about the affairs of the estate so that he would know how to manage it when he grew up and was in charge. It was all havers as far as he was concerned. After a week in gloomy Glasgow with its smoke-blackened buildings and sooty fog, he would have preferred a walk up the Campsies.

But his mother was insistent and they sorted through stacks of papers. Some were so old that they felt as dry and crisp as autumn leaves. The faded ink was almost too dim to read, the lines thin and fragile as a spider's web.

'These,' his mother said, handling them as gently as if they were newborn kittens, 'will go to the museum in Edinburgh because they are historical documents back to the time of James V, and some even further back than that. The Lammondsons are an ancient family.'

Jamie knew that. Age-darkened portraits of his ancestors, men and women in fancy dress, lined the corridors and inhabited the bedrooms in the old part of the castle. Some of them resembled his father, and there was one, a boy with red hair, who reminded Jamie of himself.

'He was called Red Tom,' his mother told him, standing before the portrait with her hand resting on Jamie's shoulder. 'He fought for Charles I under Prince Rupert. He died in the battle of Marston Moor. The portrait is a Van Dyck, and should be in a museum along with the papers. Perhaps we should have named you for him instead of for Jamie Graham. He is very like you, isn't he? Strange how family resemblances keep cropping up.'

He so resembled Jamie that it was like seeing his own reflection in a mirror, if he should ever be fool enough to dress up in such lacy, prissy clothes.

'He was only a few years older than you are now when he was killed. His diary is in the library. Would you like to read it?'

That script, too, was so faint as to be almost the same colour as the paper, and the letters were formed differently and the words spelled in an ancient way. But there was a sketch of the battlefield which Red Tom had drawn, with blocks of soldiers drawn up facing one another, pennants and men on rearing horses; the supply wagons and cook fires, the bridge of boats across the River Ouse. Red Tom was no Van Dyck, but Jamie could almost feel the action and excitement. It must have been a grand thing to be fighting against the Roundheads and a pity that Red Tom was killed.

When he told Liam about it Liam said it was better to plant a bomb and be away than it was to charge a cannon. Jamie refrained from saying it was Liam's father's own bomb that had blown up and he hadn't gotten away.

His mind was full of Red Tom when they went back to Uncle Sean's the following Sunday. It seemed no different from the usual Sunday aside from the fact that there were new faces there. It was Liam who whispered, 'Something is going on here. Something is different. Can you not feel it, Jamie? It's all electric.' After a few moments of thoughtful scowling he added, 'It's the new ones who've come over. That's it! Cor! I wonder what they're plotting.'

Uncle Sean was enclosed in the second sitting room with the men. All the men, that is, except Patrick and Norrey who were playing their harp and penny whistle as usual. They never seemed to do anything else. When their music stopped so they could catch a breath or take a swig of ale, the boys could hear the low voices in the other room. Sometimes the voices rose in stifled anger and hard fists hit the table. When Pegeen, Uncle Sean's wife, tapped at the door and went in with tea, whisky and biscuits, a sudden silence would fall until she came out again, closing the door carefully behind her.

One of the new women, Mavis, couldn't sit still. She paced the room, lit a new cigarette from the old stub, and kept brushing her hair out of her eyes with the hand holding the cigarette. Jamie expected her Medusa-like red hair to catch fire any moment. Everything she said, accompanied by gestures and stances, reminded him of a cinema star. Maureen watched her with ill-concealed scorn. Liam was hypnotized.

When next the musicians stopped for a drink Mavis grabbed Patrick by the lapel. 'Patrick, you are with us, are you not man? It's only for a week. We'll have you back in Glasgow before your bed is cold.'

Roughly he jerked loose. 'I'm no' goin'.'

'You *are* going. What are players without their musicians? Where is your patriotism, man?'

'My patriotism doesna' include losin' my wages to sew up mail sacks in Belfast gaol.' He took a long swig from the ale bottle. For a moment Jamie thought he was going to spit in her face. After holding it in his mouth a moment he swallowed very slowly, his Adam's apple moving up and down. 'Get Peddar and Hugh. They play.' He picked up the whistle and began a mournful tune.

'Peddar and Hugh *are* sewing mail sacks, as you damn well know. And were they not, if the Specials saw *them* in the van, the all of us would be sewing mail sacks.'

He stopped playing long enough to say, 'I'm no' goin', Mavis.'

'Bastard,' she said under her breath. She turned to the harp player. 'Norrey, you are coming, are you not?'

'Aweel . . .' He cast a sheepish sidelong look at Patrick. 'Aye. I'm owing Bryan for helping me escape from Derry, so it seems I should go. Aye.'

'Good man.' She kissed her finger tip and touched his forehead. Norrey wiped it off and winked at Patrick who scowled over his whistle.

Mavis said, 'Patrick owes Bryan as well, Norrey, but *he* is not willing to pay.' She turned her back on the musicians, lit another cigarette, and went over to stand by Maureen, looking down on her and her knitting as a queen might look down on a lady-in-waiting who didn't rise to curtsey to her Majesty.

'We'll be needing Liam, Maureen.'

Liam's head jerked up, a glass of ginger beer halfway to his lips.

'That you do not. I lost my man. I am not losing my son.'

'He will not be lost. Nor would your man have been if he had not fiddlefaddled with the wee bomb which was already set.'

'Hold your tongue when you speak of my man, and forget my Liam, woman.'

Mavis turned from Maureen, smiled at Liam and arched an eyebrow. 'We need a young one or two to give us authenticity.'

'There are young ones a-plenty in Ireland and the half of them orphans from the guns of the English.'

'We need him for the *crossing*, Maureen and for the road. You've gone soft living in Scotland, Maureen. You've gone grand living in a castle, even if it is only the kitchens.'

'I am safe and my lad is safe, and he is getting a fine education.'

'Not an education that will make him a hero of Ireland.'

'Perhaps a different kind of hero for Ireland. One who is alive and neither in gaol nor his grave.'

Mavis dismissed that with a wave of her cigarette, leaving a trail of smoke and sparks. Before she could say anything more, Uncle Sean came out of the other room, leaving the door open behind him.

'It is good work we have done this day and a wee toast is in order. Maureen, you and Mavis fetch the whisky from the kitchen—the malt, mind you—and clean glasses to go with it, and spare the water. Tell the wife 'tis time to serve the cake.'

He waited until they were out of the room, then said to Liam, 'I am wanting a word with you, lad, for your ears only.'

'I'll go, Uncle Sean.'

'So that fool woman has spoken to your mother. I told her to leave the speaking to me. What did Maureen say?'

'She's not having it, but I'll go. I want to do my bit in memory of my Da.'

Uncle Sean took his pipe from his pocket and tapped out the ashes. 'Against the wishes of your mother?'

'Need she know. She'll be at the castle and we don't go there every weekend. Mavis said we would be back in a week. So she told Patrick, didn't she, Pat?'

'A week if they're no' caught and taken.'

'You're not with them then, Patrick?'

'I've had my share of gaol. Bloody dreadful it was, too.'

Carefully, Uncle Sean refilled his pipe and touched a match to it. He puffed at it so long that Liam began to fidget.

'I should like to go along as well.' The words were out of Jamie's mouth before he knew he had said them.

Liam gave him a grin and a punch on the shoulder.

'Well, now, that could be a bit sticky, Lammondson. Your uncle could raise a stink that would spoil the party.'

The kitchen door opened and they heard Pegeen saying, 'I'll bring along the cake, but they'll hold it in their fingers. I'm washing no more plates and two sets of glasses as well.'

'See me tomorrow after you're dismissed from the Academy.' Uncle Sean scarcely moved his lips as he spoke, clenching his teeth. 'Mum's the word, lads.'

Jamie was unable to accompany Liam the next day. He had promised to take young Charles to play ball in the park. His mind was not on tossing and catching a silly red ball. The young one could neither catch nor toss, being too busy leaping about, clapping his hands and shouting.

Liam arrived home only a few minutes before Uncle Charlie who, for a change, was home early. It was exasperating. Jamie's curiosity was near choking him. After supper Uncle Charlie challenged them to a game of Muggins, two wins out of three.

At long last everyone was yawning and Charlie sent them off to do their homework. He was going to do the same, having brought home his briefcase.

Jamie and Liam raced one another up the stairs. At the top Partland came out and hushed them. 'You'll wake young Master Charles.'

They tiptoed to Liam's room. 'Huh! No doubt The Young One is sleeping like a stone after all that jumping and hollering this afternoon. You'd have thought it was a soccer game and him the crowd. So tell me. I'm nigh bursting.'

'This is the way of it. Mavis is the organizer because it's her fiancé they're to rescue. He's in gaol in Berkshire—'

'Berkshire! That's England.'

'Aye. He was caught there after setting bombs in London along that street the troops march for the Changing of the Guard. They didn't go off 'cause he was spotted and got as far as Berkshire before he was caught. Stupid careless, I call it, and think of the horses—even if they are English ones—had the bombs gone off. He's been on hunger strike, but last week he went on thirst strike, too. Once you go on thirst strike you're done. You shrink to nothing at all. Scarce enough fit to bury. He's going to be transferred to hospital, and we're to get him from the ambulance between prison and hospital.'

'How?'

'The transfer will be done at night so's the other prisoners don't know. We're driving down in a van, posing as a travelling acting company, a family affair like, which is where I come in. Once we have Bryan, we take the van to Ireland and then the real fun begins.'

'What about me?'

'Uncle Sean said the Maccallums have too much power to risk including you.'

'I'm not a Maccallum. That's my mum.'

'But your Da was a bloody Hon, and your mum's away, and your Maccallum uncle is in charge of you. They'd send every ship in the yard after you.'

'Havers.'

'It's a big thing that's planned. Too big for risks.'

'What am I to tell Uncle Charlie and Partland when you have gone missing? What about school?'

'Tell Uncle Charlie I'm staying with my mum at the castle

for a week as she's feeling lonely. Tell the Academy I've gone sick.'

'That's lying.'

'Lying is excusable in a noble cause, Seamus. They tell lies in wartime to make the public angry enough to want to fight. It's no different from wartime, this. Your staying behind is a noble sacrifice.'

'Mavis said she needed a young one *or two*. If it's so big a risk why should it be allowed to fail for want of me?'

'Tell you what. I'll telephone her. Maybe she can put it right with Uncle Sean.'

'Even if she can't, I'm going anyway.'

Everything fell into place so easily that it seemed that fate was on their side. Liam telephoned Mavis as he had promised. She said that Uncle Sean was being a sticky old bastard because Maureen objected to Liam's joining them. However, *she* was all for it, and if Jamie wanted to come, the more the merrier. Best they did not show up at the house, but wait at Queen Street station with their luggage and she would pick them up on their way south.

When it came to handling Uncle Charlie, fate again helped. He was taking a night train to London on business which would keep him away a week or more. Jamie and Liam could not believe their luck. Mavis had promised they would be back in a week. No one would suspect, no one would know. Except, of course, the Academy. There was the real problem. A problem that, incredibly, solved itself.

The boiler which supplied a modicum of warmth to the classrooms burst. Without heat, the plumbing pipes froze, causing flooding, noxious waste which had not yet passed through the pipes, and useless water closets. Classes were suspended for the week or ten days it would take to repair the ancient equipment, parts for which in the long run proved impossible to replace, and new equipment had to be ordered and shipped from England, if it could be had at all.

They told Partland that as long as there was no school they would spend their unexpected holiday at the castle. Liam's mother was lonely, what with the Lady gone and no excitement around there. Jamie's mother's last letter had contained orders about a few things which needed attention. And, best of all, they could get in some hiking in the Campsies and work on their Nature Study reports.

Mrs Partland swallowed the story as if it were sugar and cream. It would be good for them to get in the fresh air and have some exercise. She knew Liam's mother would enjoy his company, and of course, Master Jamie must start learning his responsibilities. She gave them money for their train fare and told them what fine laddies they were.

Liam guffawed all the way to Queen Street. 'You're a fine little laddie, that you are indeed, Seamus, and here's a shilling for a sweetie to eat on the train.'

Jamie punched him. They boxed good-naturedly all the way to the underground.

A fine drizzle dampened the street as the boys hurried to the station. The street lamps were on, the shop windows misted over, and Sir Walter Scott on his pillar in George Square wept tears which dripped from his nose and his plaid, which was draped over the wrong shoulder. In a sudden momentary cessation of traffic noises, they heard the yelping toot of a tug on the Clyde.

Either they were early or Mavis was late. Jamie shivered in the wind sweeping dust and papers in front of the station, and Liam paced up and down, his damp hair plastering his forehead.

They scarcely recognized Mavis when she swooped upon them. Her hair was hidden in a scarf tied under her chin, and she wore a tatty old cape which billowed around her. She hugged Jamie and kissed Liam. His face turned the colour of pickled beetroot.

'Sorry I'm late, darlings. Was your train on time? The motor's round yon corner.'

For a second they stared at her uncomprehendingly, then nodded simultaneously and burst out that the train was late and the food horrid. She trilled a laugh and led them away, her arms hooked through theirs.

The van was not 'round yon corner' at all, but a good four streets away, parked in a narrow, garbage-strewn alley. It was decorated with curlicues and flowers and birds on the wing. Green letters proclaimed, 'The Harp Singers'. Norrey, his cap pulled low over his face, his coat collar turned up, was hunched over the wheel. Two men, introduced as Laurence and Don, were in the seat behind the driver. Liam and Jamie were instructed to climb in the back where there were thick, rough blankets, several tins of white, water-based paint, thermos jugs and a picnic basket. Mavis told them to help themselves to a sandwich each and that there was ginger beer in the string bag if they could find it. But under no circumstances were they to touch the box labelled tinned milk . . . 'or they'll never find enough of us to put us back together again.'

'Paxo', Liam whispered to Jamie. 'Gelignite. Pow!'

They wound their way through the back streets of Maryhill. The tyres went sh-sh-sh on the wet streets and the windshield wiper went whump, whump, whump. They stopped in front of a tall tenement and Norrey tooted da-da-da-daaaa. After a few moments, just as Mavis was asking, 'Where is he, damn his eyes?' a man climbed into the front seat beside her.

'This is Terence, lads,' Mavis said, half-turning. 'Liam

you know. The other one is Jamie. We were about to go off without you.'

'Glad to make your acquaintance. I remember your Da, Liam,' Terence winked over his shoulder. 'Nah, Mavis, my darling, you can't fault a man for taking a last piss for the road. Anyway, 'tis your own selves who're late.'

'Sean went for paint and stopped at the pub on his way back. Norrey had to fetch him or we'd be later still.'

'Drowning his sorrow that Pegeen will not allow him to be a party with us.' Terence nodded and looked to Laurence and Don for reassurance. 'Proud to have you gentlemen aboard. 'Tis a fine thing for Ireland we'll be doing tomorrow night.'

It was too dark now and the rain too heavy to see where they were going, but Jamie knew they were on the road to the south. The motion of the van and the sound of the rain made Jamie drowsy. He rolled himself up in one of the blankets and fell asleep.

When he awakened there were no other vehicles on the road and the rain had ceased. Long clouds hurried across the sky, swirled around a white, shrunken moon. The men and Mavis were singing:

> The state of man does change and vary
> Now sound, now sick, now blyth, now sary
> Now dansand mirry, now like to die
> *timor mortis conturbat me . . .*

It went on and on, mournful verse following mournful verse. Jamie knew his Latin. *Fear of death troubles me.*

> Sen he has all my bretheren tane—

Mavis interrupted them. 'There's the lay-by. Pull in,

Norrey. Terence probably needs another piss for the road.'

They stood in the lay-by drinking strong, milky tea from thick mugs and eating sandwiches of lamb and Pegeen's oatmeal bread. Low hills huddled around them, grey in the moonlight. No houses were to be seen. No sheep bleated. The silence and emptiness seemed to stretch forever. A wave of terrible loneliness surged over Jamie. He wished he were back at Uncle Charlie's, safe in bed.

'Here we are. Wake up, you slug-a-beds.' Mavis seemed as wide awake as if she had had a night's rest. Jamie thought she had sung all night, some songs mournful, some merry, some with words he could not understand. The men had joined in on the choruses, and when Terence had taken over from Norrey at driving, Norrey had played his harp. The sound of the harp and the lark-like voice of Mavis had invaded his sleep and his dreams.

He crawled out of the van, stiff, sour-mouthed, and blinded by the brilliant sunlight. They were parked in an old, cobbled carriageway in front of a barn covered with moss and thick-boled ivy. Heavy oak doors stood open and no sooner were the boys out of the van than Norrey drove it into the darkness beyond. Terence and a stranger swung the doors shut.

Beyond the barn was a meadow, flower-sprinkled, humming with bees, singing with birds. Mavis led them briskly up a path to a house as cloaked in ivy as the barn, with small peaked, leaded windows glittering in the sun.

The kitchen door stood open and a woman waited in the shadows within. 'God save all here,' Mavis said.

'God save ye kindly,' the woman answered. She was as ancient as the house, Jamie thought, but she patted him and Liam on their heads, standing on tiptoe to do so. She sat them down at a deal table where porridge steamed in cracked bowls, there was toast and dark marmalade, and cream so thick it had to be spooned into the cloudy tea.

They spent the entire day in that house while springtime taunted them through the rippled windows. They did a jigsaw puzzle on a table that wobbled on the uneven plank floors. They searched a dusty bookcase and almost quarrelled over who could have a first read of a tattered copy of *Tarzan of the Apes*.

The men were busy in the barn, and the old lady carried their luncheon out to them in a basket. Mavis took a bus into town and didn't return until late afternoon.

By then the men had finished whatever they had been doing. They spent a long time washing up in the kitchen, but even then Norrey's face was spattered with small white specks.

'They've been painting the van,' Liam guessed. 'To look like an ambulance, see?'

After dinner the four men dressed in white uniforms and Mavis in a blue and white pin-striped nurse's dress, with a starched white apron and black stockings and shoes. Her hair was pulled back in a tight knot and pinned under her cap, and she wore the tatty black cape. Liam whistled in astonishment and Jamie felt as if he were gazing at a stranger.

'You laddies try to get some sleep, but don't undress, because we'll be off as soon as we're back and wash the white paint off the van and put the seats back. Pray God it won't rain between now and then, but on the morrow it can rain all it wishes and take off what we can't.'

It was difficult to sleep, knowing what was happening. Besides, the two beds hadn't been slept in for years and were so dusty both Liam and Jamie went into paroxysms of sneezing.

They awakened when they heard the van return. Liam leapt up and started fumbling for his shoes and pulling on his jumper. It was only when neither shoes nor jumper fitted that he realized he had Jamie's. Patiently, Jamie found matches and lit the lamp. Clothing was sorted out. When they emerged into the hall Mavis ordered them back into the room.

'Not yet. We have to change into our own clothes and the paint has to be washed off the van. Bryan's so weak he must be given some broth. I can carry him in my own two arms.' She left them, removing her nurse's cap as she strode down the hall. Her fiery hair, released, writhed down about her shoulders.

Dawn paled the sky and cocks crowed in the distance when once more they were on their way. Jamie rode in front this time so Mavis could be in the back of the van to take care of Bryan. The quick glimpse Jamie had of Bryan was not re-assuring. He looked more like a skeleton than a flesh and blood man. A frilled granny cap on his head made him look the more grotesque.

'It's me old Granny who's fallen ill to the death and we are taking her home to Dublin to her own parish to die and be buried in the family plot.' Mavis laughed at Jamie's shocked expression. 'You have to be devious in this game, Lammondson, if you don't want to be kneecapped or kicked until your entrails fall out of your arsehole. There's one am-bulance driver who'll never walk like a man again after to-night. He objected a little too strenuously to our taking Bryan.'

Norrey drove as if he were in a chariot race. It was so early that the roads were empty. Lorry drivers dozed in lay-bys, farmers in their beds. The slow, early rays of sunrise lay se-rene and soft on the land. Norrey and Terence talked over Jamie's head, but they were so guarded in what they said that he could make little sense of the plans they discussed. He did make out that they were headed for Liverpool from whence they would embark for Dublin, and that they would leave a bit of luggage in the Customs office there 'to be picked up later', a statement which caused them both to guffaw.

Several days later, when a similar 'luggage to be called for' had been left at several Customs huts on the Eire-Northern Ireland borders, Jamie realized why the men had laughed. The luggage left for a non-existent member of The Harp Singers contained bombs. One explosion had blown the house next door to bits, killing two children sleeping in their beds. Jamie tried to tell himself that war was like that. He had heard tales of the London blitz and Coventry, and, from Aunt Mairi, tales of what had happened in Germany. But he was liking this adventure less and less.

Waiting in line at the border or in villages along the way, the van would stop and Norrey would play his harp, Mavis and Terence would sing or do an Irish dance together, while Jamie and Liam passed caps amongst the crowd to collect a few coins. In the van Bryan lay semiconscious, smelly, and more and more shrunken.

'He's not keeping the food down,' Mavis announced. 'All this travelling about is doing him ill. We must get him to a loney, a safe house.'

They were headed north by then, leaving the border stations behind. An appearance by The Harp Singers on the BBC station in Londonderry had been arranged. Norrey was against it, for already the van was under suspicion, but Terence argued that appearing would confirm their innocence. Mavis had to be persuaded with a promise that they would take care of Bryan immediately afterwards. There was a safe house in the hills outside Londonderry, still unknown to the authorities.

'We won't be unknown to the authorities after the

bomb goes off at the BBC.'

'It is set to go off two days after our appearance, woman. By then we'll be away and the van repainted. You're going soft because of Bryan.'

'We didn't save him to let him die. He could have done that in gaol.'

'We *need* that appearance,' Terence said firmly and Mavis gave in with a shrug. 'It's a bold move,' she said. Too bold to be healthy.

Mrs Partland was not unintelligent, but her intelligence had never been put to good use. She had married too young, been a good wife and mother until her husband and her child were killed when a bomb hit their house. For a long time she had felt guilty for not having been at home to die with them. She had gone to visit her husband's sister who had just given birth to her first child. She could no longer bear to live in London and had returned home to Glasgow to begin a new life.

She had been fortunate to obtain the position in the Maccallum household after Mr Maccallum's shameless young wife had deserted him and her child. But in another year Master Charles would be in school, and her usefulness would begin to come to an end. Sometimes she prayed that Mr Maccallum would marry again. A wife young enough to produce children, and that she, Mrs Partland, would continue to be needed.

She realized that she was not a success with Jamie and Liam. They were at a difficult age, she told herself. More child than adult, but adult enough to be no longer children. She felt that she always said the wrong things to them and that they laughed behind her back.

She was glad when the school called the enforced holiday

and they went to the castle. She did not trouble herself—they would resent her interference, however well intentioned—to telephone to ask how they were.

The plumbing problems at school carried on for two weeks, then notice was sent that classes would resume. It was then she telephoned the castle. Maureen was out 'going messages', the maid who answered said. Nor were the lads there. She seemed puzzled about classes being resumed. Mrs Partland assumed she was young and not very bright. The lads were probably tramping in the Campsies and perhaps had not even told her of their unexpected holiday.

Several days later the headmaster telephoned to inquire why the boys were absent. Exasperated, Mrs Partland telephoned the castle again. She suspected that the stupid girl had not relayed her message.

Again Maureen was out and the same maid, Dora, said that she remembered Mrs Partland calling with a message. But the lads were long away.

Mrs Partland had no way of knowing that 'long away' referred to a long-ago weekend rather than taking the train to the school. And Dora thought Mrs Partland a daft old hen to be worrying her with dafter messages. It was not until Mrs Partland replaced the receiver that she thought she should have asked if Dora had given them the message. Charlie returned that evening and was surprised to find neither Jamie nor Liam at home. He listened in bewilderment to Mrs Partland's confused account of the boiler and broken plumbing pipes and the lads being at the castle, but that they had not returned to school for some reason, probably because the maid had not passed the messages on to them. He was thoughtful for a few moments, then went to telephone the castle.

Mrs Partland sat beside the fire, hands clenched, with a

dreadful feeling of foreboding. She began to cry as soon as he returned and she saw the expression on his face.

'They are not at the castle and have not been at the castle all this time, Partland. Stop sobbing, please, and tell me all this again.'

This time he listened more patiently, interrupting only to assure her that it was not her fault, but some mischief of their own, and that she would not be dismissed. When she had finished, he said, 'That means they have been missing for over two weeks. I must speak to Maureen again. I have a strong suspicion that she knows something.'

The line to the castle was engaged. It was half an hour before he got through to her and he had another sobbing woman to deal with. By the time he had finished speaking to her he had enough of the story to suspect that the boys had gone with Mavis without the permission of Maureen's brother Sean, who had sworn by the graves of their dead parents that he had forbidden Jamie to go, and urged Liam not to go because Maureen had objected.

'If they are with that lot that is going about bombing Customs stations they'll get themselves imprisoned, or worse still, be killed. I'll go see this Sean chap myself. He should be able to tell me how to deal with the authorities without risking their lives. And—yes—I shall cable Lady Lammondson. Pour yourself a sherry and calm down, Partland. We are fortunate they haven't been abducted.'

He was not as confident as he sounded. Abducted with a demand for ransom seemed infinitely preferable to wandering around Northern Ireland with a band of rebels who were bombing Customs stations. He cursed himself for having allowed Jamie—there had been nothing he could do about Liam—to attend those wild Irish gatherings at 'Uncle Sean's' house.

★ ★ ★ ★ ★

Mrs Partland was still up when Charlie returned home. Breathless, she met him in the hall before he had removed his hat and coat.

'Oh, Mr Maccallum, after you left I had the sherry you offered so kindly and sat down to watch the television thinking it would take my mind off this terrible affair. There was a singing group from BBC Londonderry—The Harp Singers, I believe they called themselves. It was very beautiful. Old ballads. And at one point the camera roved over the audience and there in the front row I am sure I saw Master Jamie and Liam. Only for a second, mind you, and I could have been mistaken. But it did look so like them, I waited up to tell you.'

'If the group was The Harp Singers it very probably was them. The trouble is, Mr Grogan convinced me that the worst possible thing we could do would be to call in the authorities. It could result in a shoot-out. He's making inquiries of his own. With that, we have to be satisfied, whether we wish to be or not.'

Mrs Partland finally quietened down enough to stop apologizing and go off—reluctantly—to her bed. Charlie poured a stiff whisky and sat down by the guttering fire. This was the crowning touch to an unsuccessful business trip and a disappointing meeting with Amelia. Tomorrow he would have to tell Fa that not only had the contract for the seaward defence boats gone to Yarrows, but that the boys were cavorting about in Ireland with a cell of the IRA.

Fa paid little attention to the yard any more. For a long time it had been his main interest in life, but that interest had died along with Memsah'b. The only time he interfered—perhaps, in fairness, that was not the term—in the yard's affairs was when Charlie suggested introducing new, post-war techniques. In Fa's eyes they were radical because they were new. It did no good to point out that Yarrows had gone ahead, coming to terms with the new ideas, and it was Yarrows which was surviving.

Charlie had not yet told him that new orders no longer came in as fast as they once had done. That they were far less than five years behind in fulfilling contracts. It had been good, too good, while it lasted, but now the world shipbuilding capacity could handle double the world's requirements. And countries other than Scotland could build for less.

As for Amelia, he had cajoled her mother into giving him her London address. After she had given in, she had seemed almost pleased with herself. 'She was always overly fond of you, Mr Maccallum. But I always warned her, it wouldn't do. Class must stay true to class, Amelia, I said. Otherwise it's courting disaster. I suppose you're wanting her to come back as your secretary. Good help these days is so difficult. These young girls think of nothing but nylons and boys.'

He had not told Mrs Maclean that it was not as a secretary that he wanted Amelia, but as a wife, and class differences be damned. When she had resigned she had admitted that she was in love with him. He hoped that, during the long time that they had been apart, her love had become deeper, as had his. In a few months he would be free. Perhaps he was a fool to try again to win her, but try he must.

Perhaps her mother had warned her, but Amelia had not seemed surprised when he had telephoned her. She had agreed almost demurely to go to dinner with him.

They had met at a small, quiet, upstairs French restaurant where they could talk undisturbed. The change in her had surprised him. Poised, chicly dressed, Scottish accent gone, she was a new Amelia and even more desirable. He was in love with her as he had never been in love with Meg. When he had told her that she had given him a Mona Lisa smile.

'I admit I sometimes miss you, but I have learnt to do without you. The days no longer begin and end with you as they once did. And I doubt I could ever return to Glasgow or to a—a situation I am not sure I could handle. Let us settle for being old acquaintances.'

Old acquaintances. Did she think she was in a play?

She allowed him to kiss her good night, but hers was a passionless kiss and she released herself from his embrace gently, but definitely.

He had cancelled his train ticket and flown home because London was full of disappointment. The fire had gone out. His glass was empty. He could still hear her voice. 'I have learnt to do without you . . .'

And somewhere in Ireland in a van full of gelignite, were his nephew and Liam, and God knew how he would get them back again.

Charlie had spent a sleepless night. His interview with Sean Grogan had been brief and angry, conducted on Grogan's doorstep.

'There's no call for you to come storming my house and threatening me and demanding their return. The young scoundrels duped us both and any meddling on your part will only result in disaster to all concerned.' He slammed the door in Charlie's face.

When Charlie met Tad and Jan for luncheon the next day he was already finishing his second whisky, which was doing nothing to cheer him nor was it resting well on the breakfast he had half-eaten.

'London must have been a gruelling ordeal,' Tad observed. 'No point in asking if the trip was a success. It shows on your face.'

'What I returned to was worse than London. Jamie and

Liam have run away and are busy blowing up Ireland.'

'They're with that crew that is in the news just now?' Jan was incredulous.

Charlie attempted to explain over yet another whisky. Tad's face grew grave. He tugged at his moustache, drummed the table with his fingers, and left his drink untouched.

'You had no information or satisfaction from the uncle?'

'None. I suspect he has some idea of their whereabouts, but he wasn't telling. He advised me that if I want them safe, I should do nothing.'

'He is probably right about that, but there are other ways. Thank God Fionna doesn't know.'

'She will soon enough. I cabled her asking her to telephone. I thought she should know.'

Tad groaned. 'So, we shall have to move fast. Let me think a bit.' He sipped thoughtfully at his drink while Jan and Charlie remained silent. Charlie no longer had thoughts enough to think. After a short silence Tad emptied his glass. 'No more whisky, old friend. Food is what you want and so do I. Then we see this uncle. If he knows where they are, he shall tell us where they are.' He signalled to the waiter who had been hovering restlessly in the background.

'If he wouldn't tell Maureen for the sake of her son, or me, why do you think he will tell you?'

'Polish persuasion. I'll have the ploughman's lunch and a pint of bitter, please.'

Sean Grogan was not happy to see Mr Maccallum and the Polish Major with the unpronounceable name ushered into the room he called his office. Pegeen knew that room was sacred territory, but she was still angry with him for having slammed the door in Mr Maccallum's face the night before. 'Not only is your own widowed sister weeping her heart away for her son, but you've got the gentry on you as well, and who knows what will happen now,' she had said. 'A real gentle-man would have asked him in, sweetened him with drink and talked to him man to man.'

And sure enough now, they were scarce in his office but she had brought the bottle of Irish and the best Waterford glasses. The Bible erred in referring to Satan as a male, Sean thought. Satan was female, no doubt about it.

He gave them a surly greeting, some of the surliness di-rected at Pegeen and a bit left over for the precious whisky. He attempted to seat the gentlemen with their backs to the map on the wall, but the Major spotted it at once, and exam-ined it before he took his chair.

'A fine map of Ireland you have there, Mr Grogan. I take it the pins mark their progress. The black pins are the marks they have hit, the blues are the various cells as we called them in the underground. The red, I would guess to be new targets, and the green their present location.'

By the saints, the man was clever. 'Aye. They are in a loney, that is, a safe house in the hills. But I'll no' be telling you where it is.'

'I can see where it is, but not that it is safe.'

'I am telling you it is safe or they'd no' be there.' The arro-gance of the man. That was officers for you. Maccallum, on the other hand, seemed to have aged ten years since last night. Well, Sean had been in that situation himself many a time, living on hope, fear, whisky, and little else.

'You think Jamie and Liam are safe?'

'As if they were in the pocket of God.' Sean had a feeling that his voice betrayed the conviction that he did not feel. 'Mavis can be a bit of a bitch, but she'll no' let the lads be harmed. She'll send them packing at the first smell of trou-ble.'

'On their own?'

'Well . . . aye. They're no longer babes.'

The Major, glass in hand, rose again and studied the map. 'This is the main road and this a long country track leading off it to the house, right? And this, where the hills come together? Is it a footpath?' Sean nodded. 'This is the house? And this broken line?' Tad waited. 'Mr Grogan?'

Sean cleared his throat. 'A—a tunnel. Scarce large enough for a hare. It leads from the cellars.'

To his and Charlie's surprise, Tad took a camera from his pocket, clicked on the flash button, and snapped three pictures of the map before Sean could protest.

'That tunnel is the way Mavis would send the lads away if there were trouble?'

Mesmerized now, Sean nodded.

'Then that is where I shall await them. I will alert no authorities, make no trouble, betray no one, including you. If you are in touch with this woman, tell her that a poor wandering musician will be loitering in the hills, waiting for the lads when they emerge from the hare's burrow. And if they do not emerge, every British patrol in Ireland will know the location of the safe house.'

'There's no way I'll be in touch,' Sean said hoarsely. 'The house is not on the telephone and the post does not deliver there.' He poured another round of whisky and tossed off his drink. 'You'll never pull it off, mannie. You are a fool to try. The main road'll be mined. The dawn patrol goes out and picks off every loiterer.'

'Show me where the mines would be. Tell me how to avoid the patrol.'

Beaten, knowing he was beaten, wondering how it had come about, Sean rose to his feet and went to the map. When he had finished he sat down heavily. 'You'll have to trust Mavis. She's no' a bad woman for all she's a bitch.

Strong-willed, aye. Persuasive. Doing what she is doing for Ireland. I am taking your word you'll not betray the cause. It's only the lads you want?' His voice was pleading.

'Rightly or wrongly, it's only the lads.'

'Then,' he sighed, 'go with my blessing and may the saints go before you and guide you when you return.'

The safe house was an old, greystone farmhouse, riddled with passages and unexpected corners and rotted window frames. The panes rattled in the slightest breeze, cold air seeped in through the gaps in the wood. There was little furniture and many of the chairs had only three legs and the upholstery worn through to reveal dusty horsehair and bulging springs. The carpets were moth-eaten. The kitchen smelled of sour milk. The basement was cached with weapons taken in raids on the barracks of the territorial army.

Housed there were fifteen or twenty—Jamie could not be sure of the number because they came and went so often—young men in green battledress who were armed with US army surplus war equipment.

Bryan died a week after The Harp Singers arrived. He was buried at a distance from the house where there were mounds of other unmarked graves.

Mavis wailed and sobbed. Liam called it keening. Norrey said Bryan was well out of it, and Mavis leapt on him like an angry cat and tore out a handful of his hair. Norrey clouted her and they fell to the floor, kicking and wrestling. It took Terence and Laurence to separate them.

They were still gasping for breath and glaring at one another when the radio, which was kept turned on all the time, announced that there was a mountainside search under way for the suspected bombers of various Customs stations and the BBC.

Mavis forgot her sorrow. 'The van. We must get rid of it. I knew that BBC appearance was a daft idea. But no one would listen to me. Norrey, you and Terence take the van away. Far away.'

'Oh, aye, and how are we to do that, with the roads bristling with traps and soldiers behind every stone wall?'

'Don't ask me how to do it? Are you a man or a snivelling brat?'

Norrey shrugged and jerked his head towards Terence. They went out together, jingling the ignition keys and muttering.

The young men in green left for various lookout posts in the hills, and others mounted guard on the loose slate tiles of the roof.

It had been a long week, but Jamie and Liam had been allowed to play on an old overgrown bowling green with some balls they had found in a dusty cupboard. But this day they were not allowed out. The sagging shutters were closed and they sat in the semi-darkness of the house, waiting.

Once there was gunfire in the distance. Later one of the young men was carried to the house, his green blouse stained with blood.

At four o'clock the radio asked everyone to stand by for a special announcement. Jamie nearly fell off his chair when he heard his mother's voice.

'This is Fionna, Lady Lammondson, in Glasgow. I am speaking to my son believed to be somewhere in Ireland. Jamie, I am back from Africa. I want you to come home. I know you hunger for adventure and to do a grand thing, but I beg you, come back.'

He was glad the room was dark enough that no one could see his tears. Mavis started to speak, but another voice followed. It was Maureen and her voice was not controlled as

Fionna's had been. The sorrowful anger came across as clearly as if she stood before them.

'Liam, do you want to end up like your father. Not enough left of you to bury? Ireland may be worth it, but our history is a history of martyrs and, God help us, nothing has changed. Nor will you change it. It is your choice. Stay and carry on the fight or come back and, as an educated man, work for the reconciliation of Ireland and the country which gave us refuge. Whatever choice you make, I bless you and pray God will keep you safe.'

'Damn mothers!' Mavis exploded. 'Tying you to their aprons, hiding you under their skirts. Coward-makers is what they are.'

'Nah, Mavis, be kind,' Laurence said.

'You heard her say she'd let me make the choice. I'll stay with you. That I will.' Liam's voice was choked.

'We're not wanting you. Away with both of you. You're nothing but worthless burdens. It was a daft idea to bring you at all.'

'Be kind, Mavis.'

'Leave off telling me to be kind, Laurence. Kindness is not needed here. It's gunfire against gunfire, blood for blood, death for death.' Jamie had a feeling she would have gone on striding up and down, catching her heel in the worn carpet and kicking it free, her voice growing shrill, her words tumbling over her lips, smoky as her cigarette. But one of the guards outside banged the door with his rifle butt. 'They're closing in! Better take cover! Jaysus! They're an army!'

Laurence grabbed Jamie by the shoulder. 'Quick. Down the cellar. There's a passage out to the hills.'

Jamie cast an agonized look at Liam, hoping he would follow. Liam's eyes were glazed. He seemed hypnotized by Mavis. Laurence was shoving Jamie before him, pushing him roughly down the worn stone steps into the damp, black cavern beneath the kitchen floor. Dark as it was, Laurence knew his way through the darkness.

'This way. You can't get lost. It leads nowhere but out. Sorry there's no torch, but you can feel your way along the wall. Once you're free, start running. You'll be safe.'

'Thank you, sir. I wish Liam—'

But Laurence was already hurrying up the steps. Jamie heard the door slam behind him. This was how it felt to be blind. He could not see the walls which he touched, he could not see the way before him or the cavern behind. Hesitantly, he took a step, then another. The walls were damp and cold, the air dank and stale. Gradually, his steps quickened. Once he fell over fallen earth. His heart pounded. The walls or the roof of the passage might cave in and he would be trapped forever, never found. He got to his feet and went on. Silence reverberated like waves in his ears.

Now the darkness dimmed. He could see his hands and the gleam of seepage on the wall. The passage became so low, so narrow, he had to crawl on hands and knees, and finally, wriggle completely flat, pushing himself forward by his feet. There was light ahead, bright light which hurt his eyes. The opening was so small that he had to put one shoulder through at a time. Then he was lying, head down, in grass so tall that he was completely hidden. Cautiously he knelt and looked around. He was in a narrow cleft of hills which sloped steeply downwards to a fold scarcely wide enough for a farm cart.

Far away from beyond the hills came the echoes of gunfire. It sounded as harmless as the champagne corks which exploded when a Maccallum ship was launched. He hunkered on a mossy stone trying to think what to do. The sun was warm and the air so fresh after the tunnel that it was like coming back to life. He wished Liam were with him. Liam would have a plan. Not that Liam's plans were always the wisest, Jamie now knew.

Deep in thought, at first he could not believe what he was hearing. It was a guitar and Jamie knew the tune as well as he knew his name. His mother, Uncle Charlie and Jan used to sing it while Koko played the guitar which had belonged to the Uncle Carlos Jamie had never known.

> There's a valley in Spain called Jarama
> It's a place that we all know so well . . .

Jamie stood up slowly, as if he were a sleepwalker. He had died in the tunnel and it was all a dream. No longer blinking in the unaccustomed light, he saw what he had not seen in his first dazzled look around. A tramp, a tinkerman, sitting on a rock at the base of the hills, strumming his guitar. 'You will never be happy with strangers . . .'

He began to run. He ran as he had never run before, stumbling over his own feet as he negotiated the steep slope of the hill, catching his foot in the long grasses. Panting, he grabbed the tramp by the arm, grinning with happiness, grinning at the shabby clothes.

'Koko! Oh, Koko, you—' he laughed. 'You look as if you're dressed for Guy Fawkes Day and you're the Guy.'

'From the sounds coming from over the hillsides, I'd say it *is* Guy Fawkes Day and the fireworks have begun.' Tad put the guitar into its case and swung it over his shoulder. 'And it's time we were on our way.'

'I wish Liam had come.'

'That may be him creeping down the hill now.'

Jamie looked and gave Liam a hail. Liam broke into a gallop, leaping over the grass like a hill pony.

'I heard my mum on the radio,' Jamie said. 'I wish you

would marry the woman and put some sense into her head.'

'We were waiting for you to come back and give her your permission. Ah, here's Liam. I told Maureen that I would bring you back. Your uncle showed me where the tunnel opened out. You are both fortunate, you know. I suppose it was a great adventure to begin with. That's how wars are made.'

'I'm a coward to desert them, but Mavis threw me down the cellar steps and bolted the door after me. Wars should be left to women like her. Violent is what she is. So, where do we go from here?'

'Home. Right, Koko?'

'Right.'

7

'Mairi dear,' Fionna's letter read, 'please come to my wedding. I want you to meet Tad, and it would do Fa a world of good to see you. He asked if he might give me away and how could I refuse? He is getting old, Mairi. (Well, aren't we all?) At my age it seems a bit daft to be "given". Presumably, I am at an age to know my own mind. The ceremony is to be in the long south room at Milkstone, *your* Milkstone now. So you should be here.

'There is to be a real, old-fashioned *ceilidh* after. Comrades from our war: Spain. Tad got in touch with many of them through a printer he met in Edinburgh. One of them actually worked at Maccallums' from '41 to '47—and I never knew, nor did Charlie. There's a great lady whom you would like. She lives in Fife now. I didn't know her in Spain, she was mostly in a small hospital near Barcelona. We shall probably end the evening singing the old songs, boring everyone but ourselves.

'Please, can you come, will you come? Do you still hold out hope that Erich is alive after all this time? Or should I not ask? There are other men, Mairi. And there is always Milkstone which belongs to you and you should see it again, give it your love. If Erich did come back, he would find you . . .'

Before Mairi had finished reading the letter the answer was forming in her mind. 'No, I cannot come because, yes, I still have hope. I would know if he were dead. He would have said goodbye to me. I have never told anyone before, but

Memsah'b came. I was in the garden picking lilacs. Do you remember old what-was-her-name, the upstairs maid at Milkstone, thought lilacs were bad luck and scolded whenever Memsah'b said to cut them and that the only bad luck about lilacs was that they harboured ticks? I was thinking about that as I picked lilacs, and suddenly Memsah'b was with me. I don't know how to explain it. It was not herself, but as a presence, surrounding me, everywhere. I could feel her, almost hear her although I was not conscious of her speaking. She was there. I spoke her name and said, "Have you come to say goodbye?" as if I knew that she had died. I cried for her and the next day Fa's cable came from Calcutta. If Erich were dead he, too, would have come. You know yourself that we Scots have a touch of the fey.'

Should she tell Fionna that there had been other men. There had been Maxl. There had been a man when she had worked at the Embassy in Bad Godesberg. The affair they had was one of the richest experiences of her life. It had been their love, which she did not trust, her need of him, the temptation to give in, that had caused her to leave the Embassy and return to the *Schloss*. She had come into Memsah'b's money by then and no longer needed to work. But the need did not subside slowly. He had written to her at Christmas saying that if she ever changed her mind he would be waiting . . .

There were many—too many—times when she was tempted to pick up the telephone, to hear his voice, to say 'It is Mairi . . .' He would understand at once. She would go to him.

Then, on a day when her hand was actually on the telephone, there had come that mysterious cable from the German Embassy in Istanbul. 'Do you know Erich Eduard Christoph Trötzen stop Claims to be your husband.'

She had cabled, offered to send money, demanded more information. A month, six weeks, passed, before a stiff, formal letter came. 'The person about whom you enquired, Erich Eduard Christoph Trötzen, is no longer in contact with us. He did not return to the Embassy after his initial visit. We have no knowledge of his whereabouts.'

Nor did she, but she would wait, as Penelope waited.

Wait in idleness, as wasting days passed. Long empty evenings sitting on the balcony watching the evening mists of hot summer drift up from the river, to flow along the streets, then slowly, oh, so slowly engulf the houses, swirl around the golden cock on the church steeple, lap at the road up to the *Schloss*.

She seldom thought in English now, but last night a nightingale had awakened her and Keats' Ode had come to mind. 'Thou wast not born for death . . .'

Others could doubt, she knew Erich was alive.

The mist turned to spindrift just short of the moat. The dampness drew out the scent of the garden, cooled the heat which had warmed the stones of the *Schloss*, muffled the sound of the church bells ringing the hour.

A figure formed in the mist, moved unevenly up the steep road, becoming clearer as the mist thinned. A limping man, fleshless as a ghost. She felt a pang of fear. She was alone in the *Schloss*. The maids and cook went home to the village at night. Hannes was in Switzerland on his obligatory holiday with Maxl and Vikki. Edu had gone to France to visit Lilli and George.

'Who are you? What do you want?'

The man halted, turned his face up to her and raised his arms. 'Mairi? Mairi? It is Erich. I have come home.'

On a late April day when the ground was thawing enough

to be soft underfoot, but had not yet turned into the deep, spring mud, the Governor had come to Erich's office and asked him to accompany him on a walk. Something in his face made Erich quick to agree.

Janek watched him, silently, as Erich weighted down the papers on which he had been working and shrugged on his coat. As they walked Janek talked in generalities, gesturing at the mine facing from time to time, commenting on the weather, the number of men in hospital, the increasing number of deaths which always came with spring.

'They are underfed and live in miserable conditions,' Erich interrupted.

Janek gave him a reproving look. 'It is always so.' He said no more until they were a long distance from the buildings and the workings. The birch and wild shrubs were budding and spears of small wildflowers penetrated the softening earth.

Janek took Erich's arm and gestured with his other at a flight of birds flying northwards. Then, still looking at the sky, he whispered, 'Stalin is dead.'

'What!'

'Lower your voice, comrade. Who knows what devices they have that may hear a whisper even at this distance? Yes,' he continued in a normal voice, 'what a sight to see a flight like that. I remember times before the war when the sky was black with birds and the sound of their wings beating the air surpassed all other sounds. Spring cannot be far away. He died on March the third. I am to be rehabilitated.'

'I do not understand.'

'You think I am here by choice? What innocence. It was a trifling matter, but I am free now. I shall be leaving in a week.'

'How does this affect me?'

'Officially, not at all. Unofficially, you are going to disappear. There will be a delay before my replacement arrives, poor fellow. He backed the wrong horse, but at best he has not been purged. Now the loss is his and my ticket has won.

'I have a bit of money put aside. I believe it is called padding the accounts. A dangerous business, but what could they do when I was already in exile? Well, send me to East Siberia, perhaps, to work the mines myself instead of sitting in an office. I intend to share some of the money with you. You cannot accuse me of being an unmerciful man, Trötzen. I will tell the others and leave word for the replacement that you have gone, on my orders, to Tom'-Usk where they are having equipment problems. The replacement will be new here and too dispirited to be concerned at first. The man at Tom'-Usk is also being sent home and *his* replacement will know nothing of your supposed visit. I doubt there will be any hue and cry for some time. By then, they will have trouble tracing you, if you are careful. They may not even bother.'

'Why are you doing this? And is it possible?'

'The possibility depends on you. As to your other question, I am doing it because you, too, were, in effect, a prisoner of Stalin. Other Germans have been exchanged. There have been enquiries about you left unanswered. You made yourself too valuable, too efficient, to be released.'

'And if I had not?' Erich's voice was sharp.

'Who knows?'

'What about the others? The prisoners? The soldiers?'

'Ah, those.' Janek spread his hands helplessly. 'For them there is little hope.'

'That is outrageous.'

'It was the fault of your Hitler. I can do nothing for them. It is a delicate matter.'

'If other prisoners have been exchanged, why not these?'

'No orders have come for their release. Perhaps it has been

forgotten that they are here. Perhaps those who knew them died in the air raids.'

'Set them free yourself.'

'For them to wander through the countryside, living off the land, to be arrested or shot? There isn't a peasant in Russia who wouldn't shoot them on sight.'

'Is that what I am to expect? To be shot on sight?'

'You will be alone, not a battalion of ragged prisoners escaped from a penal colony. You have learned enough of the language to communicate. You are an intelligent man, a gentleman. You will have a bit of money, but you must spend it cautiously. I have prepared maps for you. Do not stray into Mongolia. From there the only way out is into China. My advice is to head for the Caspian and cross it however you can into Georgia. The Georgians are good fellows. Friendly. Hospitable. Someone there will help you into Turkey. Once there you should be safe. It stayed neutral in the war, having learned its lesson in the first one. There is a German Embassy there. They will help you.'

Erich listened in growing disbelief. 'You are talking of three thousand kilometres or more as the crow flies. How am I to get there?'

'By your wits and your feet.'

'There is no chance of taking the railway?'

'You will not have the proper papers.'

'I have no papers at all,' Erich reminded him. 'They were taken away when *I* was taken from Poland.'

Janek put his arm around Erich's shoulder and gave an affectionate pat. 'It is freedom, comrade. Isn't freedom worth the risk?'

The risk of wandering, being shot, taken prisoner again and sent God knew where that time? Wasn't it better to grow old here? He had long suspected that all the letters he had written had never been sent or that Mairi was dead, killed in the Allied air raids. But unless he tried, he would wonder about her forever, just as he wondered about Marya.

'When shall I go?'

'Tomorrow?'

'Tomorrow!'

'The country is still in turmoil due to what we shall call recent events. The sooner you leave, the better. I myself shall drive you the first stage of your journey on the pretext that I am accompanying you to Tom'-Usk to visit my friend there and see to the trouble there myself. I shall return alone, saying you needed to remain. By then, I shall not be here to answer questions.' Janek cocked his head at Erich, rather like a questioning bird. 'Are you game?'

'Only a madman would say yes. Only a fool would say no.'

'*Horosho!* Or in your language, *wunderbar!* We shall plan all tonight.'

They spent the evening poring over maps, discussing various routes. 'I suppose there is no chance that I could return by way of Silesia,' Erich said.

'That *would* be the act of a madman. You would never get that far without papers. There was a woman there, wasn't there? I see. To return, even if you made it, would do nothing but harm to both of you. Take my advice and head for Turkey. Now let us see how best to get there . . .'

Was it better to avoid cities or villages? Cities ensured anonymity, but also contained efficient police. Villages would be suspicious of strangers, but unlikely to report one unless he stole or made trouble. Villages, too, wished to avoid the police.

'Depend on your instincts as an animal would do. Danger has a smell about it, an electricity which prickles our prehistoric senses. Never mistrust a rising of your hackles. Be alert to the feeling that all is not well.' Janek folded the map carefully. 'Do not lose it. Study the stars by night and the sun by day. It will be a great adventure, comrade. I half envy you.'

Erich grinned. 'That is a lie, Janek. You cannot wait to return to Moscow.'

'I am not so old that I do not hanker for adventure. So! I will call for you at dawn and we will be off for Tom'-Usk by way of nowhere.'

Erich spent what remained of the evening packing a rucksack with supplies. Potatoes, onions, dried peas, vodka, rye flour, matches, an old-fashioned tinder box, a stew pot, and some dried meat.

Without undressing, he tried to rest, but sleep evaded him. He was up pacing the floor long before he heard the small truck. The sky was dark and full of stars, and the lamps of the truck scarcely pierced the darkness. Janek was in a jovial mood.

'So, I have my little adventure.'

'It seems to me, after our discussion last night, that you could have escaped any time, Janek.'

'To go where? I am Russian. Any country I attempted to enter would send me back immediately. Nor would I want to be anywhere but in Mother Russia.'

He threw the truck into gear and set off at a pace as if they were pursued. He drove so wildly, swinging around corners as if they did not exist, swaying from one side of the road to the other, that Erich half-feared they would overturn. When the sky began to turn grey Janek left the road to follow what seemed to be little more than a long-unused cart trail, but he did not slacken his speed. They jolted on and on, tall grass bending before them, birches slapping the windows. The forest stretched endlessly on either side and often the road was so swampy that mud was flung against the wind-shield. After a while Erich fell asleep.

When he awakened the sun was overhead. Janek had pulled into a clearing scarcely large enough to accommodate the truck. The only sounds were the cries of birds and the whine of mosquitoes.

'A rest and some food,' Janek said. 'You talked in your sleep, comrade.'

'What did I say?'

'A woman's name.' He went into the trees to relieve himself and Erich did the same. Then Janek produced vodka, bread, slices of ham, and hardboiled eggs. They ate standing, slapping off mosquitoes, gulping vodka and water. The meal finished, Janek refilled the tank from a gasoline tin. They drove on and on. Late in the afternoon as darkness gathered the forest thinned. They passed a *dacha* of grey, unpainted wood. The door hung from one hinge and the shutters had been smashed, Janek leant on the brakes, throwing himself and Erich forward. Then he reversed and pulled to a stop in front of the building.

'Here we sleep.' He jerked the door off its remaining hinge and peered inside. Two stools, a table with a leg missing and two wooden bunks built against the wall were the furnishing. Janek grunted with satisfaction.

Night gathered quickly and they ate by lamplight. The meal was the same as they had had at noon. This time the vodka was undiluted. Erich slept poorly because Janek was restless. He was up and down a dozen times, peering out of the door, taking a swig of vodka, cursing the mosquitoes. Finally he awakened Erich by shaking him.

'I am leaving. I dare go no further without more fuel. You will be all right from here on. As a child I was taught to believe in God and to pray. Then I learnt there is no God. Perhaps you still believe. If you do, I say, God go with you and protect you.'

Erich walked out to the truck with him. 'Good luck, Janek. Thank you.' They embraced, then Janek climbed into the machine.

'I left the ham and bread, but not the vodka.' He laughed. 'I shall need it more than you.'

The truck lurched off. Erich watched until its lights glowing against the trees were no longer visible and the sound of the engine was lost.

Silence made a surf-like sound against his ears. He understood what had ailed Janek. They had forgotten what silence and solitude were. It had been too long since they had been alone.

He was tired and would have liked to go back to bed, but the journey ahead stretched before him like infinity.

It was difficult to follow the old cart road. He stumbled in the ruts, and tangled grass caught at his feet like traps. His eyes grew accustomed to the dark, so he soon caught the gleam of streams and marshy ground. But he mistook bushes for bears or gigantic human beings. The rustling of the wind in the trees, or perhaps animals, alarmed him.

When dawn came he rested in a thicket, well off the road, and ate some ham and bread. He could have eaten more but already he worried about how he could replenish his supplies. Sooner or later it would be necessary to make contact with others. There was no way of knowing what that would lead to.

Towards afternoon he began to climb, leaving the birch forest behind to be replaced by pine. The ground was firmer here. Walking was easier. Patches of snow lay unmelted under the low branches. Then the pines thinned and he was on a high, windy pass, snow-deep, cold.

It would soon be dark, but he dared not sleep up here, risking frost-bite. Wearily, he went on, falling once on loose stones, aching in muscle and body. When night came he was back in the pines. He gathered cones and dead branches and built a small fire, heated snow so he could drink hot water with his frugal meal. Despite the cold, he slept deeply that night and awoke refreshed.

The days took on a sameness. Gradually he noticed that daylight came earlier and the twilight later. His muscles no longer ached. The cold lessened. Twice he saw hunters in the distance and heard their gunshot. Later in the day he saw smoke from village roofs. He longed for human company, but dared not risk making an appearance.

He had heard of men's experiences in the *taiga,* the fright and yet the holiness of being alone, the trees always whispering as if the forest were full of ghosts. To shut out his fear he concentrated on the birds nesting and their constant twittering, on the bats who came out to feed when evening came, flying on silent wings. Sometimes he sang, sometimes recited poetry to himself . . .

> Kennst du das Land, wo die Zitronen Blühn?
> . . . Dahin! Dahin!
> Möcht ich mit dir, o mein Geliebter, ziehn!

He was low on food now. Only a few potatoes and onions were left, and the onions were going soft and rotten. One evening as he was roasting potatoes in the coals of a fire he was startled to see a man standing before him. The soft grass had masked the sound of his footsteps and he had moved through the trees unseen. He was ragged and bearded as Erich himself, and Erich thought his eyes had a gleam of madness. Perhaps his own did as well.

They studied one another a moment. Erich spoke first. 'Comrade?'

'*Da.*'

Erich gestured at his fire. 'Are you hungry?'

The man nodded.

'I will share with you. Sit down.'

He tried to make conversation but the man answered in shrugs and grunts. He continually glanced uneasily over his shoulders. Erich began to wonder if he was being pursued. But when he asked the man shook his head. He would not say where he had come from or where he was going, he would not give his name. He ate ravenously. Regretfully, Erich watched his last chunk of bread disappear into the mouth of rotten teeth, his last onion eaten raw. That left two potatoes.

Having eaten, the man rolled himself in his long ragged coat and fell asleep, close to the fire. Erich watched him for a while, too uneasy to sleep himself. But it had been a long day and despite himself he soon dozed off. He awakened when the birds began to sing at dawn. The man was gone and with him the potatoes, the canteen of water, the matches. The tinder box was still there. Perhaps he had not known how to use it. His money! Did he still have it? It was there, fastened low in his trousers. Fortunately the man had not risked searching him. Perhaps he thought there was nothing worth finding. Erich was thankful he had not had his throat cut. But without food, he would now have to risk a farmhouse or a village.

He no longer knew how long he had been walking. He judged it must be mid-summer because dawn came early and the light lingered long into the evening. Birds' nests were deserted, for the fledglings now flew and fed on their own. The streams from melting snow were sluggish and muddy, and held no more fish. The mushrooms he found were curled from the heat, and the wild berries had been taken by the birds.

His boots had long since worn so badly they had to be discarded. He walked barefoot now, his feet calloused and toughened.

Light-headed, giddy from hunger, he stumbled on. In the evenings he searched the valleys for smoke that would indicate a house or a village. He saw none.

Late one afternoon when he thought he could go no further and must die alone from the torture of starvation, he heard men's voices echoing across the valley. Their laughter reassured him. Men who laughed so heartily would be merciful men, neither police nor soldiers.

Following the sound, he reached a steep slope and saw four men lolling at ease, sharing food and passing a bottle. Before he could reach them, they tossed the bottle into the bushes and stood up, preparing to leave. They had guns with them, and each had a brace of rabbits, squirrels, and large birds. Surely such men would spare a bit of food for a starving man.

At first they did not hear him hailing them. He called and called again, stumbling down the slope as he did so. They looked up, alarmed. One shouldered his gun and took aim, but did not fire.

Hands high in the air, Erich tried to run, missed his footing and slid down the hill in a cascade of loosened stones and earth. Flailing arms and legs in an effort to stop himself, he succeeded instead in catching one leg in the spiked branches of a dead bush. He heard the bone crack as the slide carried him on. Then, as pain sickened him, a stone struck his head, sending him into darkness.

When he came to, the four men were hunkered around him. They had pulled down his trousers to examine his leg, they had opened his pack, they had found his money and put it back in its waterproof packet. Seeing that Erich's eyes had opened, one man asked him a question in a language he did not understand.

A second man asked in Russian, 'Soldier?'

'Prisoner. The mines.'

The man translated for the others, then said to Erich, 'My father also. Dead now.' Swiftly he talked at length to the others, apparently giving them orders, for they nodded, took up their guns, and waved back as they departed. The Russian stayed with him. He pointed at himself saying, 'Igor'.

'I am Erich. Where am I?'

'Kazakh. I am Ukrainian. I came after the war to grow wheat. The others, they are Kazakhs. They have their own language, their herds, some are still wanderers, but many are becoming settlers, growing their own grazing grounds. They are good men. They have gone for help.'

The sky, which had been circling at an increasingly dizzy rate, rising and falling, growing ever darker, crashed down on Erich. The earth seemed to drop away from beneath him and the man's voice faded.

He was aware of being moved, for pain awakened him and he screamed before dark again claimed him. When he next awakened he was on a straw pallet in a small whitewashed room. A woman was bathing his leg while Igor tore a worn sheet into strips for binding. When she saw that Erich was awake, she wiped her hands and handed him a cup. It was a bitter drink which numbed his mouth, spread the numbness the length of his body into the leg. Not enough that he could not feel the agony when Igor set it, heard the bone crunch against bone. Tears ran down his face and he fainted. When he opened his eyes again, the leg was splinted and bound. Igor took a stick, broke it into three pieces, and said, 'Your leg. Two places.'

He stayed in that house for four weeks. Igor carved some crude crutches and eventually Erich managed to get around. They fed him well, his strength returned, he made friends with the children, and sat day after summer day watching the fields ripen. The Kazakhs came to visit and Erich learnt a few words of their language. Once soldiers came. Igor hid him behind a false wall in the outdoor privy.

He paid them a small sum every week and worried that his money would soon be exhausted. He still suffered recurrent headaches and brief blackouts. The blackouts passed quickly but the headaches often lasted for days.

One day, shortly after the visit from the soldiers, Igor told him it would be better if he moved on. 'Do you understand?'

He understood that there must have been suspicions aroused in the village. 'Where shall I go?'

'The Kazakhs will take you. They are moving their herds to new grazing grounds. They will take you as far as the Caspian. There a friend will take you into Georgia. From Georgia you must find your way into Turkey.'

The memory of that journey never left him. Because of his recurrent headaches, everything became distorted, timeless and unreal. He could never quite separate dreams from reality. The slow days, the nights of many stars, of the ever-changing shape of the moon, sleeping in the domed felt *yurts,* the diet of mutton and fermented mare's milk, the language of which he had so little knowledge, and their endless kindness. Often he wondered if they thought they were caring for a madman who was touched by God, and therefore sacred.

He remembered the trip across the Caspian in a fishing boat, the sail shifting, the wind lifting the water. The weather was cool now. Summer had passed. He no longer felt pain when he walked, but the leg was slightly shorter than the other, and he limped. He still had bouts of dizziness, but his headaches were fewer, and every day he felt closer to the end of his journey.

When they put him ashore he was still in Russia. He remembered farmhouses where they fed him, barns where he slept at night and slipped away before dawn, dogs which threatened him, and the constant, nagging fear, of being taken. Sometimes he would find himself in a village café sitting in the sun at an outside table with a drink before him. A place at which he had no remembrance of having arrived.

Then suddenly he was in Turkey, for when he tried to pay for something they shouted at him and threw the rubles back in his face. Again there were mountains and windy passes, and later flurries of snow. When he reached Istanbul, it looked like a city out of a fairy tale, a mirage which he was afraid would vanish before his eyes.

He wandered for hours trying to find the German Embassy. He asked in Russian, in German, in English, but could never quite follow the directions. At last a man guided him and was angry when Erich could not pay him.

He was acutely aware of his filthy, ragged clothing, his limp, his beard and unkempt hair. He was turned away at the door. He went back day after day, gained entrance, and told his story. They did not believe that any man could have walked the distance he had and stand before them. Reluctantly they agreed to send a cable. He should return in two days for an answer. They exchanged his rubles and told him to clean himself up before he returned.

His first thought was to have a decent meal. In the clothes he wore a restaurant was out of the question. He settled for an outdoor table at a small, dark eating house in a lowly part of town.

Halfway through the meal he noticed another diner glancing at him, frowning as if to place him. Erich knew that jowled face and the heavy shoulders, but could not remember where he had seen him before. Every time he looked up, the man shifted his eyes away. Abruptly, in the middle of drinking the thick, sweet coffee, Erich remembered.

A GPU officer who had escorted a battalion of prisoners to the mine in the last months before Stalin's death. Janek had entertained him at dinner along with Erich and the overseers.

What was he doing here? Had he trailed Erich all this distance to take him back to conditions worse than those he had escaped?

He gulped down the last of his coffee, paid the hovering waiter and walked away as casually as he could. The best place to lose himself was in the labyrinth of the Great Bazaar with its crowds, shops, and bewildering streets.

He made turn after turn, doubled back on himself, then doubled back the way he had come. He was convinced he had not been followed. But if there was one GPU officer, there were bound to be more. He sat at a table in front of a shop and had another coffee and a sticky, honey-sweetened dessert, wondering what to do. Did he dare go back to the Embassy and appeal for help? What were the diplomatic rules these days? Would they return him or protect him?

The headache which still plagued him began to constrict his forehead. The crowd swam before his eyes. He had to leave that closed, underground world before he blacked out.

The wind was blowing down the Horn, chill off the Black Sea. His only thought was that he must leave the city, cable or no cable. Along the waterfront the fishing boats had unloaded the day's catch. Tables were set up there and fish were broiling on charcoal braziers, sold at a price that even a beggar like Erich could afford. He ate octopus and a soft-fleshed white fish, crisp on the outside, flakey within, seasoned with garlic and oregano. Whatever happened, wherever he went, he needed food. Suddenly he saw the GPU man wandering among the tables. He had not yet seen Erich.

A blue fishing boat was preparing to go out to sea again. Night fishing, Erich thought, but perhaps they would put him ashore someplace. He squatted on the jetty and said in German, 'Take me?' He held out the last of the money he had exchanged at the Embassy.

The elder man eyed him suspiciously, and the son, busy with the sails looked at him, too. They exchanged glances, then the man nodded abruptly. He gave Erich a hand aboard and jerked his head to motion him below.

The cabin was narrow and crowded. There were two bunks on each side and a table between them. There was a galley with a primus stove, a stained iron sink, some cooking pots, bottles, canned food, and a primitive corner with a bucket for a latrine.

Erich hoisted himself on to an upper bunk. His head throbbed, his leg ached, and he was sweating with fear. For all he knew the men would take his money and heave him over into the sea once they were out of the harbour. He had done a stupid thing, as stupid as waiting and evading would have been. He had been a fool not to have gone back to the Embassy.

He heard the lines thud on to the deck, heard the cough and throb of the auxiliary motor, felt the boat drift away from the dock. Then the sudden movement as the sails went up and caught the wind. Through the long, narrow window he watched the lights of Istanbul slide into the night.

An hour passed before the men came below. They were

out of sight of land by now, sailing smoothly before the wind. They made coffee, poured drinks, and offered both to Erich. They spoke Italian, a little French, a little German, and in that mixture they learned about one another. When Erich told them his story, they laughed and clapped him on the back and poured him another drink. They had helped him because they had thought from his manner that he was evading the police.

They were drug runners. They showed him the packages stowed in secret compartments built into the bunks. Fishing was their cover and earned a few coins, nothing like the cargo they sold. He could work his passage, they told him, and at the end, they would put him off in Brindisi.

He was cook, dishwasher, slops boy, deck hand, and often took the night watch after he learned how to handle the sails. They stopped at Salonica, Piraeus, Crete, Sicily, Crotone, Tarranto and finally Brindisi, always sliding into port after dark, and out again before dawn.

In Brindisi, he was paid off royally, and there was a prolonged, fond, drunken farewell. Erich took a bus up the tortuous narrow highway that followed Italy's Adriatic Coast, fascinated by the chalk-white villages clinging to the hillsides, always topped by a castle falling into ruin, or a magnificent cathedral. At Aquila he transferred to a train to Rome. He bought new clothes in the market, afraid to go into a shop. He wanted to telephone Mairi, but he remembered that the *Schloss* was not on the line. If things had changed in peacetime, it would take a day or more to find out, the operator informed him.

The plane to Frankfurt was boarding, so he did not argue. He would try again when he got to Germany. But in Frankfurt, he spent a day going through Customs where he was held because he had neither luggage nor passport nor identification. Methodical, pedantic, they must send for records. He would be permitted to communicate with his so-called wife in due time.

After two days he was issued with a temporary passport, the proper papers, and a train ticket to the village. The young man on night duty at the *Bahnhof* looked at him curiously when he got off the train, then gave a shrug and went back inside to his radio blaring out music which had been forbidden during Hitler's time.

He had wandered slowly through the misty streets, remembering and, mentally, returning. No one saw him, for the shutters were closed as they always were at sundown. He felt like a ghost visiting a world that he had left. A tower was missing from the *Schloss* and he panicked for a moment, thinking everyone must have been killed. Then Mairi's voice called out to him, 'Who are you . . . ?'

He had come home.

The weeks which followed were carnival. Lilli and Georges came from France with their exuberantly French children. Edu came, sobbing like a child as he embraced his father. He had to tell his story again and again, and they told theirs. The days reeled by like a film in a cinema. It took longer for him and Mairi to cease being shy with one another, to know one another again, as if each had returned from the dead. Erich even felt jealous when he heard of 'her Yanks' and the days when they occupied the *Schloss*. But he knew so little about what had happened during the last years of the war that he had to hear it again and again.

Then Maxl, with Vikki and Hannes, came back from Switzerland. Hannes flung himself at Erich saying, 'At last I have my *Vati*.'

Mairi caught her breath and Erich saw Maxl's face over

Hannes's head as he hugged the boy. He held him at arm's length and said, 'You are the picture of your Uncle Maxl when he was your age.'

That night he asked Mairi, 'He is Maxl's child, isn't he?'

'Yes. I am sorry.' She held herself very still and apart from him.

'Then I can tell. There was a woman in Poland. She had your name. There was to be a child. I was sent—taken—before the child was born. Before I knew it was to be born.'

Mairi was silent, then she leant over and kissed him gently. 'We must find her and learn if the child is all right.'

'You would not object?'

'Only if you want to leave me for her.'

'That I would never do.'

The rejoicing and merry-making done, the family departed to their various homes. A quiet which Mairi found almost unbearable settled over the *Schloss*. She had expected Erich's restlessness to leave him once he became accustomed to being home. Instead it seemed to increase. Often she felt as if she were living with a silent stranger.

He spent day after day writing to the parents of the soldiers whose tags he had collected as they had died at the mine, a task which increased his gloom. Many letters were returned stamped 'Address Unknown' or 'Deceased'. A few came with quiet thanks, adding that they had long since given up hope. Some said they would have preferred not to know the fate of their sons or husbands. It would have been better had they died fighting for the Fatherland. These Erich crushed angrily and threw aside.

'Leave it, Erich,' Mairi pleaded.

'Leave it? Is that what you wanted? Not to know my fate? Perhaps these parents are right. It would have been better had their sons died in battle. Better that I had died.'

'Don't talk nonsense. You know I tried to find you. You have seen the file of letters. You know how glad I am to have you with me again.'

He laid down his pen and put his head in his hands, elbows resting on the desk. During the silence which grew between them, birds sang in the trees growing in the ruins of the bombed tower.

She longed to comfort him, but she no longer knew how. There was an invisible wall between them and she had no key. She started to leave the room, but he spoke her name.

'Mairi.' She waited. Then, 'I must see the death camps. Auschwitz. Dachau.'

'To flagellate yourself? Isn't it enough to know about them?'

'Do we know or is it a new lie? Could we, as Germans, have allowed such a thing?'

'It is no lie, and we did.'

He returned gaunt and hollow-eyed. He pushed his food aside, half-eaten, wandered in the garden, along the river bank, and in the family burial plot reading the names, half-illegible on the ancient markers. At night he paced the floor until, as dawn came, exhaustion overtook him. Then it was a sleep of nightmares from which he awoke screaming. Mairi rocked him in her arms until he was still.

Hannes tried to comfort him. 'Vati, I promise you, we are a new nation, reborn.'

'Reborn or rising like a phoenix from the ashes of those we murdered?'

'It will never be repeated. Edu and his friends say so, and I say so. The new youth will be the peacemakers.'

He put his arm around Hannes's shoulders. 'I hope your

dream will become reality.'

Evening came earlier, the night air had a bite, the wood
which had dried all summer was carried in to the fireplaces
and smoke scented the air. Mairi filled the *Schloss* with autumn flowers, for frost was in the air.

'I feel guilty when I cut them,' she said as she carried in
yet another basket of late roses. 'Perhaps I should leave
them for the frost to kill instead of bringing them in to die for
our pleasure. That is what the war did for me. I regret even
the death of a flower. I'll bring some to your office.' She
smiled at Erich. He had fewer nightmares these days and he
looked better. Or perhaps she imagined it. 'Would you like
that?'

'Yes. The white ones, please. I have a matter I want to discuss with you.'

Now what? She had had enough discussions. She took her
time arranging the roses in a silver urn, then carried them to
the room which had been the office of Major Kimball. Erich
smiled as she came in, surprising her. He had not smiled for a
long time. She placed the urn on the table he used as his desk
and sat in the chair opposite him, waiting.

'Mairi . . .' he was hesitant, lacing his fingers together.
studying his hands. 'I want to leave Germany. Emigrate.'

'Emigrate? *Emigrate!* Leave Germany? Our home? Are you
mad? Where would we go?'

'I thought to Scotland where we first met. To Milkstone.
It is yours now.'

'I don't want to go to Scotland. I don't want to go to
Milkstone. To me, it is my home only on paper. One does not
go back to the home one left as a child or a bride. It never
works. You know the old saying, you can't go home again.
Erich, make your peace with the past. It is over. Done. Look
to the future.'

'The guilt is too great.'

'It isn't your guilt.' She felt the chill and darkness of winter, though the sun shone, the air was still. She could not imagine herself living at Milkstone, a Milkstone without Memsah'b, with Fa grown old.

He shoved back his chair and went to stand by the window, looking down on the village, the trees turning colour, the smoke blue from the chimneys, the flag of new Germany drooping over the *Bahnhof*. He plunged his hands into his pockets. Mairi imagined them clenched, the nails biting into the flesh, his shoulders rigid. 'I am going. Will you go with me? Or must I go alone?'

Close to tears, she was a long time answering. The wall clock ticked and a fly buzzed anxiously from window to window, seeking escape. A petal fell from one of the full-blown roses. 'I will go if I must. I will not be left alone without you again.'

Now that she had agreed, the move was inevitable. She hoped they were doing the right thing. It seemed to be the right thing for Erich. His moroseness vanished. He laughed, he made small jokes, he sang, became once more as ardent a lover as he had been long ago as a bridegroom.

It was Erich who telephoned Fa to tell him the news. Erich who attended to the necessary documents, made reservations, went to Bonn to urge Edu to move with them.

Edu would have none of it. It was his duty to remain in Germany. He was involved with a group of young, politically active people who were gaining votes and popularity. 'I hope to be Foreign Minister by the time I am fifty,' he told Erich. 'I make it sound like a joke, Vati, but I am serious.'

'I hope you will succeed.'

Too soon for Mairi, their papers were in order and the date of their passage set. Reluctantly, she began to pack.

Erich's enthusiasm made the task easier and she even began to feel a quickening of excitement.

Hannes swung back and forth like a pendulum. Should he take his *Lederhosen?* Would he have friends? Would they laugh at his accent? And, 'I do not like choosing what I must leave behind. Most of all Dieter and Jurgen.'

'I do not like choosing either, but our things will be here when we come for Christmas and the summers. Then you will be glad.'

The attics took the most time, for Mairi insisted they must be cleared. Over the years they had carried boxes of things they could not bear to throw away up the twisting stairs, as Erich's parents, grandparents and great-grandparents had done before them. The attics were a jungle of dust and cobwebs and mysterious boxes.

They laughed over some things and were saddened by others. There were elegant Edwardian hats that had belonged to Mutti Trötzen, the veils dusty, the feathers barren quills. Trunks of gowns and lingerie, long out of fashion and yellow with age. Shoes and boots, children's ice skates, old medals, old uniforms, even a piece of ancient armour. Mounted antlers, heads of beasts long dead, moth-eaten, bare of fur, their glass eyes gazing reproachfully.

'What's this roll back here?' Erich's voice came from under the eaves where he crouched, dragging out the last of the boxes. 'I hope it isn't a mummy. It is rolled up like one. Did we have a mummy? We had every other kind of curiosity.'

'I don't remember a mummy. Let's see it.'

He crawled out, dragging his find. Taking his knife, he cut the cords which held it and shook it so it unfurled across the dusty floor. They stared at it in dismay. A chill crept up Mairi's back.

'What if the Yanks had found that?'

'Where the devil did it come from? I never bought a Nazi flag.'

'I remember it. We came to spend the summer. Maxl came before we did to open the *Schloss*. The first thing we saw when we arrived was this, floating over the tower. You went up after dark and took it down. You must have put it away up here yourself.'

'Yes, I do remember. Edging along the roof in the dark, thinking at any moment I would fall over the edge to die, inadvertently, for the Third Reich. Damn Maxl! It took him a hell of a long time to learn.'

'What can we do with it?'

'Burn the damn thing. Burn it with everything else.'

That afternoon they had a fire: old Christmas boxes, wrapping paper they had thought too pretty to throw away, frayed ribbons, lace turned to cobwebs, letters in ink too faded to read, papers that fell apart as they tried to unfold them, instructions for toys long since broken or lost.

'All the past gone forever, never to be resurrected,' Mairi said. 'It is sad the way things survive their owners.'

When the fire was at its highest, they cut the flag to pieces and fed it, bit by bit to the lapping tongues which scorched first, then consumed the blood-red cloth, the white circle, the hooked cross.

Smoke carried flakes of ash up the chimney, the wind caught the smoke, swirled the ash like snowflakes, and scattered it in the sky over Germany.

8

A year had passed since Mairi and Erich had moved to Milkstone. Another Christmas was approaching and Mairi made reservations to return to the *Schloss* for the holidays. She had spent six weeks there during the summer and returned to Milkstone reluctantly. Fionna wondered if she would ever settle in.

More and more, Mairi reminded Fionna of Memsah'b: grand, extravagant, preoccupied, and occasionally imperious. The physical resemblance to their mother increased as well, so much so that Fionna had playfully remarked that Mairi should wear the famous diamond in her nose.

Mairi had looked at her, puzzled. 'Why ever should I do that? Memsah'b told me she felt an awful fool when people stared at her.'

'Nonsense! She loved it.' They were in Milkstone's south drawing room, sitting before the fire. The early November dark had drawn in, rain slapped at the windows, and wind tore the last lingering leaves from the trees. 'She was a complicated lady. I wish I had known her better.' Fionna gestured. 'I mean as a person, not as a daughter-mother thing. She was complicated enough as a mother.'

'She didn't know herself, Fionna.'

No more do you, Fionna answered silently. It was Erich, the foreigner, who had been instantly at home at Milkstone. He called himself a gentleman peasant. 'Farmer, you mean,' Mairi corrected him. 'Or forester.' And had added, 'What you really are is *schlamperei*.'

'What does that mean?' Fionna had asked.

'Lazy, aimless.'

'He deserves to be after what he went through. He really is a charmer, Mairi. Even the old dragon at the village store calls him her Good German and orders Fortnum's ginger biscuits for him. No one else will pay the price.'

'More than she does for me.'

Fionna did not pursue the fact that Mairi seldom set foot in the shop. Instead she sent a list by Erich or the cook. Often as not she forgot to write the list in English, leaving the cook to puzzle out what was wanted or Erich to translate.

'I wish you would stay for the holidays, Mairi. Pa needs you. It was jolly last year when you created a real German Christmas for us. All your beautiful ornaments on the tree, the candles, the feast.'

'Jolly until we started to sing.'

Erich's voice had soared operatically through *'Tannenbaum'*, but when Mairi and Hannes began *'Stille Nacht'*, Erich had left the room abruptly to go outside, where a slow-falling snow dappled the frozen earth.

Tears had gathered in Mairi's eyes. 'It is to do with the mines. I should have remembered.'

'I want to spend Christmas at the *Schloss*,' Mairi insisted now. 'You could all come there. That would be a lovely Christmas.'

'Too dear by far with the shape the yard is in. You know how it has been.' But she wondered if Mairi did know, having been gone half the summer, and still immersed in her own brand of homesickness. 'One strike after another from the beginning of spring and carrying on sporadically until October. Orders delayed, launchings postponed, contracts cancelled. Japan and Denmark, in fact almost every other country, can build more cheaply than we can. It isn't only a case of a better mousetrap, but a better mousetrap for less money.' She stood up, preparing to leave. 'Speaking of which, I must get home and begin to gird myself for tomorrow's board meeting. List the facts I wish to present to the old boys who only half-listen because their brains are ossified by senility and their inability to accept the postwar world. Why don't you join me in town for luncheon? I'll need cheering up.'

'I must start translating the poems that Tad wants.' Her face was suddenly animated and she smiled. 'It's such a fine idea, a collection of international war and postwar poetry. I have seen some of Gerald's sketches for the decoration and they are *wunderbar!* It will be a beautiful book and do much for peace and understanding and forgiveness.'

Fionna went home thinking that Mairi might settle in after all. They would all have to think of enough to keep her mind busy, make her one of them again. Perhaps Tad could make her some kind of editor of—well—something. She would speak to him about it.

As for the board meeting, Fionna dreaded it, but Charlie needed her support. Fa took little interest in the yard these days. He was writing a family history, going back to the days before the Highland clearances had sent the original Maccallums to seek work in Glasgow.

'I wonder what I shall potter about with when I am old?' Fionna said to Tad that evening. 'I feel old already when I think of the days when the banks of the Clyde were filled with ships in every stage of construction. The sky was dark with smoke and the rattle and clang and bashing of construction could be heard for miles.'

The postwar days when the order books had been filled five or six years ahead; when Maccallums' had launched a ship and laid down a new one every week, when a completed ship had been delivered every ten weeks.

Those times had passed. Fewer orders replaced those which had been filled. The world's shipbuilding capacity could now cope with more than double the demand. Bombers had replaced destroyers. Passenger planes had replaced passenger ships. Electronics, radar, new automation had changed design and construction. A few yards had already closed down, their machinery dismantled and sold for scrap metal, their buildings rotting in the tidal mud. Only the fittest were going to survive, those bold enough to adapt to the new techniques.

How many years had she been the Cassandra of the board meetings, warning them of the coming change? She must play Cassandra again tomorrow when she and Charlie would introduce a plan which would involve voting for a loan of two-and-a-half million pounds to re-equip with new machinery and train new men.

'A last ditch try,' she told Tad. 'Maccallums' may soon be sinking in the mud along with those others.'

The meeting was worse than she had anticipated. The men would not listen, refused to concede a single point, voted down the loan, and refused to take the prospectus home to study.

Fionna slammed out of the board room before the meeting was over. She was standing at the window glaring down into the yard when Charlie joined her. He poured them each a drink, handing Fionna her glass without speaking. She gulped at it, nodding her thanks.

'Rotten wood is what those old men are. Dead wood. If they were cut they wouldn't bleed. If their heads were broken open you'd find nothing but dust. Can you fire board members or must we kiss Maccallums' goodbye?'

'Damned if I'm going to kiss it goodbye. I've called another meeting for next week and told them we would bring up the same subjects again. I have homework to do. I've arranged a meeting with a man from Yarrows. They've been wise enough to move with the times. I'll convince your rotten wood somehow.'

'Optimist. Two private yachts, five fishing trawlers, a patrol boat, two Fisheries Protection vessels, and a hospital ship aren't enough to keep us going, and you know it.'

'I am going to buy the new gas-turbines whether the board agrees or not.'

'Where will that money come from?'

'If you'll stop pacing the floor and sit down and drink in a civilized manner, Fe, I'll tell you where it is coming from. I've had an offer for the house. It's the only home left in Blythswood Square, now that all the old mansions have been converted into offices. An insurance company wants it. They made a generous offer. In fact, a great offer. One I can't turn down.'

'You would actually sell that old relic? Give it up? Where would you go?'

'Mairi offered me the other cottage at Milkstone. The one where the groom lived when Memsah'b kept horses.'

'It's a wreck. It has sat empty for years. It's probably full of rats and mildew.'

'Actually, it isn't too bad, although you're right about the mildew. It's fairly large. Four bedrooms, a sitting room, a solarium, an enormous bathroom. It needs work. New wiring, electric heating in addition to the fireplaces, paint, new slates on the roof, all the usual. I'm looking forward to it. Charles will be close to his cousins. I'll be close to all of you. You are all I have.'

'Twaddle. What about all that ghastly furniture? Are you going to stuff it into that cottage?'

He refilled their glasses and grinned at her. 'An American antique dealer came around as soon as he heard that I'm selling. After about two hours of haggling, he found he couldn't get what he wanted on the cheap. He offered a staggering sum for the pieces I want to sell.'

'Which he will sell for three times that staggering sum in America. I thought you doted on those Victorian horrors.'

'I did once. But they wouldn't look right in the cottage. There is better stuff in the attics at Milkstone. Memsah'b had good taste. There's a Rennie Macintosh dining set I can scarcely wait to put to use.'

'And with all the money from the sale of the house and the horrors, you're going to buy gas turbines?'

'What else? The yard paid for it all in the past. It may be only a drop in the bucket, but it will be a beginning. There *are* contracts to be had, Fe. I want the one for the seaward defence boats. If I get that, others will follow. I'm going down to London the first of the week and I'll call the board for the day I return. I'll have new facts to lay on the table, lower the size of the loan we need—'

'And get another refusal.' Fionna shrugged. 'I suppose it is worth a try. By the way,' she swallowed the last of her drink, and gathered her gloves and handbag. 'Don't expect to see your little popsy, Miss Maclean, in London.'

'She was not and is not my popsy. And I haven't seen her any of the last few times I have been down.'

'I think she would like to see you. I ran into her the other day in MacDonald's tea room. She's in Glasgow to see her mother who is in hospital, presumably dying. I had a cup of tea with her and told her all, including that the yard is touch-and-go and may have to shut down. She laughed.'

'Laughed?'

'Laughed. Then she blushed. She still blushes like a giddy

girl. She said excuse her for laughing, but—and I quote—if the yard shut down, Charlie would be on the dole and there goes class distinction.' Fionna opened the door and smiled, cat-like. 'I assume you know what she meant by that.'

The longcase clock by James Smith, which had stood against the wall since the days of his grandfathers, ticked sonorously. Carefully, Charlie took the telephone book from his drawer and turned the pages to the M's. He wrote the number on a pad and looked at it. Then he dialled slowly. What would he say to her when she answered? *If* she answered?

Her voice was just as he remembered it. 'Hello'? . . . *Hello?*'

'Amelia? It's Charlie. Maccallum.'

'Charlie! Hello!'

'My sister told me you are back in Glasgow.'

'Oh, yes. Lady Lammondson or that is, Mrs Kosciuszko now. She's lovely. She said she'd known my brother in Spain. That was a long time ago, of course.'

'Everything was a long time ago. Amelia, I want to see you. Will you have dinner with me tonight? Please?'

'Of course. I'll be glad to see you. I'll have to stop by the hospital to see my mum. Just briefly,' she added quickly. 'You could wait in reception while I say hello and give her a hug. She wouldn't expect me to stay for a chat if she knew you were waiting. She would rush me on my way.'

'I thought she was a staunch supporter of class distinction.'

'She's mellowed. She's afraid I'm going to be a spinster.'

'Are you?'

'Going to be or afraid?' She was teasing.

'Um—both.'

'That depends. When I heard you had been down in London I don't know how many times and hadn't called me again—'

'I didn't call,' he interrupted fiercely, 'because I thought you didn't want me to call. Because you said you had learnt to live without me.'

'I learnt to live without you, yes, but I didn't learn to forget you. I didn't learn to stop—Charlie, do you remember what I told you about why I was leaving Maccallums'?'

'That you didn't want to grow old. That you wanted an adventure or some daft romantic thing.'

'Not *that*, Charlie! Daft yourself. Because I was in love with you and had been from the first day I had reported for work. Being in London, a new position, a few attentive young men, it didn't change anything. Charlie, don't make me say it. It's you who should be saying these things.'

'I hope I know what you are saying. Amelia, will you marry me?' He heard her sigh.

'Of course, Charlie.' She laughed. At him? At herself? 'Thank you for asking.'

His own laughter echoed hers. 'I don't believe this. I don't believe it for an instant. All of a sudden, everything is turned around. Amelia, we'll be living at Milkstone in a cottage. You'll have a stepson.'

'I've never had a stepson before. And I could live in a shoe box if you were there.'

'Look, I'm closing the office right now. I'm coming around. Wait for me. Everything is going to be all right. I'll get the metric equipment, the turbines, and surely the contract. As well as you! Everything's going to be all right!'

'Don't shout, Charlie. I know it's going to be all right. Everything.'